WITHIN THE DARK MIRROR

In two thundering steps, Kendric put himself face to face with the mirror. Finally, he saw Irissa.

She stood, life-sized, within the dark surface, slightly elevated by the frame so that they were face to face. But she was not looking at him. Her Torloc eyes roamed searchingly past him, as if he were the unreal image, not she. Then he saw that she wore the robe of Rule with which Geronfrey had tempted her months ago. Behind her, he saw the long stone halls of the magician's evil tower arrowing into the distance.

Her eyes shifted as he watched, helplessly seeking . . .

His hand tightened on the hilt of the sword and he raised it to shatter the glass.

No! She might shatter within it. Kendric's thoughts collided madly, veering between two worlds, two halls, two magicians—two Irissas . . .

Exiles of the Rynth

Carole Nelson Douglas

A Del Rey Book

BALLANTINE BOOKS • NEW YORK

A Del Rey Book
Published by Ballantine Books

Copyright © 1984 by Carole Nelson Douglas

All rights reserved under International and Pan-American Copyright Conventions. Published in the United States by Ballantine Books, a division of Random House, Inc., New York, and simultaneously in Canada by Random House of Canada Limited, Toronto.

Library of Congress Catalog Card Number: 84-90857

ISBN 0-345-30836-0

Manufactured in the United States of America

First Edition: July 1984

Cover art by Darrell K. Sweet

Map drawn by Carole Nelson Douglas

For Judy K.,
midwife to many books

Right of Passage

◆ ◆ ◆

"Go back! Go back. You cannot pass."

Sound came remotely in a world so dominated by sight. The words were only a coarse, distant grating, stubborn as an unoiled hinge.

"Go back," they ordered.

Back? But there was no back. Nor forward. Only this explosion of pure, shattered color, raining around her. She looked down at her left hand—its surface was an entrancing dapple of pink and gold, rich streaks of blue veining the open palm. She had never worn jewels, but now her very flesh flashed its own gem-bright color. She had walked into a rainbow arch—now she remembered—on her way through a long-sought gate to a long-lost place. Stepped through, and . . .

A lock of hair swung past whatever part of her vision was not swallowed by the careening, undiluted colors around her. Dark hair she had, long and straight. It was important to remember such details in this state where things did not hold together with their accustomed predictability. Her hair was dark, quite dark, nearly black. The sunlight had sometimes crowned it with a rainbow circlet, brighter than Iridesium, so someone—who?—had told her once.

The strands of that hair were separating into luminous ropes—emerald, violet, saffron—and twining into a braid of their own volition. Perhaps this place was dangerous. But why? She had sought it, been promised it. It was a place of passage; she must pass through—

"Go back, I tell you. Back! Quickly."

I? Yes, the voice had an identity, a particularity, even a rough familiarity, if only she could see past the colors long enough to hear the remembered note in it.

Shades drifted by in veiling wisps—tender lavender, death-dewed purple smoking into crimson, raucous orange. Yellow, growing green . . . A band of pulsating emerald swept by, and she fixed it with her eyes until the colors stilled. The green was endlessly deep, light-shot, yet opaque.

"Go back, Irissa," the green wall urged more reasonably, the voice merely hoarse now, not harsh. "You are not yet free to pass to this world. *He* impedes you."

Irissa. Of course, herself. She who was Irissa stared at the depthless expanse of green, waiting to discern who was—

"Finorian!"

A woman's face had formed in the iridescent surface, an old face, not so much wrinkled as drawn very tight on its bones.

It was oddly easy, in this havoc of color, to focus on the woman's colorless visage and the scanty white locks clouding its edges. But Irissa did not look into the icy, pale eyes, re-calling instinctively the peril of regarding a Torloc seeress directly, just as she'd had to evade her own silver eyes in any reflective surface. Yet a mere glance, aided by her restored clarity, identified the woman who had as good as reared her, and whom she had not seen for many months. Finorian.

The Eldress' face resembled the dead white moon as seen from Rule. Rule? To go back was to return to Rule, and she could not. *They* could not.

"As usual, you come too late and too soon, child. You cannot pass, and dare not rest long within the gate. You must go back—"

"But I have sought our Torloc gate so long, and no magic worth the naming remains in Rule—"

"—or go, then, wherever your willfulness takes you. But go!" Finorian's commanding finger rose from the sea of green that buoyed her image. Although the hand moved and pointed, it seemed no nearer than any other portion of the old woman, as if the bottomless green had no depth after all, but only pure surface.

"You have some—small—powers still," Finorian went on. "Despite *him*. Perhaps they are sufficient to bear you elsewhere. But he is your anchor, Irissa; he mires you in this gate, as he once was mired by his own marshes."

He! Irissa became aware of her right hand, closed round

something. She had extended it at the last possible moment in Rule, when she'd felt the rainbowed gate wrapping its iridescent wings around her. "You bear more magic than you know, Wrathman," she had said, not really knowing why, and he had reached out his large, hard hand and followed her into the gate, without asking where or wherefore. He was Kendric the Wrathman from the marshes of Rule, a fellow voyager into chaos on her last-minute invitation.

She felt his presence then, as colorless in its way as Finorian's in this whirlwind of hue. He was dim, utterly opaque to her magical senses and quelled by phenomena even she could hardly focus upon. He was a dull black or brown or blue blur somewhere to her rear, still linked by the warm, human chain of a hand.

"Loose him," Finorian urged. "Perhaps you can yet slip through by yourself."

"Leave him? Alone in a gate? He is unmagicked—"

"Better riddance, then. If you had not insisted on inviting mortals to *our* gate . . ."

"Our gate? Then we Torlocs have finally found Edanvant?"

Finorian's white head nodded solemn confirmation. "But you cannot pass, *he* cannot pass. He is not true Torloc, he is not true magicked—"

"He is—my guest."

The old woman snorted. "You have no such powers to draw another through a Torloc gate. He is your burden."

Irissa recoiled, the cloak of her wits at last fully and protectively gathered about her within this seductively dazzling gate. She remembered all that had passed in Rule and the horror of the last days as magic drained from its many lands. Once before she had stood before a gate with Kendric the Wrathman an unseen, barely sensed force at her back. Once before she had watched Finorian waver from her sight, leaving Irissa stranded, the last of her kind in an unkind world.

Irissa had been absent from the Torloc Keep in Rule at the very instant the long-sought gate that would usher her magical and outcast kind into a place where they were welcome had opened; she had arrived in time only for the vanishing Eldress' cryptic farewell. At Irissa's back had hovered the reason for her delay, a wounded Wrathman—a great, weary warrior she had found with his full seven feet supine under a weepwillow tree and his blood staining his Iridesium mail—that odd, black Rulian metal alive and gaudy with rainbowed highlights.

And so they had joined reluctant forces on a journey through a changing, treacherous land—Kendric the magically unempowered Wrathman bearing his longsword and his hereditary distrust of the sorcerous Torlocs on his back like equal burdens; Irissa the abandoned young Torloc seeress nursing her pride and her untried magical skills as if they were wounds from opposite edges of the same blade.

Yet together they had evaded the ambitious Ronfrenc's pursuit, midnight attacks of moonweasels, two powerful sorcerers' separate seductions, the maddened turning of the six Wrathmen one upon the other—and the unasked advice of Finorian's old white cat, Felabba, whose ancient feline wisdom had dogged their every step in an all-too-articulate form.

Irissa recalled it all now, as if her quest with Kendric in Rule unrolled before her eyes in compact pictorial form. Her magical vision had healed Kendric's wounds; the bitter bite of his five-foot-long sword, a weapon passed down from each Wrathman to the next, had cleaved moonweasels and even a berserk fellow Wrathman and ultimately the ravaging beasts of the senses from Outside at the gate of Valna.

Together they had preserved what remained of Rule against invasion from a place as extraordinarily remote as their native Rule had now become remotely ordinary, locking that gate forever and leaving a circle of stalagmite-frozen Wrathmen as warders. And together they had finally found Irissa another exit, so at last she had stood on a rock in a new-formed lake under a misting rainbow arch and wept again the tears of a true Torloc seeress—born of human salt but hardening into gems of coldstone as they fell.

She had thought that shedding such tears, proof that her powers lost upon the journey were regained, would have been satisfaction enough. She remembered viewing a puzzled Kendric through a dazzling, faceted sheet of sorrow. And she remembered her joy at the sign of her restored self giving way to her surprise that she could feel as bereft standing within a gate and bidding someone farewell as she once had felt standing without a gate and watching all that she knew evaporate into it.

And so her hand had been extended and taken, filling her with a soaring sense of unison and purpose. The sword—a thing of Rule now bleeding a gem-studded scabbard—had been left to the lake and the watching Felabba. Tears of loss that had rained past her cheeks broke with a joyous crystalline clatter of welcome at her feet. And then the gate was whirling its mist of many colors around them, somehow isolating them from each other, save for an almost umbilical tug that resisted all forces.

And finally, here was Finorian, telling Irissa to relinquish the gate, or to relinquish Kendric because he had no magic. Irissa, her memory now fully solid, even if nothing else in this place was so, fixed her gaze on the curve of Finorian's cheek, as near as she dared tempt the seeress eye to eye, and revealed one final, telling detail of that time in Rule that she had not forgotten.

"I cannot loose him. We have shared bed-bond."

Finorian usually knew much that it was not quite natural to know. She had not known this one very natural thing. Her head reared slowly back on her narrow neck, revealing the emerald touchstone hanging from a chain around her stringy shoulders. The gem glowed deep viridian, greener than the engulfing green, and the flaw within it shifted warning.

"So much the worse for you! Then lie in it!"

Finorian's image abruptly withdrew. The green flickered angrily out of range, drawing blinding folds of chromium, crimson, and violet in its wake.

"Finorian!" Irissa's will plunged into a swirling cacophony of undiluted hue, trying to bind tighter the darkness she felt weighing heavier behind her. The unseen handclasp held still, but the link was stretching thin, a homespun thread about to break—and who would notice one dull, snapped thread in a tapestry of such spinning, flagrant colors?

"Finorian—!"

The green drew near again. "Go back, I said and still say."

"But where? Not to Rule, there's no magic there . . ."

"She who would pass through a gate must take what she finds on the other side. And take your Wrathman with you," the old woman mocked, her visage sucked away again by an ebb of green past Irissa's face.

The dark pull on Irissa's hand was weakening. It was only a surface tug now, nearly undetectable. Irissa felt in that faltering the invisible pull of the Eldress' power and clung desperately to one she could only sense, not see. She strained forward with all her senses, especially with her eyes, in which her power lay, determined to draw Finorian to her like needle to magnet and then push herself through the eye of that needle until the Torloc Eldress would reveal why she so needed to sever Kendric from Irissa...

It was pure struggle, in a place that offered nothing tangible upon which Irissa could anchor her Rule-crippled magic, but she was winning. Inexorably, shade by revolving shade, the rainbow wheel turned back, bringing a wash of pure Torloc green before her.

Suddenly, behind her, something snapped and swirled away. The once-evasive green flashed in waves of disembodied triumph. The green swelled to welcome her and her alone. Irissa sensed an entire world of yearning Torlocs beyond the gate and saw a smile forming on Finorian's impassive, pale face, a bony hand rising to claim Irissa's now-empty one—

No!

Irissa released her hold on the gate in a moment of utter renunciation. The rainbow exploded; acid-bright color ripped into screaming tatters. It wove through her body, combing her hair crimson and violet by turns. She was sent spinning up and down, forward and back.

There was no green at all around her now, although the other hues pulsed at almost painful intensity. It didn't matter. Irissa was determined to find one plain thread among a gaudy company, and it would stand out by default.

Chapter One

———◆◆◆———

A threshold is the most elusive of concepts—so much empty air between one room and another, between here and there, between then and now—with only one slim lintel upholding the entire frame of passage. A human body always overflows a threshold, leaving untidy remnants of elbow and heel caught edgewise between one place and another. On a threshold, entrance and exit tremble in the balance, and sometimes seem the same.

So it was for Irissa in the rainbowed gate, even after she had renounced it.

Colors still collided around her, clashing bodily and refusing to bend their hues. But Irissa kept her will focused on the feeble tug from the one dully colored element she sensed in a many-hued world, the plain brown of earth.

She found it so suddenly that it rose up to slap her before she could recoil. She was face to face with it, as with a wall, the loamish scent stinging her nostrils, her fingers spread wide to dig cool tunnels into brown loam.

It was all gone—the rainbow vortex, Finorian, the lake-bound rock of Rule—and Kendric. Irissa stared with an odd self-disgust at her empty fingers plowing empty earth, at the ground undewed by the sheen of Torloc tears. She, who had so blithely beckoned Kendric onto an alien bridge, had watched that pathway melt from under her feet—at her wish and Finorian's encouragement. Why? And where was Kendric? He was not here, and by that fact he truly became her burden, as Finorian had named him. He would not like that, Irissa thought ruefully, and then chilled to think that he might be in no state to dislike anything anymore.

Irissa finally pushed herself up on her elbows, for she was

lying pressed flat into the shaded earth of a forest. Above, dappled yellow-green trees whispered together in a dozen muted shades, leaf to leaf, bough to bough. Through the fanning limbs, she saw the pale violet of sky.

Perhaps only the gate was lost—and good riddance, she quoted Finorian bitterly. But not Kendric! No, Kendric was likely shading some nearby patch of innocent earth with his own massive form and preparing to grumble at length at Torloc gates, evasive Torloc Eldresses, slippery, silver Torloc eyes, and outright Torloc lies. At the moment, Irissa gratefully would have endured such a litany. She levered herself to her knees and dusted off her palms. There would be no finding anything or anyone unless she looked. It was strangely distressing to have no one near to share such reflections, to discuss the future course, to advise against or for, to unsheathe a great, long sword and challenge uncertainty with it. There was nothing to do but walk into such a world without Kendric, and hope it would not remain so.

The glade opened before her; she stood and walked toward the meadow beyond.

On the horizon of gently rumpled foothills floated a white-walled castle, its upper reaches breaking into fragile, blue-roofed turrets against the lavender sky, its massive base walled and windowless.

Irissa bent to brush dirt from the damp knees of her silken gray trousers, still keeping her eyes on the construction. She had never seen such a perfect castle, such soaring laciness of towers, such a profusion of pointed roofs and gilt standards flying scarlet and blue pennants. But there it stood, only the tantalizing treetops visible inside a walled garden providing a clue to any life at all within those dazzling, distant stones.

Irissa finally made herself examine the landscape between herself and the castle, and it was there her wonder died. She saw farmland, green and brown and golden in the patchwork way of farmland everywhere—or everywhere that she had seen it, which was Rule—with sheep grazing in woolly white clumps like fallen clouds, trees edging fields in strict lines, a distant bearing-beast near a two-wheeled wagon, and a thatch-roofed cluster of faraway cottages that adhered to the white-walled castle's foundation like golden mushrooms sprouting in one crowded spot. She even saw people—specks that bowed and straightened and bent again to the fair and fertile fields and who, no doubt, wore the wool of the grazing sheep upon their backs and slept under the faraway mushroom roofs. Perhaps one of them was Kendric, in search of a peasant's direction to an inn that would quench his thirst and answer his questions . . .

Lured forward into the meadow, Irissa glanced down to see her sillac-hide boots from Rule crushing a sea of tiny green blossoms. She stopped to stare again. Green flowers. This was not "back," no matter how many times Finorian had ordered it. This could not be Rule, though it was not unlike Rule. It was better than Rule, whatever world it was, prettier, as pretty as a mosaic from some new Rulian realm-map. Unless she had fallen back into some corner of Rule she had not traversed— Tolech-Nal, perhaps, on the edge of the Abyssal Sea, though even fabled Tolech-Nal had never been noted for such picture-book perfection . . .

Irissa glanced up, aware that the sunlight fell warm but oddly diffused. No, this was not Rule. The sky was pale lavender still, but smooth and opaque, with the sun glowing through it as through a globe. There were no clouds as such—or perhaps it was all cloud. And through the middle of it, looking almost as near—or far—as the perfect castle, ran a pale white arch. Irissa's gaze followed the arch to its pinnacle in the heavens and finally regarded what seemed like this world's eye—a white, daylight moon that hung there, open and staring, bridged on either side by the shining white spans, like the castle stone, save that they shone.

This was one eye that Irissa could regard directly without fearing any drain of her powers—the small powers that Finorian had said still remained. All her life, which had not been very long by Rulian standards and which was minuscule by Torlockian ones, Irissa had avoided her own image in any form to safeguard her incipient magic from trickling away. She had stepped sideways to mirrors and polished bronze, to reflecting water and armor—even to the glimpse of herself in the tiny convex mirror that was the eye of another. There had been exceptions, of course—the ambitious Rulian sorceress, Mauvedona, the dark mirror with which the misanthropic magician Geronfrey had tempted her in his many-windowed, under-mountain tower. And Kendric!

The name tugged at her again in a despairing way she dared not examine too closely. She had loosed him in mid-gate; he had been torn from her fleshly and magical grasp by Finorian. Why? Why should the Torloc Eldress, wisest of the Torloc seeresses, begrudge refuge to one who had been so useful on Irissa's quest to rejoin her scattered people? What was one marshman in a company of Torlocs to Finorian?

But now there was no company of Torlocs at all, no gate, and no Kendric. There was only this strange new world with its sky-hung moon and pretty-patterned landscape, where everything was so serene and pleasing that Irissa thought she could wander safely in this scenery for years and never be noticed. And yet to her it was an empty world. Irissa had never felt so utterly stranded, not even in Rule.

The forest branches behind her rustled, shuddered, snapped, and fell to the ground in an invisible wind. Startled, Irissa turned to see pine boughs sweep to earth and young branches drift after them with a full burden of glossy leaves, as if some unseen scythe had hacked them off with one swipe. She stood still, puzzled, at the meadow's edge. The phenomenon was speeding toward her along the verge of the forest. Then the young, shoulder-high shoots bordering the trees bowed swiftly and parted as something brushed through them and paused.

She saw a great black beast with heaving sides, furred like a bearing-beast of Rule, but with delicate long legs and a deep mane encircling its muscular neck in a coarse black ruff. The head was small and tapered to a finely modeled, silver-tipped snout where a black nose sniffed the air with winged nostrils. Silvery hair-lined ears tilted at the suspicion of a sound, and between them rose the sweeping, pointed boughs of many-branched horns, rock-crystal clear.

The beast saw her through its great, round, black eyes, one of which was glowing garnet deep within by a trick of the light. Irissa stared at it, dazed into exchanging direct glance for glance, though it was likely a mute creature and no threat to her magical vision . . .

It lowered its crystal-horned head, dug one glossy ebony hoof into the turf, then bolted past her. Irissa stepped against the back-bracing trunk of a towering oak as the creature shot past, dagger-sharp horns stripping the lower branches of their outermost leaves.

Then the mellow note of a horn sounded, dreamily distant. The black beast launched itself as if sprung from a bow down a long slope of amber-green meadow. A host of dark pursuers popped up from the long grasses, dozens of them, smaller and less dark than their prey, but loping along with an oddly repugnant gait, half gallop, half shamble.

Irissa stepped from the shade of the oak to watch the distant figures scribe a labyrinthine pattern on the pastoral scene far below. The crystal-horned beast darted and bounded, and the dark pack couldn't keep up. It didn't matter, for they sprang up from everywhere now—ahead, behind, to the side. The prey turned in tighter and tighter circles, agile for so powerful a beast, but doomed. Then others came, galloping across the serene plain below in a sudden surge. Men clad in scarlet and hunters' green came riding cinnamon-coated and russet bearing-beasts like Kendric's mount in Rule. Long manes and tails whipped behind the beasts, and their hoofed feet beat the high grasses with a rhythm that Irissa thought she could almost hear.

She barely began to discern the tiny figures of the mounted men when she noticed one chill, alien detail among all that was so familiar to this hunt scene. The bearing-beasts were unhorned, only their short ears topping their long, forelock-whipped foreheads. Not Rule! She had known before that this was not Rule. But the distant white castle immovably surveying this drama and the familiar shape of the bearing-beasts had all seemed placid and reassuring. Why should one or two missing details among so many similarities chill her so? The moon in this world did not move, and bearing-beasts did not wear horns. Two simple differences. Why did they make her think that there would be other ones, more sinister?

She felt she knew the alien beast that dodged and darted in a closing circle of hunters below. Perhaps that was because it was horned, though more exotically than any creature she had known in Rule.

While Irissa watched, the smaller dark dots closed on the frenetic, leaping one at their center. Something arched through the air, flashing a metallic wink at the overwatching moon. Then there was only a single large, dark clump in the meadow now, agitation blurring its edges. It finally dispersed as the hunt party rode away in pursuit of a clot of hounds turned to some other scent, some new quarry. A smudge of black remained after they'd vanished over the next rise of rippling green and yellow.

Irissa stepped from the forest shadows. That spot drew her with a sick-hearted fascination. She moved warily down the slope into open view. Far below and away, harvesters still bowed to abundant fields, and unhorned bearing-beasts pulled two-wheeled carts down narrow, between-field roadways. The towering castle looked on blandly with blank-eyed slitted windows. Irissa walked forward, the long grasses whispering against her silken trousers.

A twig snapped behind her. She turned. Another beast stood there, smaller than the other and shaded a soft gray. It was not horned, but its dark eyes met hers as steadily as those of the first. Irissa turned again and made for the navel of the meadow, that dark dot that had not been there only minutes before. More branches snapped behind her. She did not turn to look again.

And when she had gone as far or near as she was willing, when the dark shape laid low in the grass had resolved into the rough oblong of body and the stiff, splayed lines of once-agile legs, she stopped. The longest grasses brushed companionably at her wrists. Ordinarily they would have tickled, but Irissa couldn't seem to feel them beyond a remote cobwebbed drift, like a memory. Something else touched her then, at her arm and elbow. She raised a hand and brushed a sun-warmed coat, turned her head and met mute animal eyes.

The creature's head, low on its long, slender neck, was level with her own. In the diffuse sunlight, its gray coat blazed blue on the bone points, and the black nose in the silver muzzle shone faintly iridescent. Irissa turned, fanned her hand over her eyes, and inspected the meadow slope up to the forest-fringed horizon. Beasts like the one beside her dotted the pale field all the way to the woods. Smaller beasts wove on braced, long legs near some of the herd; their eyes were very wide and glistening blue-black.

Irissa moved forward, to the fallen beast. The creature near her stepped alongside. They all came then; she could hear them at her rear, mincing delicately through the gentle grasses, slowly to the center of the meadow that moments before had had no focus point.

She was sorry they followed her, although perhaps that was not the case. Perhaps she had only joined them. She stood a few feet from the fallen beast. Its body was transfixed by five taut lines, four for its immobile legs, one for the seven-foot-length of spear that pinned it to the ground. Blood pooled in a ragged-edged pond, dark garnet blood, like the glint of its living eye. There was no eye there now, living or dead. The hunters had hacked the head and horns away, leaving a gaping trunk. Irissa remembered the agitation of the hunting circle just after it had closed. She envisioned short swords drawn and slashing at neck and hide by polite turn, the lifeless body heaving with the blows. Helpless in death, helpless in life.

Or not quite. By one outstretched black leg lay a dark-furred thing the size of a large dog, its four feet curled into fists like an infant's and its orange-skinned, masklike face blood-dipped and gape-jawed, the sheen of protruding canine fangs on both upper and lower jaws. It wore a collar.

The silent herd gathered around her, ringing the carcass with their bowed, sad-eyed heads. They brushed against Irissa's hips and shoulders, uncaring of the stranger in their midst. Something damp and warm thrust into her palm; she looked down at the littlest of the herd, which had thrust its dark nose into her hand. Irissa stroked it idly along the velvet silvery blaze that ran between its liquid black eyes.

She was angry beyond the loss of gates and worlds that the pretty place she had stumbled into should prove itself so fatal so soon. The light-colored shaft of the lethal spear seemed an insult aimed at the placid moon. She wrapped one hand around its haft, then both, and pulled. The herd edged back. The wood slid through her palms, so smoothly that it gave no purchase; Irissa pulled again with the outrage she felt welling into her hands. The spear came out, its crimson-tipped head leaving an ugly hole in the shiny black side that no longer heaved with pursuit.

Irissa's eyes narrowed at the wound, seeing the creature's side as she had seen it first—panting, alive, whole. The unclotted blood bubbled a bit, then thickened; skin stretched to rejoin skin, and dark hair smoothed itself into place with dark hair. The wound was gone, and Irissa leaned wearily on the spear as if on a staff. So much for Finorian's "small" magic, she thought triumphantly.

The herd surged inward, pressing her close within its warm, silent circle. Dark, slanted eyes regarded her with mingled distress and gratitude. They nudged her nearer their leader, silver velvet muzzles forcing her to confront the headless carcass at her feet.

"This...this, no. I cannot. I cannot," she told them, turning in a circle and directing her answer to them all—perhaps twenty, not counting the littlest one, which nibbled now at her tunic hem. "The other was simple; at least it was once in Rule. A wound is merely a disruption of what bone and blood surround it. But this—this is absence. Not restoration, but recreation..."

She looked down at the mutilated carcass. She remembered the head so regally held, the dark eyes winking ruby, the flared nostrils sniffing the air for danger and finding only herself. It had not feared her; she should not fear it, even now.

The blood had not clotted; there had been no time for that. Irissa stared into the incarnadine shimmer, wondering if so much blood collected might not endanger her, if it might not reflect her own image back. No, there was nothing she could do, not even were her powers full and strong. Now she could only join the herd in its mourning. Her head bowed until her dark hair fell past her shoulders and veiled her face. She felt tears well in her eyes and saw them harden as they fell.

Two coldstones glimmered bright on the bloody ground, islands in a crimson sea. Irissa touched her cheeks. Coldstones—not mortal salt, worthless save for winning human sympathy, always a two-edged thing, but the gemstone-solid, clear tears of a true Torloc seeress. Perhaps her powers were not as waned as they had seemed during the last days in Rule, nor as weak as Finorian had hinted they were at the gate. Perhaps, although they were not sufficient to see her through the gate, they were still sufficient somewhere—perhaps here.

Irissa turned the spear sideways in her hands, so quickly that the herd shied back from its suddenly horizontal head. She brought the wood sharply across her raised knee. No break, but the resounding of it on her own flesh and bone. Then if force would not shatter it . . . She grasped the unweaponed end and stared at it. She had never seen wood this smooth, this welded into one sovereign substance. But her reawakened eyes undid it, strand by smooth strand, as if it were embroidery. A foot-long section broke off into her hands; her eyes unwove that into smaller and smaller splinters until her palms were heaped with them. She opened her fingers and let the sticks trickle through them into the pool of blood.

The herd pressed in, and she warmed herself at its simple animal heat. She looked around the solemn circle of heads, patted the young one once between the ears, then stared at the bloody pool, at the lifeblood of the dead beast, and at her two tears-made-stone blinking eye-bright and the sticks of spear-wood fallen into a branched pattern above the coldstone tears.

She was lost in color and memory again. The blood moved, drew into a mass, and shaped itself into forehead, throat, and long, modeled nose and ears. A bramble bush of translucent horn rose above the head, horn as crystalline as her tears. Eyes as bright as coldstones glimmered in the face; dark hair spread from the shoulders, thickening into mane, covering the neck and washing pale inside the ears, silver at the nose—how high the silver? Enough, memory said.

Irissa wove on her feet and would have fallen, but the herd pressed inward and upheld her. Irissa would have abandoned the effort—to erect what was from only pieces of something else was a task greater than any she had ever tried in Rule, and this was an alien world, where her magic might be held by leashes whose length she did not know. But the herd pressed her on as much by its mute will as by its unified body, and for Irissa there was only the beast as she had seen it for an instant and the odd native wood that was loath to break and her own native tears that were prone to fall hard and clear . . .

Too much! The attempt had been too much. A black wall suddenly shaped itself in front of her, and she had to release the blood and the coldstones and the wood from her sight. She shut her eyes, the encircling herd pinning her upright when she would have sunk to her knees. They were motionless now, and Irissa finally opened her eyes to her failure. She saw only the lucid, gleaming crystals under the lashes of the great black beast, the pale, translucent surface of his horns spreading majestically on either side above his silver-haired ears. She reached up to touch the tip of one branch. It was sharp.

The creature bowed his head and touched his perfect velvet muzzle to her forehead, just where the Iridesium cirçlet pressed her hair to her temples. His black nose came away from the dark, rainbow-tinted metal with the same many-colored sheen; the one detail she had forgotten was remedied. Irissa felt power pulsating through her. It went from her to the herd and from the herd back to her, throbbing at her metal-circled forehead as if to sunder the band. The colors around her grew solid, opaque. They all stood knee- and hock-deep in cresting, time-stopped waves of yellow and green, under a violet dome centered with one great unreflective coldstone of an eye. Color was motion, she suddenly understood, and motion temporarily had stopped . . . The phenomenon vanished as abruptly as it had appeared. The herd capered backward, away from her, hooves striking the turf in a series of vivacious drumbeats. Dark animal eyes around Irissa danced shyly.

One female, perhaps the one who had approached her first, stepped into the clearing made around Irissa and went down on her delicate forelegs. Intelligent eyes beamed steady black, but Irissa avoided too long looking, though it was doubtful a mere animal had self enough to drain Torloc powers, even inadvertently.

They pressed in again, their eyes mirroring significant meaning. Irissa glanced to the beast who led them. It was disconcerting even to glimpse her own tears live and expressive in another creature's face. But he watched her as significantly.

Sun-warmed bodies neared, forcing Irissa toward the kneeling beast with gentle, determined shoves.

"You wish me to mount her!"

Dark eyes burned brighter; Irissa was butted up against the creature's waiting side.

"But I have no saddle, no reins, nothing to hold on to . . ."

Unhorned heads lowered and pressed her gently on. Irissa studied the back before her. Unlike the well-muscled bearing-beasts of Rule, these creatures were spindly of leg, broad of stomach, and sharp of spine. Here was no hammock between withers and flanks to cradle even the most inept rider, but a long, level ridge of bone dropping away to heaving sides.

While Irissa debated, the herd shifted behind her. A spearpoint of horn between her shoulder blades urged her implacably. She twined her hands into the thick ruff around the female's shoulders and swung up, aided by a powerful shove from behind. The creature rose jerkily to its legs with its new burden, bracing them as did the young ones, then adjusting easily.

Now Irissa's face was level with that of the resurrected male. "Ingrate," she charged good-naturedly. A crystal twinkle suggested that the creature understood her perfectly. He pivoted and was at once a retreating dark flash across the endless meadow. The herd swiveled as suddenly and were flying away from her, pale pennants of farewell flashing from kicking heels and under their short, uplifted tails.

Irissa would have opened her mouth and said something about this lightning-quick passage of her new friends, save that the belly between her knees spasmed at that moment and seemed likely to flail out from under her. Irissa's hands clenched on coarse hair unthinkingly, and it was fortunate they did; that was the only part of her that seemed connected with anything corporal in the next wild moments as her body jolted on a journey rugged beyond the passing of any gates and the colors of this world swirled past in a dizzying meld of chartreuse and violet. To her left side, the distant pale castle turned into a speed-blurred falling moon and caromed past her. Dark sentinel trees in the forest to her right loomed large and threatening, and sank at her rear with a hasty, sense-deadening, monotonous rhythm. Wind whipped her hair into a knot behind her head, slunk between her and the jolting back of the beast, and tried to comb her free. It blinded her eyes until they watered and solidifying coldstones pelted her cheeks.

It ended as abruptly as it had begun. The herd was ambling along the forest verge, all signs of the castle and village gone. Irissa flexed her fingers and found them stiff. The rest of her body felt beaten. It was probably a privilege in this world, she reflected, to be invited to play passenger on these fleet, untamed creatures, but one she would forgo in future . . .

There was no future. The mellow lilt of a horn hummed through the forest. The herd bolted. This time, unprepared,

Irissa's fingers clenched on air. Her body jolted to the ground, meadow grasses tickling her nose. Above her, little legs sprang over her in a rhythmic series. The herd, moving as one and therefore with no consciousness of the one left behind, melted into the endless waves of meadow. Irissa turned to face the hunters.

The hounds came first through a tightening, hissing circle of agitated grasses. Leathery faces grimaced into bizarrely colored triumph, black lips drawn back from fangs as long as Irissa's fingers. Their oddly human faces were orange, light, poisonous green, dark purple, and bright blue, surrounded by halos of coarse black hair burning to rust in the sunlight. Their bodies were hairy, save for their long, leathery, flexible toes and fingers, and these were armed with long black claws. While Irissa stared speechless into their leering faces, they drew nearer, almost seeming to pull the ground closer with their turf-trailed hands. Silver and gold studs glinted from the wide leather collars that circled their necks; some wore black leather vests embossed with colors echoing their facial hues. Here and there, a gold earring gleamed at the base of a hugely misshapen ear.

They chattered and gibbered around her, bouncing up and down excitedly as they edged nearer, black gums gleaming wet around the daggers of their teeth. Irissa stood to face what masters held these creatures barely back from her on an invisible lead.

They were only men, a hunting party attired in dulled rusts and reds, riding creatures similar to the bearing-beasts of Rule—four sturdy legs, powerful glossy-haired body, streaming mane and tail—save that these wore no horns between their short, upstanding ears. Irissa found their naked heads nearly as shuddersome as the houndlike forms capering at their feet, now that the party was reunited.

A spearman lowered his weapon and thrust it toward Irissa, like a prod.

"What have we here? One of the Unkept come in from the Rynth? She'll regret not having a better sense of direction . . ." He twisted his head over his shoulder to wring a knowing laugh from his companions, doffing his hat to run a forearm across his overheated forehead. His head was shaven bald to just above the ears; the remainder of his hair flowed down to his shoulders.

The men laughed as expected, but one urged his bearing-beast forward to lean over his saddle horn and inspect Irissa. "Not an Unkept, I think. Perhaps a shape-slipper. She ran with the lorryk."

"No!" The men edged their mounts nearer, driving the gibbering hounds to Irissa's very fingertips, where they crouched with salivating jaws agape and almost seemed to smile. "Have the Unkept stolen a Stone from some distant Keep or other and now play sorceresses . . . ?"

"They loathe the magic arts," another objected scornfully. "What color are her eyes?"

"Ah. You think—?"

"It's been years since an ice-eyed one came—"

"And went," another finished ominously.

"She must have run with the lorryk—"

"I *rode* the lorryk," Irissa corrected.

"So much the worse." The baldheaded man redonned his brimmed hat and took up his reins importantly. "The lorryk are unridable; they die before they bear so much as one of yon lemurai—" He gestured at the capering hounds. "—on their backs. We know."

"But *she* knows nothing of this, nothing of this world, or she would not tell so obvious a lie."

The speaker spurred his mount from the party's rear. He was the only one attired in trousers and tunic instead of long, flowing robes, but his clothing was so richly embroidered with gilt silk threads that it was impossible to determine its base shade. He wore no cap, and his shoulder-length golden hair curled gently at the ends, as did the tips of a silky mustache even more gilded, perhaps by gold powder.

Despite his lavish apparel, he, too, brandished a spear.

"I think we have here the one responsible for the broken bonewood spear we found and our carcass that we did not find again. The lorryk do not bear humankind and bonewood does not break, nor do downed beasts rise again and walk headless away. You were right, Clerque; the key question is what is the color of her eyes. On the answer depends whether we return her to one of the bevies, drive her back to the Rynth, or— Look up at us, woman. Modesty is an asset in a female, but magic is not."

"Be wary, Sofistron—she may strike you with some spell!"

Sofistron smiled, and the mustache curved upward with his lips.

Irissa, her eyes still on the restless lemurai at her feet, slowly looked up as ordered, more puzzled than obedient, her glance just grazing the side of Sofistron's bland face.

"Silver!" The men raised arms across their eyes and savagely reined their mounts backward. Only Sofistron, calmly astride his quiet beast, was left near Irissa, and he was smiling.

"Yes. Silver. I have long been ready for such a one. But the Inlands have not been honored by one of her kind for many, many years. We will take her back to the Keep—"

"No!" Irissa interrupted, abruptly aware that such defiance would be received less seriously without a Wrathman at her rear.

And so it proved. At the violence of her word, the lemurai lunged inward. Facile hands tugged on her tunic hem, pulling her into their midst.

"Back, you witless scavengers!" she heard Sofistron cry. "I want her whole—"

She focused on the nearest lemurai's clawed feet; she could feel the nails scraping her back as they sought to drag her off her feet. She felt momentary panic, revulsion at the manner of her capture—alone, undefended, unresisting . . . But not quite helpless. Without Kendric and his length of ready steel, without any forged weapons of her own, she could still rely upon her native defenses.

Her eyes, fresh from the triumph of reconstituting the lorryk, scribed a fine, thin red line just before the curled black toes. A narrow sheet of flame sprang eight feet high as Irissa whirled, her glance etching a circle around her that flared into a solid curtain. Beyond it, singed lemurai leaped back, yelping. The high, nervous whistles of frightened bearing-beasts pierced her improvised wall—and Sofistron's calm tones penetrated the pulsating red as well, sounding vaguely amused.

"They say your kind passes through the Inlands on a quest for wisdom, seeress; you could do with such. Never leave yourself undefended from even an unlikely direction—"

Irissa glanced up at a tunnel of pale lavender sky above. It was too late. Before she could think to fashion a roof for her flame-made house, a great dark cloud of pure power came crashing down upon her senses like a rock. There was time for nothing but a fading regret for the willfulness that had made this world hers for a time and bitter relief that Kendric, at least, thanks to Finorian and her own unreliable powers, likely was not in it.

Chapter Two

His name was Kendric and he was a fool.

Half of that thought was familiar and comforting; the other half was not. Kendric the fool sat on a rock, which he recognized by the press of the unrepentant surface against his body through the simple homespuns of Rule.

That body ached as if beaten until a rainbow of bruise covered every scintilla of his flesh. Kendric opened his eyes. It seemed he had been somewhere unknown for an uncertain length of time, a place where not only his eyes but every one of his senses had squeezed shut. His entire being felt clenched. So he opened his eyes, seeing first the familiar dark blue cloth of his trousers and the battered orange of his sillac-hide boots, his own fists, clenched and . . .

He stretched out stiff fingers one by one; all were there and undamaged. It was agony to take visual roll call. Blinding white light danced at the edges of his vision in an arcing circle, threatening to tighten on the small tunnel of sight before him. He clung to the familiar, to the clothes woven and purchased in Rule, made from the beasts of Rule—the far-ranging sillac herds, the domesticated weaveworms . . . He tested the rock. Yes, largely gray-blue, solid, a dull-colored surface that supported him admirably, unlike that glimpsed cataclysm of color—

He took a deep breath and stood slowly, each of his limbs straightening as tentatively as had the fingers of his fists. He still tensed against something; but by the time he had risen to his full seven feet of height, the height that had made him one of only six men in Rule to carry one of the six hereditary longswords, his circle of vision had widened to include a respectable amount of rocky ground around him, and he felt his bearings return.

Of course he stood on rock. Where else would he stand now, he who but—moments?—before had stepped onto a midlake rock and into a rainbow mist at the behest of a Torlockian seeress? He cursed again all the folly encompassed in that one act of faith. That he, Kendric, should forsake a nice, simple rowboat on a lake for a jut of rock arched by a rainbow! That he should forsake Rule—an altered Rule of hot, flowing rock and flooding waters, true, but the Rule of his birth nevertheless—for a dubious gate to some world of no known character! That he should trust to a Torloc seeress, though she had traveled half of Rule with him and saved his life once and shared his bed twice! That a canny mortal from the marshlands should trust such a one, no matter how blindingly her coldstone tears rained on the rock at his feet...

He sighed and studied a wider slice of landscape. Obviously, the gate had not accepted him. He stood in what seemed to be left of the Rocklands, an endless upthrust landscape of scant soil, shrubbery, and low rocks cast into a thousand suggestive shapes, like dice in some game of giants. Transported he had been, but not to some new world, only to the most desolate reaches of the old one.

He stretched, feeling the soreness howl through all his muscles. He flexed his fingers. His hands felt empty. He had left his weapon, of course. In the most colossal, profligate folly, he had let his great longsword slide into the waters of Rindell lake to rust. His hands were bereft. He was a swordsman. He missed his hilt. Not anything other, not some tenuous grip on a piece of fog vanishing into a mist...

Something chimed from a tunic fold to glitter on the rock at his feet. He bent to retrieve it, bands of color momentarily tightening painfully on his forehead, as if *he* wore an Iridesium circlet, not she, not the one he had last seen beckoning him into mist and color and madness...

The thing glimmered small on his fingertip, a cabochon of

limpid crystal, hard, cold, clear as ice—the tear of a Torloc seeress. Once he had not believed in such phenomena—Kendric the skeptic! Now, he had seen many before this one. But it was not the believing in Torloc tears that had set him awry. It was believing in Torloc seeresses . . . His fist closed on the small stone but felt nothing, not even a sharp edge. It was utterly smooth. Kendric unfurled his large fingers and contemplated the stone. He pulled his boarskin purse from his belt and dropped the crystal into its puckered depths. A talisman—for a fool!

For a swordless one—swordless in the Rocklands! Well, he would march and forage, come to some settled place. There was little danger here but thirst, hunger, and the scrape of small, six-legged reptiles across his face when he rested at high sun. He looked up, away from the familiar rocks, to gauge the angle of the familiar sun that lighted all the well-remembered landscape around him.

The sun shone there, a single sun, past the meridian, perhaps two-thirds along its way across a light lavender sky. And above him, stretching like an airy bridge of cloud across the cloudless heavens, was a solid white arch veined with faint violet. At its apex, held by the icy arch that glittered coldstone-bright in the sunlight, hung a pale-faced, immobile moon, glimmering daylight-soft.

It was not the moon of Rule.

He had been walking perhaps four hours before he found water. He had not berated himself for the past three; the landscape proved itself alien enough to the Rocklands to make such self-admonition trivial. Nor had he looked up again to the immutable moon.

So when he spied a dun-colored bristle of leaf-bare stalks snaking across the distant gray, he bore for it, looking neither up nor down. The rocks rose higher around him and obscured the view for a time, but he walked through one last divide and was suddenly upon the two-man-high, bare trees that fringed a stone-slapping gurgle his every sense told him was water.

It was a broad, flat stream, its banks no more than rocks and its waters flowing thin near the edges. Kendric finally let his thirst free; he cast himself flat on the rough pebbles and dipped his face in the fast-running shallows. They were surprisingly icy and refreshing. He drank in greedy, throat-freezing gulps, ignoring the trickle that flowed under his chest and soaked through his tunic. He heard only the monotonous prattle of the stream past his face.

"Now here's a fellow who would wish to feed the fleshfins even while he slakes his thirst. What Keep do you think such a generous soul hails from?"

Kendric's hands dug into the stone-pocked ground as the sudden voice boomed over his head. He froze, then levered his great length over with the muscular speed of a moonweasel and faced the speaker in a crouch.

The questioner had to be the man who stood slightly ahead of the half dozen ranged behind him against the rocks only yards away—a squat, red-bearded fellow even now turning his head over his shoulder to his companions and revealing the glint of a golden ear. There was nothing else gilded about the party; they were a rude, skin-hung, tunic and trouser-draped band with a motley array of weapons bristling from their sides, backs, and hands—steel-thorned maces, ripple-bladed daggers, sickle-headed axes shining as cold and deadly as an ice-caught moon. Spiked pole axes rode high over their shoulders, with lethal steel spires rising from four-pointed stars of metal at their wooden tips.

Kendric stood warily, feeling naked in his Rulespun clothes. Oh, for the Iridesium mail he had so lightly cast away, the great longsword . . . His right hand clenched on air.

"Not only generous, Gryff, but generous of height," approved the tallest of the men, a lank fellow with slanted, deep blue eyes and yellow-white hair caught into a lock that fountained from the side of his skull. He was not as tall as Kendric.

Gryff, the red-beard, nodded. "What Keep do you hail from, stranger?" he asked amiably enough. "Or mayhap he doesn't speak. Such unnatural length may have stretched his throat too thin. Well, which Keep, stranger?"

Kendric reached into his past in Rule for an answer ironic only to him. "The Far Keep . . ." Once he had been one of the Six of Swords, six warriors known as Wrathmen of the Far Keep. No one had known what or where the Far Keep was.

Perhaps now that it no longer mattered, now that he was no longer in Rule, or of Rule, he would learn.

"He can't mean Sofistron's. We border on his circle even now," flax-hair said.

"True, Helicon." Gryff shifted his pole ax to his left hand, a gesture meant to disarm. His right forefinger thoughtfully polished his golden ear. "Is it Lacustrine's, then? Or Ivrium's iron tents? Or mayhap that madman Chaundre's Keep? Though he does not often drive men into the Rynth ... Tell us, stranger. You will soon find we rim-runners have no secrets. We can't afford such niceties."

They chuckled together then—tall and short, lean and burly, dark and light. Kendric had never seen such an ill-assorted lot, like offspring of two mongrel dogs never meant to mate. They were almost laughable.

"You seem an odd breed," Helicon said abruptly. He came over to eye Kendric. "We plains people are long of limb, but narrow for speed and grace. You seem a thickish one for your height. What Keep betrothal spawned you? He's more your kind, Gryff."

Gryff strutted over on the short, muscular legs his abbreviated leathern tunic displayed almost as a vanity. "Not ours. Sofistron would birth-banish such a long, lumbering fellow to suckle at the Rynth breast. He only kept me because coming into the world missing an ear made me a good subject for his spirit-smithing experiments." Stubby fingers stroked the golden ear again. "When I stopped growing and the ear stopped with me, it was into the Rynth with old Gryff, though I'd long planned to rim-run, anyway ... What drove you out, fellow? Tire of the monastery, did you? Looks a lusty sort. What's your name? Well, fellow?"

"Kendric."

"Hmmm. A rough-sounding name indeed," the languorous plainsman, Helicon, commented. "Perhaps he does hail from Sofistron's Keep after all, Gryff. You valley folk always did favor grunts for names."

"And you plains people are too busy pronouncing yours to every stranger you meet to have time to protect yourself. Let's see how our new man handles a bonestaff. You, Kend-ruk!

Wrest off a limb of yon bonewood tree. You'll cross cudgels with Calennian here."

Another man stepped forward, one nearly six feet tall with polished copper-colored skin and straw-coarse yellow hair. He carried only a length of thick, smooth, blond wood, but his arm, leg, and chest muscles swelled formidably.

"That tree?" Kendric pointed incredulously to an unprepossessing bristle of bare branches perhaps ten feet high.

"Aye. Bonewood. A great hulking fellow like you should be able to wrench a stout cudgel off. We'll have a friendly match. Some sport." Gryff smiled and twisted his forefinger in his metallic ear. The others grinned and laughed, long and deep and to themselves.

Kendric gave them a narrow look, but stalked over to the tree nevertheless. If they were so good as to point out a native weapon, no matter how puny, he would arm himself, even if they planned to make him pay for the privilege.

Their laughter had softened to crude chuckles. Kendric studied the tree, a stunted leafless thing, lightly anchored in the dry soil. He could see the root tracery running crimson just beneath the ground. He'd be lucky not to pull this whole meager bush out by its roots . . . And as for its use as a weapon, this wood would be as much defense as a toothpick. Why bother with a cudgel match using such fragile clubs? It proved these fellows a harmless lot . . .

Kendric curled his hands around the tree's longest limb. The wood was skin-smooth, almost pleasurable to the touch, and warm. In one rough motion, he twisted sharply to fracture it at the thick, bulging joint nearest the main trunk. The wood slid silkily through his palms, resisting the pressure. The watching men guffawed. Kendric set his jaw and wrung the branch again. He heard a crack deep inside the wood, but the joint held. Kendric released the limb, wiped his palms on his trousers, and gave the onlookers a defiant stare. Finger by finger, he wrapped his hands around the branch, took a deep breath, and wrenched it rudely. The joint screeched protest and wood fibers snapped. He tightened his grip and twisted more, using all his strength merely to keep the branch twisted to the point where he held it. Sweat bloomed on his forehead, and all his muscles twisted like the bonetree branch; he felt the sting of strain along his braced legs.

Even as he wrenched the limb slowly back and forth, Kendric realized that what he felt along his legs was no effort-generated sensation, but something exterior, something alien . . . He looked down. Red, thorn-studded ropes twined his boots and trousers, biting into the tough sillac hide and now stinging through the cloth. Kendric gave the limb a mighty turn. He heard the men laughing on the sidelines. They no longer seemed so genial or tame. What hellish thing was this? A tree with no leaves but with living, saw-toothed roots that came trellising a man? The vines were winding and embedding themselves in his thighs now. Kendric stepped back, hobbled by the entwining roots. In moments he would be thorn-encased from ankle to shoulder, all because of one stubborn tree limb. Sweat swam in front of his eyes, drawing a new annoyance—dancing red-gold gnats. Kendric blinked and pulled. He grimaced and twisted. Everything centered on the limb that would not break. He *would* have it; it was a debate between his will and that of the wood, and men were still stronger than mute matter or he would know the reason why . . .

With a sudden, echoing snap, the limb severed from the tree. Kendric's pull, released, drove him backward. The roots relaxed for an instant. Kendric stumbled out of their range and watched them tighten on air, then shrivel onto the ground. In his hands was a four-foot length of bonewood, swelling at each end to a joint, but smooth as ivory, with no sign of breakage, as if the wood had healed itself even as it shattered.

"He did it—alone!" Jaws dropped, this time not in laughter.

"Then to it, Calennian," Gryff ordered.

The copper-skinned man raised his cudgel, his hand tightening around a pierced metal sheath on its end. He stalked forward and swung the club toward Kendric.

Kendric's hands bridged the limb's length and brought it up like a bar. Wood rang on wood—not the sturdy thwonk of oak or the whiplike *whish* of weepwater tree wood, but a high, hollow sound, quite musical. Kendric lunged at Calennian's surprised copper face, bringing his own hard-won cudgel down on his opponent's bonewood near the decorative grip. Curled brown fingers shifted just in time as a deeper note rang out from the contact. Then it was all leap and retreat, with the odd, musically pitched voice of the bonewood singing in rhythmic clashes, higher and lower, depending on where wood touched wood.

Calennian's reach was shorter than Kendric's, but his blows were practiced, and he threw the force of his entire muscular body behind them. Kendric parried them until his fingers vibrated, all the time aching for a decent sword, aching most of all for the five-foot-long blade he had borne scabbarded on his back in Rule. Only fools, he thought in time to the hollow knock of wood on wood, would part with swords. He spun to avoid a powerful swipe at his knees and retaliated with a two-handed blow that just missed Calennian's broad shoulder. A cudgel was a simple but crude weapon.

The wood showed no signs of failing under the drum of blows upon it. Kendric suspected that this tough wood never broke and only bent a bit when attacked at a joint, as he had done. Torlocs, he thought, bringing his staff down square on the middle of Calennian's, seldom bent and never broke, either, and thus this current situation . . .

Calennian was tiring, his burnished face fading to gray, his movements ponderous. Kendric grinned and beat forward until the bonewood rang like hard rain. He was winning, driving Calennian back to where Kendric had made certain he himself would never retreat—within reach of the vengeful bonewood roots. Already free of the surface dirt, they rose up in waist-high concert and snapped at Calennian's untrousered legs like the jaws of a thorny-toothed beast. Calennian finally spoke—or swore, rather.

"Curse these ground thorns; they leap upon a man like a lemurai pack! Runners of the rim, the words, quickly!"

At bay, sweat polishing his swarthy face, Calennian held his cudgel two-handed before him and began chanting.

> "Stonekeep stand and notice take,
>   Overstone shine and bonewood—break!"

The chant echoed from among all the men behind Kendric, and then the pale wood in Kendric's hand fell noiselessly in two, leaving him brandishing a uselessly short shaft. He stared at the stump in his fist, a surge of rage at being so easily disarmed tightening his grip upon it. If only he had his sword from Rule, these rude fellows would not make cheap sport of him; he'd demonstrate some of the more persuasive arts of war to these savages . . .

His desire was so great, his eyes painted the likeness of the familiar hilt over the useless wood in his hand—runic-embossed metal well wrapped with sweat-stained leather, and then the wide, thick swath of ancient-forged steel shining dull silver, ready to cut or crush. He wished for it so ardently that for a moment the image of it hung there in his hand; he could almost feel metal and leather instead of bonewood . . . He looked up, aware that he had momentarily forgotten his still-armed opponent. Calennian stared, too, at the wood in Kendric's hand, as did the entire band.

Kendric looked back to his shadow sword. It was not a shadow, not an illusion. It was there, as it had felt and looked in Rule, except that beyond the first foot of steel only a ghostly gray suggestion of a blade protruded into the pale daylight. No! Kendric's fist splayed open; with fingers fanned in denial, he dropped the phantom sword. Bonewood fell to the ground, ringing a last, wistful note.

Gryff was there, picking up the broken wood reverentially. He blew softly across the broken end. A mournful whistle sounded. "Welcome to the Rynth, Kendric of the Far Keep. Wherever that is, it matters not. We rim-runners, through much practice and acting in concert, have learned some few things. But such magic as you have—"

"Magic? No magic." Kendric snatched the broken wood from Gryff's hand and examined it. Hollow—that accounted for the sound. And as for the other, the illusion, *his* illusion, though these headstrong men seemed bent on sharing it . . . He turned the wood in his hands and studied the shattered end, which had splintered like the bone for which the wood was named.

"We can cast break-spells," Helicon said in his smooth voice, stepping over and fixing Kendric with vivid sapphire eyes. "But none of us—none—can use make-spells. Only they—" His flaxen lock of hair nodded toward some far distance or location. "—have make-magic, and they do not share, the Stonekeepers. They and the ice-eyed ones who come, from time to time. Welcome, Kendric, to the Inlands of Ten. You will share fire with us."

Kendric shrugged. He was suddenly weary, bone-sore, and flesh-stung from the bonewood root inroads on his legs. A wind had risen during his battle with Calennian, and the sky had dimmed to deep amethyst until the arch-caught moon shone soft silver. This place they called the Rynth, never warm, had cooled. His tunic clung damp and chill. He was of no mind to dissuade these gullible fellows of his "magic" if it would get him fire, food, and company for the night.

And he had all that in the low caves of the rocks where the band camped. He finally understood why they had jeered at his face-first quaffing habits at the riverbed. Dinner that night was river-skimmed fleshfin, small, flat fish equipped with large thistly suckers.

"Blood," Gryff said shortly. "Their favorite food. From anything that drinks directly from the Rynthian rivers. Blood of bonefish, blood of lorryk, blood of lemurai, blood of man."

"And blood of woman," another man put in.

They laughed, the laughter of men discussing women when there were no women about. And there were no women about. What women would live in this wilderness? Kendric wondered, already homesick for the comforts of Rule.

The band settled for sleep, their backs against the rocks, the fire embers warming their boot-clad feet. Kendric remained awake. He finally slipped outside to sit and stare at the pale, immobile moon, large as his fist in the black night sky, looking as near as a walk along the sky bridge would take him.

He pulled out his boarskin purse and delved for the small stone at its bottom. He was a warrior without a sword, with a purse empty of all but flint and steel and one Torloc tear, in a world where magic still reigned. He sighed. Somewhere among the endless rocks, some wild creature stared at the moon as he did. The act ended in the howl he heard now—wild, riding up and down a lonely ridge of piercing rage or anger, ending in an ululating series of sobs.

Kendric dropped the clear stone back into his purse. Where was Irissa? In the new Torloc world now, no doubt, safe and content and most forgetful of him whom she had drawn through a gate on a whim...

Kendric leaned his head back against hard rock and continued his silent communing with the alien moon. His name, he told it solemnly, was Kendric and he was a fool.

Chapter Three

There had been a moon in Rule that went through decent moonlike phases—fat and full at one time, sickle at another, amber like a moonweasel's eye on some nights, ripe orange on others...

This moon was one constant, pale open eye, and Kendric did not like it. It watched him, this moon, thought its own secret thoughts about what it saw. At the moment, it saw Kendric still sitting outside the low caves that served as temporary shelter for the rim-runners. Kendric was unsure if the moon heard as well as saw. If it did not hear, it had another advantage over him; from inside the caves, magnified by low, echoing stone ceilings, came the sturdy snores of sleeping rim-runners.

Kendric ran his hands along the length of supernaturally smooth, broken bonewood beside him. He did not know what beasts of prey hunted this wasteland, but if the shallow river waters held fish that could drain a man's blood, he imagined there would be things that did as well for themselves on land. A man wanted more between such things and himself than the night music of his comrades.

The Rynth was a desolate, meager land, bleached into a pattern of light landscape and sharp shadow by the glow of the never-waning moon. The land lay like the skeleton of some gigantic beast under the dark purple sky—upthrust rocks here some crumbling hipbone, low line of distant bonetrees there some disintegrating ribs . . . Kendric shook his head until it rattled. Mooning. In Rule, a full moon was held to stir strange rhythms in the blood, and activities were avoided on such nights. Here, in this place they called the Inlands of Ten, it was worth speculating what effects the presence of an ever-full moon would have . . .

There was no nightly flutter, chatter, or hooting in such flat terrain. The Rynth was much like the Rocklands of Rule, after all, where only six-legged lizards scraped a living from creeping and slithering things . . .

Something was snaking across the distance now, visible because of the full moon and the flat landscape. Above Kendric, a pulse of sizzling mauve color flashed along one side of the sky arch holding the moon in place, followed by a lightning bolt of copper. From far, far away came another throbbing howl of anguish. Kendric tightened his loose fist on the broken cudgel at his side and wished for a sword. He watched the thing snaking along in the distance. It was nearer and it was not a beast, but a train of men, back-burdened until they resembled hulking beasts on hind legs. Kendric retreated into the darkened caves and shook awake the first man his fingers found.

"Some party comes."

"What?" Gryff barked out in mid-snore.

"Strangers come."

Gryff shuffled over to the low cave entrance and peered out across the stark land. The train had grown larger now. Kendric blinked at the sight.

"There are no strangers in the Rynth but you, friend," Gryff finally grumbled. "If they are not rim-runners, then they come from one of the Stonekeeps, and few from there venture here. So why wake me?"

"Something is out there! Perhaps these men from the Stonekeep hope to catch you snoring. In my world, we were not wont to lie meekly waiting for whatever phenomenon the night threw at us—"

"Your world?"

"The—Keep—I come from."

Gryff nodded sourly. "Mad Chaundre's, likely. I don't know why the other magicians tolerate him. Very well, Kendric of the Strange Keep, I will stand watch with you until yonder party comes near enough to declare itself." Gryff folded one burly bare arm over the other and stared into the distance without saying more.

The train wove nearer, clearly distinguishable now as having twelve or thirteen individual members, some wearing a bow's sharp thrust above their shoulders. Kendric watched them approach with unflagging suspicion, but Gryff was silent until his arms slowly unfolded and he stared sharply at the newcomers, who were still beyond hail. His elbow suddenly jabbed Kendric in the hip, for such was the difference in height between them.

"You did right to wake me, friend, very right," he commented jovially, turning to bellow into the cave mouth. "Wake up, you lemurai-loving sluggards! Some company comes!"

About time for the alarm, Kendric thought, reaching for his cudgel. Gryff's hearty laughter stopped him. The rest of the rim-runners circled Kendric now, their hands empty of weapons, their ill-assorted eyes abrim with good-natured ridicule.

"That's not the weapon you'll need for *these* visitors, Kendric," Gryff said broadly. "If yon party is not the Unkept women, my ear's made of tin and Ivrium has wasted sixteen years of spirit-smithing—well, be about your barter, runners of the rim. I've got a special offering to fetch."

Gryff ducked back into the caves while the other rim-runners set hide-wrapped bundles on the ground and sat cross-legged behind them, staring eagerly at the approaching party. Kendric remained standing, arms folded noncommittally across his chest, palms itching for the pommel of some weapon.

The night was still luminous, the air chill. The only things moving over the bones of the land were the antlike forms growing ever larger, advancing with processional certainty to the rim-runners clustered about the rocks.

"Who are the Unkept women?" Kendric asked flax-haired Helicon, the man sitting nearest his boot toes.

The lanky plainsman, his seated form jackknifed into four sharp angles, spoke without glancing up. "Outcasts from the Stonekeeps, as we are. Or rather, runaways. They are bevy-women gone rogue, who prefer the lean living of the Rynth to the cushioned comfort of the Keeps. For that they are like us rim-runners—foolish and free."

"The Stonekeeps must be dire places, then, if so many flee them for the Rynth."

"No, stranger friend Kendric. The Stonekeeps are marvelous, fair and warm, with the very winds that brush them and the air around them kept scented and soft by magic. On my lush home plains, our Lord Warden has anchored his iron tents, impervious to rain and wind, and there the bearing-beasts of the Inlands gallop free for the taking. Ivrium trades with his fellow magicians—bearing-beasts for one of Melinth's strange flying lizards or encrusted cloths from the hands of Sofistron's bevy embroiderers. All is soft and ease within the circle of influence cast by the Stonekeeps. The peasants toil and live and die very pleasantly within that space and never see or hear of the Rynth, save as a vision with which to terrorize their adventuresome swaddlings who might wander afield."

"Then why leave?"

"Why did you leave your Far Keep, friend?"

Kendric thought, then frowned. "I was invited elsewhere, by one who—"

"Was female?"

"That," Kendric finally conceded. "Among other things. But—"

Helicon's supple hand gestured at the now fully arrived party. "So also were we." He uncoiled and stood, in Gryff's absence obviously the spokesman.

"Welcome, women of the Rynth. The Overstone shines cold this night. Will you share fire flicker with us?" he asked formally.

The newcomers clustered silently along the rock-rimmed clearing's edge. Women! Kendric thought doubtfully. They were as oddly caparisoned as the rim-runners—hung with short leathern kilts and bits of fur and hide—and as oddly composed; some were man-tall, others short and slight, some dark of face and light of hair, others oppositely favored. They, too, were weapon-draped, though bows and daggers seemed more numerous than spears and axes.

The shortest of them stood to their fore, like a haughty foothill barring the way to a sharp peak, and spoke for them.

"Fire would be welcome. We have come to trade," she answered as formally. The seated men let out a sigh of relief at her words, but Kendric shifted uneasily on his still-wary feet. The Rynth was a strange land, and these strange men and women apparently had stranger still customs; he would not relax his guard until events gave him reason to.

"Will Amozel take a seat?" Helicon gestured gracefully to a sort of rock throne near the cave entrance. The woman who had spoken walked over and sat impassively. The others followed, the clink and clatter of their beweaponed passage watched avidly by the seated semicircle of men. Calennian rose, went to the unlighted tent of sticks and scrubs on the ground before the rock, and held his open palms over it as the rim-runners chanted in unison:

> "Overstone shine and ice-arch quake,
> Starshine fall and fire take."

Calennian's palms shone red briefly, then they were warming themselves over a flickering pattern of flame. Kendric almost took it for make-magic, save he realized that fire ate wood, and it was break-magic after all. Break-magic, make-magic! He was beginning to believe it all. Next he would convince himself that his longsword of Rule had momentarily lain heavy in his hand but hours ago—upon his mere wish for it! He stepped back and sank into his old place again. The rim-runners waited.

Helicon stood then and went over to the small woman perched on the rock, her booted toes barely brushing the ground. "Will you take ale with us?"

"We will take wine," she intoned imperiously. "But you may pour." Burdens were shifted off shoulders as the women clustered behind her and undid their sacks; the clank of metal hailed the appearance of a goblet for each. Helicon stepped up to the woman most obviously of his kind—a bonewood-angular giantess with her flaxen hair braided into dozens of beast tails—and accepted the wineskin she shrugged off her back. He made the rounds of each woman's cup, pouring a dark stream. He did not serve the spokeswoman. Nor the rim-runners.

When the skin was a third empty, Helicon laid it down and stood before the seated woman.

"Who will go first?" she inquired. There was quiet in the

camp, on both sides of the now strongly flickering fire. Kendric could hear the flames whispering secrets to one another as they broke the bones of the wood with fierce cracks and snaps. Something very odd was going on here, something—

"I," Helicon said. He turned defensively to the men seated behind him. "In Gryff's absence..."

They made no objection, but seemed to be holding their breath, as did the women across the circle. Helicon returned to his sitting spot and picked up his bundle. He brought it to the tiny woman enthroned on the rocks.

"Amozel, I bring you and your women—a comb." Small gasps of pleasure came from the women, though from what Kendric had seen, only the wind had ever combed their disheveled locks. Helicon flourished his offering aloft, so the leaping flames polished its many-toothed length rosy. It was white, and sharp. "Of fleshfin spine," Helicon announced importantly, turning so that both women and men could see it and admire it.

The small woman smiled tightly, without opening her lips. "A dearly won treasure indeed. I was minded to mate you with Palimoyra of your own kind this night—" Here the giantess tossed her fierce braids in disapproval. "—but I am pleased and will award you...Odalisc. Ivrium did not value her; see that you do."

Helicon bowed away, his lean, pale hand tight upon the arm of some wispy, bronze-skinned gamin who looked nevertheless as if she could chew fleshfin unfilleted. Lanky Helicon, however, seemed fiercely pleased with his petite prize, and they vanished together into the dark of the caves.

"And?" Amozel asked into the silence that was broken only by the fire's flapping in the hushed night air.

"And I." One of the seated men scrambled up, his bundle small and unpromising across his palms. He eyed the standing women, licked his lips, and pulled back the rough cloth. "I have a...well, several actually, enough for three or four." He elevated something like a jewel between his thumb and forefinger, but the firelight shot right through it. "Archer's ring. For dainty fingers. Made of—carved from—bonewood."

Their gasp rose as one even as Amozel rose also and advanced to take the object from the man and stare through its center. "So it is, and much carving these bangles must have cost you."

"Since your last visit," he admitted, ducking his head.

"Enough for three or four..." Amozel's small hand dove greedily into the pile of wooden rings; she let them trickle back onto his palm as coins; certainly they rang with the telltale musical clink of true bonewood. "Then, my good carver, you shall have three—or four. Who of my archers will, do so," she ordered with a crisp nod of her head. Behind her, a trio of women broke from the rest, pausing only to claim their rings from the man before surrounding him and escorting him into the caves to the accompaniment of giggles.

Kendric shifted on his feet. He could not comprehend this odd ceremony, and Helicon, his guide, had been first to go. So Kendric stood and glowered in the shadows as, one by one, the hardy rim-runners approached the imperious little woman, offered one item or another, and were awarded one woman or another. Bit by bit, the opposing groups dwindled. Kendric could now see individuals among the women, the fire painting their features with a certain barbaric beauty, whether they were slant-eyed or straight, tall or short, buxom or slender. One particularly he noticed finally, though he realized then that she was the one the waiting rim-runners let their eyes slide to most frequently. She was neither short nor tall, and thus could match either height with dignity. The fire rinsed her hair crimson, but Kendric guessed it was a gentler shade in daylight; even in moonshine, her eyes glimmered a faint, feline green. She stood, calm, singled out by every man's eye, if not by Amozel's choosing, one long, bare leg gracefully flexed, her longbow carelessly playing cane to her relaxed posture. Kendric did a quick count on both sides of the fire. There were more women than men—this seemed to be a universal condition in every world. It was possible this woman would not be awarded this night; it was impossible to tell whether she preferred to be assigned or to remain unchosen. That mystery alone enhanced her desirability.

But as the last of the rim-runners announced their gifts—a lorryk-horn-handled dagger and a long leather belt studded with a few pieces of metal—and took their granting, the women dwindled, but the flame-haired one still remained.

"And you?"

There was silence and few to break it.

"Well?"

Kendric stared at the tiny woman across the fire from him. "Me? I am just a stranger, I, uh—"

"Strangers bring strange goods—" the woman began severely, but there was an interruption.

"I bring something even stranger." Gryff strode into the clearing on legs of such stiff pride that he strutted. His bundle was thick and clumsy; the cloth barely covered it. Gryff held its selvage edges together until he stood directly before Amozel, then let them spring apart. "I bring this!"

Amozel's small, strong hands flew back in surprise; her pointed little face lighted with wonder. Then her narrow fingers were delving eagerly into Gryff's bundle, and she hoisted out some shimmering length of white.

"A hood," Gryff said gruffly. "Warm. Fowlen fur from the Cincture. Nowhere to be found in the Keeps, but fit for a queen, a queen of the Rynth."

Amozel's tiny hands flourished the thing about her head. It settled over her shoulders, a rough-shaped pelt of fur so white it shone silver at the hairtips. A feathery ruff flared from the pointed skullcap formed where Amozel's dainty features peeked through what once had been the wild thing's visage. It was hard to imagine what the creature had worn for a face after seeing Amozel's floating there amid a spray of feathers and fur. She smiled, showing even, white teeth, frightening in their perfection, and crossed her arms upon her breast to plunge her hands wrist-deep in the pelt furring her shoulders.

"Bravely done, Gryff," she purred. "Beautifully done. You shall have Demimondana this night and six more."

The statuesque redhead straightened to sudden life as Gryff tried to stammer out his gratitude. She leaned her bow against a rock and moved fluidly to Gryff, taking his arm and leading him deep within the cave's dark mouth.

Kendric watched them go in wonder.

"Strange gifts from a stranger, I still say," Amozel said.

Kendric turned to face her. The fire was sinking to a pale orange glow at his feet; no matter, he had some "magic" of his own to make it flare again—a flint and steel from Rule in the boarskin purse at his belt.

"I—I am a stranger, yes. But I bear no gifts. I beg to be absolved."

Amozel's lips quirked. "The begging shows a proper orientation, but no gifts... Surely such a strapping fellow as you can at least match one of these rim-runners. Have you never taken down a lorryk stag by the horns, my giant, or skeined fleshfin from the meanders that riddle this place? You must have something—one thing—that would buy you a night's respite in the lap of one of these."

On this she gestured to the remaining three or four women, and Kendric tried to mask his horror. As bandy-kneed, motly, and rag-hung a group of malebanes he had never seen—not since first sizing up the various members of the rim-runners. Yes, they suited one another well, but not him, thank whatever overgods there were in this moon-hung world. Here, as elsewhere, the best were claimed first.

"Nothing," Kendric said, fanning his large-palmed hands in demonstration.

Amozel's eyes, dark and birdlike, now that he noticed it, narrowed. "Step nearer," she ordered softly, and he saw the hands of her remaining henchwomen move surreptitiously to their bows. He stepped nearer.

She was quite impressive close up, a sword-backed little woman quite prettily made, but with iron underlining every contour of her. He saw why she ruled the lank, the strong, the young, the lovely, and the headstrong equally. The fowlen pelt hooded her aspect in even deeper mystery, and Kendric shuddered a bit at the hard, dark burn of Amozel's gaze from the regal surround of white feather and fur.

"Something, you must offer me something, surely," she coaxed, but there was nothing of persuasion in her voice.

"Only a—a broken cudgel," Kendric said. He retrieved the thing and held it out to her. "Uncarved, you can see, quite useless. Hardly an offering."

Her face averted from his suddenly, her small hand thrown up before it with bird-claw intensity. "Make-magic. It has been remade in your image. Away with it! I scent it, the spell. Away!"

Kendric was happy to toss it from him; it had served him ill until now.

Amozel calmed and turned her face back to him. The feathers on her headpiece stood separated and ruffled, as if still on their living owner.

"You wear a purse at your belt of some kind of skin. I will extract some tribute from you for the fault of bringing magic to my eyes. Empty it."

Her pale palm was extended, tense and open. Kendric shrugged and shook his boarskin above it. Two objects tumbled out.

"Flint and steel. Almost worthless in my—in my Keep. But you may like them—they make fire—" As he suspected, the word "make" alone was enough to repel her. She thrust her palm at him and he took back the items. One last thing tumbled out of the still-gaping purse into her palm then. Amozel's breath drew in, in fear and horror. She stood, as if drawn upright by some force in her hand. Her dark eyes drilled into Kendric's, humanly beseeching.

"This thing, take it, I beg you, take it from me!"

He stared at her palm. There, cradled in its very center, lay a quivering bit of quicksilver, mirror-bright. Kendric could even see a minuscule image of himself staring gape-mouthed into the tiny cabochon.

"Take it!" Amozel screeched.

Kendric slowly touched a fingertip to the alien silver. It leaped for his flesh as if for home and solidified there into a teardrop of clear, hard coldstone. His thumb pinched it safe only an instant before it would have fallen to the ground.

"Magic," Amozel intoned, holding up her palm. The center of it glowed faintly luminescent green. "Strong make-magic. Keep your purse, stranger, and your powers. You bear a stone, an alien stone, and neither I nor mine will have aught to do with you this night or any other. Away. Leave us in peace."

Kendric retreated to his rock-backed post, sliding his rangy length to the ground. He elevated the coldstone to peer through it to the fire's last glowing embers. Make-magic indeed, if it could make three harridans back off from a man and keep their rather formidable selves to themselves. Kendric tossed the clear bit of glitter up in the air and caught it neatly as it came down.

He grinned. Perhaps the tear of a Torloc seeress was more useful than he had thought.

He frowned then, but the Unkept women had turned their backs and were making themselves snug against their own territory of rock. Perhaps even a Torloc seeress was more useful than he had thought, he confessed to himself as he adjusted his weary frame on the hard ground, remembering certain satin lengths of impeccably combed hair and eyes that of neccessity refrained from drilling a bird-sharp gaze into his and demanding tribute. She had asked, not ordered, him hence, the Torloc seeress Irissa, and it was just as well she had escaped this place where magic was despised by some and envied by others. On that thought he fell asleep, being a man who would rather sleep with unbidden memories than with forbidding realities.

Chapter Four

———◆◆◆———

Before, it had been all black. Now, it was all white. There had been no transition from one color to the other, from one state to another. One merely *was*, then the other.

Gradually, the white began to assume a corporeal presence. Irissa lay on the white—some cold, stone floor—and looked up at the white—some icy inlaid ceiling in the same relentlessly milky hue. When she sat up, the white walled her in, luminous, pale, almost mockingly sentient. She had the impression of many foggy figures surveying her from somewhere beyond the translucent walls. Only one was in the chamber with her, if indeed anything so smooth and all of a piece could be a chamber. He was as light in his way as the room; his full head of shoulder-length gilded hair merged with a mustache even more gilded. His pale-skinned, unwrinkled face watched her closely.

Irissa braced her fingers on the pavement and was shocked to feel a chill seep up through her bones, as if she sat on ice . . . Yes, that was what seemed to surface this room, some artificial sheet ice—clear yet cloudy, cold but not truly frozen.

"The chill stems from the nature of the stones," the man told her, observing her shudder, "and the fact that no hearth or great number of humanity present alters its innate coolness. This chamber is seldom used," he added dryly.

He walked nearer, but Irissa, her attention drawn downward, saw that his feet had stopped at a tiny ridge of silvery dust. Her eyes followed its miniature topography until her head would turn no more; her gaze jerked over her opposite shoulder.

"Yes, a circle. A circle laid to contain you. It has been here a long time, a very long time. Likely since before you were born. Ah, conundrums make you impatient, do they? I should be patient in your place, Torloc. You will have little else to do now but learn to be patient."

"How do you—"

"Ah, yes, now the how; later the why. Very well, I have no dislike of sharing my hows. Let me answer you fully before you ask. It will exercise my logic."

The man began striding along the gleaming frosty walls, making a circle and only then bringing home to Irissa that this entire chamber was circular. She twisted to follow him with her eyes, still oddly aware of a shifting line of grayish ghost figures immured in the white stone.

"How do I know that you are Torloc? Simple. Torlocs have come to the Inlands of Ten heretofore. Next how. How long have you been here?" The man stopped and fixed her with his eyes. She avoided the direct glance, though not before she noted that his eyes were as colorless as his chamber walls— blank, unrevealing eyes, with neither warmth nor true iciness of intent. Irissa had the terrifying thought that if she did dare his direct gaze, she would see right through it to the smooth, white, veiling walls in which something moved with graceful regularity. "Only hours," he answered his own question.

"Next how." The man was obviously enjoying her wonder, her silence. "How did I bring you down and bear you here? The bearing was the simplest part—what else are bearing-beasts made for, and what else would hunters do with their prey but sling it over a hindquarter and convey it back to the hall? Not that I had anticipated more than a prize set of lorryk diadem this particular day. As for the bringing down—" The man stepped very near the silver circle and held out his open palm. "I am Sofistron, you are in my Stonekeep, and my Stone is the Lunestone. 'Tis no great honor to me; I merely inherited it in my time. But it takes its powers from our ever-shining moon, hence my own powers wane neither night nor day. I am become Overlord of all the Inlands magicians and I have some small skill at overcoming the senses in a variety of enchanting ways, including striking even a Torloc seeress quite senseless."

A milky stone glowed in his palm. It was a small, smooth thing, a pebble really, save that it gleamed with uncommon vivacity. Sofistron closed his parchment-pale fingers; a bit of the stone's light leaked through, painting his flesh faintly blue.

Irissa's glance recoiled.

"Yes." Sofistron laughed. "Wise Torloc. Avoid looking upon the Lunestone, by all means."

She opened her mouth to speak, but the admonishing raise of one long forefinger stopped her.

"Now. Not how—but where. Where indeed? In my castle, my pretty white stone castle. In a chamber within my castle that has been prepared for a Torloc for many doublings and redoublings of time upon its tracks. Longer than even I would care to sum up."

Sofistron pushed his trailing gown sleeves impatiently behind him and took another circuit of the room.

"There are some—all nine of my fellow Stonekeepers, I fear, were I to count, who would consider this chamber and what it holds—you, dear Torloc lady—" he said with a gallant bow that made Irissa twist up the corners of her mouth, "who would call this the veriest folly. Luckily, I rule in this Stonekeep and can keep what I will within it—in this case, you."

"And if I do not wish to be kept?" Irissa demanded.

"Ah. An 'if' question out of you. That I had not anticipated. If does not seem to be a potent word in the vocabulary of a Torloc seeress penned in by mirrors . . ."

Irissa darted her glance around the slick, pale walls. Mirrors! Not really, but if even half-true, then the gray figures that shifted as she moved must have been—herself!

"Polished commonstone. And a circle, you see, so there's

no avoiding it. I had to send my hunters, bailiffs, and even some rather grumpish bureaucrats out into the Rynth for wagonloads of it. Commonstone pebbles carpet the many meanders that run through the Rynth. And it's a bit too bright for true mirroring, but it will serve, I think. Poor fools. One or two were lost to the fleshfins. A small price to pay for an Inlands wonder—one round room capable of containing a Torloc. You have another 'how' for me?"

She looked at his bland face—not at the eyes, for that would have been courting greater danger than what lay in the commonstone refracting around her. But in Rule she had become adept at reading men's faces by their edges. It was only when a Torloc attempted to read the center that she occasionally went wrong. He was perfectly pleased with himself, in command of himself, this Sofistron. It was unlikely that he should not be in command of her, as he had said.

She finally asked it, though she recognized that her question signaled another victory for him. "Why?"

He might have smiled; at least the beard shifted a bit. "I mean you no bodily harm," he answered obliquely. "You shall not suffer. I mean only to use you. Too long have the Inlands been a mere footpath for those of your kind, on your mysterious errands to places we dare not go, consorting with powers we dare not think upon. I, Sofistron, will be the first to dare. And you will make it possible. I cannot bid you make yourself comfortable on such barren stone," he admitted with a host's regret. "But I can at least see that you are tended by my bevy. Do not cross the silver sand; it was ground at great risk from the smallest sliver of my Lunestone. The bevywomen may pass things through to you, but under no circumstance are you to cross the invisible plane the sand represents, unless you wish to confront your own image face to face, for the zone is also a veil, and these gray shadows of yourself wear but a fraction of the intensity they would in unfiltered light. So rest, Torloc. That really is all that is left for you to do at present."

He stepped back into the stone, ebbed to a gray figure, and was gone. Truly a veil separated her from the limits of the room. Irissa put her hand slowly out to a point directly above the shining sand. Her fingertips trembled forward, paused, plunged, and drew back, seared. She looked at them. The skin was white, dead white, the blood frozen from it in an instant. Irissa's hand curled in upon itself as she sat back on her heels and took another survey of the walls. The phantom figures' heads turned with her; there was not merely a single reflection, which was danger enough, but a whole multiplication of them, reflecting one from the other until they magnified into an army of Irissas bent on containing their original, on holding her captive. They were a force more threatening than any gibbering, snapping ring of fang-toothed, human-fingered hounds, because they were herself.

She slept; it was one way to foil the watchers that were herself. But she woke weary, her back cramped from lying on the remorseless stone that even reflected her image downward, although her features were blurred by the depth of reflection.

More gray figures surrounded her—not the images of the wall, but individual women, all attired in the same flowing, silken gray, with even their heads veiled. One flowed forward.

"I bring you bread," she said breathlessly, suddenly thrusting a common woven basket across the sand-indicated line. Irissa was so surprised she took it.

"Sofistron says you are to be well cared for," the woman went on nervously in her light, piping voice. "We of the bevy will see to it."

"How can you see to anything?" Irissa wondered, gesturing at their heads, which were veiled from crown to upper lip, the fabric held fast to their temples by circlets of some greenish metal. They reminded her of the Iridesium circlet still binding her own forehead, once a veil-holder in Rule but now only a reminder that she had doffed all veils in exchange for true vision. "How can you see at all?" she asked again.

Their silence was suddenly replaced by giggles. "The shivan-cloth is transparent outward, opaque inward. We learn all our lives to weave it close-threaded but fine, so we see more out than others see in. Are you not eating your bread?"

The speaker seemed to be their spokeswoman. Irissa broke the soft white loaf into pieces and nibbled at one to placate them. It tasted salty and bland. "What is your name?" she asked, though names seemed useless among women so impossible to differentiate from one another. But she had to start someplace if she were to puzzle her way to freedom and find Kendric.

"Name? I have no name. It would give someone other than Sofistron power over me, and that would be most unseemly. But I am Lady Ward of this Stonekeep. That is name enough for me. The others are bevywomen and do not signify."

At this offhand dismissal, they all burst into giggles.

"Lady Ward?"

"I am first chosen."

"You are all wives of Sofistron?"

"They are wives," the spokeswoman answered contemptuously. "I am Lady Ward. Here. Some wine to wash down the bread. The goblet's metal has been black-breathed upon by Sofistron, so you need fear no reflection."

"Most considerate," Irissa noted, taking the flat, black metal cup the Lady Ward handed her. The woman's hands were as pale as Sofistron's, but Irissa noticed that the other women's hands ranged in shade from yellow or copper to brown or pink, a veritable flesh-toned rainbow.

"And you all come from this Stonekeep?" Irissa swallowed from the dead black goblet; its surface was cold and unsleek, repellent, but she detected no spell in it other than the veiling of its natural glimmer. The wine within was as flat as its container.

"We come from the Inlands over," said one who had not spoken. Her voice was deep and rich and matched her copper hands. "We are First Daughters; the magicians woo one another assiduously for our addition to their bevies."

"But you are not Lady Ward, Ryantha," the first woman snapped, as if angry that her role as sole speaker had been superseded. "You plainswomen learn pride in Ivrium's iron tents and are the bane of every bevy. I am surprised you did not slither away to the Rynth, as so many of your kind—"

"In any Stonekeep but Sofistron's, *I* would have been Lady Ward," Ryantha challenged, her veil trembling above her lips at the vehemence of her words.

"Would have been," the Lady Ward mocked in her lilting, arrogant voice. "All of you are 'would have beens.' Only I *am* Lady Ward. You would do well to remember it, or I shall have the bailiffs tickle the soles of your feet with the switch."

They were silent then. Irissa noticed that while the bit of their feet that peeped out from the veiling hems were strapped with jewel-set gilded leathers, these phantom sandals had no soles.

"Surely your feet must be chill on such icy stone," she suggested. A dozen gray shoulders shrugged.

"We are used to it," a third voice said philosophically—a new speaker, but which one was impossible to tell, for all mouths were still by the time Irissa had surveyed the group. At least with these eye-veiled women Irissa need fear no self-reflection in their pupils and thus a lessening of her powers . . .

Power! What power did she have in an enchanted circle where the warders were herself? It was a self-generating trap Sofistron had created for a Torloc. The longer she remained, the more she caught some inadvertent glimpse of her shadowy self on the outer walls, the more her power ebbed to the walls. Commonstone, he had called their surface. In Rule the same rocks would be called coldstone, some of them the once-living tears of a Torloc seeress, as rare as Iridesium. Irissa put her seared fingertips, still numb, to the circlet at her forehead. She felt a faint tingle; her hand came away unfrozen. If coldstones were only commonstones here, perhaps Iridesium remained potent. In Rule, linked into mail, Iridesium could repel sword strokes with magical ease. No one had yet forged the metal into service, other than as decoration or defense; perhaps it also had a cutting edge, a magically cutting edge . . .

"And I will have you women of the bevy to attend me all the time?" Irissa inquired, munching docilely on her bread.

"All the time? Indeed not! We have embroidery to do. Our Lord Warden depends heavily upon our needle arts to encrust gifts to his fellow magicians, so they can carry on the trade among themselves that makes our masters comfortable."

"I am sorry, Lady Ward, if I have taken overmuch of your time. Here. Your wine cup. I am finished."

The Lady Ward snapped her small, pale fingers. "Ryantha. You take it. You will have to scour it clean again before we use it at Keep table. Sofistron can't be bothered to unspell it; he has much to do, he told me. We are to keep her fed and clothed and well. And first we shall weave some proper skirts for her—and Keep-thongs. Look at those great, clumsy boots she wears—like one of *those* women from the Rynth!"

"Perhaps you do not want to expose her feet," Ryantha suggested silkily, her copper hands tight on the black goblet's stem. "Perhaps if they are too fair, Sofistron will decide he wants her in the bevy. And then, if she is an empowered woman, perhaps she will rise to Lady Ward."

"I'll keep my boots," Irissa nearly growled, drawing her feet hastily under her.

The Lady Ward's gray veil lay still about her upper face. It suddenly blew forward with her words. "Yes, keep your ugly things; we will feed you—when we must, and no sooner. So do not be ambitious yet, outlander; remember, you are in our hands until Sofistron has time to deal with you as he intends to."

They swept away in a gray scudding cloud; with them went the little warmth their mere presence had lent to the chamber. A phalanx of gray figures remained in the encircling walls, waiting to move when Irissa moved, gray because Irissa wore the gray silken tunic and trousers of Rule, quiet now because Irissa did not move. She thought.

There would be no harm to her but the loss of her freedom and containment within this barren circle—at least for now. Yet that was harm enough. There were only the bevywomen to watch her, since Sofistron apparently put all his faith in his commonstone walls and silvery sand. Yet even if she passed the searing wall that only she could feel, she would be ringed by a clear-seeing set of her own images; it would take great concentration to pass them and to find the one point in the seamless chamber that provided a door for those who knew where to look for it.

It would be a comfort to have someone of Kendric's simple blunt attack with her now. He would doubtless merely lumber through the sand directly to the door, his warrior's confidence of dealing with things physically arming him against considering a dozen different paralyzing alternatives. But that was because he was wont to carry a weapon; it was harder to be so venturesome when one's weapon was oneself. Unless...

Irissa's fingers stretched to her circlet again, their tips resting lightly along the metal. She felt the same slight stir of power;

perhaps the commonstone reflected its native strengths back at it. She wrenched it off, turned the plain metal band in her hands. Its black was as muted as the goblet's, and the streaks of color that reflected in it were elusive—violet, gold, bright azure; they shifted as she turned it, racing her eye to the edge of the metal. It was smooth and seamless, but Irissa knew that mortal fire and human-held hammer had forged it. The Torlocs mined the Iridesium in Rule, but Rulians bought, sold, and made it into something. Ergo, there must be a seam somewhere. She turned the circlet in her hands until the metal warmed. Still her fingertips sensed no weld mark, no ridge, however slight, in the metal. Yet Iridesium did not grow round, like fruit on trees. There must be a seam. She honed her eyes on the circlet, chasing the fugitive colors around and around the narrow metal band, watching for an interruption, a place where they should leap some tiny metallic chasm...

She found it, a spot where the color stopped and danced momentarily like a waterdrop on a hot tong. Her forefingers marked the spot and then she set her eyes to warming the metal, melting the solder into a thick, viscous silver-gray pool, and stretching the circlet until the metal edges showed a seam. Her hands pulled hard at the well-sprung metal; her eyes released the solder; it dripped to the commonstone floor, hissed in protest, then coagulated into a hard, steel ball.

Irissa strained to straighten out the still-curved metal. Oh, for a bit of brute strength, for a bit more muscle and less brain... The metal remained semicurved, but one raw end was fairly straight, like an untapered blade. She pushed herself across the smooth floor to the miniature mountain range of piled sand that surrounded her. Gently, she touched the Iridesium edge to it. Sand shriveled away, creating a gap. Irissa raised the Iridesium to the air above it. There was a windborne hiss. She put her finger to where she thought the Iridesium had touched, then pressed slowly forward. Nothing. She felt nothing but air. She would cut a door in Sofistron's trap, and the Iridesium circlet—now straight—would be the key.

There was no time in a room where the walls reflected back a constant milky glow. Nothing told Irissa how long it had taken her to etch a door-shaped oblong in the air before her. Nor was there anything to tell her whether the lines she had drawn had dissipated the nothing that had hemmed her in. There was only one way to test her hopes—step into the space that once had seared her fingertips, using her whole body as testing ground. Irissa had never had to risk her physical body. Her sight, yes, even her powers; a Torloc seeress expected such risks. She had never contemplated annihilation of the simplest, most mortal part of her. Once beyond the barrier, should it be bridged, she faced a gauntlet of mirroring images. Those she would deal with as inspired at the moment. Her need at this moment was merely to step forward into the painful, searing passage of what was more felt than seen. Her body braced for the instant of motion. She held the Iridesium pointed before her, like a sword.

She stepped over the silver sand. The hiss of a thousand Abyssal Sea waves washed over her in a dry, icy gust. A ring of bright light tightened on her, and in it the Iridesium band in her hand curled back into a circle, like a living thing huddling into itself for shelter. A hundred figures moved toward her from the walls, but Irissa spun her glance so fast around them that they merged into one, solid gray mass. She stepped forward again and again into the blinding white. She had chosen to exit the circle nearest to where Sofistron and his bevywomen had seemed to enter and exit. So it was simply a matter of stepping forward and forward, inexorably, using her body as a kind of blunt instrument, driving mindlessly on, beating back the dazzling light and mirrored walls, and passing through as easily as through air . . .

There was gray all around her—not the crippling gray of her reflections, but the gray of torchlighted stone walls. Irissa stood in a hall. She turned back and saw a portal ablaze with white, a figure at its farthest recess turning to see her, a figure dressed in gray, like her, with unbound dark, streaming hair and eyes that . . .

She moved on, farther into the safe, solid stone passage. Escape was now merely a matter of following the spirals of the Keep, of eluding oncoming footsteps, and of plain mortal wiliness in slipping quiet as a thought through so much space and time and coming out on the fields she had seen, perhaps through the garden. Then through the long grasses until safe at the forest edge. Perhaps she would find the creatures that the huntsmen called the lorryk. Perhaps they would bear her far away. Perhaps she would find Kendric.

The gray walls seemed suddenly to rush inward at her, to the hiss of soft, flowing fabric. She had not heard the bevy-women coming, for their sandals had no soles, and there was no betraying slap of leather on stone. She was taller than most of them, but they pushed inward on her, as inexorably as a noose, and herded her back to where she had come from.

"No," she told them. "You don't need to stop me. None could blame you. I have magic and you have none."

They pressed on, silent, their mouths all the same straight, uncompromising line, whether etched on copper, cream, or amber skin. Their gray veils fluttered unrevealingly around their heads. They did not even need to touch her; they just nudged her back and back, mutely, relentlessly. As one, they surged forward and drove Irissa back foot by reluctant foot to the commonstone chamber that was her prison.

She stumbled backward, blinded suddenly when she crossed the threshold into the room again. She shut her eyes and retreated until her body was finally free of the feel of the bevy women. She was inside the silver sand. Sofistron was rushing into the room, gray figures parting to make way.

His long fingers held the Lunestone over the broken sand chain and it drew together, grain by grain. Behind him, the women gathered into a tight, silent gray mass.

"Your circlet will not unbend again," Sofistron told her. "The undiluted reflection of the outer walls has forged it shut beyond the workings of your magic or even mortal muscle. Here you are and here you shall stay until I say you may go."

He wheeled to leave, the bevywomen dropping as one into deep bows before him. The Lady Ward remained half-erect, having bent to a curtsy only. Irissa recognized her white hands holding wide the shapeless gray stuff of her skirt. They would have been ludicrous, these servile women, had their mindless press not just foiled her escape so effectively.

She sat again on the cold floor, careful not to look beyond the bevywomen to the seated gray hummocks of herself that mocked her in the veiled white walls. It was a good thing

her diminished train and to continue to be completely ignorant of whatever Rynthian customs were being enacted within.

"Stone." Kendric mulled the word. Stones evidently had a potent reputation in this place. It was a pity they were of no use to him, whatever Amozel should think. "Well, I save the stone for important uses."

She nodded approval, the white feathered ruff hooding her features and lending even more dignity to what was forbidding to begin with. "You are not a true Stonekeeper, then; they are forever flourishing their Stones and their powers about. It is good to hoard such things; whatever the service they do you, the ill they return is twelve times the benefit."

"Quite true," Kendric said fervently.

"You seem oddly indifferent to magic for a maker of it," Amozel observed, her features lightening for the first time into simple curiosity. She was even more fearsome then, for she merely looked wise and pretty, and Kendric knew that to be a deadly combination in the female of any species.

"You loathe magic," he answered instead, "yet you consort with the rim-runners, and they have their chants and disconcerting little spells . . ."

"*I* consort with no one, Stonekeeper."

"Kendric."

"What?"

"My name. I would rather be known by it than by the possession of any pebble in my pocket."

"You keep the stone in the hide-skin purse at your belt," Amozel noted suspiciously.

"A mere figure of speech." Kendric sighed. "But for one who despises magic and its making, you appear to venture routinely into the rim-runner camp."

Amozel's lower lip curled. "That is business. Trade. Unkept women do not live by bow and arrow alone. We need forged metal, and that takes muscle. We need other things that it is more convenient to bargain for than to get for ourselves. And Gryff and his men see to it that their offerings are untainted by any magical shortcut of manufacture. Except you—"

Kendric stood impatiently and stamped his booted feet to get the blood moving again. "I. You seem to convict me of magic as if it were an odor you scent. I know only the magic of edged steel and sometimes blunted brain. I have seen magic and have known those who make it—or break it—but I myself am only the butt of magic, its victim. Ask Gryff, who brought the bonewood to break in my very hand. Ask another, who brought me to a magical gate and then left me to be spat out of it as a piece of gristle. They may keep their magic, the magicians and the sorceresses, and you may keep your suspicions of me quiet."

"Perhaps." Amozel sounded amused. "But even magic may wear a rude and honest face, though I grant you it does not often do so." She drew the white fur closer to her throat and shut her eyes, leaning her regal little head against the stone wall behind her.

Kendric moved back to the rock that had pillowed him for the night. He had been willing to plead lack of magic, but not quite in such homely terms. Even a Torloc seeress, the most sophisticated of a magical breed, had found him more than that. He curled watchfully into his cloak, and was not surprised when a form scrambled over to join him soon after. It was Helicon. Across the now-roaring fire, his wiry woman for the night before rejoined her kind and squatted on her heels to sample a mealcake.

"Transaction completed?" Kendric inquired indifferently.

Helicon grunted an affirmative. "You spent the night alone on the rocks?" he demanded then, somewhat incredulously.

"Not alone. I had *them* for company." Kendric gestured at the women across from the two men.

"Yes, but none of the comforts of their company, friend Kendric."

"Then it's as it appears, you rim-runners barter for the women?"

"Does it never happen so in your part of the Inlands?"

"In—my Keep occasionally; but more often, men and women go together by an exchange of—of wills, not worldly goods."

Helicon laughed. "What hard feelings that must make for. Oh, of course we rim-runners hope to have our own women to keep, in time. But for now, the Unkept will suffice. After all, this is what we came into the Rynth for."

Kendric was incredulous. "For *them*?"

"Aye. A handsome lot. Bare-faced and leather-soled. Oh,

we know the best women are kept close behind bevy veils, but these will do for now. They will not show their feet, more's the pity, but doubtless they are not great prizes in that department, else they would not be Unkept."

"If the better women are in the Stonekeeps, why did you not stay?" Kendric demanded.

Gryff's voice answered from behind them. "Because the women of the Keeps are not for us, or for the bailiffs or the bureaucrats or even the warriors and huntsmen. Not even for the One Son when his appointment is full made. The bevies belong to the Stonekeepers alone, and the rest of us keep to a single lot, unless we grow weary of our own company and strike out for the Rynth and the willing though dear consort of the Unkept women."

It had been a long speech for Gryff, but he had spit it out while still standing above the two men. Now he crouched beside them, his knees creaking, and stared into the dancing fire.

"Oh, Demimondana's hair teases like the lick of flames, and I've six more nights for the fowlen fur. It was worth the Cincture and the tracks along my back. I swear, not a fairer face lives beneath even bevy shivan-cloth. After this, I'll raid my bevy wife and settle to peasantry at the edge of some Keep and stay happy until they till me under."

"*You* were awarded Demimondana?" Helicon's copper face flared even duskier. "It has never been done, to my knowledge. We all thought Demimondana was to be kept to tempt some Stonekeeper away from his docile bevy . . ."

"You should have stayed later, Helicon," Gryff said with a wink. "But you were so keen to rush that stringy morsel off to an inspection of the caves—"

Helicon pummeled Gryff to silence and gave Kendric a chance to ask a few of the questions that were nudging one another at the gateway of his mind for equal egress.

"These women consort with the Stonekeepers as well as you?"

"When it suits Amozel's purpose, though she likes it not. Of course, the magicians have to leave their blasted stones behind, and few are quite so hot to do that as they are to slip their Stonekeeps now and again."

"And what is this Cincture, Gryff, and this fowlen fur, and these fowlen . . . ?"

For answer, Gryff stripped his rough tunic off his shoulder to reveal a serrated track of pink and white skin crisscrossing his muscular back. "Fowlen beak. Once it starts gouging, it never stops until the cursed thing's dead. It took the men of the rim three solid hours of solemn con-chanting to stop the bleeding when I came back from my expedition, bearing *that*." Gryff nodded across the fire to Amozel and the pelt draping her head and shoulders. "Suits her, doesn't it? I feared she'd be so pleased with my gift that she'd break all custom and offer herself as reward." He shrugged his tunic shut again. "Luckily, it was the divine Demimondana, whom no living man has shared bed with—until Gryff the Golden-Eared." Gryff rubbed his one polished attribute pridefully. "But you, Kendric. You had cold comfort last night, I warrant, unless your make-magic conjured up a sleep-siren."

"I like my own company. And I *have* no magic," Kendric growled. "I just finished telling Amozel that and now I tell you."

Gryff and Helicon exchanged dubious looks.

"Of course, Kendric," Helicon said smoothly. "You are wise to keep your powers to yourself. We rim-runners must exercise our crude magic in concert and would offer no threat to a possessor of his own magic like you, but if you choose to keep up the pretense—"

"I choose to tell the truth!" Kendric exploded. "And if you care to let me have a weapon other than your singing, stubborn bonewood, I will prove the truth of my magic with the chatter of it on your thick heads . . ."

Kendric had finally produced a string of insults long enough to have possibly infuriated the rim-runners, had they been listening. Instead they had risen with him, not to heed his challenge, but to squint into the diffuse light of the dawning Rynth day and watch a lone dot come zigzagging toward the camp.

"Calennian," Kendric announced, recognizing the lanky cudgel master who had rung bonewood with him. "He has been gone all night."

"Of course," Gryff said. "He had a mission. And if he has succeeded, I would be almost minded to cede one of my nights with Demimondana to him." Helicon stared. "But not quite. Well?" Gryff demanded when Calennian finally stood panting before them.

"True," the man gasped out. "I have been all the way to the foundation of Sofistron's Stonekeep. There was more flutter than a downed lorryk in the meadows. An ice-eyed one."

"An ice-eyed one? You're certain?" Gryff's red-brown eyes kindled with a fever that seemed totally unrelated to the night before.

Calennian nodded, gasping. "Taken within. The peasants were out in their fields and abuzz with it. Taken alive. Are you sure you want *him* to hear?"

The three rim-runners turned to look dumbly at Kendric. Gryff's face was feverish, triumphant. Calennian's expression was exhausted—and worried. Helicon frowned.

Gryff rubbed his hand over his mouth instead of his ear for a change. "What harm can he do? And mayhap he'll help. 'Tis certain not all of our brothers of the rim will want to storm a Stonekeep with an ice-eyed one as prize, not even with the lure of bevy booty."

"Bevy. Stonekeep. Icy eyes." Kendric was more confused than angry. "Can't you fellows speak plain and straight?"

"Straight, aye? All right, Helicon, your tongue is as silver as my ear is gold, I swear. Tell him."

Helicon brushed a hand through his pale hair while he made up his words. His voice was low and musical. "From time to time, Kendric," he explained, "we raid the Stonekeeps and the bevies for our own women. With such, we are full men again, not merely rim-runners, and free to settle in the circle of the Stonekeeps with whatever we have managed to acquire—usually it is one wife; with unholy luck—sometimes two or three."

"Settle as peasants?"

Helicon ignored Kendric, but Gryff did not. "'Tis better than a lifetime of the Unkept—for one Demimondana there are a hundred lesser ones—and better than a lifetime at the tame behest of a Stonekeeper."

"And this, this—"

"The ice-eyed one," Helicon said patiently. "They come, from time to time, from somewhere else. They pass lightfooted over the Inlands—some say Cincture-bound, though none but fowlen live there. They wear great power in their eyes, power enough to challenge a holder of a Stone. At first, some Stone-keepers tried to docile them for the bevies, and then there was much grief. Ivrium's iron tents were so much mush before the last one dusted her feet of his sands. It is better to kill such a one on sight than to be sighted by her in turn. Her eyes glow silver, like the moon—and strike ordinary men to stone, it's said. Only the Stonekeepers have magic enough to deal with such a one and they deal her death—if they can. But Sofis-tron—"

"Sofistron grows ambitious," Calennian interrupted, now that his breath was restored. "You can count on me for your raid, Gryff. If you think we have mutual magic enough to control an ice-eyed one . . ."

Gryff's square hand clamped around Kendric's forearm, or what of it he could encircle. "We have make-magic now." Kendric would have objected, but Gryff only had ears for his own voice, and one of those was metal. "We will take what we can from the bevy, to lure the rest of the men who might otherwise steer clear of our true prize. But she is our goal, none other. It is lucky that friend Kendric came to us with his magic just as such a one stumbled into whatever trap Sofistron wove."

The other two nodded.

For once Kendric was not hasty to deny his magic. Luck! Not luck, but logic. Kendric had dared a gate with a silver-eyed seeress from Rule, a Torloc by the name of Irissa. She must be the "ice-eyed one" the rim-runners both feared and coveted and whom the distant Stonekeeper Sofistron had cap-tured for purposes of his own.

Very well, Kendric would join them on their venture. Cer-tainly he planned to see more of this world than its forbidding wastes and the face of Amozel across the firelight. And, in the way of this world, if what one earned by deed or by barter was one's own, then Irissa, however hunted in this world, would be better off under his protection than left to her own devices. Besides, he would be relieved to see her again.

Chapter Six

—◆◆◆—

Kendric stood in the moon-washed, perpetual midnight glow of the Inlands night, his seven-foot length pressed against the foundation of a white stone castle, trying to be invisible.

On either side of him, a handful of rim-runners were attempting the same bit of natural magic, not much more successfully. They had marched all day through the endless Rynth, crossing shallow meanders with a careful eye out for fleshfins, watched only by the faithful moon. It had been an uneventful trek, almost boring, and Kendric had become ever more unenamored of the Rynth and more puzzled why anyone should seek it out, even as an exile.

He wondered about that even more when, at the very hinge of night and day when the distant sky played purple curtain on the vistas ahead, the party mounted a rocky ridge. Before them lay a rolling gold, lavender, and green expanse of meadow and forest. The rim-runners brushed past the dumbfounded Kendric to plunge down the last incline into this sudden wonderland, their weapon-bristling silhouettes adding an ominous profile to the soft, glimmering scene ahead.

Kendric stuck out one massive hand and halted Gryff summarily by the arm as he began to brush by, the last man down the incline.

"'Tis a marvelous land," Kendric murmured. "I had no idea that any place as fair as this existed in your reach."

"There's more to the Inlands than Rynth and Cincture," Gryff growled, unimpressed by the scene. "This is the border of Sofistron's Stonekeep and its lands. Of course it's fair, by his lights; he'd be a poor Stonewielder if he could not make a pretty pasture for his peasants. But he fences it well, friend

59

Kendric. We'll keep to the forest verge, lest any wandering lemurai pack scent us in open meadow."

Gryff lunged on into the deepening twilight, but Kendric remained behind, watching the spreading deep purple of night make the land look like a rich and many-colored cloak carelessly thrown groundward by some giant. Some one-eyed giant. Kendric glanced up at the moon, paler now than by day with the darker sky behind it. It shed enough light to mark well the rim-runners' forward march. Kendric sighed, stopped gawking, and strode after them in easy, long-legged paces. It appeared that Irissa, with a Torloc's luck, had fallen into softer circumstances than he had.

But now his face was pressed against hard, cold stone, and he could hear his heart beating a hunter's rhythm between his chest and his backbone. They had given him an intricate battle-ax, and Kendric shifted its short, unfamiliar weight in his hand. Perhaps a sword was too cumbersome for indoor fighting; perhaps that was why the rim-runners were armed with every implement but the one Kendric knew and understood as well as he knew the workings of his own hand. Still, he wished for a sword for perhaps the twentieth time in this place. If wishes were fishes, he told himself ironically in the old rhyme of Rule, here they'd likely turn out to be fleshfins and would leech the wisher bloodless for his trouble.

The Stonekeep was larger than Kendric had imagined, a towering icy mountain of pale stone, cresting in a series of jagged turrets. It might have been a fitting prison for "an ice-eyed one," but Kendric wondered how the rim-runners expected to find Irissa in such a place. Where would Inlanders tend to store a misplaced Torloc seeress whom they feared—in a below-ground dungeon, a narrow turret room, or somewhere in between?

"Sofistron's bevy is above us," Gryff whispered harshly. "He keeps his women's feet well off common ground. We'll make our way up as quiet and quick as we can; then it's each man for himself to catch what bevywomen he may and escape with them. You, Kendric, seem to have a foreign taste in these matters. You will help me with *her*. Your make-magic will be needed to contain her."

Kendric opened his mouth to object to the slights Gryff had

managed to pile one on top of the other, but decided that this was their terrain—or had been—and he would leave matters to them until he and they were all back on common ground and could discuss such things later.

"Give Helicon a hand," Gryff ordered, and Kendric obliged, finding that he was literally expected to play ladder while the rangy plainsman leaped to his shoulder and from there eeled through an unpromising-looking wooden shutter in the foundation. The castle's true windows loomed many dozens of feet above, narrow and high. But Gryff appeared to know the place; it wasn't long before Helicon's hank of yellow hair was waggling outside the tiny square. "The door is open around—" he whispered with an impatient nod.

The rim-runners edged along the gently curved stone, Kendric in their midst. Suddenly they tumbled through a narrow wooden door into utter darkness. Kendric felt his toes stub on unexpected steps and heard muffled curses all around as the party stuttered its way up a cut-stone corkscrew in the blackness.

A square of dim light fell into their midst from the open window where Helicon had hailed them. They stood on a landing of the stairs, and Helicon swung the shutter closed again on Gryff's command. In the restored dark, Kendric was pushed upward by the press of the rim-runners, all keeping so close to one another that he felt the prick of another man's weapon more than once. Kendric drove the decorative curlicue of his ax into the man ahead as similar goads to movement jabbed behind him. And so, self-spurred, the rim-runner party twisted and stumbled its way up a narrow spiral staircase into midnight.

"Wait!"

Gryff's command caused the train to halt abruptly and with decreasing success, so that several protesting muffled yelps announced the crash of man and weapon into man and weapon.

"Quiet, you slime-worms!" Gryff led them slowly through another rude door into a broad, torchlighted hallway. "Service stair," Gryff explained to Kendric, nodding his ruddy head back the way they had come. "Sofistron's peasants are so docile that the Keep never expects trouble from that quarter. They should all be playing dreadnoughts in the great hall or asleep on their narrow, knightly pallets. They've had a hunt recently and should be properly exhausted, the whimpering gang of lap hounds. Even the lemurai are likely to be penned below. We've chosen our time well—"

The shuffle of feet on pavement echoed softly from far down the corridor. Kendric and Gryff jumped back behind the door simultaneously, driving a train of rim-runners back into one another's weapon points. This time there was no sound but indrawn breaths. They had come too near to risk even gasps. Through a crack, Gryff, with Kendric peering out above his head, watched a veiled party of women flutter down the passage, some covered dishes in their hands.

"Ah, tasty!" Gryff smacked when they had gone. "It's a pity I'll be too busy acquiring the cursed sorceress to see to my own bevy."

Kendric stared at the rim-runner leader in the crack of torchlight leaking through the door. There had been naught to see of the women, if women they indeed were, other than their veiled faces, flowing garments, and—oh, the rather chilly sight of their bejeweled bare feet flashing out from under their hems. He himself was more interested in the contents of their platters, after a few days of the Rynth's bare bounty . . .

Gryff's elbow dug into Kendric's hip; Kendric would have to straighten the man out about the location of his ribs when they got back to the Rynth. "Look here, Kendric. You and me'll follow the bevywomen." There was a murmur of dissent from the rear. "Shut up, you lemurai-heads. The full bevy's just to the right down that passage. Go and do your best or worst. We'll trail these others to our prey and join you below. Successful hunting!"

Gryff leaped out into the passage with Kendric at his heels. The others rustled off in the opposite direction, but Kendric and Gryff moved with stealthy speed past the flickering torches until they caught up with the women's shadows, which trailed like wafting, ghostly trains.

The turret's inner wall curved more markedly than its outer one. Still, it was of formidable size. Kendric wondered how long they could walk through it without curving back on themselves. He glanced at Gryff, who was looking back down the passageway, doubtless envying the bevy raiders their opportunity. What a bizarre world this one was . . .

Turning, Kendric discovered he had stepped onto the shadow of the woman he was following and was brushing against the back of its caster. The women had paused, but Gryff and Kendric had not.

The women screamed. Screeched was perhaps a better word. Every stone in the hollow tunnel that was the passage echoed their chorus and magnified it. Their solid pewter platters clanged to the stones, adding a deep timbre to the general soprano cacophony. Gryff stood paralyzed, one hand pressed to his golden ear. Kendric saw only the eddying flutter of gray clothing agitating in the middle of the passage, a half-dozen open mouths below the concealing veils, and the flash of a jeweled dagger. Beyond them, he sensed a milky-white glow farther down the hall. The moon must be at full power, he thought, to cast such light into a turret window. He wished he were outside looking at it right now.

One of the gray figures launched itself at him, fists flailing; it was joined by another and another. "I will never be in keeping to a Rynthman!" "Nor I!" "I would die first!"

They were brave, bold sentiments, but the bevywomen were hanging on Kendric more than beating him off; still, it was effective. He was nicely impeded. He moved his ax hand behind him so none of them should impale herself on its blade. Gryff was similarly besieged against the other wall. It was like fighting off an attack of large, rather noisy moths; there was only the flapping of the women's swathing gray garments, their concerted cries, and the irritating clinging of their milling arms.

"I don't *want* you," Kendric ground out between his teeth. "We have come for the other—"

Veiled heads paused long enough to turn in concert to the glowing doorway down the passage. Kendric's eyes followed their glance, and that was a mistake. One figure who had remained pressed to the opposite wall came flying at him the moment his attention was distracted, the glint of a drawn dagger flashing jewellike from her gray garb.

"I am Lady Ward," she challenged in a light, indignant voice. "No one shall interfere with the bevy or myself!" She leaped right at him, the blade making a futile upward arc toward his face. Kendric pushed off two of the engulfing bevy with his left hand and tried to catch and turn the dagger before it wounded one of the women. The blade hit the wall behind him and scraped along on a nerve-chilling screech, breaking just as Kendric wrested it away. He thrust the encrusted hilt into his belt, nevertheless.

Gryff had succeeded in brushing off his screeching flock. The women finally stood away from the two men, panting and momentarily quiet. Into the sudden comparative silence, broken only by ragged breathing, came a distant sound of cutlery being wielded at a banqueting table, the solemn scrape and clang of knife and three-pronged fork working in concert. Except this was not dining, but—

"Fighting," Kendric announced grimly. "Back down the passage."

Gryff looked regretfully at the last bevywoman in his grasp, as faceless and shapeless as any of the others, but within his reach. "We could take just this one and be out the narrow stair in a thrice."

"*You* could," Kendric said, "and welcome to her! *I* go to help the others." He turned on his boot heel and ran down the corridor.

Gryff called after him. "It's every man for himself—don't be lemurai-brained!" But the words faded with distance.

Kendric spurted past the open wooden door that had ushered him into this idiocy and along to where the ring of metal on metal announced battle. As he saw at once, it *was* one man for himself. A burly rim-runner Kendric had never conversed with stood back to the wall, his ax flashing a lethal semicircle of defense around him. Another flock of gray-draped women cowered near a wide doorway. Six fighting men circled the lone rim-runner, and they were well armed with short swords. Kendric swept his ax blade across the first man to turn and thrust at him; the man dropped to the stone floor with a moan. Short swords meant little threat to a man of Kendric's reach; in a few moments he had beaten his way to the embattled rim-runner and they stood back to back—or rather rear to rear, as Kendric's back was a good deal higher than his squat battle companion's.

"The others?" Kendric asked between the rhythmic clang of their weapons.

"Down the stairs—some with their prizes, some empty-handed. And Gryff?"

"Gone, too, I think—empty-handed if he is not totally empty-headed."

Two advancing men engaged Kendric's ax blade. While he turned their swords, a third man rushed into the opening created. Kendric sidestepped with an agility they obviously had not expected in so hulking an opponent. The sword ran aground on stone and mortar; Kendric's descending ax numbed the third swordsman across the wrist with the fall of its unhoned edge.

But these were well-equipped and fit fighting men, not a ragtag company of rim-runners. Ax blade and hardwood handle would not be proof against them, and neither would sheer brawn, in the long run. Kendric wished once again for the familiar length of longsword sheathed across his back, then drew the broken dagger from his belt so both his hands should be weaponed. He could at least bruise if not cut, and it was easier to parry a blade with metal than with flesh. The Lady Ward's small jeweled hilt dug into his clenching palm; it was a toy more fit for jabbing meat at table than parting ribs at steel point. His hand reverberated from the downward stroke of an encroaching sword across the truncated dagger blade.

A fierce ax swipe drove back his attackers a bit. Behind Kendric, a grunt and the soft collapse of a body against his own told him the nameless rim-runner had been wounded. Kendric dropped the dagger to prop the man up against the wall before the advancing swords should finish him. Only the constant slash of his ax blade kept the five swordsmen from making a lethal advance.

Then came one who could only be Sofistron, an unarmed lord with a glitter-dusted mustache that Kendric took an instant dislike to. The man stepped measuredly to a spot behind the five swordsmen. Kendric noticed then that their unprotected heads were all bald to above the ears, whence their hair fell flowing to their shoulders. Sofistron was fully haired—and well tended as well.

Sofistron opened his palm, where a plain stone lay, glowing softly argent in the hot torchlight. It drew Kendric's eyes, this stone so like the stony-faced moon outside. For a moment he thought that was all it had been meant to do—distract him.

Then he felt the wooden ax handle in his palm thicken, swell, and force his fingers apart. Unable to hold it, he dropped it to the floor, as once he had dropped magic-broken bonewood. The handle took root there, standing upright, growing knee-high. The intricately cut blade began sprouting sharp, silver branches, shooting up and out at eye-blinding speed. A fence of metallic nettles penned Kendric and the limp rim-runner against the wall. The baldheaded men smiled wolfishly as the magician closed his fingers and dimmed the stone's moonlike light.

"We toss bevy raiders to the lemurai pit," Sofistron announced blandly for the intruders' benefit. His light eyes raked his own exhausted swordsmen. "I don't know what we do with so ineffective a set of heirlings," he muttered, "except consider sending them Rynthward."

The men leaped as one to reach their arms through the metal hedge and take custody of their prisoners' arms, eager to show their supremacy, now that another had won it for them. Though the huge, jagged thorns snagged the men's brocade tunic sleeves, they did not cut flesh. Kendric saw why; beneath the rich fabric, the men wore silver mail. In all ways, this had been a doomed contest. No wonder the rim-runners ran! Once again, Kendric the fool had rushed headlong into uncertainty. Well, he did not know what these lemurai were, beyond the anxious invoking of the rim-runners, nor what or where their pit was, but he didn't imagine that a night spent with the lemurai could be any worse than one spent in the company of the Unkept women. At least Sofistron seemed uninclined to kill them outright, for the half-unconscious rim-runner was dragged away with Kendric, once Sofistron had allowed his metal barrier to melt into limpid moonbeams on the passage floor.

The two men were half-led, half-dragged down another endless corkscrew of dark stairway, this one dimly lighted by a few torches to show lichens blooming sulfurous yellow and blue along white stone walls gone gray with the dampness seeping through them.

A stench rose up to tease at Kendric's nostrils. His head reared away from it, but he and the barely stumbling rim-runner were impelled further into the depths and the dark, until the passage broke open into a large, low-ceilinged cave. With a last, farewell shove forward, Kendric and his companion were hurled out into unsupported darkness. They fell, landing moments later with bone-rattling impact. Kendric grunted; his partner in durance only moaned. An instant later something hard and sharp rebounded off the dirt-packed earth to strike Kendric's knee.

"Your lady's dagger, rim-runner!" A pale face hovered like the moon over the pit's edge. "Perhaps the lemurai will need a toothpick when they're done with you. We'll leave the torches; they don't mind dining by dark, but mayhap you do."

Several moons hung above the pit edge now, bald pates glowing slightly silver in the firelight. The Keepmen's laughter held a malice Kendric found hard to fathom; there was a certain ring of envy to it. But why should well-caparisoned and well-cared-for soldiers to a powerful magician envy the exiles of the lean and rugged Rynth? Then they were gone, and Kendric was left in the rancid stench and the faint light of faraway torches, with a wounded rim-runner for company and a broken dagger for defense . . . No, not only a wounded rim-runner for companion, he amended. His dark-adjusting eyes searched the pit's distant expanses and found constellations of avid scarlet eyes glowing ruby-hot within the mouths of many passages leading from the place.

The advertised lemurai, he assumed, whoever or whatever they were. Kendric picked up the ragged-edged dagger and dragged himself and his unconscious companion over to a length of pit wall not populated by the paired gleams. He put his back against damp, fetid earth and made a slow sweep of the unblinking eyes. They were large and more numerous than he cared to count.

He wondered if his own eyes—amber-brown by day— gleamed any particular shade in the eternal twilight of this place. He doubted it. His name, he told himself and the nameless watchers, was Kendric. And he was a fighter.

Chapter Seven

No food was brought for beast or man. The unknown rim-runner still lay semiconscious and fevered. Kendric did what he could to staunch the wound in his side, using the blunted dagger to twist a strip of makeshift bandage tight.

Above the pit lip, the torches flared at the same weak, flickering rhythm. If anyone came to refuel them—and some-one must have done so as the hours went by, seeming days—Kendric neither saw nor heard a sign of it. And no more taunting faces hung moonishly out of the darkness.

But the glittering eyes that jeweled the farther pit wall did not show signs of advancing, though certain spine-chilling shrieks and snorts emanated from the dark now and again. And Kendric's fellow rim-runner moaned.

At least the stench was no longer detectable; breathing any-thing long enough made the tortured human senses become willing to take it for air pure and simple. Kendric knew if he should be elevated out of this place and then returned, the overwhelming odor of it would knock him off his feet. For now, he was of the pit, and there was one small mercy in the numbing of his sense of smell.

He stood and surveyed the distant ledge of the pit that was made to contain whatever lurked in the caves and tunnels open-ing onto this space. Surely it was made to pen an Inlands man from time to time. Yet Kendric had seen none of those who could match him for height. Perhaps his length of limb would make a ladder for his escape. As he drew nearer the wall, his hopes heightened—the pit lip was not so high or far as when viewed from where he had stood. In his eagerness to measure it, he stepped forward without looking—and nearly plunged into a deep trench cut into the earth. Kendric threw himself onto his stomach and draped as much of his head, arms, and shoulders over the edge as he dared. A slither of such scaly rasp and prolonged duration oozed from the depths below that he immediately rejected any thought of seeking downward for his escape. What lay below was there to contain what hid in the tunnel mouths. It was better to face an unknown enemy than to challenge the unknown meant to keep that enemy caged.

He stood and made an uneasy circuit of the pit. The trench was semicircular, a grinning sickle of an obstacle that ended where the sheer upward wall of the place began—the wall that was punctured by darker tunnel mouths up to a great height and that housed the glittering, vigilant eyes.

In the center of the pit lay a island of rocks, leafless tree limbs springing from their midst. An inspection there revealed the pale sheen of bone—bones strung necklace-neat over the ground. Some were small. One intact pile showed the swell of a rib cage and the long, delicate leg bones of some large, fleet animal. One particular suggestive grouping caused Kendric to stretch out his arm and imagine the bone that formed it bare, then shrunken somewhat to a length more common to Inlands men . . .

He paced back to his mute partner in imprisonment. The man needed water, but so did Kendric. Kendric sat beside him, weary from a long day and night's march, a lost battle, and too much thinking. What he really needed was a Torloc seeress to heal his companion's wound, conjure a light from the darkness, squeeze some water from a stone, and perhaps mind-forge him a sword or mind-weave a rope. Reputedly there was one near at hand; perhaps she would escape by Torloc trickery and—

No, if Irissa were here and had not yet escaped, she was not about to do so. Perhaps these Inlanders were more formidable opponents than they seemed.

If only he truly had the "make-magic" the rim-runners ascribed to him, he thought ruefully, then rejected the idea. No, a man made his own magic, by ordinary muscle and brain. That was how Irissa had sought to console him, back in Rule when he had been foolish and regretted that he bore no special magic, as did his fellow Wrathmen. "Ordinary," she had said, was its own kind of magic, because it held to simple virtues.

She had also said, "You bear more magic than you know," standing oracle-impressive inside the shining rainbowed arch just before he had leaped to join her.

Now he was here, in a fetid place he could no longer smell, with a red-eyed firmament above when he leaned his head back to contemplate the dark wall across from him. The rim-runner beside him murmured feverishly. Kendric had never learned his name. He did not think he ever would.

Time passed slowly in the pit. The anonymous eyes in the wall were content to watch. Kendric finally slept; if being in a place made one immune to its odors, perhaps sleeping would make one immune to its realities. He was awakened by a feeble series of gasps and moans. It took a few moments for his eyes to make out movement on the pit's floor; then he spied a many-headed monster writhing near the trench edge. He reached to rouse the man beside him and found only empty space.

Kendric's searching hand came upon the broken dagger and tightened on it. Several pairs of ruby eyes flashed in his direction as he stood. The shadow-thing writhed into a patch of torchlighted ground, and Kendric made out the form of the weakened rim-runner with several smaller forms attached to it. He ran toward the struggle, and one of the forms hurled itself upon him.

Something furred, warm, and strong clung like a child to his neck. The thing's hot breath swept his face, a carnivore reek flooding his face. Kenric tore the thing loose and held it at arm's length, though it weighed as much as a small man. Its own hairy arms still struggled for a grasp on his throat and were nearly managing it, despite the length at which Kendric held it. Was the creature able to grow its limbs longer at will? But Kendric's big hands had it by its powerful neck and were slowly squeezing the air out, both in self-protection and in revulsion. The thing's head lolled back into the light. Its face was a leathery blue mask of pain and fury; formidable finger-long fangs at the front of its narrow jaws gleamed ivory-sharp. Kendric throttled harder in a surge of self-preservation and hurled the finally limp creature into the trench behind him.

Before he could turn, the rim-runner gave a cry of utter denial. Kendric spun in time to see the shadowy mass of man and monsters tilting on the trench lip, the lemurai too busy at their devouring to notice the danger, as the man must have done. The greatest mass of the bulk suddenly pushed itself backward—over nothing. Man and monsters fell into the deeper pit together, the lemurai giving a sudden, cognizant screech. Then there was silence. After that came a great agitated slither, followed by a random crunch or two.

Kendric picked up the dropped dagger and retreated to his former post by the wall, where he lay shaken and panting, regretting even his heavy breathing for the waste of water it was. But surely there must be some water somewhere for these lemurai? Back, in the tunnels? Or here, in this central place? He dragged himself over to the rocks where the dead trees grew and the dead bones were scattered. The bones lay under the trees, now that he noticed it, as if someone had crouched on a branch above and dined. So the trench served to pen creatures that might, given time, even scale a high pit wall. These lemurai climbed, that was it. And so could a man.

Kendric pushed up through the rocks, avoiding the piercing of tree branches. In the formation's center, at the rock island's highest point, he found a huge flat stone with a scooped-out center. His fingers plunged into warmish water, paused, then thrust into his mouth, where he sucked the wetness from them. His fingertips had skimmed some slick bottom surface of the rock well, but Kendric didn't want to think about the source of his water. If it was wet, it would serve. Here, at the top of the rocks, the torchlight fell strongly; the terrain was as desolate as the Rynth. There was some comfort in the light. Kendric stretched out his long frame, tired from crouching in the pit. Perhaps from here there might be some way to leap or swing to the pit ledge. But then he realized that if the distance was sufficient to keep an army of long-armed, climbing lemurai captive, it would keep one heavy-boned human nicely contained.

There was always the trench, of course, for the quick way out that the rim-runner had chosen. Kendric did not fancy the trench. He looked across at the wall where the bright eyes still shone. If the tunnels honeycombed the rock walls of this subterranean kingdom, perhaps a wily man might elbow his way out where a pit full of lemurai might be too stupid to challenge.

But he was not a wily man by nature, and by nature not built for eeling deep into the earth, likely getting caught between rock and rock and then lying there while lemurai lunched on him from behind. If only he had a weapon, something that gave him a literal edge! With one slender piece of steel in his hand, he could deal quickly with lemurai or patiently with rock, scraping his way to freedom. Kendric contemptuously eyed the dainty dagger beside him. It was worse than useless, a reminder of how effective real steel could be. Might as well throw the thing away now—

The slide of some dislodged rocks interrupted his motion. Below, ringing the stones, was a chain of dark shapes, some eyes gleaming ruby among them, others in too much torchlight to shine with anything but dark, unallayed appetite. They did not come closer, but waited for him to weaken, as he must. Kendric glanced to the nearest tunnel mouth, just opposite him at this height and tantalizingly near. If he climbed that tallest tree, inched out on that thick branch there, and managed to swing himself over before it broke under his weight, he might be able to scramble inside the vacant tunnel and perhaps to freedom deeper within the rocks.

It was not much of a chance, but it was better than a plunge to the trench or waiting for the inevitable rise of lemurai around him. If only he had a weapon! He looked at the half-dagger in his hand. If it had a whole blade, not only whole but broader than before, perhaps with a nice, lethal curve in it that a man could twist into lemurai hide to make short work of it . . .

If he were going to wish himself something, Kendric decided, staring deeply at the dagger's slight shape, he might as well make it something worth wishing for.

Chapter Eight

❧❧❧

Irissa had a headache.

She could not say when it had begun, though she had mortal reason enough for a headache. Perhaps it was after Sofistron and the bevy had left her to herself—and to the reflected selves that outposted the chamber. She had never looked directly at these reflections, but their mere presence had a certain draining effect. She tried to keep her gaze fastened on the chamber doorway, which was a soft, unreflective oblong. Yet she sometimes lost sight of it and would find that her tired glance had slipped sideways to the dangerous coldstone wall. They called these polished walls commonstone, but Irissa, like most prisoners, grew stubborn in protest. In Rule these clear white stones were called coldstone, and a room so paved with them would have been worth six magicians' ransom—were there any magicians still in Rule or any willing to ransom them.

But her head ached bitterly. It had done so ever since she had thrust the rejoined Iridesium circlet on her temples after her useless escape attempt. The gesture had only been intended to keep her flowing tresses captive and to claim one of the few things left to her. Now her temples throbbed. She eased the circlet off. It looked no smaller than before. Her fingers tested the metal. Seamless now, truly, as Sofistron had said—sealed seamless in the blinding glare of coldstone walls reflecting off coldstone walls. Then the space created by the silver sand, the barrier she could not pass unaided, *was* a kind of veil . . .

It was easier to think now, for her headache was subsiding. She laid the Iridesium circlet by her side. A mirror image of its almost black surface appeared in the floor. She idly pushed it a bit farther away. Her head was mending rapidly now, so rapidly that . . . Experimentally, she nudged the circlet farther from her. It was as if an invisible band around her forehead loosened. With her boot toe, she pushed it farther still. The headache was nearly gone; in fact, a flood of well-being was washing over her temples. The circlet was nearly touching the silver sand. One small push more and... Perhaps she could *shove* the sand aside and make a pathway out—

Irissa got to her knees and pushed the circlet farther, over the ridge of sand. The metal rose by some force not its own as soon as it came even with the sand. Although the circlet was half out of the zone now, the sand was not disarranged. The circlet would be allowed to pass through, but not Irissa. Allowed? The circlet was being *invited* to pass through, as Irissa was being invited to thrust it from her, the one thing of power she had left to herself. No! She snatched back the metal and crowned herself with it in one sweeping motion, before she should hesitate. The pain settled back on her like a pall, heavy and dark. He was persuasive, Sofistron, and had realized he could not take the Iridesium from her without violating the central rule of magic; power must be given freely. But his Lunestone ruled the mental senses; he had said so himself, and he could certainly afflict Irissa in such a way that she would eagerly cast the circlet aside.

Well, a Torloc seeress' head was harder than it looked and sometimes more stubborn than wise. Irissa folded her arms and shut her eyes against the pain. An Iridesium-colored rainbow of dancing lights cavorted on the dark of her closed eyelids— violet and bright blue-green, spinning crimson and gold. It was easier to dare the bright light without than the dark confusion within. Irissa opened her eyes to find an afterimage superimposed on the vague doorway. It stood about seven feet tall, was mostly blue and brown, and paused blinking on the threshold in a most aggravatingly indecisive way—

"Kendric!" She stood, so suddenly she momentarily outstripped the pain before it tightened on her forehead again. She reached out a hand, in disbelief or welcome. The vision lumbered forward. Kendric's dark hair was disheveled, his face and hands earth-smudged. Hardened streaks of red earth—or blood—creased his tunic and trousers. And even through the barrier erected over the silver sand came the reek of some place very foul. She couldn't keep the most natural question contained.

"Kendric! Where on earth have you been?"

"*Under* earth," he answered grimly, still advancing to the sand's edge. "It *is* you? That shapeless gray thing in the center of this, this . . . milky bubble with some colors in it that reminds me of your cursed rainbowed gate?"

"I can see you clearly enough through it. Don't touch it. It is some spell of Sofistron's, the magician who—"

"Yes, I've met the fellow." Kendric walked a bit around the construction so obvious to him, so invisible to her.

"You came here after all!"

"Here?"

"To this—world."

"The Inlands of Ten," he corrected, folding his filthy arms and contemplating the air between them intently.

"It could be the Inlands of Twenty for all I care. It was not where we were meant to go," she explained.

"Hmmmm," Kendric said dubiously. "I take it this Sofistron intends to keep you in here. Wise fellow."

"I tried to escape with my circlet. The Iridesium was the only thing that would cut the barrier, but I was turned back by the bevy."

"The bevy turned you back? A simple gaggle of silly women turned back a Torloc seeress? I thought your magic was restored by the rainbowed gate—you were shedding enough coldstone tears to populate a meander with commonstones."

"You know about the bevy? Where have you been, Kendric? What is this meander? Would you stop roaming about and do something to free me from this nothing that pens me in?"

He made a fist and rapped his knuckles sharply on air. A hollow sound came. "It may be 'nothing' to you, but it's solid to me, almost like a glassblower's construct. I wonder if it shatters?"

Irissa sighed. "It's magic-made, so it's no use, Kendric. You cannot disperse a spell with a rap of your knuckles; only other magic will displace it, and any magic that remains is inside with me."

"I have my weapon," he began, drawing something from his belt.

"In Rule your sword was a bit more than weapon; it carried its own magic. Here, whatever steel you have will not suffice," she said sadly.

Kendric lofted a slice of metal as long as his forearm, with a wicked, innovative twist to the blade.

Irissa shuddered. "Native steel, I take it. Lethal on flesh and bone, but useless on magic bubbles. Put it away."

"Not native," Kendric said, regarding it with stolid wonder. "It is of my own—manufacture."

"Now is no time to boast of your skills! So Halvag the smith's son from the marshes of Rule has made a demon's dagger on the Inlands of Twelve—"

"Ten," he corrected calmly. "You always insisted that numbers had a certain magical integrity of their own. We would do well to be careful of them in a strange place."

It was his almost unnatural calm that unraveled her where adversity had not served to do so before. "Mere metal will not work to free me; it must be magic!" she shouted in exasperation.

Kendric tipped the dagger point toward her, almost as if dubbing her this or that, a token kind of touch. It touched on nothing, and nothing cracked. A dark lightning bolt raced jaggedly around the chamber and remained in place, simply a free-standing, circular zigzag line etched on air. Where Kendric had touched, a door-sized space was outlined. Kendric offered his hand; Irissa, speechless, took it and stepped through, like a dancer through a pattern. Behind her, the suspended crack in nothing collapsed into dark dust, falling to the floor in a circle and smothering the silver. Irissa was examining Kendric closely, but Kendric was examining his weapon.

"I suppose if I had used the hilt, nothing would have happened," he considered, turning the ludicrously small haft in his hands. "Only the last half of the blade was . . . made. Perhaps I should have tried the hilt first, just as a matter of comparison."

"Perhaps we should leave first and consider alternate courses of action later?"

He looked at her then, directly, though he knew the danger of it. "You look pale, Torloc," he told her with narrowed eyes that contained an odd mixture of concern and suspicion.

Irissa found herself holding his gaze longer than she was wont to allow. His eyes were the same innocent amber she remembered from Rule. Despite his lamentable state and the pungent perfume of the lemurai that clung to him—she recognized it now, she who had been ringed by their carnivore greed—she was tempted to invade the space behind his eyes for the deep looking that would reassure her that all was well, that Kendric was as he had always been. It was good to know in a world of gates gone unreliable and Eldresses suddenly unsympathetic that certain things still held and that foremost among them was Kendric of the Marshes—stalwart, dependable, and untainted by more than the slightest stir of magic. Even that should be gone now, since he had left the reason for it—the sword—behind in Rule.

She could only look deep with his permission, and nothing in his eyes extended that. Perhaps it was not safe at the moment. Women, even Torloc seeresses, were prone to moon and stare during critical reunions; warriors wanted to get on with it.

"Other than being muddied and bloodied, you seem to have survived the gate," she noted in turn. Now that they had each taken formal stock of the other, they could resume as if there had been no interruption, no unaccepting gate, no separation. But it was not as it had been at the last moment in Rule, the moment when Irissa's and Kendric's eyes had met within and without a rainbowed gate and an instant's impulse had both joined them together and torn them apart on a journey of dubious outcome.

Kendric seemed to feel this, too, for he quickly lowered his eyes to his weapon that his fingers toyed with as if they could not quite release it.

"It was the Lady Ward's," he noted. "Hence the hilt."

Irissa stared at the small jeweled haft he shook at her like an admonitory finger demanding or expecting an explanation.

"Yes. Very pretty, Kendric. But why are you so fascinated by a borrowed dagger when our greatest need is to leave Sofistron's castle?"

His eyes caught hers. "*You* see nothing intriguing in this weapon? In the blade? I thought Torlocs were gifted with true sight to the center of all things."

"True sight, yes. Sometimes. If the Torloc is true and there is magic in it. But I have been long in Sofistron's polished cage, and—and I am getting a headache again. Can we not move on and discuss all this elsewhere?"

Kendric nodded, thrust the dagger into his belt, and started down the gently curving passage. Relieved, Irissa followed him, wondering if some resentment of her for inviting him into the gate lingered. Yet that moment had been so inevitable, how could any ill seem to come of it?

Kendric stopped ahead of her, and Irissa, thinking deeply, came up short of his earth-caked back.

"They guard the stairway now and likely the bevy beyond it. We'll have to try the other direction," he decided.

They turned and retraced their steps, passing the empty glow of the commonstone chamber and moving on through deserted, torchlighted halls. A sudden break in the inner wall's stone showed a spiral of cut-stone stairs. Kendric paused, shrugged, then plunged up it.

"Is this not a dark and close passage to follow?" Irissa wondered as she followed him through the unlighted turns.

"A lot less dark and narrow than the lemurai tunnels," Kendric said shortly.

After a dizzying progression, the stair opened onto an arch and then a balcony beyond it. Irissa and Kendric stood surveying a high-timbered hall; far below, tapestries lay against the white stone walls and rushes carpeted the floor. They were up among the timbers supporting the high, arched roof.

"If we could fly . . ." Irissa suggested.

"Perhaps we should wish for wings," Kendric retorted. "Or you could make us some."

"Make—? Perhaps I could, had I a feather or two. The most extraordinary thing happened when I came to this place. I found my magic restored, working in ways it had not done so before. I was able to create from one substance the living reality of another, not merely to alter what was. Perhaps going through the gate—"

"We did not go through the gate," Kendric interrupted. "At least I did not. I remember nothing of the gate but a blinding flash of colors and the distinct sensation of being spat free of it. Nor have I seen any Torlocs in the Inlands of Ten. Except one I already knew too well," he added accusingly.

"Kendric, I cannot blame you if you regret joining me in attempting the gate; it was but a moment's whim, I suppose—"

"Whim? You call leaving Rule, my Rule, leaving my sword behind in some unnamed lake, leaving all that behind a whim? The Circle was right; Torlocs are a dangerous breed, particularly when they talk. A whim indeed!"

"I named it whim," Irissa said stiffly, "so you should not be bound by my naming it anything stronger. Why do you not simply redub it 'regret' and put a true face on it, if Rule is so much to be mourned?"

"I do not wish to put names on anything," Kendric said. "Not even on myself." He turned abruptly to study the scene below, and that in itself was disquieting, for Kendric of the Marshes had not been abrupt. "It's odd. There's not a soul stirring below, yet the torches flare. By my estimation, it is still near midnight . . ."

"We could find a window slit and see how the night progresses," Irissa suggested.

"By what? The moon? The Inlands moon has neither phase nor motion. The night turns the same bland face from dawn till dusk."

"Would Wrathmen were so constant," Irissa murmured. But Kendric had not heard her; he was searching the adjoining walls for another exit from the balcony. He found one.

"Steps, along the wall."

Irissa went over to peer down a steep stretch of narrow stairs that plunged to the stones far below. They would have to travel it unguided by torches, without so much as a rail to hold on to. At times the course lay in total darkness; at others, the stone risers seemed to waver by the light of some powerful torch below.

She hesitated while Kendric started down two steps, then paused. "Your hand," he offered.

"The wall will be sufficient," Irissa answered, spreading the fingers of one hand along the cool stone and starting after him.

They were silent on their descent, though no one roamed the hall below to hear them, had they spoken. There came only the soft footfalls of rhythmic boots on stone and the whisper of Irissa's sleeve against the wall. Finally, Kendric's boots touched level floor.

"Empty," he said, his voice ringing off the stone walls. Not even a tapestry stirred in alarm. "Then if the castle sleeps, we've only to find our way out and will be free."

"Only! How many doors do you think lead off from this place?"

Kendric took a quick survey. "A dozen or more. But with doors, it is merely necessary to start with one. Your choice."

"I have no luck with gates," Irissa demurred. "You choose the door; perhaps you will be more satisfied with what you find behind it."

Kendric strode without comment to an open arch, paused, then plunged through. Irissa, following, found herself in a deserted passage. They followed it through some hanging tapestries and into the castle kitchen, where the stone-topped tables had been scrubbed clean for the next day's preparation and kegs and vats of foodstuffs piled a pantry corner.

"A courtyard exit—there," Kendric guessed, heading for a low-arched wooden door that had an external look to it, indicated by the heavy bar across it. Once through, however, they found, not the eternal moonlight of an Inlands night, but, oddly, another dark passage. They followed it, becoming ever more secure within the castle's silent, unpopulated common rooms.

A final turn brought them to an armory where metal gleamed upon the stones in lethal profusion. Kendric's grim face lightened at the sight of several swords scabbarded on the walls.

"They look a bit short, but—"

Irissa, however, was drawn by a broken spear lying propped against a wall. "Kendric! Here—this lance. I told you that my magic had found another dimension in this place. See this wood?"

He grudgingly came over to touch the broken end. "Bonewood," he confirmed. "And you broke it—with your eyes?" She nodded. "Something of an achievement, I confess. I was asked to do it with my arms and not expected to succeed. But what is so astounding that a warrior breaks even stubborn wood, or that a Torloc seeress unravels it with her eyes? We are merely acting true to our kinds, as we should," he added significantly.

"It was not the unweaving of the wood I marvel at. There

was a fallen beast in the fields when I came, transfixed by this very spear, its head and horns wrested away for the hunters' prize. With the pieces of wood I unwove from the spear end, with the beast's own pooling blood, with my tears—"

"Torloc tears again," Kendric grumbled. "They do not seem to be valued in this place," he warned her. "Nor does anything Torloc bring much welcome."

"I see that," she replied. "But Kendric, I was able to—restore—the beast. It stood before me, the blood beating in its hide and heart again, its head reshaped, this—bonewood, you called it?—this bonewood grown into a crown of horns and my coldstone tears made into eyes..."

"It sounds like a children's tale to me," Kendric said. "Perhaps your eyes were still gate-dazzled."

"No! It stood, whole and hale. It walked—"

"And talked?"

"No, not talked..."

"Well, that's some relief. The one advantage I have found to this world is that nothing four-footed talks. Although the lemurai gurgle a bit when throttled..." Kendric folded his arms dubiously. "From what I can tell, a Torloc's tears are worth only a passage to trouble in this place. And as for your tale of the dead beast, even a seeress cannot make rise what has lain down lifeless."

"But, don't you see, it was not a futile gate. My powers are restored—look!" Irissa turned around the spear's broken end and stared fixedly at the splintered wood. She could not believe that Kendric would disbelieve her, especially in this hurtful, openly doubting way. Perhaps Finorian had been speaking only the truth; perhaps mortal men were not meant to pass through Torloc gates; perhaps by asking him to join her, she had altered him in some indefinable way...

She was thinking more of Kendric than of the task before her; this was no way to prove anything. She needed to recapture the feeling of utter joy when she had discovered that her magical vision worked as never before, a joy almost as complete as the herd's freedom in its romp across the endless waves of grass. But that had been before she'd known Sofistron's descending black cloud and his coldstone chamber, before her head had throbbed to the confines of her own Iridesium circlet, and before she had been reunited with Kendric, only to find them puzzlingly disunited . . .

"It's no use. I can't concentrate here. Perhaps all the weapons around—"

"Your weapons are your eyes," Kendric said quietly. "Let me see them."

Was he *asking* for deep vision now? The bonewood spear remained unchanged in her hands. Puzzled, Irissa finally looked up to Kendric's eyes. He did not look at her long, eye to eye; there was no risk that she should see her own image in his iris and drown.

"I thought so." Kendric took the spear from her hand and set it against the wall so gently there was no sound of wood on stone. "I had missed more than I thought. How long were you in Sofistron's chamber?"

"Almost as long as I have been in this world; there is no time in a mirror."

Kendric sighed. "Two, perhaps three days, then. The cell was made to contain you, to mute your powers."

"Of course. Apparently the people of this place are wary of Torlocs, for what reason I know not. Kendric, you prided yourself on speaking plain in Rule. Have you lost that facility in the gate as well?"

"No, but you have lost something in Sofistron's chamber, I think. I glimpsed it, but had another reason for avoiding naming it. Your eyes, your sorcerous silver eyes—" He put his hands on her shoulders as if to hold her still for his next words, but she hardly felt them.

"My eyes? Tainted? Gone amber? As after Mauvedona? But I can see! I'm not blind as I was then."

Kendric shook his head. "Not amber, but— There is only the slightest ring of silver around your eyes now, the rest is—"

"Is what?"

"Gray. Common, mortal gray. I do not think you could move a hair from one side of a part to another with those eyes, much less mend bonewood."

"But . . . if you had seen it, Kendric, seen the power! It was all around, beyond anything in Rule, as if I tapped some colossal well of pure coldstone-clear water and it ran through me.

And the beast, standing there blinking crystal eyes at me. Such a magnificent creature, all bone and blood and magic. *My* magic! I have not found much joy in being of my kind, but there I saw, for a moment, the wonder of it. It was beyond gates, beyond Finorian's cautions, beyond myself—oh, you cannot understand! You cannot mourn the loss of what you had never had!"

She hid her face in her hands, her once-silver eyes closed to the weapons around her, to the sight of Sofistron's castle, and to the careful watch of Kendric's eyes. It no longer mattered if she avoided them for his sake or her own.

"I can mourn the *gain* of what I never had," he said.

"The gain?" She raised her face from her hands. No tears would come, neither coldstone nor commonstone, not even mortal salt. She was wrung dry by her own image.

Kendric had drawn the oddly balanced dagger with its dainty hilt and oversized blade. He held it out to her, blade foremost.

"You miss magic. Then hold this. Fold your hand around it. If you press too hard, it cuts. Yet it does not exist. A half-day ago, it did not exist beyond a broken stump of metal. It is mine; I made it in the lemurai pit. It is why I stand before you now, instead of serving as a community dinner. Yet I wonder . . ."

"*You* made it?"

Kendric smiled. "With my eyes, my tainted, mortal, amber eyes. And only most of the blade. I cannot claim credit for the hilt or the jewels. I cry no coldstones."

"You?" She held the blade still in her hand, feeling it twist artfully through her palm, feeling even the powder of dried blood along its shining surface. Kendric held fast to the hilt.

"Torloc," he asked, "why did you come to me in Geronfrey's under-mountain castle?"

"Must we talk of that? It was in another time and another place, and besides, the mage is dead. Geronfrey is so much powder with his mountain in the altered Rule we left. We are here—"

"You came to me, wearing your silver eyes and Geronfrey's proffered velvet robe and no shoes. It was dark and chill. You sought me in the dark and the cold. Why?"

"It was—I was . . . It was escape. Geronfrey was a powerful magician, he wanted . . . and I wished to elude him, to remain free. And we had traveled long together, you and I. It seemed—"

"Geronfrey wanted more than your velvet hair and your silver eyes; Geronfrey, the most powerful magician in Rule, wanted more of you than a foolish mortal man would take and think himself well pleased. You did not merely choose to find me in the night; you were forced!"

"No. I had a choice. You were my choice. I had that still. I had choice."

"And what has this signal honor brought me?" he demanded.

"Brought you? What does a man benefit from the coming of a woman to his bed? Warmth. Satisfaction. Whatever magic they can weave together in whatever night is theirs. It is over. If it was a mistake, it is an old mistake. There. I forget it, if it troubles you. You are as free to forget—"

"Not with this blade between us," Kendric said, his huge hand pressing tight on hers until she felt the honed blade edge press into her flesh. "I made it, Torloc. Myself. Make-magic, as they call it here. Why?"

She felt what seemed like tears well in her eyes; they would not fall, could not fall. "Kendric. It was as Geronfrey told me. If a Torloc seeress' first flesh falls to a man of power, then he achieves her powers. He desired to harvest both me and my powers. You and I were as good as prisoners within his premises. I could not permit him the ambitious possession he wished and could demand. I thought if I disarmed him, made what was valuable in me worthless to him—"

"It was not mere vanity that enraged him, then, when he discovered you had left him whole and come to me?"

She shook her head violently, until her dark hair made a whirlwind around her face, obscuring it. "No. Geronfrey was never one to unleash his full rage for reasons of mere vanity. I was no longer of use to him after I had been in your bed. Was it so terrible a barter? Did you reap no benefit at all from it? I am told that mortal men hold some value to such simple exchanges. I did not take from you anything you were not willing to give—"

"But you *gave* me what I was not even asked if I cared to receive! Oh, foolish Torloc who thought you could have power and behave like an ordinary woman! Why do my thoughts take visible form? Why does my looking make a dagger blade? I never asked for magic. I never asked to leave Rule. Yet I am here, in an alien land, with a dagger in my hand of no man's making but my own—"

Kendric released the dagger hilt so suddenly that the weapon fell to the floor between them, naked and shining. There was nothing more to say, nothing more to do, but for Irissa to mourn the loss of her power, and Kendric to mourn the acquiring of his.

"We are the opposites of our kinds, then," Irissa said dully. "An impotent Torloc seeress and an empowered mortal man. Perhaps that is punishment enough for the past—"

"The present shall be punishment for the past, and you linger here long enough," a deep masculine voice said. It was not Kendric's. Bitter as he was, he knelt quickly to retrieve his magic weapon.

"Who spoke?" he demanded, stabbing at the air around them.

Only weapons winked reply, an armory's worth of forged and fearful steel, hung formally on walls, lying carelessly across benches. He and Irissa were as alone as before.

"There!" Irissa pointed to the wall above, where a great beast's head hung from a wooden shield, one of a series of beasts that ringed the room with their dead, stone-eyed presence. They were so much a part of the gray stone, so much a part of the weapon-hung room, that neither Kendric nor Irissa had noticed them until now.

Now Irissa walked under the heavily muscled neck and proud head she had observed.

"It is most like the beast I restored. Even its eyes seem to blink a coldstone sparkle . . . Oh, but see the rock-crystal horns of this beast, its glory and its bane! Not even in Rule did we have such extravagantly crowned creatures."

Kendric walked over to join her in staring up at the mounted head.

"Most impressive. Perhaps someday I shall become adept enough to attempt the crystal horns. It is no use to wish for what was, Irissa. Leave the beast dead as it belongs. We still have to find our way out of here."

"And will not," the same deep voice said authoritatively.

Irissa shook her head bewilderedly at Kendric.

They faced the mounted head again. And the black lips moved. "Great silly creatures," the head said, quite clearly. "If you wish to bid Sofistron's castle farewell, you must spell your way out. A spell of his keeps intruders circling endlessly the halls and stairs and towers. Only something purely natural can see you out."

"And *you* are natural?" Kendric challenged.

"I am Bounder," the head returned. "And not many hours past I was the most natural thing in the Inlands. I was stag, with a herd to follow me and none to bar me passage. Then I saw her of the silver eyes and met the lance that wounds forever. But she of the silver eyes came after, with the herd, and with a power that flows around but not within, she brought me to my hooves again."

"The lorryk do not speak," Irissa said, moving forward to stare up at the head.

"The lorryk do not speak," it repeated. "I am not lorryk. I am the head that was carted behind the heels of the bearing-beast back to Sofistron's walls. I am the magic you breathed into what remained of me in the meadow. It could not reside in what was natural of me. I am Bounder and I reside here. If you would leave this place, you must take up the spear that wounds forever. On its head lies lorryk blood and on Sofistron's stone lie the drops of lorryk blood. I was dragged raw and oozing across these stones, so eager was Sofistron to set my crystal diadem on his walls. The maids scoured the stones clean in my wake, but the spear that wounds forever will find and follow every drop. Take it, she of the silver eyes—"

"She of the once-silver eyes!" Irissa said unflinchingly.

The stag's great dark eyes blinked once. "Follow the blood of the once-bounding stag to the still-bounding stag. You will find the lorryk waiting to bear you away from this place so deadly to my kind and yours."

"The lorryk do not bear riders," Irissa objected. "I heard the huntsmen discuss it."

The head spoke without a pause. "As long as there are lorryk, you and yours shall have ride-right. So take your once-mortal Wrathman with you."

"Leave me out of it," Kendric grumbled. "I can walk."

Irissa turned to him, waiting.

He sighed heavily and jammed the oddly shaped dagger inside his sillac-hide belt.

"I suppose," he noted direly, "I may need this."

Chapter Nine

——◆◆◆——

It was as Bounder had said.

The spear Irissa carried point-down illuminated a faint red glow on the pavement as it neared a place where stag's blood had fallen. Apparently a good deal had spilled as the huntsmen had rushed the trophy head to the great hall where Sofistron's magic would in an instant bind it to the wall; the stones that reddened to Irissa and Kendric's passage were only footsteps apart. Their ruddiness faded when the spear point moved on to the next bloodied stone.

"Convenient," was all Kendric would say of Bounder's magic—or Irissa's role in it.

The very passage that had led them to the kitchen, then back to the hall, now took them directly to the castle's supply courtyard, into the open air and under the cool survey of the ever-overhanging moon.

Irissa stopped to stare. "It's beautiful by night. No wonder Sofistron calls his talisman the Lunestone."

"Yes, I've spent more than enough time craning my neck up at that unnatural sky globe. We'd best be well out of Sofistron's way by dayshine, and that could come at any moment. Sunrise is as sudden as sunfall in this world. It's a long march Rynthward."

"You sound well acquainted with this Rynth. Is it a fairer place than this?"

"No, but safer."

That seemed as much as Kendric had to say about the Rynth. Irissa held the spear point-up, using it for a staff as they walked quickly past the castle gardens and pathways toward the surrounding meadows. They had not gone far when a rustle stirred the long grasses. As the head of Bounder had predicted, the lorryk herd came sweeping over the gentle hills. The restored Bounder himself led them, the littlest lorryk running smoothly by his side. The stag stopped abruptly at their very boot toes and lifted his horn-crowned head inquiringly at Kendric, nostrils sniffing delicately at the air, his crystal-clear eyes level with the man's.

One powerful black forefoot uprooted turf. He shook his head and horns, a snort of negation adding an explanation to his gesture.

"He scents the lemurai on you, I think," Irissa warned.

"If he did not, he would be a poor excuse of a beast." But Kendric's hand joined hers on the upright spear between them. With the tips of his diadem calculated into his height, the male lorryk was perhaps nine feet tall. The moonlight polished the muscular swells of his massive black body and made his bone-colored horns almost seem to shimmer; the glint of his icy eyes was sharp as lightning.

"You . . . created this?" Kendric asked.

Irissa reached for the silvery blaze between the coldstone eyes. The living Bounder mutely lowered his head for her touch. "Yes." She glanced obliquely at Kendric. "I was able to reweave your flesh and blood in Rule. Why do you think I could not do as much—or more—for another one wounded in another world?"

"With Torlocs, it was more often a case of 'would not' than 'could not,' as I recall traffic with their kind in Rule. But I did not think you would part with your tears so lightly. Perhaps that is why Sofistron was able to siphon the silver from your eyes in his commonstone circle; you had already overexpended yourself on the stag."

"No! They were true Torloc tears, and you of all creatures should know I have more than one or two to shed. My magic only strengthened from using it to aid the lorryk."

"We'll have no proof of that, of course," Kendric noted. "I

warrant I'll have to look cross-eyed at this beast, too, now that he wears your tears for eyes."

"You need not look directly at either of us, though there's no danger in it," Irissa said, stamping her foot impatiently, like the stag. "Both Bounder and I appear to be limited to the purely natural now." The littlest lorryk, mistaking her gesture, nudged protectively between them and braced its four slender legs, turning aggressively toward Kendric. "Now even the smallest beast thinks we quarrel," Irissa observed.

Kendric laughed suddenly and waved his hand in denial. "No quarrel. It is impossible to quarrel with a woman or a Torloc, as they are always right, even when they are wrong. So. Bounder has sent us steeds—of a sort. Do we ride all twelve or twenty in turn?"

"I have ridden the female before." Irissa nodded to the pale gray doe at Bounder's side. "You will have to mount the male; he's the only one high enough to carry a Wrathman of Rule without causing your ankles to trail in the grass."

Kendric's mellow humor suddenly soured. He walked consideringly around Bounder, the lorryk's coldstone eye sharp upon his every motion.

"Ride the stag." Kendric rested his wrists lightly on the beast's sharp backbone as he stood deceptively casual at its side. "With no saddle, no reins, no spurs...of course, no spurs," he added hastily as four hooves churned earth restively at the word.

"He has a fine ruff, even thicker than hers," Irissa pointed out. "It should suffice to cling to. And then there are always the horns." She was already astride the doe, having curled her fingers in the ruff and swung herself aboard.

"I do not need hair or horn to cling to," Kendric said, suddenly slinging his long legs over Bounder's back.

The impulse surprised the lorryk as much as it did Kendric. While Irissa watched, the stag bucked once, dug his sharp hooves for purchase in the sod, and shot off into the open meadow. There he zigzagged over the ground, his silver-haired heels kicking their way over one rise after another, his powerful hind legs propelling him through the grasses. Through it all, a certain stubborn dark lump clung to the beast's back. At times, it seemed Kendric had not only his hands fisted in the lorryk's neck ruff but his long arms wrapped around the proud neck. At other times, he appeared in danger of slipping sideways to the ground.

The pair vanished over a ripple of ridge, then reappeared again to pause on the horizon. The sunrise Kendric had warned Irissa about was upon the meadow. Dark sky was rapidly warming to rosy lavender. Against the dawning color, Kendric and the stag were silhouetted in detail so sharp that Irissa thought she could reach out and prick her finger on one of the lorryk's diadem points. She held her breath. Kendric had ridden a bearing-beast in Rule, a high red-coated creature with two straight horns and its own crooked way of doing things at times. Surely in this place it was not so great a difference between man and beast, even if the old divisions still lay heavy between man and Torloc. It was important that the lorryk accept Kendric. Bounder had said that the herd would carry them both away, but the speaking head of Bounder was only a residue of Irissa's now-drained magic and the rough animal spirit she had animated. The stag was its own creature, despite its wise head hanging elsewhere and its borrowed eyes and horns. It would accept or reject on its own instincts.

Irissa saw the horned head bow a bit and shake from side to side. The man sat very straight on its back, a feat not easy when the backbone was one spiny ridge from withers to tail. Kendric leaned toward the neck again, then straightened. Bounder pawed the turf. The sun painted the meadow bright green and yellow; Sofistron's castle stones began lightening to their ordinary daylight dazzle. It was late; soon bevywomen would be dropping their platters outside the empty coldstone chamber, lemurai keepers would be searching for a set of long bones they could not find, huntsmen would be out on their own bearing-beasts, hunting...

The creatures on the horizon wheeled, backs to the sun. They came hurtling across the field, in a straight line very alien to lorryk. The stag stopped abruptly before Irissa, but not so abruptly that Kendric was dislodged.

"It is agreed. The lorryk will take us to the Rynth," Kendric announced.

"So you have found a four-footed beast to speak to?"

He shook his head. "We both have thought awhile—separately. It is often the way with beasts and men. They can arrive at the same conclusions without words."

"It is a pity it is not often the same with man and man," Irissa said. "Or with man and woman."

Kendric glanced at the spear in her hand and frowned. "This is the weapon that—"

"The spear that wounds forever, Bounder called it."

Kendric reached for it, turning its haft distastefully in his hand. "It has served its purpose. Let us leave it for Sofistron." The stag backed up, his weight on his powerful hind legs, almost as a prancing warhorse. Kendric raised the spear and flung it far. Irissa sensed a burden lifted from the lorryk herd with each moment of its passing farther away.

The spear finally found earth, straight and true, in the center of the meadow. It quivered there for a moment, then stilled, thickened, split and split again, branched, and separated into spreading fingers that thrust at the sky. In moments, a tall, leafless, many-horned blond-wood tree stood aloof at the meadow's center, resembling nothing so much as a giant set of lorryk diadem.

Kendric looked at Irissa, and Irissa at Kendric.

"Did you—?" he asked.

She shook her head violently, the Iridesium circlet casting a rainbow of reflection in the brightening daylight.

"It must have been some spell of Bounder's head . . . some lingering Torloc magical taint to it," he suggested. "I only meant to have a thing of senseless death no longer with us when I cast it away, for the injury it did the lorryk—that it does the lorryk still."

"You wished it were other than what it was." Irissa's tone was statement, not accusation, but Kendric's light amber eyes darkened to stormy brown.

"I did not do this. A man hurls a spear from him—it was a simple act with a simple spear. I cannot help it if the very ground of this place grows magical trees at the slightest pretext."

Kendric's trousered knees clenched on the swell of the lorryk's side between them. The beast wheeled as if signaled and darted away down the meadow, away from the spear-tree, the castle, and the climbing sun behind the constant pall of cloud.

Irissa tightened every muscle she could on her own mount, waiting for the rippling mutual motion of the herd to reach her. They were off only instants behind the stag, the drum of their hooves pounding earth, the wind their true and only running mate. Even the littlest lorryk lengthened its stride to great, galloping adult length.

Irissa's fingers shamelessly curled into the female's thick gray neck ruff. Lithe, she would call her mount. The belly between her legs leaped with recognition. The lorryk had sensed her name. Kendric was right, there *was* something unspoken between beast and man—or woman. It was something she had never known before. Torlocs who could turn whatever their eyes saw to their own uses had never had need of creatures of bone and blood to serve them. But now bone and blood bore her at a jarring pace through the magical environs of Sofistron's lands to safety in the unfair and unmagical Rynth.

"You bear more magic than you know." In Rule she had told Kendric that, more from a Torlockian intuition than from any true insight. Perhaps she, too, bore more magic than was inherited through her silver eyes. Natural magic. Ordinary magic.

And Kendric . . . The thought came to her roughly, jarring her almost as much as the spring of lorryk limb over ridge and level land. Kendric now knew more of magic than perhaps he could bear.

She didn't know which of the two of them to feel more pity for.

Chapter Ten

———◆◆◆———

"It is an unprepossessing place." Irissa sat upon Lithe's narrow back, gazing at a landscape as flat and barren as Sofistron's had been undulating and fertile.

"It is the Rynth," Kendric said. "And we now join the other exiles of the Rynth—the rim-runners, the Unkept, and whatever four-footed beasts share this retreat with us."

"Not the lorryk." Irissa patted the sweat-dampened withers before her. "They have been restive since crossing the last meadowed ridge of Sofistron's reach. I think some predator on their kind lives here."

Kendric smiled grimly. "Only the rim-runners, the Unkept, and whatever four-footed beasts live in the Rynth." He slipped sideways off Bounder, his hand loosely curled in the thick black ruff. "Yes, it's time to release our many-legged mounts to the mercies of a magical land where only men hunt them—and then for vanity. Here hunting is serious. I don't think I could persuade the rim-runners or the Unkept to spare food or hide for the sake of a ride, and that a rough one." He patted the stag's black shoulder. "I've had smoother steeds, but never fleeter."

Irissa swung her leg over Lithe's back, then slid down the lorryk's sun-warmed side, her arms tightening across the doe's spine to gentle her arrival on immobile earth again. She felt faintly dizzy, for the lorryk had sped across Sofistron's magical meadow with its almost rhythmically perfect swells of earth at great, ground-gulping bounds. Even when their hooves had hit the Rynth's rocky shale, they had hardly slowed and had leaped their way with the sharp-hoofed precision of a rock ram over the few dry stones making a path through the shallow meanders.

As soon as Irissa had dismounted, the littlest lorryk minced over for a scratch and a rub, pressing its slightly panting side against Irissa's hip and butting her hand with its forehead.

"I'm glad these creatures seem natural enough and mute," Kendric said, watching. "To have been dogged by a conversant stag would have been worse than having been kept company by Finorian's prattling old cat in Rule."

"Do you most fault Felabba for having voice at all—or for holding her tongue so successfully in your presence that she seemed an ordinary cat?"

"I fault no one. I merely state a preference. Beasts should be beasts, and men—men."

"And Torlocs?"

Kendric looked straight to her eyes. Now that they were dull, common gray, she no longer had to fear that seeing herself in the eye of another would strip the silver from them, and he no longer had to fear that their sheer power would by chance deal him some harm.

"There is something in the stones," he said, seeming to evade her unspoken question with a clumsy change of subject. "In Rule rin-mined coldstones are beyond price, and only a silver-eyed Torloc seeress could weep coldstones at will."

Irissa shook her head. "Not at will, Kendric, at woe. A Torloc's tears well from the same spring as anything mortal's. It is the human part of us that weeps, which is why the water makes itself stone—and immortal. And it's why they are such a sign of power."

"I am not an epicure of tears," he said. "I only know that here in the Inlands of Ten, which is utterly unlike any part of Rule, what we would call coldstones carpet the Rynth—and are considered so worthless folk call them commonstone." Kendric bent and scooped up a fistful of the softly glittering pebbles at his feet. "There is some link in this—some link and some disruption. If we could fit the opposite sides of this conundrum together, we might solve why the gate sent us here, instead of to the Torloc paradise you sought."

Irissa smiled at the "we" inserted so unthinkingly into Kendric's struggled reasoning. "At least we travel with muted beasts," she pointed out. "And I shall not have to avoid your eyes because of the power of my own."

"A thing should be what it is, to the nature of its kind," he answered. "I would rather you keep your powers and your silver eyes in this place, despite the danger—and that in Rule you had kept them to yourself."

"You regret what passed between us?"

"Your powers passed between us; the rest belongs in a ballad," he answered angrily.

Irissa didn't reply to this, but bowed her head until her dark hair veiled her face. "The lorryk have gone against the nature of their kind to come this far into alien land on our behalf." Irissa absently stroked the small doe's forehead blaze. "We should release them."

Her words did it, or perhaps they read the farewell pat she bestowed on the young one. The stag wheeled, then the entire herd followed. They were springing away over the low, rocky terrain, stitching a moving black zigzag line across its monotonous folds.

Irissa turned to see them go. She watched for a long time, her back as immobile as the moon above, until Kendric shuffled his boots for attention.

"You weep?" he asked cautiously.

"I cannot. But I had grown fond of the lorryk. It is sad to lose what is friendly to one."

Kendric said no more, until Irissa finally turned back to him. Then he gestured to the unpromising distance.

"I trust I can find the same hummock of rock that I left with the rim-runners—and that they still camp there. It would be lean living in this waste without decent weapon or company."

They started off on foot, their rule-cobbled boots still sturdy, the thick sillac-hide of Kendric's impervious to the sharp rocks. Irissa's were fashioned of a softer gray hide, but they, too, were tough.

The never-waning moon beamed down on them. High in the sky, seeming far above the ice-arch, though that was unlikely, some wide-winged birds soared. Nothing else moved in the Rynth, except the slow-flowing waters of the many meanders that snaked ahead of them.

They picked their way across the meanders, Kendric warning Irissa to be wary of fleshfins. The waters were so cold and clear that in the shallows she could easily see these flat, silver-scaled fish with their round, blood-red eyes and the thistly suckers that lined their sides. She saw, too, the profusion of coldstones that winked bright beauty from the waters. Even without power, they were pretty; how was it that the people of this place held them in such disregard as to christen them "common"?

But she was also common now, her glamour stripped from her with her magic gaze. Perhaps it would not be so bad to be common, Irissa considered. There was comfort in the common. Certainly Kendric would not so bitterly regret a union with a common woman as he did the exchange that had apparently transferred some—or all?—of her incipient powers to him. Why? It should not have been. Only a magician like Geronfrey would expect to acquire a Torloc seeress' powers with her first womanhood. Yet he had been so greedy for this possession— for with Geronfrey all commerce with a woman would have come down to that—that she had fled him for the common comfort of another man's bed. Man, not magician. Of all things Kendric had been, good or ill, magic was the least of them. No wonder the stir of it within himself galled him so . . .

She was thought-lost, exploring the meanings and emotions of another time and picking her way over the rough Rynth stones at the same time. The weight of Kendric's arm descended heavily across her shoulders.

"I see the bloom of a rim-runner fire near those rocks," he said, pointing to an undistinguished hummock on the horizon and twisting her to face in that direction. "I think we can trudge there before the last warmth of day is gone. The Rynth at night turns a colder shoulder to its creatures than a glacier."

Irissa smiled palely and said nothing, but she did not shrug his arm off her shoulders. And they marched in relative companionability toward the horizon.

Chapter Eleven

◆◆◆

"By the Overstone, you bagged it! I feared for your skin, friend Kendric. You must be not only brave of heart and long of limb but as quick of brain as the lorryk are fleet of feet. Mind you keep her well behind you, lest her icy eyes freeze us all to the ground we stand on!"

Gryff, the red-beard, was torn between pounding Kendric on whatever part of his back he could reach, peering around Kendric's shoulder at the walk-weary Irissa in his wake, or sending victorious winks over his own shoulder to the leery rim-runners massed behind him.

"What a triumph, eh? An ice-eyed one in the hands of us poor Rynthian exiles. Now the Stonekeeps can tremble. Better Sofistron should have slain her. But you're sure we suffer no blight from her presence, Kendric? Do the flames flicker? No. A storm come? Perhaps a chant to disarm her . . ."

"She is disarmed," interjected Kendric, who stood somewhat amazed at the fear and awe one footsore Torloc could instill in the rugged rim-runners. On the campfire's other side were gathered the Unkept women. Amozel was as erect and stiffly disapproving as ever.

"Of course, of course, friend," Gryff soothed. "You would not bring such a one into the heart of our camp unless she were well under your control, isn't that right? Let us see her better."

Despite their trepidation, the rim-runners were slowly edging nearer, spreading wider, the better to view the figure still half concealed behind Kendric.

"We have never seen an ice-eyed one," Calennian explained, his bronze face a bit sallow, his knuckles white on the cudgel with which he had earlier challenged Kendric and seemed dangerously likely to do so again, should any sudden wrong sign strike him.

"A Torloc," Kendric corrected suddenly. "She is Torloc."

"Tor-loc." Calennian pronounced the name delicately, as if to say it was to risk invoking it.

It was odd; these people clearly knew *what* but not *who* a Torloc was. "Torloc," Kendric repeated. The sooner Irissa became something other than the feared "ice-eyed one," the safer they would both be.

"And this Torloc," Gryff said, grinning confidently to his men, "it is under your control?"

"*She,*" Kendric said, so shortly that several rim-runners stepped back nervously.

There was a pause. Gryff began again, a bit less authoritatively. "So. This . . . she-Torloc is safe, then? Not likely to make the moon's face turn crimson or the meanders rise or the fowlen rush in from the Cincture and devour us all?" He was being jocular, for the sake of his men and his own uncertainty. "You have her under your control?" he demanded again.

"No," Irissa said, stepping forward.

"Yes," Kendric said, barring her way with his arm.

There was another silence while they all regarded one another, or rather while the rim-runners regarded Kendric. They kept their eyes off Irissa, who glared at them over the barrier of Kendric's arm, nevertheless.

"Her magic is . . . unmade . . . at the moment," Kendric explained. "She could do you no harm, even if she were so inclined. She is safe."

On these terms, Irissa could not deny it, though it was not strictly true she could do them no harm; she looked at the moment as if she could do them a great deal of harm, personally.

"Would I have traveled all this way from Sofistron's Stonekeep in her company and remained unharmed, were she dangerous?" Kendric pressed on.

The rim-runners had no answer.

"Bring her to me. I can tell you how unmade her magic is."

Amozel's iron voice startled the men. They were unused to hearing a woman intervene in matters of masculine discussion.

Kendric's arm wavered in front of Irissa, but she pushed it down and started forward. "No," he whispered in warning.

"She might know how deeply ebbed my powers are," Irissa rejoined, brushing past him to walk around the waist-high fire to Amozel on her rocky throne.

"Seeress," Irissa addressed her.

Kendric groaned to himself. The mistake was natural; in Irissa's world wisewomen held sway; seeing Amozel installed with the fowlen pelt hood might make one take her for the woman of power in the Rynth—which she was, in purely natural matters.

But titles had no sway with Amozel, for good or ill. She stared at Irissa, studying the knee-worn gray trousers, the boots, the circlet binding her hair. Amozel's small hand stretched out imperiously, yet with caution.

"You are not a bevywoman, nor yet an Unkept. You are like a bit of both and still utterly alien to both. You are called—"

"Irissa."

"Irissa. It is not an Inlands name. And your eyes—" Amozel blinked, owllike, then focused her burning dark eyes on Irissa's. "Your eyes are empty. There is no magic in her," she announced in tones the entire party could hear. It was an official declaration from the only official the Rynth could call its own— Amozel, mistress of the Unkept women and bestower of their company.

Across the firelight, relieved and jubilant rim-runners circled Kendric in congratulatory triumph. His rough, dark head loomed from their midst like a mountain from its foothills. Before Amozel, Irissa stood shocked and silent, staring numbly into a face that knew her not and thus should have no reason to lie.

But the rim-runners were no longer concerned with her, now that she had been officially declared powerless. All their concern was for her keeper.

"Ah, Kendric, my lad." Gryff practically cooed. "I'd wagered my ear we'd not seen the last of you. You're not one to serve as lemurai meat; the pack would choke on you. And to have brought back this, er, prize, though how you have muffled her magic enough to fool Amozel, I don't know. But that's even better. I'd not like to drive her and her flock of Unkept off over soon . . . But tell us how you fared, once we had parted in Sofistron's turret."

"He's dead, the rim-runner I found outside the bevy chamber, wounded by Sofistron's guard, or whoever they are—"

"The Keep-brothers, yes. We thought that Nallor was a dead man. And you, too, friend. But such are the risks of a bevy raid."

Kendric noticed one friendly face missing and looked about the tightly gathered circle. "Where's Helicon?"

"Such are the benefits of a bevy raid," Gryff said, smiling widely. "Helicon made off with a bevywoman, striking out directly for Ivrium's Stonekeep to settle with her. Now that he has one of the Daughters for a wife, he will be first among Ivrium's plainsmen. It was a pity he snared only one; with the beginnings of a bevy, he could have demanded land-right. Ah, well, Kendric here has made up for our meager catch. One big fish is worth a dozen minnows."

"Helicon always liked the life of the Rynth less than the rest of us," Calennian said. "The plainsmen are made for a life on beast back, not for pacing through this waste. I do not blame him for returning to the Keep, now that he has earned entrance-right."

"We shall all return to the Keeps on our terms," Gryff predicted. "Now that we have the, the—Dorloc."

"Torloc," Kendric said.

"Whatever you call it—or her—it will be enough to make the magicians clutch their stones, the heirlings grind their teeth, and the bevies shake in their soleless sandals to hear that the rim-runners have such a one. We'll celebrate this night. Break out the nettle ale and pour a large cup for our friend Kendric of the Foreign Keep."

"The Far Keep," Kendric corrected. The very, very Far Keep.

"The rim-runners are reckless tonight," Amozel observed from across the fire. "If they break out the ale, they consume a full season's brewing. I think, Demimondana, we had better have our own wine this night; and we begin with you. Whether the rest have new trinkets to offer or not, you are sworn to Gryff for five more nights."

Irissa watched a handsome woman with dark red hair bring out a wineskin and fill the goblets passed around.

One was handed to Irissa and she drank from it gratefully. She not only was thirsty after a long ride and march but wanted to soften the stings of the day, which were many, not the least of which was watching Kendric being lionized across the fire for achieving something that was little to his credit—her company.

The wine was slightly chilled from the night and bittersweet with a faint overtaste of honey. Irissa let a drop fall on her finger and studied it in the firelight. The wine was colored bright blue.

"Barrenberries make our wine," Amozel said. "They grow, rarely, around the largest of the bonewood trees and must be harvested one by one and slowly fermented in a commonstone-lined container. It is the only thing the commonstone is good for. But the barrenberry is a living jewel to the women of the Rynth, a jewel that weeps blue wine in time."

"You do not drink yourself," Irissa observed.

"I do not need to, I do not consort with the rim-runners."

"Nor I!" Irissa sounded indignant.

Amozel leaned forward; it seemed to Irissa a great white wolf dove at her from the darkened sky. Amozel's small hand fanned over the top of Irissa's pewter goblet, the nails pale and sharp.

"Do not spurn the barrenberry wine, you of the unmade magic. Bevywoman would rather die than drink, but you are here in the Rynth, in the keeping of yon giant; if you wish to keep your freedom, you will drink. Perhaps you do not count him a rim-runner because he is new to their camp, but it is the same thing."

"But why is this wine so valued?" Irissa took a deep draught under Amozel's approving but disconcerting stare.

"It keeps the swaddlings from my women's feet forever; it permits them to bed the rim-runners for the best of their barter but to remain always free to wander, to remain Unkept. We did not flee the Stonekeeps to become brides of the wastelands. That is why I share this wine with you. You fall between kinds, though I fear you are more of the bevy. With this wine, no swaddlings will come to force you into settlement within a

Stonekeep's throw after you bed this night or many after with your giant—"

Amozel paused. Choking, Irissa spat a startled spray of azure wine into the firelighted darkness.

"I am sorry to waste your wine," she apologized breathlessly when she could speak again. "But why would you think that I and that— Listen, Amozel. If I share no man's bed, I need drink no wine, if I understand you rightly."

"But you are kept."

Irissa shook her head. "No."

"You are not Unkept," Amozel insisted.

"Yes. Not as you are, perhaps, but—no one keeps me but myself."

"He keeps your magic contained. Were it not so, the rim-runners would have skewered you before now, and I and my women would not tolerate you within a meander's width. I have seen the stranger's silver Stone of power. And now he holds yours as well. If a man may keep your magic, how are you not kept?"

"It is—not as it appears," Irissa said, realizing for the first time that to show magic would make her an enemy of everything in this world, and not to show it made her a victim of everything in this world. "And why do you tolerate magic of him, then, if it is so forbidden to me?"

Amozel shrugged, the pelt rippling silver over her small shoulders. "The rim-runners have some crude chants. It is nothing to rival the magicians, and they keep their break-magic well away from us. If the stranger giant were to wield his Stone of power, he would have to leave the Rynth and challenge some Stonekeeper or other, or erect his own Stonekeep on whatever part of the Rynth he could hold. It was all Rynth once, you know. You have seen Sofistron's fair fields, but there are many Keeps more wondrous. Yet there is a certain beauty to his fields and forests, and there is no more glorious Inlands Keep than his shining white-stone castle with its blue and red pennants flying . . ."

Amozel sounded as soft as a woman of her iron bent could be. Irissa waited a moment for her to speak further, then asked the question that suddenly troubled her.

"You have—seen—Sofistron's Stonekeep; you are not purely of the Rynth?"

"Of course I have seen it," Amozel said, cocking her head solemnly at Irissa. "Sofistron is my father."

Chapter Twelve

"It is necessary," Kendric said.

"Oh? I have heard many reasons for it, but necessity was never one of them." Irissa folded her arms.

They stood in the last flare of the dying fire. One by one, the rim-runners had approached Amozel with various tokens, these much more common than the offerings of the two nights' previous; and two by two, the men and the Unkept women had paired off and vanished into the caves.

Amozel still kept watch, though, and Irissa was most conscious of the woman's bird-bright eyes upon her.

Few remained on either side of the fire now; those who did were destined to remain for the night. Kendric, unlike before, did not plan on being one of them.

"It is only a rush mat on a cave ledge; I will take the floor."

"No. I told Amozel that I was Unkept."

"And so you shall be. In reality."

"Not if I vanish meekly into the cave with you."

"If you do not, I shall lose face among the rim-runners—"

"But it is all right if *I* lose face among the Unkept women *and* the rim-runners!"

Kendric flushed in the last rays of firelight. He lowered his voice in direct proportion to his urge to raise it. "Irissa, this is not Rule. Even in Rule your kind was mistrusted; here it is destroyed—unless these people see a value in it. We must accede to their customs, at least in a surface sort of way. If the rim-runners believe that I do not govern you, their fear of your kind will lead them to slay both of us. Had I my sword, I would put it between us—"

"That was not wholly effective in Rule," she reminded him.

Their eyes blazed at each other. It was a new experience, this luxury of surface staring, to those previously restrained by Torloc evasiveness. Kendric decided that gentlemanly restraint was not called for in the Rynth, either.

"Perhaps we should honor these customs fully; perhaps if we shared bed-bond again, I might pass your precious powers back to you—the powers you tricked me into taking unwilling!"

Now Irissa's cheeks warmed in the light of the fire's last embers. But she turned to face the cave mouth, away from Amozel. "Then you may use your dagger as token of your innocent intent. Since it is magic-made in part, perhaps it will cry warning if you violate your oath."

"Were there a dozen lemurai at my throat, I could not be persuaded to it," Kendric swore as he followed her into the darkness.

The rocks themselves were low. Kendric had to bow to the cave ceiling more than once as he sought the place Gryff had originally assigned him. The caves were sprawling, with many offshoots into which the rim-runners and Unkept had vanished. Its common area was lighted by low-burning torches, and some natural chimney pulled most of the smoke upward. But when Kendric came to the passage he recognized, it was as dark and uninviting as a lemurai tunnel.

"You'll need to fetch a torch," Irissa said.

Kendric cleared his throat. "No. Go ahead." He prodded her rather summarily into the dark. The instant they were fully enveloped by it she knew why.

"A light! It is your dagger—because it was mind-forged," she diagnosed.

"Is that it? At least you are useful for explanations. I first noticed it in the lemurai tunnels."

Kendric seemed less than enchanted by the phenomenon, but he pulled the weapon from his belt and elevated it torchlike. The blade burned with white fire two-thirds of the way up, then the glow softened toward the hilt. Still, it was strong enough to flood through the jewels bedecking the haft and spin a gaudy constellation of red, orange, blue, green, and purple reflections onto the cave walls.

"Sofistron's taste in metalwork leaves much to be desired," Kendric said sheepishly. "I liked the single emerald eye in the hilt of your mind-sword in Rule better. Perhaps you can carry this rainbow, since you go ahead."

He thrust the dagger at her, hilt first. Irissa couldn't help smiling at the blend of wonder and embarrassment that formed Kendric's approach to his newly discovered powers. But her smile uncurved when the gleaming hilt was warm within her hand; the light quenched, leaving not even an afterglow. The metal chilled at her touch.

"It is yours," she said, thrusting it back at him. "You made it; it will respond only to you."

"But your mind-forged sword remained lambent in my hand in Rule, and I had no magic then."

She held the dagger pointed at the dark until she felt his hand reluctantly curl around hers and take it back. "Perhaps my magic was stronger than yours is now," she said impatiently. "Perhaps I am so utterly drained now that magic of no one's making will cling to me. Perhaps we had a link in Rule that is now broken—"

"Or perhaps all three," Kendric said thoughtfully as the reviving hilt light bathed his features in a parti-colored glow. The effect was one to make Irissa smile, if ever she would smile again. She sighed instead.

"You promised me a rush mat," she reminded him.

He gestured forward with his dagger hand. The passage ended in a cul-de-sac and a sort of rock-formed bench, piled high with dried grasses. "The rim-runners occasionally cross Sofistron's borders to poach a lorryk or harvest his meadows for mattresses. I have not slept here myself, but it looks soft enough."

"Not slept here? But surely there was a similar ritual to this night's the time before this? From what Amozel implied, all men must offer for one of her women. She does not brook indifference."

"I was on the march to Sofistron's Stonekeep the night before this," Kendric pointed out. "We all had only the moon for a bedmate, or the snores of our fellows, which were as plentiful as stars."

"And the night before that?" Irissa sat on the dried grasses and started when she sank into them deeply.

"The night of my arrival I was invited to sue for the favor of Amozel and her women, but I had no gift to offer that was found worthy. It seems the mechanical things of Rule are taken for magical here, so my flint and steel were of no use, and my one trophy of the place so far, a bonewood staff, was magic-tainted by my eyes upon it."

"It appears the powers you took from me are a grave disservice after all," Irissa said, lying on her side on the mat and sinking deep into the lingering fragrance of the grasses. "I would not have put a leash on your courting practices for the world."

"This world or any other?" Kendric demanded.

"All. A Torloc seeress does not need to bind men to her by magical means."

"Worry not. You do not bind me, Torloc," Kendric said, letting his back slide along the rock wall until he sat on the ground beside her. "And there are women other than the Unkept." He laid the dagger beside him, its light cast mostly at the rocky ceiling.

"Yes. The bevy. No doubt you would find them more docile." Irissa rolled onto her back and contemplated the variegated colors fanning onto the dimpled rock surface. "Amozel is Sofistron's daughter," she announced. "She told me so."

"Sofistron's daughter? Then why does she live the hard life of the Rynth when she could be safe within a Stonekeep? And why do she and her women disdain magic so?"

"That is something for us to think upon. If we come to understand the ways of this place, perhaps we can find our way out of it."

"To where? Another gate?" he demanded skeptically.

Irissa cradled her head on her hand and supported herself on an elbow. "Finorian said, in the gate, that you could not pass through a Torloc portal, but if you acquired Torlockian powers from me, even unknowing—"

"Especially unknowing. I still do not accept the full burden of that fact. Perhaps this magic of mine is merely a phenomenon that fades; perhaps it simply stems from association with a Torloc."

"I am not empowered now," Irissa reminded him almost impishly. "And your dagger hilt still casts a gaudy glow. I think only you can take the credit for such a display."

"Another cursed blade to carry through another world gone mad; that's the price a simple marshman pays for consorting with a Torloc," he grumbled, leaning his elbows on his bent knees, resting his back against the rock to sleep, and looking quite forlorn.

"Past sins are always paid for in the present, when we cannot enjoy them," Irissa said, brushing the back of Kendric's hand with the slightly coiling end of a lock of her long hair.

His eyes flew open and his hand caught and held her wrist. "Do not bait me, Torloc. I may be a simple man from the marshes of Rule, but this is another place and other circumstances, and I do not think we can afford to take them so simply."

Irissa stared into his eyes. There seemed no danger in that now, and she recalled many times when she could not do so and had wished to. Now all she saw was wariness and confusion, nothing magical about either. Apparently those who acquired rather than inherited Torloc powers did not need to guard their eyes from looking too deep into the gaze of another. So Kendric had her powers, without the leashes upon their nature that she'd had to suffer, and still scorned both powers and possessor. Yet now he had to include himself in that harsh judgment.

"When we met," Irissa began, "you said that we were fated to travel together—a woman who had never wept and a warrior who had never bled. Now I have wept, wept coldstone clear and coldstone dark, wept mortal salt even, until I can weep no more. And you bled in our journey, many times. We have, I think, passed deeply into the darkest ways of our kinds; perhaps we have passed beyond them."

"Torloc powers or not, I still bleed like a mortal man."

"Be wary, then. I cannot heal you now. I cannot even weep for you."

"I require neither your healing nor your weeping," he replied.

"You asked for—demanded—my healing powers once," she reminded him.

"I thought such things came cheaply then."

"The only thing that comes cheaply is hindsight," Irissa said.

"You may have lost your magical powers," Kendric said, "but you have not lost the power of speech, and dire speech, too, as is the way of Torlocs."

"The way of Torlocs is your way now, if you truly acquired my powers."

"I do not have to use them. Geronfrey knew from the first what he wanted and how to get it. What I took from you was unintended and shall be unused, now that I know it's there. Perhaps disuse will discourage it from sticking to me."

Irissa laughed. "Oh, Kendric, power is not something to come and go at your command or a stray cur to be kicked unwanted from your side. Use it or not, it is yours, and there are many who would not be so ungrateful at its acquiring—"

"Yes. Geronfrey gave you too long a leash in hopes of drawing you to him gently, and you slipped it to come to one who put no leashes on you. I will remember this and keep you well fettered. I will not use my unwanted powers and I will not look upon you as ordinary man looks upon ordinary woman. Thus both sides of our natures will be muted. It should make our travels through this place much easier."

"Yes," Irissa agreed, staring at the many-colored ceiling, "much easier."

Her tone had been intensely ironic, but Kendric, having declared himself, was at peace and already sliding into sleep. The hilt-cast light softened; all the vivid colors paled to pastels. It was gone, crossed over with Kendric into the purely natural world of dream he inhabited for the night.

Irissa remained awake on her soft, scented bed and felt she lay on thorns.

Chapter Thirteen

In the morning, Irissa awoke in the dimly lighted cave with Kendric gone. She emerged to find him with the rim-runners, gathered in a circle while they broke their fast on dried fish and a flat bread the Unkept women had brought.

Kendric had exchanged his lemurai-stained tunic for rim-runners' garb. Indeed, it seemed that every rim-runner had volunteered something from his stock, for now the orange boots and blue trousers of Rule were topped by a green tunic, a white fowlen-fur vest—obviously Gryff's gift, made from the remainder of the pelt Amozel wore—and assorted belts hung with implements useful for a journey, including an intricately bladed ax. The dagger was nowhere visible.

Not to be outdone, the Unkept women invited Irissa to their side of the camp and offered her a leathern skirt and a bright blue vest. She refused the skirt despite her ragged trouser knees, but gratefully accepted the vest.

"It is light but warm," Demimondana explained, "and filled with moonhawk down. They say that fowlen feathers are warmer and softer, but of course we do not venture into the Cincture, and the fowlen seldom pack in the Rynth. And our arrows would not bring down a full-grown fowlen, anyway."

Irissa took the opportunity to ask a question that had, among others, worked ill at her understanding all night.

"Demimondana, do you not mind that Amozel trades you like so much merchandise to the rim-runners?"

The woman's gray-green eyes met Irissa's full on. "Amozel does not trade us. She merely applies order to what is our choice—to live free in the Rynth and freely do what is necessary to survive here."

"But would you not prefer to choose your own companion? To be parceled off at Amozel's whim of a night—"

"It is only a night. In the Stonekeeps, we would have been assigned for our lifetimes to one magician's bevy or another, to spend our days veiled and bootless, to tend swaddlings until they became heirlings and were wrested away, and then to attend only to our petty precedence, until we died."

"But surely you would prefer a man of your choice?"

"We choose no one; therefore, we can prefer all." The woman's eyes sharpened. "Only a bevywoman would meekly go to a Stonekeep of her father's choosing and there stay with one Lord Warden until her days end or a new One Son becomes Stonekeeper and decides to keep or replace her. Sometimes entire bevies have been driven to the fields after the time of the Exchange, to starve among the peasants. But that does not happen often. The Stones prolong their holders' lives, and promising One Sons have lived and died without so much as a new wrinkle touching the face or a white hair showing up in the beard of his father."

"It is most confusing. Amozel is Sofistron's daughter—"

"And I am the daughter of a Stonekeeper. Yet I prefer the Rynth."

"And Gryff?"

"And Gryff. He is a rim-runner; he does not simper about the Stonekeeps in hopes of rising to the place of Lord. He does not smother his own hopes in the ambition of succeeding another. He does not abjure women because it suits the vanity of his father-magician. And he ventures into the Cincture for the fowlen fur, which makes him a better warrior than any of his highly trained eunuch-brothers in the Stonekeeps."

"*Gryff* is a magician's son?" Irissa demanded incredulously.

"We are all sons and daughters of the Stonekeepers," Amozel said, coming over and sitting on a nearby rock. She had doffed the fowlen hood, evidently deeming it a ceremonial headdress not suited to daylight. Her hair hung, waved and golden, about her shoulders, but her eyes were still fierce. "Is it not so with you and the giant?"

"We come from—farther away . . ."

"The Far Keep." Amozel nodded. "A mysterious place we have never heard of, nor have we ever met someone from thence until now. But we cannot contradict you. The ways of the Rynth are devious, and the meanders flow through many places and touch on many things—ten Stonekeeps that we know—and the Cincture itself, of which we know nothing and are glad of that mercy."

Demimondana shivered, rose, and returned with a white bone comb. Irissa combed her wind-ridden tresses while Demimondana watched her consideringly.

"You still say you are not kept?" Amozel asked.

"I am not kept," Irissa answered firmly, sweeping the comb from the circlet down through the distant curling tips of her dark hair.

"There is no magic in you now, as there is in the giant."

It was beginning to irritate Irissa to be continually told that there was no magic in her and to hear Amozel continually label Kendric by his height. He was tall, yes, but she herself stood six feet, which was long among womankind. But one tended to forget how tiny Amozel was—to her, Kendric would seem a walking tree, and Irissa perhaps more of his kind than her own. It was odd that so delicate a woman should rule it over the sturdier of her kind, rim-runners and Rynth, but there was no oddity in how she managed it. She did so by the natural force of her character and integrity. No one forced Amozel to his or her wishes; not even, Irissa understood now, a magician-father.

"There is some slight magic in *that*—" Amozel pointed one disdainful, sharp-nailed finger to the Iridesium circlet. "But it is very weak and you could always leave it off . . ."

"Leave it?"

Amozel nodded slowly. "You could join us, travel the Rynth with us, trade with us. If you are not truly kept, it is not meet that you should partner with yon giant. It is not the nature of things here to unite kind with other kinds for more than reasons of necessity. If you are not kept, you should not consort in other matters with the man."

"I am not kept," Irissa repeated, "but necessity propels us together. We search for the history of my kind, each for our own purpose."

Amozel shrugged daintily; she was much less forbidding in daylight. "Do not decide until after we and the rim-runners share Stonelore tonight, as we always do before breaking camp and going our separate ways. If you seek the cave again, I shall know the Unkept remain at our original number."

Amozel rose and rejoined her women, while Irissa continued to comb her tangled locks and muse. Join the Unkept women? And come into the rim-runner camp to be assigned at Amozel's command? How was this worse than being sent by one's father to the bevy of a fellow magician? Irissa had never known her father, had barely seen any Torloc males at all, for she had been born after the Torloc place in Rule was waning; only empowered Eldresses like Finorian ruled what meager roosts were left to undefended Torloc women who kept to castle ruins like hens to henhouses. She found it hard to fathom the idea of one's sire trading his daughters off as if they were so much grain or goods.

Then Irissa remembered Finorian's ambition to wed her with the last Torloc man of power left in Rule and reflected that customs merely wore different masks in different places. Still, to be traded for the odd night here and there by one's own kind did not strike Irissa as much of an improvement on more formal subjugation, although at least the rude arrangements of the Rynth permitted the objects of the bargain to benefit from it. Perhaps the very comb in her hand had been won by some woman's body! Irissa let it drop to the ground.

Odd, Amozel spurned the dim magic of a metal circlet as if it were tainted. And Irissa kept to her circlet and found an ordinary comb distasteful. There was much to puzzle out here, and no reason yet to say why any Torloc seeress should want to touch so much as her great toe on one scintilla of this benighted land.

"Fleshfin skeleton, also dearly bought." Kendric had traipsed over to retrieve the fallen comb, not so much out of courtesy as from a desire for conversation. He sat on Amozel's vacated rock, and Irissa watched anxiously over his looming shoulder for some stir at this liberty. There was none.

"How do you like my caparisoning?" he asked in resigned tones. "These folk seem bound to make a rainbow of me one way or another. But the rim-runners have been generous; I should not object to the color of their generosity."

PANEL

43

"So, too, with the Unkept. Amozel even generously offered that I should join them."

"You? Join the Unkept? Ridiculous. It would be like a wolf among lambs."

"More like a lorryk among the fowlen. You forget, I am quite unempowered now."

"I was not thinking of powers," Kendric said, frowning heavily.

"You must admit it would solve the matter of our sleeping arrangements."

"There is no 'matter' there, except that the customs of our world and this are at cross-purposes."

"I'm afraid you are right. It seems that a woman has no honor here in the Rynth unless she takes some gift in return for herself."

"There was nothing given," Kendric grated between his teeth, but leaning forward to speak low so the rim-runners should not hear, "except misery. And besides, you had the grasses as thick as a new-mown field and no ground drafts to tickle at your nose all night."

"That is between the two of us; as far as the rest of the camp is concerned, I am as good as a bevywoman. I might as well be veiled and unbooted—"

"Here!" Kendric pulled some object off a loop upon his belt and slapped it into her palm. "Now that I have something to offer, you can have something to show to your cursed Unkept women."

Irissa turned over a small knife in her hand, suitable for cutting fish or bread. "It's very nice, but it might be more useful if it would glow."

Kendric slapped his hands to his knees and stood, leaning down to her one last time. "A wolf among lambs, I said. I hope you *do* decide to join the Unkept; I could not imagine a better undoing for them." And he stalked his way back across the camp.

Irissa smiled and tucked the small knife into an inner pocket of the woven purse Demimondana had given her. It would be a shame to grant Kendric's wishes too easily; if he would learn magic—and he would have to, whether he wished it or not— he would have to earn his reward first.

* * *

"Make fire, stranger friend. It is good that we have strong magic at the beginning of a recital of the Stonelore; even Amozel cannot gainsay your make-magic at such an occasion."

Gryff nodded encouragingly at Kendric, who glanced across the camp to Amozel, surrounded by her women. It was odd how he couldn't look at the woman without thinking in terms of asking her permission for something.

But Amozel sat still and ceremonially silent now, the fur and feathers of her white hood breaking against the dark night behind her like spray against rocks.

Above, the luminescent moon cast light enough to wink brazenly from the weaponry among the two bands gathered near the caves. It flashed from the metal tip of Demimondana's bow that rested against a rock and glimmered off an ax blade on the opposite, rim-runner side. Amozel's white hood shone silver in the unchanging moonlight, Kendric noticed—or rather, it gleamed like snow, fresh snow as fine as coldstone dust. Why did he think of frozen phenomena when the Rynth was chill enough in its own, unfrozen way and an ice bridge arched the sky from side to side like a frozen white rainbow? It was cold enough here, fireless, without musing on ice and snow.

Kendric shivered, then applied his flint and steel expertly to the high-piled wood—pine branches poached from Sofistron's forest, not the hard-won Rynthian bonewood.

The sparks danced between his icy fingers as the rim-runners murmured their approval; Kendric couldn't help wondering if one place's magic was always another place's practicality. Soon a respectable sheet of flame was shaking in the slight night wind. The warm flames reflected off the gathered faces, polishing them ruddy and making Gryff's golden ear look molten. Firelight painted Amozel's frozen expression a shifting pattern of sweet and severe; it turned Demimondana's tresses to liquid vermilion and danced bright reflection in the smooth dark locks that cloaked Irissa's shoulders where she sat at the fringe of the Unkept women.

Kendric stepped back to his own circle. Together, the two groups almost met in a flattened arc around the high-burning fire—almost, but not quite.

Gryff leaned so close to the fire that his red beard shone crimson and began speaking in a singsong, ceremonial voice:

"We gather here, exiles of the Rynth, both men and women, rim-runner and Unkept woman, with two of a farther Keep. We gather here, under the Overstone that sees all and says nothing, to speak of the Stones that rule the Rynth and the Stonekeeps and the Inlands of Ten unto the very Cincture at the ends of the earth.

"We are not Stonekeepers, though some of us could have weighted our palms with this heavy magic, but we speak the lore of the Stones, so it is not forgotten by those who come after, and so we remember that common men like ourselves first found the Stones in the shallows of a meander and learned only slowly over great time and many generations to use them to their fullest powers.

"We speak of the Stones as keepers of powers both good and evil, as there is good and evil in all men and all things, as fire both warms and burns, as ice both cools and kills, though may we be preserved from the Cincture and live not to see its frozen wastes.

"We ask of the fire, which was ignited by strong make-magic, that it break to our voices into the nature of the Stones we celebrate in turn, as we raise our voices together and invoke the Stones."

There was a pause, with the indrawing of many breaths, and then the men began chanting:

> "Shinestone, Sandstone,
> We name thee, we count thee.
> Nightstone, Floodstone,
> We live by or beyond thee
> Skystone, Lunestone,
> To the Inlands thou brought breath.
> Gladestone, Bloodstone.
> Stoneless the Rynth bringeth death."

As the rim-runners chanted, the flames separated into individual tongues that spoke in new shades, in colors to be glimpsed in ordinary fire, but seldom seen clear and overpowering as now. The flames grew gold, then copper and coal black by turn. The sudden opaque sheet of ebony flared clear, like water, so the Unkept women were seen through its veiling dance of flames. The tongues suddenly spoke in unison a blue so pure and true that mere earthly azure seemed an insult. From blue they paled to silver; then flared to an emerald green so hot and liquid it shimmered jewel-bright on the night air. Immediately, a sheet of deepest, ruddiest crimson was shaking its fiery fingers at the seated circles, seeming to stretch so close it would singe their eyebrows and flow into Gryff's red beard as one.

The effect ended with the echo of the rim-runners' last-invoked talisman—the Bloodstone. The fire faded to a yellow-orange color and snapped wood ferociously, once returned to its natural state.

But the invocation was not over. Only eight Stones had been called upon. Gryff leaned back and lowered his voice slightly.

"And we invoke the Stones of no-color, whose power is found not in the flames, whose strength comes in their oppositeness—"

The rim-runners picked up the chorus, their voices blending with Gryff's to begin their chant with two plain words:

> "Drawstone and Shunstone
> That stand at the ends of the Inlands,
> And keep Cincture for Rynx alone.
> Drawstone and Shunstone,
> As long as ice-arch curves and Overstone stands,
> Keep all to itself and each to its own."

No flame-flung color shifted above the burning wood on the last chant; as the words died, the fire cringed and burned lower.

"Calennian, you begin with the finding of the Sandstone and the spelling of the iron tents."

The bronzed-faced rim-runner drew his crossed ankles tighter to his body and began speaking slowly.

"It was in the days when Rynth and Rynth alone extended from one side of the ice-arch to the other and Overstone shone only on man, lorryk, and fowlen. The Rynx ruled the fowlen and the fowlen roamed Rynth and Cincture equally, and the ways of the Rynth were as harsh as they are now, save that all was Rynth.

"Then Ivrium came to a meander to catch fleshfin for his tribe, bold Ivrium, who alone could skein the meanders for food and remain fingered. His quick hands found a stone among the white commonstones—a rare colored thing that shone like the sun when it falls to earth each dusk and climbs the sky each dawn, all bright copper and red-gold.

"Now Ivrium placed the stone within his sack with the few fleshfins he had netted and returned to camp. But Ivrium's tribe were many, the fish few. As he laid the sack at the feet of the forefather, in the way of his tribe, he was humble at the lack of his skill, rather than boastful of the bounty of it, which was still more than any of his tribe could bring.

"And Ivrium said, 'I would wish that herein were enough fish to feed the entire tribe, but I am a poor skeiner only and this is all that I have.'

"And, lo, the fish flowed like water from the sack of Ivrium and fell to the forefather's feet until they piled above the height of his head standing, and the whole tribe came and ate of the fish; and when the last and smallest swaddling who could walk had been fed, Ivrium's sack was empty, save for the small, orange Stone that shone like the sun at dawn or dusk.

"And Ivrium took the Stone and wrought great wonders with it and became forefather after and turned the Rynth within a wide circle all around into rich, shifting red-brown earth that gave comfort to all of his tribe. Upon the earth he erected his iron tents against the winds of the Rynth, which still would blow across his rich earth, no matter what he did. And none of the other tribes crossed into Ivrium's sphere. Ivrium built a high, peaked place for the Stone, where he lived with his offspring and ruled the people, and it was the highest and hardest of his iron tents, and still stands to this day, as does Ivrium of the Sandstone."

There was silence after Calennian had finished speaking, except for a few affirming grunts among the rim-runners, who had heard the tale before but now approved that it was retold with all the proper details.

Irissa's and Kendric's eyes met across the campfire, the first long look they had exchanged all that day. They watched each other in deep interest, though their ears seemed tuned only to the words around them. For now, all the alien places and names they had each heard in their separation were drawing together. The Stonelore might have been fable or remembrance or the fever dream of an old people guessed faintly from its infancy, but the words were real and the Stonekeeps still stood.

"Gonfallon," Gryff ordered.

A swart, stocky rim-runner spoke on command in a dusky baritone, as rich as bonewood when rung at its widest part.

"I speak of Lambard of the far sphere, whose Stonekeep borders on the very Cincture itself, may the Overstone protect him and his tribe.

"Lambard was a tender of the lorryk herds, for in those days the lorryk were meek to the uses of man. And one day a pair of fair twin lorryk young wandered to the meander and fell prey to the fleshfins. Lambard found one already bled dead, but the other he took up in his arms. Stepping artfully on the shallow dry stones that crossed the meander, he brought it safe to the dry land of the Rynth.

"But barely had Lambard touched lorryk hoof to dry land when his eye spied a bright spark of green at the running water's very edge. He plucked it up and put it in his food wallet and forgot about it, except from time to time to take it out and admire it. But the Rynth always grew green around the hooves of Lambard's herd from that day forth, and in time he spread the green into a great circle round and gathered the people to him. When the forefather was no more, Lambard was forefather and had many heirlings. And the people lived on the fair summer terraces that Lambard erected upon the green stone, with woven reed pavilions that rippled in the wind. And the lorryk grew wild and fled to the far ends of Lambard's Stonekeep and even to the other Stonekeeps and would accept the hand and staff of man no longer. But it did not matter, for, since the finding of the Stone, they were no longer needed. And the people gathered around Lambard and knew prosperity and forgot the ways of the Rynth."

Gryff barked out another name. Another rim-runner began a similar recital, and another, some mentioning Stonekeepers whose names were known to Kendric and Irissa, others who were foreign.

There was Sofistron, who had ventured to a meander in dead, dangerous night to slake a fever thirst and thought himself dreaming when he found a pale, luminous, blue Stone among the paler commonstones. From then on, he commanded the senses of living things around him and built a salt-white stone castle for his Keep.

And Lacustrine, whose Stone came to him as a drop of living water sprayed upon him from a meander, but of a shape that was hard as adamant. From then on, the meander waters flowed clean and fleshfinless around Lacustrine's very feet. In time, he erected a dazzling city of floating bridges upon the plentitude of the waters and installed himself and the Stone in the loftiest one.

There was Elodien, whose Stone winked ruby at him from the meander verge, whose Stonekeep always shone vermilion like the setting sun, and whose temper was as hot.

And Melinth the hawksman, whose Skystone blew great translucent blue bubbles of a Stonekeep around him and his people at his command. The ice-arch above Melinth's lands always played backdrop to huge, fluttering armies of birds, and the other Stonekeepers would pay dear to import them to their own Keeps, as they paid dear for Lambard's efforts at establishing sprawling green gardens near the Keeps, no matter if it were Ivrium's sandy copper terrain or the waters surrounding Lacustrine's Keep, from which sprang a lacy tracery of greens in a living, airborne trellis.

There was Jacine, whose gilt domes so like the sun sprang from his finding of a glowing golden Stone in yet another meander. And mysterious Reygand of the black-draped towers, whose jetblack Stone ruled the night that never was in the moon-drenced Inlands.

Finally the recital paused.

"I will tell of mad Chaundre," Gryff announced, "since none of his people have fled to the Rynth to journey among us.

"Chaundre, the youngest of the Stone-finders at the time of the finding, who was also the most foolish. Chaundre was but a swaddling who crawled unwatched to a meander to plash in its cold waters. In so doing, he lost the tips of two fingers but gained the possession of a plain, dun-colored Stone with but one property, that of pulling other things to itself. With the

Drawstone, despite his youth and foolishness, Chaundre came to be forefather also in his time and to draw his tribe to a Stonekeep remarkable for its plain madness of invention. And there he sits, still in command of the Drawstone, of his Stonekeep and his people, but not, in truth, of his own sense."

Another pause fell over the lashing flames as the rim-runners solemnly and sadly contemplated the madness of Chaundre.

"You speak only of the men who found the Stones." Irissa spoke abruptly, as the thought occurred to her. "Was there no woman who happened across a talisman?"

The rim-runners were silent, whether from outrage that a stranger and a female had broken their Stonelore ritual or from lack of answer was not certain.

"Her name was Hariantha." For the first time, a voice had come from the Unkept women's side of the fire. The speaker was Amozel.

"Her name was Hariantha. She was First Daughter to Banil, who was firekeeper for his tribe, in the days when the tribes had not enough make-magic to generate their separate flames. She had gone to the meander to beat linen upon the rocks in the shallow waters, risking fleshfins, as women did in those days, but the work must be done; it was not only swaddlings like Chaundre who lost fingers in those days," Amozel added accusingly.

The rim-runners stirred uneasily across the fire at this unprecedented turn the Stonelore had taken, with an alien woman questioning and Amozel breaking long silence to answer. There was not the formal turn of phrase to Amozel's tale of Hariantha and the Stone she found caught in the wet folds of linen by the meander's edge; the tale was not one repeated often. Perhaps it was even a bit disconcerting that Amozel knew it. Certainly, many throats cleared on the rim-runners' side, and eyes fell.

"It was a Stone of plain hue, but it was soon clear that in Hariantha's hands there was little plain about it. Meander waters would turn from it. The bonetrees grew away from it, as in a strong wind. It was useful for shaping the Rynth around, and Hariantha used the Shunstone to divert water where it was needed and to drive the chill wind away at night. The people of her tribe were pleased; some even said that she should succeed her father.

"But her brother Fanis Firstborn saw Hariantha use the Stone and win the people's favor. No longer did she sit by the meander and pound cloth upon rock. No longer was it important that Fanis Firstborn's arrows flew farther than other men's; there were no wonders that he could wreak by might of arm that Hariantha could not overrule by the powers of the Shunstone, even to turning Fanis' arrows in their flight.

"So Fanis watched Hariantha one day as she set the Shunstone down on the Rynth ground and turned a meander to a more favorable course. He whose arrows would be turned from her body while she carried the Shunstone came upon her with fair and courteous words; and when Hariantha had turned from him, he took the arrow he carried behind his back and plunged it into hers.

"That none would know the deed of Fanis, he used the power of the Shunstone to scatter Hariantha to the near and far curves of our world, and there she remains to this day, all around us. Her bones became the bonetrees; her brother-blind eyes, the morning and evening stars that appear only for a few moments before the Overstone shine outgleams them; her pale hair is the cloud that veils the sun, for she is ashamed that any look down and see the deed done by Fanis Sisterslayer."

There was another long pause.

"It is true some tale of this sort has been whispered among women from time to time," Gryff admitted. "Even in the bevies. But the Stonelore says naught of this, only that Fanis holds forth alone in a place where all things rush away from him, that his is the Shunstone, and that its possession is, of all the Stones, the most dire. His bevy and heirlings have shrunk to nothing with time, or if they escape, none of them come Rynthward. He has little to do with anything of the Inlands, save that he makes it the Inlands of Ten by his presence. And he enlivens the Stonelore with such legends as you spin, Amozel."

Gryff stood, stretching his short legs. "It is done. We do not bargain tonight, in deference to the Stonelore."

The rim-runners began drifting away to their caves, and the Unkept women started settling onto their meager bedrolls at the base of the rocks. Amozel remained seated, staring into the flames. The flickering pattern etched the hood's shadow onto her features so she looked more mask than human. Irissa sat on, too, at the edge of the fire, her knees tucked up, her arms locked around them, her chin sunk on her knees, and her dark hair fallen across the sides of her face.

A large hand suddenly shaped itself firmly on her skull. Kendric crouched beside her, dropping his hand away when he had her attention.

"An intriguing ritual," he commented.

"A gruesome tale," Irissa agreed, staring up at the ice-arch and shuddering a little. The fire had burned itself down to embers, their red glow reminiscent of the Bloodstone flames.

"Do you think these Stonekeepers are as long-lived as the tales imply, that the first is still the same?"

"Magic lengthens lifelines, marshman. See your own palm."

Kendric made a fist. "I never had it read before; a reader now could say that my line was short—and therefore had been longer, or was long—and had been shorter. That is not prediction, but fraud."

Irissa smiled without looking at him. "That is not knowledge speaking, but skepticism. I think—there is so much talk of heirlings—I think each Stonekeeper, no matter how long-lived, is eventually succeeded by a son who takes his name. Save for one Stonekeeper who was not long-lived."

Kendric snorted. "Tales. Tales belong on bearing-beasts. I know one thing. Torlocs did not tread through the wastes of this world for want of sense. There is something here that drew them—"

"The madman's Drawstone, perhaps?"

"This is no time for merriment."

"Oh, I know that. Believe me, I know that."

Kendric paused before speaking further. "Nor is it a time for petty disagreements. I propose we venture forth tomorrow, into the Rynth and onto whatever path may draw us out of the place."

Irissa didn't answer directly or look at him. "I have been offered the opportunity of traveling with the Unkept."

Kendric rose to his knees and glared at the distant Amozel. "I see. And I could join the rim-runners, I suppose. They assume that I have as good as done so already. You do not seriously consider this?"

Irissa ached to give an answer that would shake his incredulity. She finally shook her head.

"In this world, the only fates for a woman would appear to be to become one of many to one man, or one to many men—or to play stars and cloud and bonetree. I may have lost much magical power, but there are certain natural powers I will exercise—and one of them is the privilege of keeping myself to myself."

"I also am not one for many, or one of many for one," Kendric said. "I may bear magic unbidden, but I, too, have privileges. And one of those is that I will not exercise my unnatural powers. To remain among the rim-runners would be to have them constantly nipping at my heels for some new trick or another," he grumbled. "It appears the only sensible course is for us to venture forth. If Torloc seeresses before this have come and gone through this place, perhaps we can leave also."

Irissa only nodded, the embers casting a rainbow of reflection on the Iridesium circlet and the dark of the hair it constrained. Kendric's hand paused heavily over the tresses draping her shoulder, as if he would have petted them, had she been as docile as a bearing-beast.

"If you wish to sleep in the cave this night, I can remain here. I am used to sleeping on rocky ground," he offered gallantly.

"I had the grasses last night," Irissa said, turning charcoal-dark eyes to him. He barely discerned the faint rim of silver circling them. "Besides, if I am to be merely ordinary, I might as well become accustomed to ordinary discomfort."

Kendric stretched to his feet, towering so high above the seated Irissa that his face was out of fire reflection. "It is not chivalrous," he objected to no one in particular.

Irissa answered with a smile. "No. But perhaps it is fair."

Kendric left, the last to rustle off into the darkness of the caves.

Across the bright red glow of the fire's last embers, Irissa and Amozel watched each other cautiously.

Chapter Fourteen

◆◆◆

At times even the most private decisions become public policy through some mysterious, unspoken process. The next morning, the entire camp seemed to take it for granted that Irissa and Kendric were equipping themselves for a journey apart from the rim-runners. Gryff, having been convinced finally by Kendric's assurances, Irissa's demeanor, and Amozel's testimony that his prized "ice-eyed one" was of no magical value, seemed relieved to see her gone and Kendric with her. He offered as a parting gift dried food in pouches to hang from the many belts draping Kendric. The Unkept women gave Irissa a belt of her own, a length of rawhide that looked suspiciously like lorryk, studded with metal. Irissa dared not decline Amozel's forbidding generosity, although Kendric glowered heavily at the Unkept's dainty leader, as if certain a simple belt were more constraint than was evident.

"You will travel some way with us," Amozel said then.

"Our path is different," he objected.

Amozel smiled, her thin lips curving like a scimitar. "How do you know until you have walked it? But the Rynth is dangerous for a stranger, even a giant, and you will do better at first in the safety of our company," she declared.

Kendric wondered, but his questioning glance to Irissa was returned by a brisk nod.

They left the rocks that had been Kendric's only home in this place without ceremony, striking out into the shadowless wasteland under the tireless moon's ever-open eye.

Only a few wheeling birds were also alive and moving through the Rynth. Kendric watched them scribe their seemingly aimless yet lofty circles against the ice-arch somewhat enviously. Apparently there were no ready mounts in this place,

124

save for the bearing-beasts reserved for the Stonekeepers' use and the skittish and sharp-boned lorryk. Kendric winced as he recalled the results of his last bone-rattling ride on them.

"You miss your rim-mates already?" Irissa had dropped to the party's rear to keep him momentary company.

"No, my bearing-beast of Rule. Now, there was a creature admirably constructed to carry a man, even one draped in Iridesium chain mail and full battle gear. They were meant for carrying a rider—"

"Meant to—or made to?" Irissa asked. "Even the lorryk were tame until the Stones were found. I wonder if all tame beasts are only a delusion of men."

"Well, if I have such a delusion, I'll ride it, thank you," Kendric said. "And what have you learned from that untamed delusion up yonder?" His dark head gestured in Amozel's direction.

Irissa grinned. "Only that we are being led in the direction of Ivrium's iron tents, where we should receive a friendlier welcome than from most of the Stonekeeps."

"That I'll believe when I see it," Kendric interrupted.

"And Ivrium's sphere contains most of the Inlands' bearing-beasts, since he breeds and trains them for trade with his fellow Stonekeepers."

Kendric's face and steps lightened simultaneously. "Every journey on foot should have a bearing-beast at the end of it."

"Next you will be wishing for your sword," Irissa noted, "and if you are not careful, you may actually have it in the palm of your hand—there!"

Kendric looked worriedly at his right hand. No, it still swung at his side, gently curled as if ready for the holding of something, but empty. He would have rebuked Irissa for making light of what was heavy enough for him, but she had slipped forward to rejoin Amozel at the party's head.

She was becoming remarkably friendly with the women Kendric would always think of as "Unkempt" more than "Unkept." He frowned. It was natural, of course, that kind call to kind. He had been welcomed into the rim-runner ranks, weaponless as he was. Now Irissa was weaponless in a sense, and all the more fit for the magic-hating Unkept women. And he supposedly held the seeds of her power and would let them desiccate and blow away before he'd use them. He and Irissa were of two different kinds even more than they had been in Rule, he realized; and further, each had been driven by circumstance against his and her very natures—she, unmagicked, to watch another scorn to use what she would prize and he, unwillingly magicked, to bear the burden of a power unsought, and therefore as heavy in its use as in its abandonment. Kendric would have continued musing in this melancholy vein, except that the party had stopped.

He glanced up to see a black, cruising dot in the sky abruptly pause and drop earthward. Kendric ran to the party's head to find Demimondana lowering her bow.

She had threaded another arrow and was gesturing by sweeping the bow along an imaginary path across the sky. "Draw your arrow along the curved path of the ice-arch so, for steadiness. Then, when the bird crosses it and is clearly outlined against the white, let fly, but let the prey fly into your arrow, for both are fleet and must be given time to meet at the exact moment of crossing."

Irissa nodded intently and reached for the bow. Irissa? Kendric stepped forward.

"It takes more than an arrow and a bit of taut string to develop the archer's eye," he warned. "Or the archer's arm."

Her glance at him was as perfectly aimed as a defiant arrow shot to some enemy's feet. She drew back the bowstring and aimed the arrow along the upcast angle of her eyes. "I may not be an archer born," she admitted, "but perhaps I can put my eyes to a purely natural use. I would see how true I see by only mortal means—" On the last word, Irissa released the bowstring. The arrow thwanged on its course, low but long enough to be respectable. A cry from Demimondana indicated a hit; they glimpsed the prey only long enough to discern a winged shape before it plummeted to the Rynth.

The Unkept women ran forward to retrieve it in case it had fallen into a nearby meander and the tender custody of the fleshfins. Kendric and Irissa remained behind, staring into the flat and cloudy sky, equally astonished.

"A good shot," Kendric allowed at last.

Irissa let the empty bow drop while she massaged her right shoulder. "Not very long—"

"Long enough to meet the prey."

"Or very strong."

"Strong enough to bring down the prey."

"Or—very accurate."

"But you bagged a bird on your very first attempt with the bow. Most, most—amazing aim."

"In truth," Irissa said, keeping her eyes on the ground, "I was aiming higher." She looked up then and, with the arrow of her pointing finger, drew a curve across the ice-arch to a distant, dancing dot of black. "I know not what I pierced that flies so near the ground; likely it was a windblown barrenberry branch; Amozel says they grow nearby."

"Or perhaps a flying fleshfin. I wonder if they are edible?" Kendric said, laughing ungraciously. "At least you did not skewer the ground merely a few paces in front of you—usually the fate of novice archers."

"And my arm hurts," Irissa complained, kneeding it absently. "Now they will laugh at me as well as you—"

But the Unkept women were not laughing; they were circling in the distance and gesturing for Irissa and Kendric to join them. Demimondana signaled a hit, and one they were excited about.

"I did it? I—bagged—something? Perhaps I had seen it all along, with some inner eye that directed the arrow to the likelier prey—"

"Not likely," a chagrined Kendric said, clumping off after Irissa and her flying pennants of hair.

She arrived there much before he did, being eager to confirm her kill, and stood in the circle of Unkept women, her head bowed down like theirs, all eyes on something in the circle's center, which they were discussing with high, excited, birdlike chirpings. Kendric came up behind them. He was not excited, as he knew that one bird could feed only a few stomachs on a march, particularly a young or wounded bird caught flying near the ground.

"What is it, Amozel?" the slight, bronze-skinned one trilled. "It has an alien sheen to its feathers—and there, it is half-molted, isn't it?"

"Half-eaten, it looks like," another said disdainfully.

They continued debating the merits of Irissa's prey, but the successful archer did not join in the verbal dissection. As soon as she heard Kendric's heavy step, she drew back from the circle to make room for him and turned stricken, quite ordinary gray eyes upon him.

"Kendric. It's a falgon. A dwarf falgon from Rule. I've killed it."

He didn't believe her and brushed by to take his place within the circle. There, lifeless and arrow-pinned to the turf, lay a good-sized bird; or rather, it was half a bird. Its wings, chest, and crested head were magnificently feathered in indigo, violet, and green that glittered softly in the always veiled Inlands sun. Its muscular hind legs looked plucked to the Unkept women; to Kendric, who had seen and even ridden an empress falgon, they looked patterned in the smallest of golden scales, all marching neatly across and down to the end of a long, lizardlike tail, now frozen into a gentle arc.

"You have seen its kind before?" Amozel herself was asking now and required an answer.

"Yes," Kendric said slowly. "And never thought to see it again . . ."

"Well?"

"Well what?"

"Well, is its flesh edible?"

Kendric stared at Amozel, at the bright eyes burning so urgently. "Edible? I—I don't know, we never . . ."

"What good is it to know the kind of a thing if you do not know its uses?" Amozel asked impatiently. "No more use than to kill a thing without knowing its kind. Demimondana, your bowstring is empty. Sunfall comes."

The lithesome Unkept woman stepped over to take the weapon from Irissa's numb fingers. In minutes, the women had fanned out at Amozel's directions, the archers among them sending a flock of small, feathered spears flying at the aloof ice-arch and the tiny dark patterns that flashed across it. The rest fanned out over the inhospitable Rynthlands to retrieve the kill.

Kendric watched them go. "It strikes me that Amozel is unduly harsh for one who encouraged this experiment," he noted.

Irissa had knelt by the abandoned carcass and touched a

fingertip to its brightly feathered crest. "If I still had my powers at the full bloom they had when I first came to this world, perhaps I could—"

"Reanimate it? Do you deal in magic or blasphemy? It is dead and by your hand, dead quite naturally, however misdirected."

"I wanted only to *hit* something, not to slay it. And a dwarf falgon, a dwarf falgon from Rule, like us an exile in an alien place, alone—"

"Are you sure alone applies here?" Kendric had remained standing; Irissa had to squint into the limpid glow of the Overstone haloing his head to see his expression. It was, as was becoming usual, suspicious.

"What do you mean?"

"Only that I have seen nothing that even hints of the existence of the Rule we knew in this world. Nothing, except you. And me. And that."

"You speak of it as if it were a hateful thing. I would think you'd be glad finally to see something familiar, something from your long-lost Rule—"

"Perhaps not so long and not so lost. Where one is, two may be. May be—"

"A pity it is dead and we cannot follow it—perhaps right to a gate and out of this world, back to Rule, as you so desire—"

"Irissa. You killed it, and now you know what it is to have a thing beyond wishing back in any form. And I do not say I desire to return to Rule. Only think—if this thing of Rule is here, within this other place, may not *other* things of Rule be here as well? Are we the only ones to try a gate? Remember, the Rule we knew was caught in some cataclysm. Its very mountains were crumbling, the Abyssal Sea had risen to drench even the marshlands . . ."

"It seemed a Rule worth leaving," she said tonelessly.

"We may not have been the only ones so to conclude."

"You mean—you think other creatures of Rule live here, came here through a gate, if not with us, then before us—or after us?"

Kendric nodded slowly. "Perhaps long before us, or a goodly time after us. And perhaps not only creatures but . . . persons."

"You mean magicians!"

He shrugged.

"But they were all dead, mere ghosts of themselves when I tried to invoke their aid during the last, dreadful moments in Rule."

He shrugged again and changed the subject. "If you like, I will bury the falgon."

"No!" Irissa said. "*I* will bury the falgon."

Chapter Fifteen

———◆◆———

Kendric and Irissa stood with the Unkept women; the last meander they'd crossed was at their backs, and their first step was yet to be taken upon the red, shifting earth that was Ivrium's.

Like all Stonekeeps, Ivrium's dyed the land around its own peculiar color, not only in the shade of soil and what grew out of it but in its unique character as well. Even the air seemed vaguely copper, as if the clouds filtered the last rays of sunfall through an orangish veil. The moon had exchanged its pale silver coinage for gold in the feverish, dusky air that hung over lands as rolling as Sofistron's—but empty.

Also, as was true of all Stonekeeps, Ivrium's started abruptly. One foot could stand on solid if unpromising Rynth ground; the other could sink ankle-deep in the shiftless soil the wind sculptured into solid-seeming rills all the way to the horizon.

"It is like the gate," Irissa said.

"How so?" Kendric asked.

"There is no subtlety to the spheres the Stonekeeps cast. One must either pass into it or out of it, with very little time for dawdling in between."

"I thought I seemed caught in the gate an eternity," Kendric said fervently.

"That is because you are so long of limb," Irissa teased, "and could not fit, but left great clumsy bits protruding into both worlds. No wonder the gate refused us." But she remembered her own curious experience in the gate, of both time flowing faster and herself moving more slowly, of time and her at each other's throats, and Finorian in the middle serving as translator and then, somewhere behind her, some stubborn, ponderous tug that would not be discounted, no matter how many flying colors impaled themselves on the gate and ran crimson . . .

"This is not good land for walking," Kendric observed, still surveying the deserted landscape.

"They do not walk here." Demimondana came striding over on her long legs and eagerly brushed her hair from her face to see the desolation better. "It is—was—my home Keep. And there are your boots for Ivrium's Keep, stranger." Her bare arm pointed to a red cloud rising along the summit of the farthest hill. The dry red earth boiled and foamed, rising tower-high. The dust cloud churned toward them, and they finally heard the muted thunder of what charged their way with the swiftness of an earthcrack on firmer soil.

The sound was of hooves beating the soft earth to powder, hooves hidden by the very dust they raised.

"Bearing-beasts!" Kendric peered hard into the oncoming cloud, his hands over his eyes, his voice excitement-taut.

And on they came, their bobbing heads leading the train of red dust at their rear—beasts red as the earth, or russet, carmine, sorrel, or copper, all lunging forward.

Dust rose in front of the party from the Rynth until it curtained off their view of Ivrium's lands. Then it began settling to the ground, revealing the forms of the bearing-beasts—and the men who sat them—as if the earth itself had sculpted them. The riders were well wrapped against the dust in flowing robes that fell into shapes as fluid and rhythmic as the shifting ridges. The bearing-beasts snorted red dust out their heaving nostrils and soundlessly pawed the sand. Amozel stepped forward, no higher than the shoulder of the tallest of the beasts, and spoke.

"Ivrium, of all Stonekeepers, gives warmest welcome to the Unkept," she said.

One of the swathed riders answered. "True enough. We will take you and your women swiftly to his iron tents. But this other—even Ivrium has no fondness for rim-runners . . ." The man rose in his hidden stirrups to survey Kendric. "Does he stand upon some rock or—"

"He is as high as he appears," Amozel confirmed.

The riders' fabric-draped faces leaned together as their mounts brushed gleaming belly to belly. Finally their spokesman sat forward and addressed the party.

"We will bear you all to Ivrium—including the giant; he might be just what is needed to impress Ivrium."

"Impress Ivrium with what?" Kendric demanded, but the Unkept women were already hurling themselves up on the backs of the bearing-beasts behind the riders. Even Irissa had caught one copper hand and was swinging into pillion place on some broad, copper-colored hindquarters. Kendric sighed, stepped into the red earth before him, sighted the highest of the steeds— it was the spokesman's crimson-coated mount—and threw himself up behind the muffled rider just as the party wheeled, churning up a whirlwind of red dust as it cantered off toward the unmarked horizon.

The ride, though swift, was fully as uncomfortable as it would appear to be for unprotected passengers; Irissa and Kendric, when not lost in their own coughing fits, could hear the rack of the Unkept women's.

But at last the thudding of the hooves softened and slowed, the dust swirled and then settled, and they could begin making out the peaks of some dark, hulking roofs ahead of them. The riders dismounted into the red fog.

Kendric found a bit of gray and snagged it. "Irissa?"

She coughed instead of answering, but he recognized a familiar note in it.

"This is worse than the gate," he complained. "I can't see so much as the end of my arm."

"At least you rode a proper mount," Irissa said consolingly.

"Unhorned. I find such bearing-beasts alien. They can't even lower their heads and charge an enemy or skewer an ambusher. Oh, their gait is smooth enough, I suppose, for such soft soil, but they are not as swift as the lorryk, and I find I like the lorryk's looks better."

"Bounder should be overjoyed that he meets your approval. I'll tell him when next we meet—" Irissa's promise ended without a period, for Kendric had taken her arm urgently.

He nudged her toward the dimly seen shapes huddling immobile through the still-churning dust motes around them. "Iron tents, indeed. This place must stand as high as Sofistron's loftiest tower. I like not the look of it—no windows, nothing but this mass of rusted metal. It smacks of a prison."

"Where are the others?" a suddenly alarmed Irissa asked.

"Gone. Leaving us to our own devices—mountless, guideless, with your marksmanship and my magic for a defense . . ." Kendric slapped at his chest and raised ruddy puffs from his accoutrements. "I wish a little dust would banish Ivrium and his entire tent from my sight."

"I think it's too late." Irissa put her hand on his sleeve and tugged for his attention. "I think Ivrium has discovered you."

Whether it was Ivrium himself who stood at the tent's dark mouth was difficult to say. He was a tall man, by the lights of this place; certainly he was Calennian's equal. He, too, was shrouded by the brick-colored robes the riders wore, which made man, dust, and mount at one with each other. But this man stood, not rode, his feet braced. The glint of jointed metal was visible on his feet as his rusty robes stirred around them. A breastplate of rust-colored metal held his robes to his chest, and gold-scrolled thigh and arm pieces fleshed in his form; otherwise, he was as elusive as the dust. His face was masked by a decoratively pierced metallic oval so expressionless and chill that it rivaled the tent's forbidding iron facade.

Kendric unhooked the ax from the baldric at his side. "It appears we have a greeter."

The figure strode forward, any metallic grindings on its person muted by the sand.

"I do not like his aspect," Irissa began.

"I would like his aspect better could I see it. And I would like yours were it some distance to the side. Look, I see the Unkept by the tent opening. You had better join them."

While Irissa lingered, uncertain, the figure turned its featureless metal face toward her. "Go," it ordered in not very encouraging tones. She glanced for confirmation to Kendric, and he nodded.

But Kendric was less concerned with Irissa's going than with the figure's steady coming toward him. When it had turned its head toward Irissa, Kendric had seen only the head shroud and an even chiller sight than the metal mask on its face; a similar mask guarded the head's rear with the same configuration of depthless black holes suggesting eyes, nose, and mouth. Either it was a fanciful way to discomfit a rear-attacking enemy, or the creature had eyes and a few other sensory organs in the back of its head.

Kendric felt the hairs on his neck stiffen. He braced his feet and flexed his knees in readiness.

"I am Ivrium's heirling," the figure announced pridefully, "and I challenge you, giant of the Rynth, to combat here before all. Who wins shall gain honor; who loses shall stain his robes with blood and dust and dishonor. Raise your weapon or have it struck from your nerveless fingers!"

The figure drew from its garments a triangular-bladed sword of no great length that curved into a sickle halfway down the blade. The challenger came grinning at Kendric then, a taut steel smile on the face of the red dust.

Kendric stepped back more easily than the other seemed to have expected and struck upward at the passing steel. The unhoned edge of the ax hit it obliquely, driving the sword wielder's arms sideways.

It was the first honest ring of steel on steel that Kendric had heard in this world and it gave him heart, despite the strangeness of the place and his attacker and despite the fact that his only armor was woven thread and the slant of a leather baldric across his chest. He lunged inward in the wake of his ax blade and sliced through the dust his sudden motion had raised. A piece of robe fluttered leaflike to the ground.

But his opponent was swinging his weapon back the other way, like a mighty, timed pendulum. Kendric sprang back, to see the lethal curve at the sword's end swerve by his midsection at the very moment he retracted it from the oncoming edge with a desperate indrawing of breath and muscle. The blade's hook made it hard to judge how close or far the weapon came, a handicap far greater than lack of mail within the agitated arena of dust the two men were creating. He wondered then at his unnamed enemy's formal challenge, which implied witnesses, and he wondered what witnesses there were beside the women and the looming structure behind them. Most of all, he wondered how witnesses could see any contention at arms amid the ceaselessly swirling dust.

Then the blade that curled into itself was slicing by him again, and Kendric had no time for wondering about anything other than the natures of the man and the blade against him— how they were balanced, how hard-honed they were, whether there were any weak or half-weak portions forged into the length of either . . . He did not think that there was any magic in the man, if man he truly were, and that was one blessing, for he would rather risk himself upon his might than upon his magic. Besides, he had sworn to Irissa that he would not use any such unwanted artificial advantages in this world, and he did not like to break his word. The dust rose in a choking fog, and Kendric leaped into the middle of it, a man who fought a phantom, and not completely sure that it was not himself.

"It is murderous!" Irissa glared down at Amozel's unperturbed little face. "What ritual is this with which to greet a guest?"

Amozel smiled the lean little smile that made her look lupinely mischievous. "The way of Ivrium's heirlings. They are high-spirited and wish to prove themselves on ever more impressive foes. Yon giant shall give them great opportunity to test their mettle, and Ivrium likes to keep his heirlings distracted from his bevy. Unlike the other magicians, he does not overestimate his own, unmagicked charms. He is a jealous Stonekeeper, Ivrium, but also accepting of the Unkept—after all, Demimondana was his most beloved daughter."

"You *knew* Kendric should be set upon thusly, and still led us here?"

Amozel's black-brown eyes slid calmly to hers, saying "yes" more plainly than any articulated monosyllable could. Irissa longed to delve the self-contained, yet ferocious depths she sensed welling in Amozel's eyes and very being. If only she still had deep seeing or had progressed to Far Focus, so she could read beyond what most people left written on their faces. Amozel's was blanker than most. She was a puzzle, this Stonekeeper's daughter who led other women, but only through the same, unwinding corkscrews of the Rynth. She was a trader in flesh, but kept her own to herself, as she did her truest thoughts. She was made of blood and body, but she never quailed at the sacrifice of either—especially if they belonged to another. And she loathed magic as something tainted and tainting, when she herself was more contradictory to her nature than anything else Irissa had yet encountered in the Inlands of Ten.

But now the loss of magic that made it possible for Irissa to travel in company with the Unkept women made it impossible for her to read more than ordinary human emotion—or lack of it—in Amozel's eyes. And the more impassive Amozel was, the more Irissa felt her own emotions slip their leads.

"You cannot permit this to continue! Kendric is ill-armed against a strange opponent who challenges him for no reason. You brought us here—"

"You chose to come with us. Besides," Amozel added complacently, "he bears magic. Those who bear magic do not need mortal aid. They can take care of themselves."

"*If* they choose to! But Kendric is foolish—he has made a foolish vow to refrain from using it. He will not, though he die for it."

One of Amozel's pale eyebrows arched. "Interesting. I have known no one able to practice magic who voluntarily withheld it. You, for instance. You would use what powers you could, were any available?"

"Gladly," Irissa said in exasperation as the sound of metal on metal rang more urgently from the carmine fog rising before them. "And the first magic I would do would be to show you that no power is as misdirected as that of human sympathy withheld."

"The Rynth does not teach sympathy," Amozel said implacably. "Nor do the Stonekeepers. But fear not; your friend is strong and has magic for a shield. I think it is Ivrium's heirling who must falter."

Her golden head nodded to the column of dust spinning before them and the sight of a two-faced man backing out of it, his sword arm trailing a lowered weapon, his arm plates hanging by their severed cords and bridged by a deeper red soaking through his robes.

Kendric lurched out of the dust after him, his clothing dust-powdered, his ax still defensively held, his face tired and triumphant but smeared with slashes of wet crimson. He stood as he saw Irissa's expression reflect his appearance and rubbed his fingers at his forehead. They came away sticky, and he frowned, then shook his head.

"Only sweat and dust," he said to reassure her.

"Stranger," a voice hailed from the iron tent's entrance. "You have vanquished Ivrium's heirling. I am heirling also and I challenge you with the might of my many-bladed ax."

Kendric paused, then turned back to the voice. This man might have been shorter, but his robes were as securely tied down by plates of gilded copper as the other's. His face was masked, but in a different pattern from that of the first. It was no less fearsome. And the ax he hefted in one copper-mailed fist spoke with as many separate tongues of steel as a company of swordsmen, so cunningly was it worked into dangerous metal spurs. It seemed a thing more of lace than of armorer's art, but Kendric knew from his father's forge in Rule that the more inventively pointed the metal, the crueler and sharper it would bite. By contrast, his homely rim-runner's ax was blunt.

He started for the place where the dust still rose. Irissa called his name, but he didn't pause. A name was not strong enough natural magic when a battle was already in motion. Her mind flew to magic means of stopping him—a wall of flame, a chain materializing out of air and looping around him . . . A waste of time; she was armed with nothing more than her wits, and those were dull from long reliance on magic. She could invent a dozen ways to *make* something that would in turn make Kendric stop—make-magic, the rim-runners called it. But magic was no longer her servant. At the moment, she only wanted to make him pause—such a small task! Another man might do it with the force of his body, but she was not strong enough to stop him; she doubted anyone present was, save Kendric himself.

"Wrathman!" she called, using the once-despised title of Rule, using the pull of that which was lost like a spell lightly thrown and then tightening to the strength of a steel wire.

He stopped slowly. She did not think that he would ever turn back to her, but he did, finally. "To call me Wrathman now is akin to calling yourself a Torloc seeress."

She ignored the truth of his taunt. "The Wrathmen of the Far Keep had weapons worth fighting with, the great longswords that only a Wrathman true-chosen was worthy to carry. Five feet long from where the steel met hilt to the honed triangle that ended it. One used to such a weapon cannot long be content with an ax."

"One who used to have such a weapon and relinquished it must make do with what's at hand." He began to turn again.

"What could be at hand—" Irissa stepped after him, her own hand extended, curling slightly around air. "—could be whatever you wished. I brought you your sword once in Rule when we met. I asked for it back when I was leaving. We both held it for a moment—I the blade, you the hilt. We can make that bridge again. I can help you make that sword live again."

"No! It changed in my very hand, grew gemstones along the scabbard. Why do you think I left it behind? What other Wrathman in the history of Rule was ever separated from his sword? Your magic wrought some transformation as you stood within the gate. It was no longer mine, and I abandoned it."

"Or *your* magic begemmed the scabbard as you touched sword to me and thus to the force of the gate. It was your sword, and even its hilt glow reflected your unknowing, incipient magic. I never exerted magic upon it, not even during those last moments of parting in Rule. My only magic was what I felt—"

"I have promised never to use what I gained unknowing."

"You made that promise in my presence, but it was not given to me or any other, but to yourself."

"Then that is the least breakable of promises, and even a Torloc should know that."

"This Torloc knows only that he who has magic and refuses to use it shall not long survive against the grain of himself."

"Then if I die at the hand of another, does it matter?"

"Yes," Irissa said.

"I will not use magic," he answered, setting his jaw.

"I cannot make you."

"Then release me to do what I must do."

"I do not hold you, I cannot hold you. I have no magic."

"Release me," he repeated stubbornly as she stared uncomprehendingly into his eyes.

Irissa realized then that she had been doing what no empowered Torloc seeress would have ever done voluntarily—

staring directly and simply into the eyes of another with no purpose of magic in it. She had been looking straight at the surface of Kendric's eyes, directing all the persuasion in her toward the purely ordinary human act of seeing. And there was a kind of power in that. They held him, her unsilvered eyes that could not so much as turn a single hair on Amozel's head from gold to black; yet they could rivet seven feet of battle-bound Wrathman to the ground.

It was horrifying, such a breach of privacy. Her entire life as a seeress, brief as it was, had been dedicated to looking deeply and magically—or indirectly. Could this be why the Torloc seeresses were enjoined from any communion with the eye of another, because there were powers more seductive than magic?

Kendric waited. She wondered if he read all her questions in her eyes. Certainly he read something, else she would not have had the power to hold him. Or was it nothing that welled from her, but some compulsion of his own, like his promise, that welded him here, frozen, waiting upon something she must do? And do it she must. His will was bent another way, and she could not unbend it without risking breaking one or the other of them. It was not a risk an unempowered Torloc seeress was willing to take.

Irissa let one last question rise to her eyes and saw Kendric brace himself infinitesimally, as against something hurled. Then she looked sideways and down. A moment later, she heard the thud of his boots on sand and the faintly scraping metal advance of another of Ivrium's heirlings.

This time it was ax-to-ax work; both blades flashed upraised out of the spinning dust and descended back into the cloud on a ringing clash. And this time the contention lasted longer. The end, when it came, was dramatic. There was the strange, half-muffled sound of a blow, and an ax head came spinning out of the confusion, detached from its handle. All eyes watched the orbiting blade until it fell to earth. The settling dust motes finally revealed its shape—the unmistakable, lacy profile of the heirling's ax. The heirling himself staggered out of the dust zone, choking behind his metal mask. Kendric followed and started for Irissa, an I-told-you expression settling on his features like its own form of mask.

"You have defeated Ivrium's heirling. I am Ivrium's heirling and challenge you to duel," came the words behind Kendric, from the next robed and armored figure to appear at the tent's gaping entrance.

Kendric sighed heavily without turning. His glance went to Amozel. "How *many* heirlings does Ivrium have?"

She might have smiled slightly; with Amozel it was impossible to tell. "Ivrium keeps the largest bevy in the Inlands."

"And the more bevy, the more heirlings," Kendric noted with heavy resignation. "Are they always so feisty a lot?"

"As long as they hope to win individual glory from it and elevate themselves in Ivrium's eyes. They all hope to be named One Son of their generation."

Kendric sighed and ran a dust-streaked hand over his mouth. He looked to be made of red clay, more a caricature than a man, with all his features and his clothes equally dusted red, so that only the creases showed a bit of true color through.

"I suppose I could refuse." His statement was a question.

Amozel's small head shook slowly from side to side. "They would all join to attack you then and carve you into pieces so that they all could claim the glory of vanquishing you. You must either meet and conquer them one by one or convince them that there is less to be gained from challenging you than ignoring you."

"I've sent two of them scurrying off behind their metal masks already."

"The others think themselves more valiant than those," Amozel answered.

While Kendric considered, the newest challenger rebellowed his message. Into the silence that maintained around Kendric, Irissa spoke.

"The heirlings are right. You will tire beyond repulsing them eventually, and one will claim the glory of defeating you, perhaps even of killing you. So they will fight on, each with the hope of being the one to wield weapon at that inevitable time—"

"Yes, it's clear that you and Amozel have a solid grasp on the difficulties of the situation; what of a way out of it other than battering my way through an endless parade of these contentious fellows?"

"A resounding defeat," Amozel suggested. "Slay one, or at least lop off a limb."

"That is not my way," Kendric growled.

"Impress them magically," Irissa put in.

"Nor that." He thought some more, hefted his edge-dulled ax, and turned to meet the next heirling.

This man fell quickly, but if Kendric had hoped that quick work would impress the heirlings, he was wrong. One after another, they appeared in the tent mouth—battle-armed, battle-ready, undeterred. And Kendric, coughing in the alien dust, with specks of it creeping into his every pore and his eyes squeezed shut against its gritty incursions on his sight, kept doggedly banging away at the challengers, finally driving them off, but never decisively enough to discourage the next.

Irissa stood beside the impassive Amozel on the sidelines, dust mantling her shoulders and the tops of her hands. It seemed a curtain of red dust had settled on her eyelashes and made them heavy. Her fingers curled into fists and her lips tightened. Had she not so utterly trusted the Unkept women, they would not have led Kendric into this unending battle with an army of individual enemies. To hear Kendric tell it, had she not meddled with his fate in the first place by inviting herself to his bed, he would not have the incipient power he so resented and had forsworn. As it stood now, neither of them had power. Once the mere glance of Irissa's silvered gaze could make a sword blade glow light or grow heavy—too heavy to be lifted. That was how she had stopped a senseless conflict before. But now she could only watch, helpless where she was not used to being helpless—utterly helpless to stay the crash of steel on steel for a single moment.

Or perhaps not . . .

Irissa took a step toward the milling men and the ground where boots and metalled feet stamped out a battle rhythm on the earth. It was hard to tell from moment to moment which was Kendric and which the latest heirling to confront him. Both men were red-powdered figures wielding vermilion-edged blades. Irissa took another step forward. Her eyes had been her weapon and her shield. Now, without their aid, she must go herself to stop this thing that could result only in disaster.

"Stop!" she ordered, but her voice seemed a very small

thing in the circle of clangor the weapons forged around themselves, the very private circle of contention that she, a watcher, was violating with her body. She took another step nearer.

"Stop!" she repeated, more to signal her advance than in hopes of either man heeding her. They could not heed her without risking their lives.

She stepped nearer still, almost upon the very ground that was roiled by their strivings. There was something horrible about how large they were and how mindless and strong in their need for self-survival. A lightning bolt could have sizzled to the ground and failed to separate them. Irissa could conjure no lightning bolts now; she could use nothing that did not already exist here and now. Two things did—she and her will to use herself.

She moved between the two combatants, feeling the noise hang suspended and the dust pause in its whirling, seeing all as red and misty with silver metal ax faces pendant over her.

"Stop!" she cried between them, but they did not stop.

One ax blade swiped past her shoulder; the other engaged it at her wrist level and pushed until both blades broke away. The first blade came striking over her other shoulder and was parried. Kendric's face came clear in the confusion, as much a mask of fury as that of his opponent, eyes red-rimmed and shocked. He jerked her to the side, and she heard the axes ring heavily upon each other in a series of repetitive blows. The heirling was bowing backward out of the circle, leaving it to Kendric and Irissa.

"Are you mad?" he demanded. "These bevy-born men would have no conscience at striking down a woman."

Irissa ignored the statement; she knew it was too true to contest. "If you had a sword, your old longsword from Rule—"

"It is gone, even if I wished it back," he objected.

"You made a weapon once with your will—"

"I was sore tried, and besides, I didn't really believe I would do it."

"Yet you did. Where is it?"

"I buried it under some rocks in the Rynth. Give me good, dependable, fire-forged steel," he said, swinging the ax in his hand.

Irissa glanced at the battered blade. "If you had your sword, the length and like of which none of these heirlings have seen— if you could wield it quickly and devastatingly against one— perhaps the tide of their challenges would ebb."

"Perhaps. And on a perhaps, I am to meddle with a magic I never wanted."

"Perhaps. That is all I came to offer this time, merely perhaps," Irissa said, smiling amid the settling dust.

Kendric glanced through the red miasma to the tent door, where the next heirling stood ready to challenge.

"How do I make this simulacrum of a sword?"

"It will be no simulacrum, but as real as you remember it; and the more deeply you remember it, the more real it will be. You must see it in your hand, Kendric. Feel it, beyond the mortal metal of it to what it was—is—to you. You must call it to you, let your hand caress it, let the weight of it form there, in your palm. It will be more real to your mind, more sharp to your eyes, than anything else at this moment. You must *hear* it, the sound it made as its scabbard scraped upon your back, its heavyhearted cleaving through air, the crush of it on metal and bone. You must know its every nick, every brave and true blow it has dealt, every impact it has taken, every time you struck. You must know its good and ill, and see it there in your hand. The sword you have never stopped wishing for—it's there in your hand. See it!"

Irissa had unerringly taken him into the deepest remembering of a thing he had ever experienced, so that he knew it in every dimension, in attributes it would not seem to possess. The sword had sung as it struck, and he suddenly knew the one true note in the world that was made by that particular congregation of steel and iron and leather. The sword had a single sharp eye at its tip that saw straight to the place where his arm aimed it. Kendric faced that invisible eye and looked through it and up the great length of steel, inch by agonizing inch, until he had journeyed forever on the shining silver road of the sword and now climbed the ridge of its guard to the hilt, the rune-carved, leather-wrapped hilt. Here he paused. He wanted no runes of Rule in a place that was not Rule! His eye blinked the hilt clean and wrapped leather around it—good, plain, sweat-darkened leather with the scent that came so reassuring to his palm. It was complete then, from the hilt to the five long feet of steel trailing from it to the ground. And now that he had seen the sword with every sense, another sense— a frightening, expanding sense that suddenly engulfed both him and the sword—sang through them together in one wrenching moment.

"You have it!" Irissa's voice entered his consciousness on the same alien tone.

Kendric looked to his hand and the sword that had bloomed there on its long silver stalk. The same, in every respect, except for the hidden matter of the runes. What difference would that one conscious omission make? Kendric shook his head as if dislodging cobwebs. None. It was a sword, mere metal, of his own manufacture. His sword. He noticed the ax where it had fallen on the ground, precisely when, he didn't know. The ax seemed alien, tawdry, a child's toy. He raised the sword's familiar length and clasped his other hand around it. The weight felt the same, but it had been some time since he had hefted it. He would be awkward at first, feeling his way with every sense but that strange, added one that had thrilled through him for a moment. Did Irissa feel that when she made magic? Or only he?

The puzzled heirling advanced, seeing the new weapon, wondering at it, but still determined to challenge. Why not? He bore a long, lethal pike. Kendric had conjured his sword just in time. He nudged Irissa back, and she gave way surprisingly docilely, which was not like her; but he had no time to think of that. He must get reacquainted with his sword before he made the acquaintance of the ten-inch barb that ended the pike.

Amozel withdrew into her hood as Irissa neared. "Magic," she intoned dully. "I saw it dance at the edges of the dust. Make-magic."

"Not mine," Irissa said quickly.

"No. But too near." Amozel drew away to her women.

Irissa shrugged and turned to watch the contest. Kendric with his own weapon—and a magic one—might prove more of an uncertainty than these ambitious magician's sons wished to confront.

Blade and the pike's long metal shaft met. The heirling thrust savagely with the point, but Kendric leaped away and brought his blade swooping across the man's midsection. The robe tore away and the point scraped the breastplate in one long, ragged scratch.

The dust rose higher. Out of its obscuring veil rose the fanged tip of the fork-tongued pike and the last foot or so of Kendric's mind-forged blade as the blows were struck harder and higher. The sword suddenly scribed a circle so wide it shone out of the dust before it plunged back into it. There was a groan and the clatter of something hitting the ground. The heirling made the obeisance of a wounded man as he backed away from Kendric, a long rivulet of red gushing down his arm and branching into many streamlets between his fingers.

There was an "Ahhh" made by many indrawn breaths from the tent door. The dust settled slowly, draping the new-made blade with a fine powder and coloring Kendric's once-dark hair as red as Gryff's. He stood in the center of the sifting earth, the sword held in his right hand, surprised at the retreat of his foe and still dazed by the remaining sight of his sword.

Irissa alone walked up to him. "It appears Ivrium has run out of heirlings, swordsman. Do you regret your magic so bitterly now?"

Kendric looked to her, then back to the sword. He seemed about to answer when an unreadable expression crossed his dusty countenance. He shook the sword slightly in his hand— and once again. His face grew consternated, then dumbfounded.

"The cursed sword. I cannot loosen it. My hand—I cannot unhand it. It's stuck!"

Irissa clapped a hand to her mouth, then lowered it. "You were too successful at seeing the sword as an extension of yourself. You must see it also as its own thing. Otherwise, otherwise—" She clapped a hand over her mouth again and fell laughing to the red dust, raising a small cloud that wafted back to earth soon after. Irissa rocked back and forth, laughing until she should cry, had she coldstones or salt to shed. "Oh, Kendric, I should have known that you of all mortals would take my meaning too literally. It can be fixed. I will help you. As soon as, as soon as—" She was off into another paroxysm of laughter.

Kendric glared.

Chapter Sixteen

◆◆◆

A warm ewerful of water poured smoothly down Irissa's dusty tresses. A dozen helping hands pushed her deeper into the oiled and steaming bath water. For the second time since her arrival in the Inlands, Irissa was in the hands of a bevy.

This time, however, it was as a guest, not as a prize prisoner of a Stonekeeper. From beyond the flutter of the surrounding diaphanous curtains, Irissa could hear Kendric being subjected to the same insistent tending.

"Away!" he bellowed. "I can wash myself. And leave the sword!"

Irissa smiled and leaned back into the copper tub, so that her head tilted up at the dark night sky of Ivrium's tent interior. It towered high above her, black and forbidding as the iron it was made from, yet paradoxically molded into the swagging lines of fabric, so the ceiling curved to a point. Against it, a myriad of mobile floating lamps twinkled starlike, creating an ever-spinning pattern. It was odd that in a world with an anchored moon, tastes in interior lighting should be so dizzying.

She tore her gaze from the lulling ceiling lights as a massive splash in the adjacent compartment indicated that Kendric, alone at last, was either entering or exiting his bath water. Irissa was content to be tended by the veiled women who surrounded her, taking comfort in their anonymity, their unquestioning acceptance. Their Lord Warden had invited Kendric and Irissa into his tent—or rather, he had invited Kendric, and

Irissa had been included indirectly, more as an inconvenient, superfluous appendage than as an individual.

Irissa wiggled her toes in the warm, silken water until ripples lapped at her chin. The water wore a veil of red dust, which the oils swirled into lovely serpentine patterns. Irissa was happy to have the dust off her person and webbed to some other element. The bevy finally dredged her reluctant from the soothing waters and draped her in thick-woven towels to dry. They brought her clothes, still dust-ruddied, and drew them slowly through a deep bowl of white sand kept heated over embers. The gray cloth passed through the sand and hung unwrinkled, unbegrimed, even untorn from their hands when they presented them.

No, journeying to Ivrium's Stonekeep had not been a mistake, after all, Irissa reflected. She and Kendric were both benefiting from some decent tending, and Kendric had been forced to fall back upon the despised staff of his magic. He might have paid for resisting it with a few bruises, but a good night's rest, a—

"Out, I said! Away! And leave the clothes."

—a bit of bevy-pampering, and he would be as good as of old. Probably better. Irissa smoothed her clothes into place and looked around for her boots.

"Here," one mouth said from beneath its gray veil. The bevywoman brushed aside a curtain to show the boots standing side by side, still dusty.

Irissa started for them. The bevy had forgotten to clean her boots, but that was quibbling when they had done all else admirably. The woman dropped the curtain closed and stood before it, barring Irissa's way.

"My boots—"

"No. You wear no boots in Ivrium's tent, but go unshod, like a proper bevywoman." The woman waggled a nearly naked foot in demonstration. Irissa was struck again by the symbolic nature of their footwear—merely a few jeweled chains draped here and there, serving no useful purpose to speak of.

"I am not a bevywoman," Irissa said, starting again for the boots. Once more she was circled by the passive, resistant power of the bevy. The women ringed her and would neither let her advance nor retreat. Their spokeswoman shook her drapery-hidden head until the veil hem danced above her lips.

"You will leave the boots. All is carpet."

Irissa glanced to the ground. Ivrium's tents had been raised on bare red sand, but were lined from iron wall to iron wall with heavy woven rugs in shades of orange, black, and gold. "But—"

"We take you now to the feast, which you are fortunate to attend, being neither bevywoman nor Unkept woman, but the giant's Lady Ward."

"I am not anyone's Lady Ward!" Now the exasperated tones were rising from her side of the intervening curtains, Irissa realized. She sighed heavily, pushing her still-water-weighted hair behind her shoulders, and marched—barefoot—beyond the encompassing draperies to where the bevy shepherded her.

The center of Ivrium's tent was supported by an iron pole as wide about as many men. From it hung a canopy of richly embroidered cloths, spreading wide at the bottom to mock the shape of the outer tent. Under this enthroning edifice of fabric, installed in semirecumbent splendor upon a pile of carpets, lay Ivrium.

He was a man as ample in his way as one of his sprawling tents. But where his Stonekeep was iron, Ivrium seemed made of some opposite substance, for his flesh overflowed his robes, or at the least raced them to their limits and strained there for release.

Irissa was led to some mounded pillows and left to sink down upon them. Once installed, she was ignored, except for the occasional speculative twinkle directed her way from Ivrium. She did not twinkle back.

At last, when Irissa had concluded that there was no new novelty upon which to occupy her gaze and when she had studied the light-swirling ceiling until it dizzied her, Kendric came in.

His clothing was as restored as hers, and he had been allowed his boots. His right hand, however, was swordless.

"Well?" she asked as he settled beside her. "It *did* work?"

Kendric flexed his fingers and rubbed them across his palm, as if it itched. "The sword and I are now two different things. It was merely a matter of . . . I'm not sure how I did it, any more than I know how metal can shape itself in my hand upon my thinking of it—and then stick there as if welded, merely because I did not think it quite right."

"You don't know how you did it? But you must. Kendric, that is the key to magic, to know how the chamber turns each time so you can unlock the same effect at will."

"At will or at won't, it's all the same to me. As I told you before, I will not rely upon these three-times unreliable secondhand powers of yours."

"What is mine is yours," Irissa returned just as the bevy-women wafted in like a silent-footed wave crested with platters of foodstuffs. It was all alien, though some looked suspiciously like fleshfin floating in a blood-red sauce. Kendric heaped the empty platter he was offered with pieces of everything from each dish. Irissa was about to snare a few edible-looking items for herself, but the bevy skittered away before she could touch finger to so much as a spice-rolled fruit.

"Wait!" She caught the tardiest bevywoman by her skirt fabric. "*I* have not selected yet."

The gray veil blew in the invisible wind of the woman's breath. "You do not select; you take what is left from *his* selection." And she tore herself loose as if she were irredeemably breaking some law for lingering even this long.

Irissa flexed her fingers, which smarted from the fabric burn of the bevywoman's flight. She looked at Kendric. He was devouring his food with the relish of a warrior who was not particular about what he ate or how fast he ate it. Kendric might not have heard that her dinner depended on his bounty, but Irissa resolved not to bother him with such a trifling matter. Her stomach growled loud dissent.

Kendric looked about. "Does this Ivrium keep those lemurai hounds? It will be a long time before I toss those man-eaters so much as a morsel from my plate, if so. This is quite tasty, I think. Bonefish stewed in some greenish mess, but quite edible. Much better than rim-runner fare." He zestfully speared a piece of orange flesh with his knife and popped it in his mouth. Irissa looked away.

"You have a fine appetite, Kendric Swordmaker." Ivrium's plump fingers hovered over a plate piled with food to his very chin, then plunged—bare—into the feast. "That's what I look for in my most promising heirlings. Appetite. Appetite always separates the heirlings from the Keepmen. But you are a man of heroic size, like myself, and must eat heartily."

"*His* heroic size is all horizontal," Irissa whispered sourly to Kendric. He ignored her.

"And it takes heroism to manage an ice-eyed one, even with her eyes at but a fraction of their power. Believe me, I know." Ivrium chuckled richly while tossing some bright turquoise grapes into his mouth. "I must admit I had ambitions in my younger days to add such a one to my bevy. I'm not like those sniveling Stonekeepers who tremble and quake at the very report of an ice-eyed one passing through our spheres. They would wish to keep well out of our way, at any rate, for their purpose here has naught to do with us."

"What is that purpose?" Kendric asked, masticating stolidly.

Ivrium shrugged and wiped his fingers on the dappled gray, curled beard that covered his chest. "Overstone only knows. Not I. Oh, they are a lively lot, the ice-eyed ones. You have a particularly fine-footed specimen there, Kendric Swordmaker," he added, actually bestirring his great bulk enough to prop it on an elbow and leer genially over his dinner plate at Irissa's unshod foot. She indignantly tucked her feet under a swell of carpet and glowered back at Ivrium.

"I keep hearing something *growling*," Kendric noted in a puzzled undertone as he wiped up the colorful melange of sauces on his plate with a piece of soft yellow bread.

"Worry not, friend." Ivrium's heavy hand delicately admonished the air before him. "I do not envy you your prize. When the ice-eyed ones come, the meanders rise, the Stonekeeps shake to their very foundations, the Stonekeepers curse, lemurai milk curdles, the fowlen prowl the Rynth, and the shadow of the Rynx is felt on the land; the bevy do not bear heirlings and the Overstone is seen to glow green, as if sickened by the sight of such disruption upon the Inlands."

"I know the feeling," Kendric murmured sympathetically.

"Sofistron was most foolish to believe he could contain, much less direct, such a one."

"A foolish man may be dangerous," Kendric noted, finishing his meal with a trial nibble at a turquoise grape. "He was not properly grateful at the removal of his trophy and may plan to pursue us."

"Pursue you? Into the Rynth? Never. We Stonekeepers keep to our Stonekeeps and the sphere around that reflects our powers." Ivrium shifted ponderously on the dunes of pillows that buoyed him. "We are too comfortable to bestir ourselves into the teeth of uncertainty. I was the one mad experimenter who would have such a one—not for her power, mind you; I have no need for a woman of power, but as an exotic addition to an old man's bevy. She had hair as silver as the Overstone—the last one to pass through—and eyes to match. And a temper, I think, for though my drowning sands trapped her and I used my Sandstone to pitch an iron tent about her, by morning half my tents were lying limp on the sand like shivan-cloth and she was gone."

"So the Stonekeepers are not likely to stir from their Keeps." Kendric nodded. "Then we are free to travel the Rynth in relative safety—"

Ivrium laughed, throwing back his head and revealing the pink, ribbed roof of his mouth. "Free to travel the Rynth? But certainly. You can claim it for a kingdom if you wish and if your sword can hold it. But safety—oh, my vertical friend, only for those who must go into the Rynth, and then their lives are short. It is a hard life and a hard death to be found there. Sometimes even the fowlen prowl. You must join the rim-runners and leave her to a bevy or the Unkept women, for no one survives long in the Rynth unless he runs in a pack."

"He may leave me whenever he likes," Irissa interjected, "but I will choose my company. It may be that I will prefer my own alone."

Ivrium's head shook soberly. "Not in the Rynth. Not with your powers shrunken to a thin silver band around your inner eye." His glance returned to Kendric. "Listen, Swordmaker, you will find the company of such a one as this a heavy burden from both sides of her nature. Magicked, she would wreak great chaos on the stable spheres of the Inlands. Unmagicked, she is of no use but to draw the fear and emnity of the Stonekeepers, for they will never believe her powers muted; they have suffered too much at the passage of her kind across their lands before. Leave her or loose her; it will be to your advantage."

Kendric shifted uncomfortably on the pillows; it was typical that what was soft and satin luxury to anyone else was thorns to one of his contrary inclinations, Irissa thought. She would not say anything to Ivrium's advice that Kendric flee her company as he would that of rabid lemurai—any more than she would deign to inform Kendric that the last bit of food he was bolting from his almost empty platter while thoughtfully listening to Ivrium's proposals was her only apparent chance at dinner!

"You have magic," Ivrium went on. "What a pity it is that you do not have a Stone. You could establish your own Stone-keep and keep whatever you wished within it. Even an ice-eyed one."

Kendric set aside his empty platter, still chewing on some last morsel of food while also masticating Ivrium's words.

"A Stone. Amozel said something—but I paid her no heed at the time. I have—" He reached slowly for the boarskin purse at his belt, drew it apart, and upended it into his palm. Something tiny twinkled there, like a cabochon of dew full-struck by the sun. Kendric made several attempts to pinch it between his large fingers before he could elevate it for Ivrium's long-distance inspection. The press of his flesh almost obscured it, save for the brilliant, sheer silver sparkle it gave off even in Ivrium's iron-dampened tents. "A Stone," Kendric announced.

"Commonstone," Ivrium said in dismissal.

"No, not quite commonstone," Kendric said. "The sheen—"

Ivrium squinted until his eyes were lost in pale dunes of flesh. "Hmmm. Most odd, now that you mention it. I have never seen a Stone of such brightness, not even the Shinestone of Jacine . . . Well, then, you have a Stone; establish a Stone-keep and then let him who dares come creeping around the edges of your sphere. And with yon female, you have the start of a bevy, although I'd keep an eye out for taint in my heir-lings." Ivrium's plump hands pounded a pillow decisively. "Now that I've solved all your problems for you, I can turn you back to the Rynth with good conscience. You've taught

my ambitious heirlings a lesson, the Unkept women are soothing their wounded pride with barter—"

"I thought only magicians and renegades were permitted to
consort with females here," Irissa interrupted suspiciously.

Ivrium ignored her, but answered the confused frown on
Kendric's broad brow. "You'd be wise to do as I advise, not
as I act, friend, when you found your own Stonekeep. I am a
bit lenient with my heirlings. It keeps my bevy safe, I get
useful news from the Unkept women from time to time, and—
well, heirlings will be heirlings! How is a One Son to take on
the duties of Stonekeeper if he's lived bevy-bereft all his life,
eh?"

Kendric nodded, confusion still clouding his face. He let
the stone roll back into his palm again and stared at its sleek,
silvered surface, so bright it mirrored back his face in perfect
miniature.

"Perhaps it is a Stone of power. But I know not how to use
such a thing; to me, it is as worthless as commonstone to a
rim-runner."

Ivrium waved a dimissive hand. "Take it to mad Chaundre,
then. There's the fellow who inquires into the natures of the
Stones. He has actually been known to leave his Keep to come
parading around asking to see our own Stones. I let him see
mine—" Here Ivrium dredged a slim but well-linked iron chain
from amid the clothing folds lapping at his expansive chest like
waves at a beach. A glowing, burnt-orange gem the size of a
small egg dangled between Ivrium's chubby fingertips. "I have
a splendid Stone, worth showing off. Some of those others are
more protective of their power. Though I think it is merely that
their Stones are puny and plain, to match their pusilanimous
masters.

"So take yourself and your Stone to Chaundre. And take
your ice-eyed one with you, if you're so bent on keeping her.
Mad Chaundre's mad enough to welcome her as an object of
study. It's certain the fellow doesn't need any candidates for
his bevy."

On that Ivrium ended his speech with a self-satisfied chuckle,
dropped his Stone back into the crevices of his mountainous
person, and drifted quickly into a deep sleep. Above him, the

flying lamps twinkled out one by one, like stars, as if sensitive to their master's slumber.

Kendric unbent his cramped legs, groaned, and glanced at Irissa. "Did you hear that? A soft growl, as of some prowling thing very near."

"Only some ill-trained beast, I'm sure, that has not yet learned that starvation is preferable to being kept on sufferance," she answered stiffly.

"The airborne lamps dim in rhythm to Ivrium's snores. We'd best retreat to our, our..." Kendric paused, but still found words inadequate to describe the iron tent's fabric-demarcated rooms. "Our curtained chambers," he finished. "And I hope those veil-smothered females, like the lamps, must mimic their master and sleep."

It seemed so, for no one rose or came to impede their way as they retraced a path through confusing layers of sheer curtains and finally recognized the hang of certain cloths.

"Ah. My boots are still here." Irissa whisked aside a curtain. "I do not understand such silliness, but they did not permit me to don them again."

"The female foot is apparently a prized Inlands attribute," Kendric explained, "though why any would treasure such a practical and homely thing—" he mused on, staring contemplatively at Irissa's feet, pinched white and turned slightly blue with cold.

She sat on the thick-carpeted floor and jammed on the boots. "Mad! They are all mad, like this madman you are told to visit. Better we forget all such pointless journeys. I can join the Unkept and keep my boots and you can take your silly Stone and set up some even sillier Stonekeep and a bevy to make Ivrium's chins quiver in jealousy."

But Kendric wasn't listening to her; he was staring at her strangely. "You. *You're* growling."

"*I* am not. Or rather, only a portion of me is. The foolish bevywomen kept me not only from my boots but from my dinner."

"Why did you not tell me? I would have given you some of mine."

"I will wait until morning and get some from the Unkept women," Irissa said firmly. "I think perhaps it is better not to eat under this alien iron roof, anyway," she added direly. "Who knows how one's food may be seasoned? Especially if one is carrying a magic-made sword and is too proud to use it—"

Kendric darted, as much as a large man could dart, around the curtains to the next compartment. He returned moments later, looking relieved.

"It is still there, be that benefit or burden." He sighed and sat on the heap of carpets that made up Irissa's bed. "I did not think I would ever miss the Rynth's hard and stony ground, but I begin to see why Gryff and the others tired of the Stone-keeps' luxury."

"And I begin to understand why a magician's daughter would flee the Stonekeeps for the life of the Unkept, if she got no boots and no food," Irissa added heartily. "Well. One more madman cannot do us greater harm than we have suffered already. Perhaps we should journey on to this Chaundre who likes to study Stones—and people."

"We have journeyed far together," Kendric agreed, leaning back on an elbow. "You promised me a green world, Torloc, beyond the gate. I am minded to travel on until I see it."

"Do you see me in any Torloc paradise?" Irissa asked rue-fully. "Yet I—we—came so near. Finorian's face hung before me in a scintillating wall of green, and she said—"

"You *saw* Finorian in the gate? You spoke with her?"

Irissa smiled at Kendric's incredulity. "The gate seems so long ago, as long ago as Rule. And we have not had much time to talk since our paths have rejoined. Yes, Kendric. I saw Finorian, and she told me that the Torlocs had come together in the place promised, so it was true, what I told you—"

"Then why did we not pass?"

"We could have, but..." Irissa's reverie ended with the sudden memory of Finorian's adamant instructions to go back, and the recollection of the remote pull on her that was Kendric. Finorian had called that pull a burden that made Irissa too heavy to waft through rainbowed gates...

"But what?" Kendric was demanding.

"The moment—was lost."

"Lost or thrown away? Irissa, was it I who made the gate impassable? For us, for you?"

"Why should you think such a thing?"

"I read it in your eyes."

"My eyes?" She put her hands over her face. "Oh, my two-edged eyes that empowered could betray others and unempowered betray myself!"

"Then it is true. I was not worthy of the gate. I was not meant to cross."

"I was meant to cross and I had invited you," Irissa said from behind her hands, her voice muffled as well as her eyes.

Kendric leaned forward. With one hand, he pulled her wrists down, so she had to look him in the eyes. She blinked, as if facing a too-bright sun.

"But *I* was never meant to cross and by trying I catapulted us both to this alien world!" he said in bitter, self-accusing tones.

"No! It was not your fault. Finorian said an unmagicked mortal could not pass a Torloc gate, but you held Torloc powers unknowing even then, so it makes no sense—besides, I *could* have continued through alone, but decided..." She paused again. There had been no time to make anything so solid that it could be called a decision. She had merely felt Kendric ebbing into some point that was their conjoined past, had sensed Finorian's approval of this sundering, and had herself released the gate, of herself, for herself, and by herself.

"You *loosed* the gate," he charged, his hand tightening on the wrists he still held lightly.

Irissa dropped her head in admission. "Yes. It was not your fault."

"Then you need not be here at all; you need not have lost your facility for coldstone tears or magic or...or inviting unwanted Wrathmen through Torloc-meant gates."

"Perhaps not," she conceded, as if admitting a grave fault.

Kendric's hands loosened and she felt them pause on the two wings of hair at either side of her face, then stroke lightly downward until he grasped and shook them slightly in frustration.

"Irissa! And you say *I* am stubborn. You journey the world of Rule over in search of a gate to your kind, then on a whim turn from it at its opening because it has limits beyond your expectation. You sit through two hours of tedious dinnertime discussion with a vain Stonekeeper and do not even ask for food because the customs of the place have denied you anything except that which is given to you! I am not sure which of your Torloc traits to blame for this, save that I think it is only honest mortal pride."

It was the longest speech she had ever heard from Kendric, and what distressed her most was that his voice sounded as if he were mastering some overpowering emotion. As if he were—

She looked up with eyes of ordinary gray that would have been watered over with ordinary tears, except that she seemed denied both Torloc and mortal release of that kind now. Kendric's eyes were not forbidden such phenomenon, and now they shone so bright an amber-brown that she knew the only tears a man was allowed to admit had come to them—the shine of merriment.

"You—laugh? At the loss of a world?"

"Look what we have gained—the Rynth! What else is there but laughter? And as for worlds—perhaps it is up to us to make our own world."

The reaction suddenly reached Irissa, and her face lightened into chagrined amusement. "With your magic-made sword and your Stone? And my wit and strength, I suppose?"

"Precisely." He caught her around the shoulders in such good fellowship that he nearly pulled her over. "Wit has been my province on our previous journeys," he pointed out tongue-in-cheek, "but I cede it to you."

"As I have given you my magic?"

Kendric grew sober then. "No, I do not think wit is so transferable. But I do know that one reputed to possess it would have the good sense to sleep—and sleep easy—on the night before a journey to find a mad magician."

He pushed himself up off the carpets, his knees cracking protest, and patted Irissa clumsily on the crown of her head.

"At least you keep the Iridesium circlet, and there may be some power in that. I hope it has the power to put you to sleep, for I intend to rise very early and shake myself free of these iron tents of Ivrium's." Kendric stared up at the almost dampened lamps above. "I do not like the feel of such unnatural confinement, however free the man is with his advice."

"That sounds like a Torloc trait," Irissa teased softly.

"And you had better beware if I contract any more," he replied before vanishing around the whispering folds of curtain that separated them.

Chapter Seventeen

◆—◆

"Chaundre's Keep?" Amusement lifted Amozel's pale eyebrows and made her straight little mouth look less severe. "Truly, your travels take an innovative twist. We will march with you."

Kendric made a negative gesture, but Amozel's eyes instantly snapped his way.

"Do not be foolish, giant. You will not find your way through the curls of the Rynth alone and you will not eat well enough to survive half the journey, especially if you rely on *her* marksmanship and bring down only alien birds you dare not eat."

"We would be grateful for your guidance—and your company," Irissa said graciously. Kendric sighed pointedly.

"And you will share barrenberry wine and night fire with us," Amozel told Irissa in a manner that was as inclusive of her as it was exclusive of Kendric.

"Naturally," he affirmed angrily and stalked off.

They stood outside Ivrium's tent. Although Ivrium was the most generous of the Stonekeepers, according to Amozel, it seemed his hospitality had an expiration time of twenty-four hours. The morning after their arrival, he had bidden his guests good journey and farewell, gathered his heirlings and bevy tight around him, and not even bothered to see them off.

Irissa was bemused. Inside Ivrium's tent, Kendric was treated with all courtesy and deference; now that they rejoined the Unkept women, it was Irissa who was turned to with favor and Kendric who felt a chill that could be attributed to more than a vagrant wind from the Rynth. It would drive them mad, this constant reversal of status, the shoe invariably shifting from one foot to the other—or rather, not shifting, if it was Irissa's turn to play downtrodden and barefoot.

"It is a very long way to Chaundre's Keep," Amozel said. "We must not only traverse our way out of Ivrium's lands but follow the Rynth around to the very Cincture edge, for Chaundre holds the Drawstone and must abide at the edge of things, lest he impel the other Stonekeeps to tumble into ruins by the pull of his."

"He holds such power—and he is mad?"

Amozel shrugged. "A thing may be mad and harmless. He has never had ill commerce with the Unkept, for he keeps no bevy and has no heirlings and therefore has no need of us. But he likes us to pause if we pass by. He says he studies us."

The leader of the Unkept laughed, a wandering, sweet rivulet of a laugh that riveted Irissa and even made Kendric look up amazed from preparing his travel burdens.

"There are some who say he is as unmanned as one of the celibate Keep-brothers, who—failing in being named One Son—are forbidden to sire sons of their own. But then even the One Son is held back from his natural bent until it is clear he will actually succeed the Stonekeeper. The Stones are old, older than the Stonekeeps, older than the Rynth, older perhaps than the Rynx. Holding them imparts some longevity; Sofistron was two hundred and sixty-seven when I was born to the bevy. He has had many sons and daughters since and he has had many One Sons who went disappointed and womanless to their graves, waiting for him to retire to his. And the Stonekeepers live on. As for Chaundre, he is the youngest, and I, who have made a study myself of the natures of man, am not so sure of his. Other than that he is mad. But it is always amusing to meet him."

Amozel, having unburdened herself of an uncharacteristically long reminiscence, went to supervise the Unkept at their packing for the trek. Irissa joined Kendric, though his work was nearly done.

"We need a guide," she told him.

He didn't look up from ladening his baldric with its assortment of knives, wallets, and other useful items. "A guide. Not fifteen."

"They are only fourteen—and only women."

Kendric grunted skeptically and stood, slinging the baldric around his shoulder with a metallic jingle. "I'll make you a bargain," he offered.

"A barter?"

"Of sorts. If you practice with yon bowwoman's weapon on our journey until you can bring down birds at will and we can quit the escort of these unnatural dames, I will allow you to try to teach me some slight tricks with these powers I seem to have contracted."

"Kendric, archery is *work*; magic is instinct. It hardly seems a fair trade."

"But I am as foreign to instinct as you are to work, so we should both be the better for it. Besides, if you can kill game enough to feed us, and I can learn tricks enough to ease small obstacles from our path, we can be rid of this unnecessary escort."

"I suspect Amozel's feelings toward you are the same," Irissa noted. Then she frowned and spoke more seriously. "But Kendric, magic is no trick to master as one would learn to throw the Tolechian dice on Rule. It is a gift and should be so honored, for its use makes it grow within one and become more than before; it must be used honestly, lest it betray its possessor."

"And I honestly tell you that I am willing to use a bit of this power to cushion our way—if I must possess it and must use it. But I will not rely upon it in battle or for anything serious. If I cannot win by might of arms, I will not use magical means. Now, that is as honest a use of such stuff as I can imagine, and you should be well content with my pledge."

Kendric finished securing his long, new-made sword in a makeshift sling fashioned of some hide Demimondana had given him, slung it diagonally across his back, and anchored it to the baldric. "I must admit a sword of a length and weight I am used to is a comfortable burden to carry again. And though this sword was magic-made, it is not an unfair advantage against any unmagicked man, for it acts as a simple sword—mere metal and the drive that mortal muscle can give it."

Kendric settled the massive length across his back and turned to join the train of Unkept women already winding its way across the sand dunes that were doubly ruddy in the glow of the rising sun. Irissa watched his towering figure bring up the rear, then shook herself free of her thoughts and ran heavily through the sandy earth to join the party.

By sunfall the towering peaks of Ivrium's iron tents were a distant dark range of foothills behind them. Ahead stretched the barren maze that was the Rynth. Irissa, already footsore, watched Kendric shift the sword upon his back as if it chafed. Amozel had sent her archers ahead; when the main party caught up with them, they had bagged a dozen gray birds, which lay at their boot toes like a trophy bevy.

At Amozel's nod, the other women began to pluck the birds and pulled out short knives with which to divide them.

"Wait!" The Unkept women weren't used to heeding male voices, but so much incredulity and command mingled in Kendric's that he had their utter attention. "Aren't you going to cut spits first, gather firewood, start a fire?"

Amozel regarded him back with as much wonder. "We travel apart from the rim-runners now. We have no one to chant make-fire for us. We must do without."

"You'd eat them *raw*?" Irissa suddenly was unsmitten with the Unkept's uncivilized ways.

Demimondana answered. "It is not pleasant, but it is possible."

Kendric reached so suddenly to the belt at his waist that leather-banded wrists tightened on bows in concert. He didn't notice, being occupied in drawing out small objects from his purse.

"Amozel, look. You held these once in the rim-runner camp, and they did not repel you. With these, I could make a fire in moments, if your women gathered wood."

Sunfall was already making it difficult for them to see. Amozel squinted into the pale cup of Kendric's hand. He gently shook the contents until they rattled together, like dice.

"It's a tool, a simple tool. It works quite naturally, though I cannot quite explain why. That was left to men of wisdom in my—Keep. Let me make a fire for you."

She nodded then, curtly. Shortly after, her women came back from foraging with armfuls of dry brambles. These they cast into a pile and Kendric knelt to it. There came the scratch of flint and steel; the sound so common to Kendric's and Irissa's ears seemed to run roughshod over the Unkept women's senses. They set their teeth and moved back. But no sparks leaped between Kendric's fingers, and the wood remained cold and uncaught.

Irissa came and crouched by Kendric. "What's wrong?"

He raked flint against steel until they rasped again and again. "I don't know. They are stubborn tonight—they won't strike sparks."

"Perhaps now that you have used your powers to make your sword, you have lost the facility for natural marvels."

"Nonsense. Flint and steel are flint and steel. And—they—always—work . . ."

"Not even magic always works, Wrathman, but you could try it," she whispered.

"I told the Unkept—"

"Magic does not have to announce itself. Use your flint and steel."

"But how?" he exploded, then dropped his voice. "I am not a fire-breathing maul-worm. I cannot create heat and light on a whim!"

Irissa's hands lay lightly over his, calming his dogged striking of flint on steel. "Peace. There is heat within you, within the blood that flows as red as flame through your fingers, until you can feel it pulsing on your fingertips. There is light within your inner eye, where you have seen flame a thousand times and let it be a mere dancing impression to be reflected in the mirror of your eye. You need but see that flame, draw it through your veins, feel it hot upon your hands, within your hands, without your hands , bridging you and wood, becoming flame only, consuming wood . . ."

Sweat instantly pearled Kendric's face. He felt a fever wave wash through him and bubble down to the fingers that held their useless metal poised over cold wood. Yellow-red tongues flared from his fingers, met wood, became entwined with it. The flint and steel fell in among the brambles as Kendric, with a curse, drew back his hands. He held them loosely curled, palms up, and blew upon the fingertips.

"Burned!" he said accusingly to Irissa in an undertone.

"Oh. You are *so* literal. It is most hard to work through such an *opaque* medium. You hold everything to you—your sword, your flame...Magic is a going out, a directing out. Don't make a fist, you'll injure yourself further. I would help you, I would have you heal yourself, but you would probably knit your fingers together!" Irissa leaned forward and blew fiercely across Kendric's seared fingertips, already glowing rosy on their own in the fire's flicker.

Amozel came over and stared down into the rising warmth, unaware of its magical origin. "And you say that these tools have made the flame, not magic?"

"Yes, flint and steel can make fire," Kendric hedged, quickly dropping his hands to his sides. Now that he had exercised magic, he thought it important to avoid direct falsehood wherever possible, lest magic somehow rise up and decry him.

"And you—throw—these objects into the flames once they begin, as a sort of sacrifice?"

Kendric sighed and watched his flint and steel grow slowly red-hot in the fire's now brightly burning heat. "Sometimes," he said dourly. "And when the fire cools, I retrieve them for another time."

Amozel nodded soberly. "It is a trick mad Chaundre would find some amusement in. He is ever fascinated by these talismans that create various effects. He, too, insists that they all need not be magical. I was not minded to believe him—being a man, he finds it easy to lie—but now that I have seen you use such things, Kendric, perhaps there is something to Chaundre's ravings, after all."

Amozel withdrew while the other Unkept began preparing the fowl for the spits they had made from the thicker brambles. Kendric slid back from the rising flames and draped his wrists across his raised knees. Like Amozel, he assumed he had done enough to ensure the preparation of this meal to avoid any further work in the getting of it. She had given her permission and he had delivered fire—at the cost of a few fingertips and one small white lie.

"I'm sorry," Irissa said, joining him. "If magic is not bred within one, perhaps it is a bit cumbersome to use at first."

"And at last, as far as I'm concerned," Kendric said, blowing with methodical melancholy over his fingertips. "I'll not be able to rend hot flesh with these hands tonight, and dare not tell Amozel why."

"Then you shall have to fast," Irissa said lightly as she rose to leave. "As I did, last night." And she did not seem to have any more sympathy for Kendric's plight than that.

By the time the small birds were basting brown and dripping juices that sizzled into the still-hot and heaving fire, Kendric had withdrawn to the very edge of the firelight to lick his wounds. Irissa remained with the hungry Unkept women, who'd eaten leanly from their own food packs while camped outside Ivrium's tent the night before.

The birds made succulent but messy fare, and there was much talk and laughter in the company around the fire. The Unkept women shared a mutual humor and ease that were not apparent when they mixed with other groups or with the men whom they regarded oddly as a blend of prey and predator. Demimondana talked bitterly of the heirlings who had tried Kendric's strength the day before. They were empty boasters, her bevy-brothers, she said, who flattered Ivrium and who magnified their small achievements until everything was obscured but their mighty self-pride.

There were some things sheer strength could not accomplish, she said, and not one of Ivrium's heirlings could lace a wing-borne bird so nearly through the heart that it would take much searching to find the wound, as she could. But she had been destined for the bevy of some distant Stonekeeper, not for the role of One Son. And so she had left and walked barefoot into the Rynth. Not all who fled the Stonekeeps survived. Many missed connecting with the nomadic bands of rim-runners and Unkept women. Some were discovered when only their bones remained on a meander verge to tell that they had come—and gone.

The Unkept women fell silent, mourning those who had not lived to swell their numbers, those of their number who had died—and even, Irissa thought, those of their kind who had remained behind. Irissa gathered up the square cloth she had used to wipe her fingers so she should not soil her sand-washed clothes and tiptoed away into the dark beyond the waning fire.

The Overstone shone as ever, so taken for granted a part of the Inlands' day and night landscape it could be overlooked, like one of Ivrium's floating lamps. Yet the moonlight painted the land dark and light and it picked out the profile of Kendric, sitting on some rocks nearby.

"Here." Irissa unveiled the center of her kerchief. Several pieces of fowl lay there. "They are quite cold to the touch."

Kendric's fingers hovered over the food, like the nose of a wary hound over meat that it feared was hot. Then he took the cloth and began eating with his usual heartiness.

Irissa sat beside him. "What do you do out here alone?"

Kendric raised his head to the horizon yet gleaming in a stiletto-thin red line. "Listen," he said, chewing hungrily.

"There is naught to see in the Rynth, except desolation. What is there to hear?"

"Loneliness. I have heard something howl, far away on the rim of things, something so lonely and isolated that even to speculate on it is a sort of invasion. It is a thing by itself, long by itself, ever by itself. It is fearsome..."

"More fearsome than an empress falgon?" Irissa teased to lighten his mood. "Or than the sight of fire flaming from your fingertips?"

"An empress falgon had its own proud reason for being. This thing doesn't. Or has lost it. And as for fire-spitting fingertips—mere foolery. Could I really heal myself?"

"Properly guided."

"Hmmpf. I will leave that to nature, which is vastly more experienced at it than I, or even you. Listen—did you hear it, faint but it cuts through one's very bones, the anguish in it?"

"What?"

"Shhhh!"

Kendric put a hand over her mouth, and Irissa shut her eyes. With two of her senses muted, it seemed a third was finally strong enough to pick out a desolate, ghostly wail that went ranging up and down the chords of despair. It sounded as unreal yet chilling as if the Overstone had suddenly unhinged a mouth and begun speaking from it.

Irissa pressed her hands to her ears and shuddered. "It is

dreadful, dreadful, such pain, such fury. I have never heard a sound so designed to pass the misery of its maker on to others. It is distant?"

"Yes, yes. More distant than we think. It is somewhere alone. And that is odd. On what we have seen in this world, nothing travels alone, not rim-runner, not lorryk, not moon-hawk, not Unkept woman—"

"Except the dwarf falgon," Irissa remembered. "It flew alone, quite low to the ground. There was only one, for the Unkept are archers who have lived long off bird flesh and they never saw its like before."

Kendric paused before he spoke again. "The falgon was a thing of Rule, and remains a mystery. What cries beyond the horizon belongs to this place, though it likes it not. And if it is a mystery, it is one more to itself than to us."

"How do you know all this?"

Kendric's easy answers stopped. "Know all this? I—I have heard it before, the night I first spent in the Rynth. I *feel* that I know it . . ."

"Feel it?" Irissa stood, and her features vanished into the dimness of the night, except for a circular silver twinkle from her eyes. "Be wary, man of Rule; you are developing instinct, and from there it is a very short slide to the depths of magic itself."

She was devoured by the dark. Moments later, Kendric saw her silhouette limned against the cheery fire glow. He kept to the dark and his watchfulness. And though he did not like the sound of it any more than Irissa had, he seemed to lack her abhorrence of the weird, unhappy cry that pierced the night's edges. His ears pricked for the agony-ridden wail of the lone thing at the Inlands' end. He heard it again, and he wondered.

Chapter Eighteen

The way to Chaundre's Keep was, as Amozel had promised, a long journey. During it, Irissa became fairly proficient with the bow under Demimondana's tutoring, so much so that she was given her own to carry. But she never relished the first moment of rushing up to see her prey. She always feared that a set of rainbow-colored feathers would lie limp on the Rynth's barren ground. Yet the specks she brought down from their wheel across the icy curve of the Overstone's arch were invariably gray and invariably the moonhawks that inhabited the Rynth's upper air. She began to wonder if the dwarf falcon her first unlucky shot had found might have been an illusion, a kind of lingering wish-for-it that her depleted powers somehow had still summoned from the deepest, most remote magic in her.

Kendric didn't think so, when she voiced her doubts.

"It was a dwarf falcon, certainly," he pronounced. "As real as rain. And were we not so sentimental, we might have spitted and roasted it and had some supper to show for your efforts."

His fingertips had healed within a day, and Kendric had become the solitary firestarter for the party. He had to drop flint and steel into the early flames, then retrieve them from the ashes the next morning, as Amozel had taken accident for design and assumed this ritual was part of the tool's effectiveness.

Irissa watched him closely as he struck the two rasping surfaces together. It took a certain adept strength to strike sparks from two such contrary surfaces, and then luck alone to have one leap just so among the gathered sticks to start a blaze. Yet the Unkept women never gathered around unlighted faggots these nights, and there was no talk of eating their game raw.

167

Irissa suspected that Kendric had learned to assist the sparks with his own brand of generated heat—without burning his fingers or betraying the source of the flames. But she couldn't be certain, and dared not ask him for fear of stifling even this small reliance on his powers. And he did not seek her aid in mastering any other "tricks," no matter how trifling.

Twice, Amozel led the party away from the endless, un-dulating expanse of the Rynth to the very edge of a Stone-keeper's lands. Each time the approach was unpromising; then the ground beneath their boots suddenly shifted character and unrolled to the horizon like a living tapestry woven with all the wonders a single mind could imagine.

The first Keep border they paused at seemed merely a mean-der that had risen and stretched to the horizon. In its still waters, as murky lavender as the clouded sky, a reflected ice-arch scribed a half-circle and a twin to the pale-faced moon floated there, forever staring up at its original.

Vessels so delicate they looked blown from glass darted over the waters' surface. From the horizon rose airy edifices so tall and spindly they seemed constructed of spun sugar and bridged by strands of lace.

"Lacustrine's waters discourage all but invited visitors," Amozel said, "and the Unkept are not among them."

"It is a pity, for Lacustrine's Keep is said to be a city wherein all the people live, and they skim the water from place to place in small boats shaped like giant water-bound birds," Demi-mondana added.

"And it was to Lacustrine's bevy you were promised," Amozel said sharply, "so you could have seen all this for yourself, had you not preferred the ways of the Rynth."

Demimondana sighed. "Seen it? Yes, once. And then I would have been confined to the bevy quarters ever after. It is better to view it from a distance—free."

"It is marvelous," Irissa admitted. "And Kendric, does it not remind you of the City That Soars in Rule, which was balanced between the mountains' teeth like a fallen snowflake?"

He only nodded. The last view he and Irissa had seen of that fabled city showed it fallen and shattered on the mountains' foothills.

"Snowflakes? What is that?" Demimondana's light green eyes gleamed with curiosity.

Irissa looked to Kendric, mystified, then tried to define it. "A frozen waterdrop, but lacy like frost, and light. It falls from the sky when the air is cold. Do you call it something other?"

The Unkept women exchanged puzzled glances. Amozel spoke for their mutual incomprehension. "Nothing falls from the sky here, save moonhawks when we pierce them."

"Not even rain? Water, waterdrops," Kendric insisted, gesturing upward.

"The water runs in the meanders and has no need to turn itself on its head, rise up, and then drop down, unless some Stonekeeper commands it to do so for his amusement," Amozel said.

"I hear that Lacustrine can command the water to dance so, in great shafts that spring up from his canals and shatter into a thousand sparkling drops like commonstones and fall back," Demimondana interjected.

Amozel fixed her with an eye of deep brown disapproval. "Then perhaps you had been better off to have meekly gone at Ivrium's command to the bevy of this water-wizard."

"No! It is merely that I have heard it is a wondrous Keep, most opposite to my father's earth-rooted lands," Demimondana finished wistfully before falling silent.

"Well, we are not for it, nor it for us," Amozel concluded, drawing the party from the dazzling mirror of water and sky by turning her small, straight back upon it and marching away.

They followed her; such was Amozel's power of persuasion that she drew things and people after her like some many-membered, docile train.

Irissa leaned in to whisper to Kendric as they brought up the Unkept's rear. "She would make a Stonekeep an imperious Lady Ward. That seems a novel concept for this place; I would like to see her become Lady Ward."

"I would not like to be her Lord Warden," Kendric returned. "She has but one tune to march to, and that brisk and of her own composition."

"But it must make one harsh to be born as child to one of these proud Stonekeepers and then to have no value but as one of many trinkets to be traded to another."

"Better than to be made weak by being born to be a Stone-keeper's ever-fawning heir, forbidden the most natural freedoms of man and made to joust one's brothers for the dubious likelihood of following the old codger when he finally grows senile enough to let his immortality ebb." Kendric shuddered at the thought. "These so-called Keep-brothers have no brotherly loyalty to one another. Far better to rim-run in the Rynth and do one's own will than to vie to please another's will in some magically supported sphere."

"Then if we must stay, we have allied ourselves with the right parties for our preferences," Irissa concluded.

Kendric stopped walking long enough to let the Unkept women march far out of earshot. "Stay? I think not. Where is your talk of Torloc paradise now? Or of gates? I swear, should I see a rainbow arching yon rock, I would leap into it this instant." He slapped the crossbar of his sword where it rode his shoulder-blade. "Only this time I should keep my sword."

"This time it is fully yours," she answered. "You truly think that there is a gate from this place to—another?"

"We entered by one. But perhaps it will not look the same; our greatest difficulty may be in recognizing it. If naught falls from the sky here, as the Unkept say and as my experience confirms, there will be no rainbows to make gates."

"But Torloc seeresses have come before—and gone. Sofistron said they came here to learn wisdom, and he seemed to have made a closer study of my kind than any of the other Stonekeepers. Ivrium cared only for the vanity of adding an outland woman to his bevy and—"

"Sofistron made a closer study of your kind because he wished to cage it," Kendric pointed out, "which makes him a canny hunter but no source of all knowledge. No, we must find why the seeresses came here and why they went again, before we can determine the most vital thing—the *how*."

Irissa smiled and took Kendric's arm. "Strange. When Sofistron held me within his silver circle, he taunted me for asking the unimportant hows and overlooking the whys. Now it seems I must worry over the whys if I am ever to have my hows answered."

"'Tis a puzzle," Kendric agreed, "and one I would rather

not have to solve. I am getting the vilest headache I've had since waking in the Rynth and finding myself without the gate."

"You can—"

"I know. Heal myself. So can nature, and nature is not likely to turn upon me like these Torloc gifts. They were always uncertain in you and are even more capricious in me. You are better without them."

Irissa stopped, the anchor of her hands around his arm halting Kendric, too. "No. As you would spring for any open gate to any open, other world than this, so I would take any chance for the restoration of what is myself. It is possible to walk the world without my powers, to kill some harmless flying thing for food, and to think and even to laugh. It is more than possible to laugh; it is necessary, for if I truly stopped to feel my powers' loss—I should not weep coldstones, nor human salt, which I now seem bereft of, but blood, until it made the meanders run red. You have barely begun to exercise what came to you by chance and my unknowing choice, Kendric, yet it grows within you and twines itself with your very soul. Soon you will find that you cannot deny what you have, any more than I can deny what I have lost."

He stood truly stricken. "You have not said much about your lost powers. I thought you had—adapted."

"Why speak of what renders one speechless?" Her gray eyes held his, and Kendric saw the darks of them swell until they seemed two black pits into which he could fall and never see his way out of again.

He remembered how, to heal him once from battle hurts, she had delved deep into his eyes to see within through what he used for seeing without. He wondered, now that he had—inherited—her powers, or some of them, if he had any healing prowess of his own, for internal injuries of the kind she so invisibly bore . . .

Kendric looked, deep into Irissa's eyes, then deeper still, so the drive of his questing intelligence went beyond mere looking. Then, with a wrenching dislocation, he was suddenly within her eyes—he, himself, his whole self, as a tiny figure in a vast and endless cave. It was dark and formless there, worse than the Swallowing Cavern for sheer black immensitude. He moved farther in, anywhere, merely to feel a sense of himself before it totally drowned in the empty, yawning abyss that lay around him.

His motion was unoriented; he seemed to be plunging ever deeper into chaotic darkness, an unmagicked darkness, an utter absence of light. He knew the despair of one who tried a familiar door, thinking to find familiar things behind it, only to open it onto mad, alien nothingness. Farther he went, knowing retreat was more dangerous than commitment. Now things were taking on a semblance to what he knew in the external world. His impression of a cavern solidified, grew stone walls and floors. His metaphorical feet pressed rock, and he moved farther into the distance and the dark, listening for something. Why should there be sound in an organ of sight? What did he expect to hear?

He knew. It was the night wail he had heard in the Rynth, the sound that expressed the loneliness, the sense of loss, he felt all around him here. No wonder she had quailed at the sound of that cry, when it had only intrigued him. It echoed this darkness, that cry, and mourned the loss of magic.

And he could do nothing against such despair, he who regretted the gain of magic, clumsy ingrate that he was.

Once again Kendric had reached for fire and burned his own fingers. He had plunged unprepared—unworthy again—into an undertaking of great risk to himself and to Irissa. She had often spoken of coming back mad from such deep seeing or not coming back at all. The latter was the possibility that seemed most likely. He was lost in a place where lost was a limitless word. He was alone, unguided, with one pale candle of magic he was wont to carry half-snuffed, in an inner world where unmagic made darkness tangible. He was a fool, where foolishness was its own fate—destruction.

Yet he moved on. He was a man of action and he would move as long as the feeble mote that was himself could stir. The longer he moved, the more he felt his physical attributes return, the more solid became the dark cave he walked through. It was not totally dark now. Kendric looked down and saw that he held a hilt that glowed and served as torch. It was a bizarre journey through past and present he made, and he did not question what hilt it was or how it had arrived. He had more in this world than before, and it was an improvement.

The way narrowed, and, small as he felt himself to be, he had to stoop to follow a tunnel that seemed all that was around him now. The vastness had abated; with its absence, he found a returning sense of size. The walls were black, but in the hilt-shed glow the substance glittered like jeweled coal, winking encouragement back at him. He moved on and felt his gathering confidence shatter at a sudden sense of great size again. No, it was merely another cave; the tunnel had opened into another cave, as tunnels had a way of doing . . .

Now there was light ahead beyond the circle thrown by the hilt in his hand. He rushed toward it. And he stopped—hovered really, had he cared to name the sensation. He was indeed in a great, black cave, and there before him lay two deep pits, like pools whose water had evaporated and left them but shells carved out in the earth. The pits were formed of the same dark stone that made the cave, except that they were rimmed with light that reflected from the glittering shards of coldstones that lined them—coldstones piled upon coldstones, so that their joint effulgence was sun-bright and threw bolts of crimson, violet, yellow, green, all the colors of the rainbow, around the cavern. The pits ran deep and their centers were so black he could see no bottom, but the coldstone vein ran deeper and richer than the dark.

The coldstone dazzle struck him, cheered him, and sent him reeling back down the distances and the dark. The glowing hilt spun from his hand and dwindled into the tunnel like the light seen at its end. He felt himself spring free and sucked back the way he had come, as if pulled by some powerful but unseen string. The blackness around him grew gray, thinned, and dissipated to fog.

Kendric stood in the fog and felt his hands clenched into someone's shoulders and saw himself to be standing frozen, staring down into a Torloc seeress' naked eyes.

He started and drew back.

"Kendric! What have you done?" Irissa's eyes seemed ordinary gray now, save for the faintly glimmering silver ring, but Kendric winced away from them.

"I thought I might try—"

"Not deep seeing? You who have barely looked upon the magic within yourself would venture within another?"

"Perhaps it was ill-advised—"

"*Perhaps!*"

"Perhaps," he insisted, his equilibrium returning and with it his old stubbornness. "I am not greatly skilled at such things and did not see much, but I did see that your magic still resides in you, in some degree."

"How did you see it?"

"I, or what I took for me, wandered in the dark for a while and then I had a glowing hilt in my hand and was drawn by some glow beyond. Then I saw it—magic. It had to be, shining coldstone-bright—your magic."

Irissa shook her head sadly. "Kendric, you saw so little because you have not been trained to see much. And all you see is a reflection of your own ability to discern. If you saw some coldstone glow, perhaps it was only a will-o'-the-wisp of your own desire to see something; or if it was some lingering scent of magic, you evoked it by your presence, because you must bear a magic very similar to mine—to what mine was."

"I may not have been trained, but I know what I see," he responded firmly. "And it was magic. I have not traveled in Torloc company so long that I may stumble over a bright piece of magic and not know it. And if I cannot give you back whatever magic you passed to me, at least I can tell you that some magic still resides in you, no matter how dim, so you will not have to shudder when you hear the wail of the thing that mourns its own loss."

Irissa's eyes narrowed. "You know how that sound affects me, how detestable . . . but how?"

"I know what I see."

Irissa finally let her fingers loosen from where they had clenched on his sleeves. "Perhaps you did see—a bit—within. Perhaps you did see . . . something."

"Magic," Kendric said matter-of-factly. "As real as the sword upon my back."

"Which you do not quite believe in, either," Irissa said, smiling nevertheless.

"That is different. You have always had magic. I have not always had swords of my own making."

"Very well. I will accept your insistence that some residual magic remains in me, for what it is worth—your word or my magic. But do not ever try my eyes—or those of any other—again, until you have mastered more than making swords."

"Never again," Kendric swore feelingly. "It is a most unsolid business, this floating into other people's eyes, and I prefer to keep my feet on solid ground."

"And if we had been doing that, we should not now be watching the Unkept women nearly vanish into the Rynth without us." Irissa pointed to a few dark dots on the horizon.

They turned and moved briskly after the women, not even casting a last look at Lacustrine's water-buoyed Stonekeep.

The Unkept made no comment at the return of their tardy fellow travelers. They seemed to feel no great responsibility for the safety of Irissa and Kendric; they welcomed their presence to the same degree that they welcomed their absence. But such indifference was common to the Rynth, where life and death were equally hard and equally to be taken for granted.

The party's path ventured near another Stonekeeper's lands only once more. Amozel stopped on the verge of a tree-dappled plain and pointed to a sky bright with flocks of many birds.

"Melinth the hawksman's Stonekeep is yonder. They say he builds his Keep of nets, and many more winged things fly within for his entertainment than ply the open sky. We like to pass here, for creatures of the air do not abide the precise lines of power a Stone may cast and often fly over. Archers!"

The women fanned out, Irissa with them, as a lemon-colored flock washed overhead in a feathered wave. The plain gray feathers tipping the Unkept women's shafts flew to meet it. Several pairs of yellow wings folded and fell to the Rynth.

"We eat well tonight," a pleased Amozel told Kendric. "And that is a blessing. We draw near Chaundre's Keep, and one is never sure what hospitality mad Chaundre will offer. Though he means well, his larder is most haphazardly stocked."

But Irissa did not eat well that night; as usual when she played both hunter and diner, her appetite was slight. The yellow birds, she told Kendric, were too small and pretty to eat.

He had no such scruples and accounted for the consumption of several. Yet he was most solicitous of Irissa's disposition for the night and saw her ensconced near some rocks. The Unkept women preferred to bed in the absolute open when traveling, for there was nothing to shelter against in the Rynth, save the legendary fowlen that were more spoken of than seen.

"Perhaps the fowlen howl," Kendric suggested as he settled down far enough from Irissa so the Unkept women would not suspect the worst. "And that is what we hear."

"Perhaps the Torloc seeresses pass through to find the fowlen, and when they do—from what I've heard tell of fowlen—howl themselves."

"Perhaps this Chaundre will know something. Often the mad of any place are gifted with deeper vision," Kendric said in good cheer.

Irissa didn't answer, since she had fallen asleep, that being the fastest way to assuage hunger.

She still dreamed. Her dreams were not as vivid and did not seem as significant as those before she had sat within Sofistron's coldstone chamber. Yet they had the virtue of enlivening her sleeping hours nevertheless. Once she had dreamed that Kendric, unwilling, had taken another ride upon the lorryk and could not dismount, having somehow become both Bounder and himself and most angry at the transformation. This night her dreams harked back to Rule, to the odd dream she'd had of the Rocklands' Shield-shakers thundering down from the sky and engaging Kendric in an uneven contest. She could almost hear the awesome rattle and the clatter of battle gear rolling across this serene, untroubled Rynthian sky, with its ever-beaming moon. She could feel the ground shake, feel the first few hard, wet pendants of rain falling fat and cold across her face . . .

"Kendric!" She sat up. The Rynth lay unchanged in the moonlit twilight, but something, someone, was spitting at her! "Kendric!"

He was awake, sitting up as well, his dark head leaning back against a rock. Now the Unkept women were shrieking also, and starting up and dancing around the open ground, reaching for their bows and shooting their arrows directly overhead.

The air above them roared; then a branch of indigo lightning appeared, forged forward, turned, and circled back upon itself. Six more fat drops of water exploded on Irissa's face. Kendric finally stirred and came over.

She held up a wet forefinger. "Look!" The finger shook for startled emphasis. "It never rains in the Rynth; the Unkept had not even heard of a snowflake. Yet—"

"We'd better draw back against the rocks, then, for shelter." Kendric pulled her under the overhang of a flat stone, but Irissa strained to keep watching the Unkept women as they aimed arrows at the rain that pelted them. The rain seemed to fall in only a small, exclusive area. It gathered on the rock lip above them and dripped steadily to Irissa's still-exposed knee. She drew her feet closer and huddled there. There was not much room for Kendric; the oversized raindrops were splashing on his sturdy sillac-hide boots and dampening his elbows.

"It is a most peculiar storm," Irissa said suspiciously.

Kendric shrugged. "We have never seen a storm in this world; we do not know how peculiar they can get. They must be rare, if the Unkept women are driven half-wild by a few raindrops." He leaned out to inspect the storm, but Irissa pulled him back by the sleeve.

"And *circular* lightning?"

"The Stonekeeps are circular. No doubt the storm accommodates them."

"Kendric. Have you— Did you— Is it *your* storm?"

"The weather rains on everyone equally."

"I mean did you make it—magically?"

He couldn't help grinning. "I thought I'd try it. The Unkept women had not seen rain before, and I thought to remedy that. I tried to evoke a Rocklands dry-storm, only wet. It goes on a good deal longer than I thought, once set in motion, but otherwise it is a most satisfactory storm, I think. My sopping tunic can attest to that."

"I do not think the Unkept like your rain." Irissa watched their disarray continue as they ranged in wider circles to escape the wetness.

"No," Kendric concurred.

"But you did not make it entirely for their edification."

"No."

"You see now that to have what others have not and value it cheaply is . . ."

"A foolishness that I—we—cannot afford," Kendric said. "I may not see much," he added, "but I know what I see. And to have gained what I never knew may be less troubling than to lose what one always knew and never thought of losing."

"True sympathy with the deepest nature of a thing," Irissa said carefully in an instructional tone, "is the beginning and the best part of magic."

Kendric cleared his throat. "Yes. I find I even like the rain, now that I have understood it enough to evoke it. They had an arid world here, where only death falls from the sky. My rain may be wet, it may be cold, but it makes a cheery drip, keeps me awake and alert for ravaging fowlen, and will leave water in the hollow rocks, so we need not risk ourselves in the meanders in the morning."

Irissa yawned. "A magician," she announced portentously, "will always justify his own magic." She laid her head on Kendric's sodden shoulder and began to slip back into sleep. Soon, she thought dreamily, he might manage to make a meal.

Chapter Nineteen

In the morning, the Unkept women steadfastly refused to drink the rock-caught water. They trekked to the nearby meander while Irissa and Kendric remained among the rocks, cupping their hands to the pools and sipping from their palms.

"I cannot blame them." Kendric sighed and regarded the liquid pooled in his hand.

"It *tastes* perfectly fresh and fine," Irissa said hastily.

"Yes, but the color is unfortunate. I was remembering the dry-storm, when rock crystals rained down on us in the Rocklands. Crystals violet and yellow." He let his fingers separate, and the jaundiced water trickled through them back into the rocky basin. "It was not good enough to create plain rain; no, I must color it inventively and impress them. That is the fault of magic—it invites excess."

Irissa smiled. "I fear that is not a magical trait, but another Torloc one for you to lament. After all, your powers are Torlockian, and only filtered through an un-Torlockian vessel. And Torlocs always were prone to embellishment, or so I have been told."

"And you think, last night, I was embellishing?"

"I am afraid so. It is not so great a flaw."

"I had no idea that power was so troublesome," he confessed. "No wonder the Unkept wish to keep utterly free of it. I cannot understand why Geronfrey . . ." He stopped, having arrived back at the point sorest between himself and Irissa, the moments in which both had forged their fates into one and yet had made that coupling painful. They were like a pair of bearing-beasts, looped together into harnesses that they had not seen coming, each finding the other's company both comforting and chafing. But for them, magic was the yoke they bore together, and its bonds were invisible.

Irissa stood up and stretched. "I hope we reach mad Chaundre's Keep today. I grow tired of walking. The lorryk were erratic mounts, but superior to boot leather."

"Be glad that we have not seen any of your hoofed friends," Kendric said. "The Unkept's supplies dwindle, and I think they would let fly at game as large as lorryk right now."

"How can they slay such magnificent creatures?" Irissa was indignant.

"All do not have your magical rapport with the beasts. And besides, Master Stomach gives his own marching orders."

It was true. When the women handed out the breakfast breads, they were broken into slender pieces, and Irissa noticed that the food bags hung slack. Amozel prodded the group into eating quickly and starting soon across the unchanging Rynth.

Irissa looked up at the moon while she walked. Its face seemed smooth and unshadowed, but perhaps that was because it always gave off light, so one did not see much beyond the fact that it was round and glowed. The frosty bands that held it, or seemed to, shone white and opaque, like ice. Yet neither rain nor snow fell on the Inlands, and though the Rynth was chill, it was not so cold that water froze. She walked along, staring at the sky, hearing the small stones kick from her boots with a light, rainlike chatter.

"Well." Kendric had stopped and caught her arm.

Irissa looked back to earth. It had changed, instantly, as it was wont to do under the influence of a Stone. Ahead lay a rugged, rocky wilderness of strange, Stone-erected shapes. Some were piled and balanced into the likeness of a man; others sprawled far in great, coiling congregations of rock, as if they were the frozen remains of great beasts and worms. And some of the outré silhouettes that rose from the parti-colored earth were vegetable—orange-foliaged trees that grew bent and twisted into shapes quite unrecognizable, but suggestively familiar.

"It's a madman's museum," Kendric announced, walking bemusedly into the display. With his height and the diagonal slice of the sword across his back, he looked part of the scene.

Amozel smiled and followed Kendric confidently into the maze, her women in her wake. Irissa finally joined them.

"You should feel at home," Kendric jested. "This magic sculpture garden must display a nearly Torlockian taste for embellishment."

Irissa regarded him oddly. "I am most uneasy. These shapes are not magic-made. They are natural."

"Natural? Nonsense! Nature does not toss rocks about so artfully." He looked to Amozel for confirmation and met only her most mysterious expression.

Without comment, she turned and moved further into the convoluted passages between rock-piled formations that rose ever higher and nearer together.

"At least we know we are within a Stonekeep's sphere," Kendric comforted Irissa.

"Hoping for the best is not a Torloc trait," she answered. "You must blame it on your human nature."

Yet nothing untoward happened, though the constant scrape of shifting stone accompanied their march. The stones balanced above them never seemed to move, despite the low, rocky growl all around that spoke of constant agitation.

Irissa had just grown used to the idea of being surrounded by rows of statuesque stones when she walked around the prominent profile of what seemed a leering giant lemurai and stopped, speechless.

Ahead lay a patchwork land—not the neat and logical patchwork of tilled soil, but a land literally borrowed from every-where. Rivers ran through meadow and forest—and sandy, dune-ridged desert. Rivers climbed *up* hills and gurgled across treeless plains. Fields of green rubbed furrows with fields of golden grain—and with fields of purple earth and pink flowers. It was as if a bored child had upended a box of embroidery threads and let them mingle where they would, as if everything they saw had slid together in a haphazard pile and then stopped.

"Mad Chaundre's Keep," Amozel announced with some satisfaction. "I believe we arrive in time for dinner." She started off down a sandy white slope dotted with thickly leaved plants that were topped by enormous black blooms.

"And they wouldn't drink my yellow rainwater," Kendric observed as he followed. "I can hardly wait to see what this fellow serves."

Irissa brought up the rear.

The way to Chaundre's Keep was unmistakable. After pass-ing through the initial range of small hills, the party found that everything went downhill. Even the greenery—and more often orangery—grew that way, with arrowlike branches all aimed at the center of this makeshift land.

What occupied that prominent spot eventually took shape beneath them. Mostly, it was a low place, but then parts of it soared tower-high. It was constructed of stone, wood, sand-packed blocks, and glass; and there was an entire windowless wing of iron. It was a large place that was made up of many small pieces. The long and the short of it—and there was much of both in it—was that it was madly made.

The nearer they came, the steeper was the terrain. The Unkept women let their pace increase until, drawn by the ever-inward pull, they ran faster down the slopes into the only spot the land's shape would let them find—Chaundre's front portal. Kendric turned sideways to slow his progress and dug his boots in stubbornly against the land's grain and signaled Irissa to do so also.

"The slower I enter this madman's Keep and the faster I leave it, the better I will like it," he said. "This is what magic gone amok has wrought."

Irissa, stumbling alongside him, intent on keeping her feet

braced step by step on the falling-away ground, found breath to demur.

"Not magic, I tell you, but nature. All nature."

Whether driven by magic or natural laws of descent, they were both finally on level ground, standing with the Unkept women before a wide, low door hinged in iron. It did not open, which seemed but another manifestation of the contrary nature of the place.

"What do you seek?" a voice boomed out from somewhere, then awaited response.

"Knowledge," Irissa said.

"Egress," Kendric said.

"Chaundre," Amozel said, diplomatically omiting the "mad" that generally prefaced the name.

"She who seeks knowledge seeks Chaundre," the voice returned. "He who seeks egress often finds himself both coming and going. And Amozel and her women are always a welcome diversion to a lonely Keep. Enter."

The huge door swung wide, nearly sweeping some of the Unkept women off their feet, since they had paused in its path. No one stood behind it.

"Magic," Kendric bent down to whisper to Irissa. "I know how it is done. One thinks of the hinges moving, the force of something like a wind pushing the wood—"

Irissa shook her head. "Nothing we have yet seen is magic, including the opening of that door. Magic would not have brushed so rudely by the Unkept. Only nature is so indiscriminate." Despite her misgivings, she crossed the low threshold into a high-ceilinged hall. A great grid of iron lined one wall, and from behind it came a sound like the marriage between a squeak and a grind. Behind them, the wide door swung shut.

"Well? What do you think?" Chaundre himself popped through a low door halfway up the stone wall, to stand on a small balcony thrust out over the hall.

"We think we have traveled long and could do with less thinking and more hospitality," Amozel said pointedly.

"Of course." Chaundre vanished, only to enter the hall by another low door on ground level moments after. "Follow me."

They did, back through the door, up some narrow stone stairs, down a hall carpeted in heavy-woven rugs, through a thick stone door, down a flight of broad wooden steps, across a small hall, and finally into a middle-sized room with no roof. Above them, the ice-arch stretched like the spine of an invisible dome, and the Inlands moon shone down.

Kendric's first act was to unsling his longsword from his back and lay it across the nearest wooden dining table, the blade pulled out a bit from the makeshift scabbard to show a steely silver smile.

"Ah, beautiful." Chaundre went over to let his long fingers caress the hilt. "Torloc-made, of course—now." Irissa and Kendric exchanged startled glances upon hearing what was so familiar to them finally pronounced in this unfamiliar world. "But what fascinates me is what it was in its own world, when merely made of so much fire, steel, and finely forged edge. You use it two-handed?"

Kendric nodded. Now Chaundre had referred as casually to other worlds as he had mentioned Torlocs by their true name.

"And these runes on the sword? I imagine even you know not their meaning, swordbearer?" Kendric stared at the crude carvings Chaundre had exposed, dismayed that what he thought he had avoided appeared despite him, but shook his head. Chaundre sighed. "Often the way of it. What we are left with is legend . . . Why do not people see the sense of it and write these things down?" he burst out. His lean hand pushed off the hilt of Kendric's sword, as if dismissing it. "Now. You have come for a reason, for only the mad visit the mad without reason. So tell me yours."

"First we eat," Amozel said firmly.

Chaundre regarded her fully for the first time. "Regal Amozel, ever practical. I have no barter here for your women. My people are employed as usual about my Keep, and busy in their work and their own affairs. And I myself—"

"—should not be tempted by mere earthy matters," she finished, laughing. "We know well of your habits or lack of them. But our companions were minded to seek you out, and a visit to Chaundre's Keep is always interesting, at the least."

"*Mad* Chaundre's Keep," he corrected with a twinkle in his nearly black eyes. "You need not practice diplomacy in my Keep." He turned briskly to Kendric and Irissa. "Your names! You, who, after my own heart, seek knowledge—"

"Irissa."

"An apt name, for it begins with 'I,' and that is where all knowledge starts . . . And you, who seek only a way out—"

"Kendric."

"A noble name with knowledge in it, though it may not be apparent to everyone's ken . . . Remember, he who seeks for a doorway out of anywhere must also pass through a doorway *into* somewhere else."

"So I am discovering," Kendric answered.

"No better occupation, discovery. I have a few discoveries of my own I would share with you, if Amozel can contain her appetite . . ." Chaundre directed a quizzical look from under his bushy, dark eyebrows at the Unkept leader, but she maintained a moonlike calm, refusing to respond to the seeming raillery he plied her with.

"It is odd," Irissa told Kendric quietly, now that Chaundre's attention centered on Amozel, "but this Stonekeeper seems on friendly, almost equal terms with Amozel and the Unkept."

"I think it is his nature. He is the oddest Stonekeeper I have seen yet. Look, he's seating them around his table as if they were the finest Inlands' Lady Wards instead of rude wanderers—no wonder the others call the man mad!"

Chaundre, having ushered Amozel into a high-backed chair opposite his at the long trestle table, then waved Kendric and Irissa over to sit at the long, empty side across from the Unkept women.

Watching Chaundre order their repast was instructive in itself. He had a lean, slightly stooped frame, and though he looked just past first youth, he also seemed older in a way far from physical; perhaps it was the shrewd, unfocused intensity of his eyes or his air of always thinking of something else. His face and figure were not unprepossessing, but neither were they distinctive, and his nose was overlong.

At the moment, that less than lovely feature was buried deep in some fresh green and orange leaves the cook he had summoned had brought.

"Very fragrant. And you used the powder I gave you in the growing of this lot? Excellent. We will have them herbed. And for the main course—side of lorryk?" Chaundre's quick eyes caught Irissa's involuntary start. "I think not; surprise us with something less lovable."

"How did you know that the lorryk are dear to me?" Irissa demanded.

"I didn't. Until you just now told me. I saw that the word distressed you. By the way, those greens we saw, they're the root of the reason the other Stonekeepers call me mad. It was a matter of trade. I did not want Melinth's raucous birds in cages nor Ivrium's fleet bearing-beasts nor Sofistron's bevy 'broideries nor even Sofistron's fairest daughter." Here, the Unkept women's breaths drew in as one, but Amozel remained impassive. "I was considered mad to have rejected what passes for the choicest items of commerce in this place; in short, I was a poor bargainer, or so they thought."

"What *did* you want?" Kendric asked suspiciously.

"The leftovers of Ivrium's bearing-beasts and Sofistron's lorryk herds. It would have been a simple task to collect it, and I would have paid handsomely for it. I have no ranging herds of anything in my topsy-turvy lands." Chaundre sighed. "Instead, I am forced to have my own people collect it where and when they can."

"You wanted—" Kendric was so incredulous he couldn't bring himself to articulate his thoughts.

"Dung. Exactly."

"Why?" Irissa demanded.

"It makes my greens and oranges grow better."

"You practice an odd magic, that you rely upon such—homely—potions," Kendric said.

"But it is not magic, any more than it is magic that holds the Overstone above us night and day."

"Come, now," Kendric returned. "Why would anyone do anything so silly as grow greens in dung unless some magic spell or other required it?"

"Because he is mad," Chaundre retorted, his dark eyes twinkling with absolutely sane delight.

"You mean," Irissa asked as a servingman laid a simple pottery platter before her heaped with scented greens and herbs, "that *this* was grown in, in—oh, this is worse than the lorryk!" She pushed the plate across the wood with a distasteful shove.

"His means may be mad," Demimondana said, grinning

from across the table as she ate heartily of the green and orange herbs, "but the results are always delicious."

Chaundre beamed like a praised child and patted along his trailing tunic sleeves until he found a full pocket. From it he abstracted a bizarre object, which—after some fiddling—he balanced on the bridge of his nose.

"Quite mad," Kendric confirmed to Irissa.

"You must forgive my failing—my eyes, not my wits. I have never seen well. It is hereditary. After all, the first Chaundre was so wrong-sighted that as a mere babe he lost two fingertips before gaining his Stone from the meander." Chaundre waggled his own fingers in demonstration.

"But you have lost fingertips also. Are you the original Chaundre?" Irissa wondered.

"You do indeed seek knowledge. No, all of the original Chaundre's heirlings and their heirlings after must submit to a bit of unpleasantry with the ax upon being named One Son. Chaundre the First thought no one should wield his Stone with more fingers to do it with than he." Chaundre leaned across the table and pulled all their eyes into the midnight intensity of his own. "He was a bit mad, you know," he confided disarmingly.

Irissa reared back from the next platter the quiet servingman set before her. The food upon it wafted a strong and hearty scent, and thankfully did not resemble the flesh of any identifiable beast, but she paused.

Kendric leaned closer to her. "Eat it," he ordered gruffly. "I'll not care to spend another night hearing the growling of hunger at my ear. In the Rynth one eats what and when one can."

No such misgivings haunted the Unkept; to a woman, they drove their short knives into the dishes before them and gobbled down their portions with unladylike savor—all save Amozel, who wielded her knife fitfully and often went to the trouble of cutting off a dainty piece, only to sweep it about the platter in its sauce with the tip of her dagger. She appeared to be thinking.

"A taste for knowledge requires risk," Chaundre cajoled.

Irissa sighed and began eating.

Chaundre leaned forward, his elbows on the tabletop and his elongated sleeves trailing away from them like droopy wings.

With the contraption still balanced on his nose, he eyed Irissa remorselessly.

"Good," she finally conceded.

Chaundre laughed and swept his arms back from the table. "Then eat and enjoy, my guests, while I fetch some after-feast entertainment."

But Chaundre didn't wait for them to finish eating before he returned, arms overflowing with foolscap. He dumped the scrolls onto the table in front of him and began unrolling the stiff papers with his long fingers. The loss of a couple tips hardly affected his agility, but now that it had been noted, Irissa and Kendric could hardly keep their eyes from wandering to this deliberate mutilation, another indication of the dangerous side of both Inlands and Rynth.

"Now. You wondered about the door—don't deny it, you did. Here. This drawing shows the mechanism." Chaundre pushed an unrolled scroll under Kendric's nose, practically into his very platter. "There. You see the pulleys and the ropes within the walls? Six servingmen opened my door from a floor above and a room away."

Kendric frowned at the scrawlings across the thick paper and pushed it on to Irissa, who studied it with as little success. She shook her head in mystification. Kendric shrugged. "If the fellow is mad enough to claim such marvels as men opening a distant door and raising tasty food on dung, who wishes to be mad enough to spend one's life naysaying him?" He pushed the scroll back to Chaundre and told him heartily, "Most wondrous. I have never seen the like. And the meat is most palatable."

"Your condescension is not!" Chaundre swooped his scrolls into a bundle, lowered his sharp features, and then looked up after a moment, his composure resumed. "Perhaps my spells are too commonplace to interest such world travelers as the two of you. I had hoped that someone from another place . . ."

"Now, that *is* magic!" Kendric pounced so fast he spoke with his mouth half full. "How do you know that we come from another place? All the people here assume we're wanderers from some distant Keep."

"Know?" Chaundre sat despondently at the table, his long face cradled in his narrow hands, the scrolls mounding before

him like a pile of white bones he mourned. "That is my curse.
I know much that others care nothing about. I know how the
Overstone is held to the center of the sky, I know where the
ice-arch touches earth, the temperature of the ice in the Cincture, where the Torlocs go when they come, how to open a
door from a distance, how to predict the coming of the Rynx,
where the Stones came from, and how to grow the most succulent greens and oranges in the Inlands." Chaundre's melancholy catalog fell on indifferent ears with the Unkept. With
Irissa and Kendric, it widened their eyes and straightened their
spines.

"He *knows* what we need to know," Irissa whispered in
Kendric's ear.

"But he is mad."

"He's no magician, certainly, but even a non-magician may
be wise on occasion. Perhaps," Irissa finished with no great
confidence.

Chaundre's long face lightened a bit. He smiled palely at
Amozel; strangely enough, she smiled back. "At least *you*
appreciate my natural wonders, for there is no magic in it."

"No magic," she agreed.

Chaundre sighed and swept away the scrolls. He plucked
the appliance from his nose and offered it to Amozel. Her head
reared back, but he continued pushing it at her, and she finally
suffered it to be perched on her straight little nose.

A giggle started among the Unkept, but a quiet half-head-
turn from Amozel ended it.

Chaundre pushed one scroll to her. "You can see the fine
lines better wearing that thing. And no magic to it, but the
work of polishing the stones . . ."

Amozel's blond head shook slowly from side to side, and
the appliance fell off her face and into Chaundre's vigilant
fingers. "I see nothing better—or worse."

Chaundre frowned. "Perhaps it does not work the same for
all. You try, knowledge-seeker."

Under those terms, Irissa could hardly refuse and sat docile
while Chaundre attached the contraption to her nose. It was
like looking at the world through two great, clear tears. She
had not seen through tears since losing her capacity for them
to Sofistron's coldstone wall. But now she saw not only the

table and those seated at it but strange, misty shadows haunting the chamber's background. All women, all weeping women with a Torloc seeress' silver eyes... She turned to Kendric and saw him veiled in a haze of green, to Chaundre and saw him looking precisely as he had always looked. She thought she heard a distant wailing screech start up. She tore the thing from her eyes.

"I am sorry. It is painful?" Chaundre's dark eyes were all concern, magnified as he redonned his odd appliance.

"Painful? Yes. You said it was ground from stones—coldstones?"

"Commonstones," he corrected. "I was so pleased to have found a use for something so useless, but like all my creations, it appears to be flawed."

"There are other things you can show us," Amozel said confidently. Her words were an odd mixture of both command and consolation.

Chaundre nodded consideringly. "Other things, yes. All unmade by magic, or, rather, made by me." He straightened, and the slight stoop that had seemed to cloak him vanished. It was not age so much as his eagerness to be ahead of himself that bent him early. He went from the room on a sprightly step and left those behind to contemplate their host.

"He does not seem *very* mad," Irissa said.

"And he has a nice disrespect for magic. I find that refreshing," Kendric pointed out.

Amozel smiled, a tight, bitter smile that reminded Kendric and Irissa of the fowlen head hood she wore ceremonially. "He has disrespect for things other than magic," she noted.

"Yes." Irissa looked speculatively at the woman. "Did he not say that he had refused a daughter of Sofistron's?"

Amozel's hand waved her silent. "You have traveled long with us and taken us for what we are. There are few in the Inlands or Rynth who extend us that courtesy. Chaundre is such a one also. Yet—he was tardy about beginning a bevy upon becoming One Son, too busy playing with his polished stones and orangery gardens, no doubt. My father Sofistron sought to spur the process. Besides, he wanted Chaundre to employ the Drawstone to bring gemstones leaping out of the earth for him. He offered *me* as the foundation to Chaundre's bevy, in exchange for the use of the Stone. I was considered a prize, since even Sofistron admitted I had the heart of an heirling. Chaundre refused. Then, for me, who had been highly esteemed, nothing remained but to be sent to the bevy of some insignificant Stonekeeper like Reygand—or worse, to the Shunned One himself. I chose the Rynth."

"And chose well," Kendric said gruffly. "You are a queen of the Rynth, as Gryff said."

Amozel's lips twitched self-mockingly. "Bluntly said, giant, and with a heart as huge as your size behind it."

Irissa was silent. She had always felt the loss of her magic the greatest ill that could befall her and had believed that an unempowered seeress was worthless. Yet Amozel's very nature had been her betrayer. She had lost nothing, because she had never had anything. And Irissa began to see that perhaps that was even worse.

Chaundre returned into their silence, his lean cheeks slightly flushed, making his eyes seem blacker by contrast. "Here. A natural wonder." He seemed to be speaking to all of them, but he looked only at Amozel.

He held a bow in his hand, a very long bow, perhaps as long as Amozel. Such length dwarfed the bows the Unkept carried.

"Bonewood," Kendric said, as if hailing an old friend.

"Bonewood! Yes." Chaundre's truncated forefinger speared at Kendric. "You are right. The thickest bonewood ever found in the Rynth. I wrestled it free myself."

"You?"

Chaundre turned back to Amozel. "I am stronger than I look, particularly when there is something that I prize in question. A full half-day it took to wrest this long branch from the tree. And a full year in carving—by my hand and no magic." He raised the hand in question as if tendering an oath.

"Carving?" Amozel asked sharply. Chaundre tilted the bow toward her in answer. Her fingers began tracing the intricate bas-reliefs that ran the length of the bow. "Lorryk! And lemurai. And fowlen. The Rynth. The Stonekeeps. It is all here. I have never seen a man-made thing so fair." Amozel's small hands were running possessively up and down the mighty bow, her face finally fallen into the simple wonder of a child. And the heart of that wonder unfolded to reveal an unconsidered covetousness. Amozel wanted the bow; she would have the bow.

Chaundre's lean hand tilted it back toward himself. "I would bargain for this bow."

Her eyes were dazzled by the wonder of the bow; when they reluctantly tore themselves from it to Chaundre's face, they were as soft and unfocused a brown as his had appeared—only now Chaundre's eyes had sharpened into the direct, brutal gaze of the trader.

"You?" The softness in Amozel's eyes widened, pooled, met adamant, and sharpened in turn. She set her hands before her on the table, and as they had caressed the bow, they smoothed the wood of the table, over and over. Her back was bow-straight, her face impassive, and the wings of waving yellow hair that edged that face seemed carved of amber. Nothing on her moved but her lips. "Very well. Bargain we shall. One night is sufficient?"

"Of course."

Amozel's eyebrows lifted. She thought Chaundre sold his bow cheaply; but being a bargainer of long standing, she knew no reason not to humor an unreasonable man.

"You have no special requests?"

"Only that I may choose my partner."

Amozel's eyes flashed to Demimondana, softened a bit into a knowingness it was not nice to witness, then came coldly back to Chaundre. "Granted. The bow." Her small hands shot out for it, held open and waiting, and only someone very near could see that they trembled a bit.

Chaundre withheld the bow. His eyes focused very hard into Amozel's. Across the table, Irissa audibly caught her breath. She saw it coming and gripped Kendric's arm in warning.

"Yourself," Chaundre said.

There was silence so deep in the room it seemed to smother everyone. The Unkept women froze, as Kendric and Irissa had already frozen, as if mirroring the calculated stillness of Chaundre. Demimondana's eyes flashed an instant's disbelief. But all their mutual shock ran as if down an incline and settled in Amozel's face.

"I? I—am—not—to be—bargained for. I am Amozel and

I . . ." Even as she spoke, one hand clutched spasmodically at the bow.

"Amozel has bargained," Chaundre said relentlessly. It was a wonder to believe that any of them had ever thought him mad or had ever seen him melancholy. He was a man of one purpose, and that purpose swayed before him as if spellbound. "Would Amozel turn her back on her word?"

"It is not custom. It is unwritten—"

"I wish to rewrite what is unwritten."

"It is—trickery!"

"But it is not magic."

Amozel's fingers yearned for the bow. They fanned and reached for it even while her face still reflected her reluctance. Chaundre held it tantalizingly near, but slightly out of reach.

"No magic in it?" she demanded.

"No magic. And this. An archer's ring." Chaundre peeled a plain stone band from one of his narrow fingers and thrust it toward Amozel. The stone was shaded blue and glowed.

Her head turned from it. "Magic?"

"Natural stone, worn smooth. There is no magic in anything I offer, Amozel. It's true I am a Stonekeeper, but I am a man first."

Amozel paused, straightening even more, though that seemed impossible. A flash of humor lightened her dark eyes for a moment. "We shall see," she said, extending her hand. Chaundre's ring was upon the second finger of her right hand; the bow tilted toward her palm like a scepter bestowing an honor. She wrapped her fingers around it and took it. Chaundre reached for and was accorded her left hand. They turned and left the roofless chamber, Amozel using the bow like a staff.

No one moved in their wake. The Unkept women were frozen and speechless to see their leader walk in their footsteps. Demimondana wept. Irissa and Kendric sat as immobile, her hand still clawing warning into his forearm.

"I suppose," Kendric finally said sourly, "we shall have to see to our own accommodations for the night."

Irissa sighed deeply and buried her face in the tough linen weave of his sleeve. Kendric covered her hand with his own and said nothing more.

Chapter Twenty

Chaundre's upper chambers were as jumbled as his rooms below. Kendric and Irissa climbed stairs both crooked and straight—and stairs that were a bit of both. They peered into an echoing stone room and, on moving to the next doorway, found themselves facing a cozy chamber large enough to accommodate little more than a cat.

There seemed no purpose to any of it. A room that housed a promising testered bed was neighbor to one that contained a large table and stools, as if for dining, and no other nearby bedchamber could be found.

"You rest here," Kendric finally decided. "I'll keep hunting for another."

Irissa, looking pale and fatigued, vacillated on the indicated threshold. "You may not find anything else, including your way back here."

Kendric shrugged, despite the weight of his longsword once again over his back. It accompanied him to bed as faithfully as a wife; perhaps more so. "It should be an entertaining search. And I think Chaundre will not let those who came here with Amozel remain lost in his Keep for long."

"What of the Unkept?" The leaderless women, utterly non-plussed for the first time in their lives, had refused to leave the dining chamber until Amozel's return. They now sat along the room's hard stone verge under the eye of the ever-vigilant moon—awake and on watch.

"I don't know," he said. "It's their business if they wish to pillow their backs on stone, but—"

Irissa stepped inward to put a hand on his arm, whispering into the deserted spaces of the lofty passage. "Kendric, I think—I feel—that something very amazing, something portentous,

193

has happened here this night. Something that shakes the foundations of this world, though I cannot precisely say why or how."

He nodded worriedly. "I know. I feel the same—that by going against their natures, Chaundre and Amozel have forged a new nature. But I agree with you, Torloc. It is not magic."

"Chaundre's natural magic, then?"

Kendric looked down into Irissa's smiling gray eyes. He was growing used to their ordinary hue and thought he almost preferred it, though he knew it marked a deep personal loss. Certainly she seemed safer this way, and he was not so confident of his own vaunted powers that he didn't see the advantage to having her as a guide to his magic while deprived of her own. There was less chance for contention.

"No magic is natural," Kendric said finally. "But if time and travel reveal no way of restoring yours, we can always resort to our old method of transmittal. You are more than welcome to mine."

Irissa snatched her hand from his arm as if seared; the black of her pupils swelled to meet the silver edges. "I will serve as the vessel of no man's pity. I would live a thousand years without my magic rather than spend one night with a man unwilling, who tends his body as merely a means to an end—"

"Yet they who call themselves the Unkept women do so frequently and count themselves freer for it. For were the Unkept truly willing to make unions of the flesh, they would not put a price on it. But you see how it is with us, Irissa? You say I feel the burden of your magic now. Do you feel the burden of my innocence? I thought an extraordinary woman had come to my bed for ordinary reasons, there in Geronfrey's under-mountain stronghold. But it was only a Torloc seeress in need of a safe vessel in which to store her magic from another's covetousness."

"But I *am* my magic—or was. That was the horror of Geronfrey's ambitions. My magic I could defend. Myself—I could not. I came to you in the dark of that night because I did not wish to be an untried Torloc seeress whose maidenhead was the prize of every sorcerer who sought a taste of her powers, but an ordinary woman who chose an ordinary man for ordinary reasons, as you thought. I—I would have chosen you later as well as sooner—"

"But you were *not* ordinary," Kendric said bitterly. "And now I am not, either. And we can never deal together as ordinary man and woman, for how do I know if you come to me again that it isn't to regain what you once gave to me and have since lost? And how shall you know that I do not court you because the man of Rule wishes to unburden himself of the powers you unwittingly gave him?"

"That would be no use, because I know you are not virgin." A demure twinkle animated Irissa's quenched dark eyes. "Therefore, as before, only my motives are suspect. And are you not used to pursuing women trying to entoil you? What of the sorceress Mauvedona? She had no powers to pass on with her body, yet still she seem inclined to yours." Irissa smoothed her long white hands along the worn fabric of Kendric's tunic and tilted her dark head at him with a mock-Mauvedona seductiveness.

He brushed her hands away and made an exasperated explosion of breath.

"You have learned to argue like an ordinary woman, Torloc, without words and too subtly for me. We will get your cursed magic back, by means that do not compromise either one of us. And I swear that you are more dangerous unempowered than empowered, after all!"

He left her without a token "Good night" and stalked down the hall, his boots making enough noise to wake whoever wanted waking. He resolved that he was not about to lay himself down to sleep in the face of an absent host without first ascertaining the character of where he slept—and he had much more of Chaundre's rambling Keep to explore. Perhaps enough to occupy him all night, even if he found another empty bedchamber. Or one not empty. That unwelcome thought stopped him as the passage took a sharp right turn. He paused and looked back. Irissa still stood at the chamber door, her gray clothes blending into the stone walls, her hair long and dark against the vivid blue vest the Unkept had given her. She was watching—or waiting—and in either case, Kendric felt it was better to be far away before he made a fool of himself again.

* * *

He awoke, angry at himself for having slept, angrier still for having finally chosen so hard a place to do it on. He awoke, as he had at first on opening his eyes to this world, feeling disoriented and bruised. He awoke only to find the moon's empty eye on him, glowing milky as if it had a cataract like an old cat's, and a daylight sky over him. He had the uncomfortable feeling that his dreams had been naming him a fool and that he had heard the howling thing again and followed it, only to have it turn on him in some dark cul-de-sac, wearing his face.

He sat up, cracked his elbow on the flagstones, and cursed.

A titter came from behind him. Above him, Demimondana sat upon a bench and watched him. "At least we know where *you* sleep," she noted ironically.

"They have not returned?"

She shook her flame-rinsed hair and chewed on a stale breakfast muffin from their lean packs. "Amozel has never drunk barrenberry wine," she noted mournfully. "There was never any need. I do not know what will come of this."

Kendric pushed his great length off the floor and lowered it gingerly onto the bench beside Demimondana. The other Unkept women still kept vigil at the room's rim. He looked around further.

"*None* of them have returned?"

"It appears we *all* have been abandoned," Demimondana answered calmly.

Kendric rose, stretched until he felt his spine snap, picked up the sword from the floor, and laid it on the empty tabletop. "It is a maddeningly constructed place. I'll find her." He took a few steps and stopped. "Irissa, that is. You'll have to look for Amozel yourselves."

The women were unresponsive, and Kendric felt a bit sorry for them. It was an enormous rent in their scheme of things to have their leader turn suddenly on her nature and become a bevywoman to some Stonekeeper. Or had she done so? Wasn't it merely one more transaction, worth violating custom for the getting of something as rare as Chaundre's hand-carved bow? But even as he thought that, he rejected it. Irissa, he had a feeling, would tell him that much more than a bow had exchanged hands last night, and he was tired of thinking about grand-sounding predictions that read more than there was into the simplest act . . .

He climbed the half-straight, half-crooked stairs again, missing his sword but sure he wouldn't need it. Chaundre's mind was occupied with subjects other than that of martial arts, and the man was mad in addition and likely to be as harmless as he seemed.

Kendric prowled the empty passages, feeling lost. He could not find Irissa's chamber again, but he did find a well-timbered door he had not noticed before. It was low of lintel, and he would have to stoop to enter it, but he was feeling cross-grained this morning and was hungry besides. He hunched his way through onto the landing of a spiral stone staircase that seemed to rise as infinitely as it plunged into darkness. He began twining his way upward, his arms brushing the walls in the dark, his large feet sometimes slipping off the steps' narrow inner portion. Why he went up instead of down he didn't know, save that some instinct— No! Torloc seeresses had instincts! He had his own natural way of working things out logically.

Voices sounded above, light women's voices. Kendric pushed his feet faster up the treacherous triangles of stair, his boot toes stubbing on every riser. There was no sure safety in these Inlands, and even a mad magician might work ill.

Bright white daylight poured like a fountain down the last of the tightly wound stairs.

The women's voices above cooed with unfeigned naturalness. Kendric thrust his head up past the last step into a small, round, roofless chamber with a huge table at its center, and around it sat Irissa, Amozel, and Chaundre.

It was a good thing he had not brought the sword; its length would have long since wedged crosswise in the twisting stairwell. But he still had his hands and his strength and *her* magic if he had to use it and—

But nothing very ominous was happening. The women were sitting, their chins resting on their elbows, watching Chaundre. He, as usual, was behaving madly. He had a stone, doubtless his Stone, on the table before him and was picking up nails with it. He moved the stone nearer a pile of what were likely nails meant to shoe Ivrium's bearing-beasts; a black spike flew into the air and clove to the stone. It seemed a small trick and hardly enough to entertain one of Irissa's sophistication. And Amozel would not tolerate even minor magic in her presence—unless the man had totally enchanted both women.

Kendric reflected that, if he wished to challenge an Inlands Stonekeeper, he would have to rely on magic. And he knew next to nothing about it. Still, if the situation were dire enough, a man could but try.

Kendric cleared his throat to announce his presence. Amozel noticed him first. She turned, her hair falling to either side of her face, and trained clear brown eyes on him. There was not the slightest trace of the habitual expression that made her Amozel—no severity, no queenliness, no iron. She looked like a girl of sixteen, on whom the world seldom laid any expression but expectation. Kendric glanced to Irissa, who had let his presence dawn only distantly on her awareness. Even now she was turning her face over the tresses-draped darkness of her shoulder, and Kendric was finding himself becoming very anxious to see it.

Unlike Amozel, she looked utterly the same, perhaps a bit better rested. And her eyes, half-abstracted, still sparkled with an expression he had not ever seen her wear in the Inlands, save for the few moments when she had told him of the rising of the lorryk stag. It was complete, self-forgotten happiness.

"Enchanter!" Kendric challenged Chaundre, who had not yet bothered to raise his head. "What have you done?"

"Ah, Kendric . . . Oh. I see. We—I—forgot you and the others. No food appeared, I suppose? We had quite overlooked our appetites."

He lowered his long nose back to his work of making nails dance across the table to the stone.

"What magic is this?" Kendric demanded, referring to the engrossed women.

"My Stone," Chaundre said, beaming but not raising his eyes. He paused to cradle an oval rock of no dominant color in the palm of his hand. "My Drawstone."

"Magic indeed to draw the fangs of a proud Unkept and turn a Torloc seeress into docile audience with the demonstration of a few dancing nails."

"Kendric." Irissa finally looked at him, her face still serene with wonder. "Don't you see? It isn't magic. It's some natural property of the stone—"

"Nonsense! Nails don't jump unbidden from one spot to the other—and stones can't make them do so without some spell in them. And what are you doing up here with this, this . . . seducer of Unkept women?"

Chaundre laughed and Amozel blushed. Amozel blushed? Kendric had not been long in this world, but he felt his grip on what he believed solid of it loosening. Much more mystery and he would be as dizzyingly disoriented as within the gate that would not accept him. Magic that was not magic. A hard and dangerous wild woman blushed like a bride. And Irissa was utterly forgetful of him—or herself, rapt in some nails that behaved as if infected by an itch . . .

"Look, Kendric." Chaundre came around the table, the Stone in the curve of his palm. "Hold a nail. Here. Hold it." Chaundre pressed a single nail between Kendric's reluctant fingers until only the head showed. He held his Stone at arm's length. Nothing happened. Chaundre moved the Stone nearer the nail. Nothing. "You see, no magic, but the same that accounts for Amozel's about-face—the draw of . . . affinity!" On the last word Chaundre brought the Stone within a foot of the nail.

Kendric felt the nail drawn like a thorn from his flesh, felt the metal warm between his fingers as it pulled inexorably through his tightening grip to the Stone and stuck there. "The magic is in the nails, then?"

"No magic," Chaundre insisted, looking as self-satisfied as an owl. "Better than magic, in that this is predictable." He slapped the nail back into Kendric's fingers and brought the Stone to it from afar again. Once more, within a foot of contact, the nail quivered in Kendric's fingers and lunged out of them to cling to the Stone with a small, metallic smirk.

Kendric rubbed his irritated fingertips together.

"There's no abating nature, my friend," Chaundre said, smiling.

"Can I do it?" Amozel asked.

Kendric and Irissa stared at Amozel, but Chaundre offered her the nail. She kept one small hand extended for the Stone. Chaundre paused and weighed it in his hand. "There is magic in it," he warned her. "It was used to erect this Keep, to do all a Stonekeeper would wish it to. It is merely that it has a natural side—" There was something of the old Amozel in her regal silence, in her refusal to have her motives questioned.

Chaundre looked sheepish for having withheld the Stone and dropped it into her hand. The heft weighed it down; Kendric braced himself for the visible abhorrence she had shown to the Torloc tear that had fallen from his purse. It never came.

"I am a magician's daughter," Amozel said, calmly placing the nail on the table and measuredly bringing the Stone nearer. "My loathing of magic grew from my own choice, for I had never seen that it gave a woman anything but grief. In that it was like a man. Although it is possible that I shall have to change my opinion of both . . ." As the Stone neared the predictable distance, the nail made its initial quivers, then rolled speedily across the wooden planks to unite with it. "Ah!" Amozel dropped the Stone and clapped her hands like a delighted child. "No wonder you magicians kept the Stones to yourselves; this magic is easy."

Chaundre smiled his relief and sat, tucking his hands into his long sleeves.

Irissa reached for the Stone. "Can I—?"

Kendric could not have refused such wistfulness, but Chaundre suddenly looked Amozel-stern. "No. She has never known magic and draws out only the Stone's natural qualities. But you have wielded magic—much of it—and the Stone would respond to that in you. And only a Stonekeeper may touch his own Stone." Chaundre plucked it off the table. "This was merely a demonstration to show Amozel that there can be wonders that are not intrinsically magical."

"I do not see how Amozel can have handled it safely, for even the touch of a Torloc tear pained her," Kendric pointed out.

"A Torloc tear? What Torloc tear?" Irissa demanded. "I have been unable to shed tears of any sort since the raising of the lorryk and my time in Sofistron's coldstone chamber."

Now it was Kendric's turn to look sheepish. He fished the thing from his boarskin purse—not an easy trick, for it seemed to roll into every corner to elude his fingertips. But finally he was able to pinch it between thumb and forefinger and elevate it for their inspection.

"It was coldstone-clear when I first found it at my feet after the gate had closed, but since then it seems to have changed."

It was true. The small stone glimmered more silver than crystal, and even as Kendric's fingers pressed it, it slid into an oval, flattened further, and would have dripped from his grasp had he not hastily put his large palm under it. The stone oozed into a thread, grew pregnant with the weight of itself, trembled like a teardrop, then plopped across Kendric's palm, where it lay in a quivering silver puddle.

Irissa stood—more slowly than seemed possible—and stared into the quiescent silver with her now-gray eyes. The silver still ringing her pupils appeared to pulse for a moment.

"*My* tear? You horde *my* tear?"

"It was merely a keepsake. A talisman, I suppose. The only thing of Rule or you that I found when I was expelled from the gate. I did not mean to deprive you of it. It has no worth but in memory."

Chaundre was standing, too, leaning across the table, his hands spread to support his weight, his long nose very near to Kendric's palm, and his black eyes glittering with magicianly interest.

"A Quickstone!" he breathed. "The Inlands have never seen the like. Think what it could do. A Quickstone!"

"It is as I told you, Kendric," Amozel said from where she sat, keeping a distance from Kendric's stone as if she feared getting too near and being drawn to it like one of Chaundre's dancing nails. "With your own Stone, you could claim Rynth land and erect your own Stonekeep. There is always room for another man of power in the Inlands."

"But not a woman!" Irissa's eyes flashed. "And you would erect your powers on the last remnant of mine. It is ever the way of mortals, to take what is precious to a Torloc and turn it to some tawdry ambition—"

Kendric's fist and jaw clenched in unison. With his fingers shut upon the molten silver in his hand, it seemed the light within the chamber had dimmed, despite its openness to the sky. "I do not *want* to found a Stonekeep. I do not *want* your magic or any other's. And I would not have even a single tear of yours, did they not so conveniently freeze into solid form and had you not tricked me through a gate not meant for me. Here!"

He thrust out his fist and unfolded the fingers one by one. "It is yours. Take it. If it holds power, perhaps it will restore yours. I do not need any more than those you have bequeathed me."

Irissa's accusing eyes calmed and she threw a length of heavy dark hair behind each shoulder, drew in a deep breath, leaned nearer this transformed part of herself, and carefully raised a hand.

"Ah—" Chaundre half-grunted a warning.

Irissa ignored him and stretched a thumb and forefinger for the thing. Kendric's palm still shook slightly from his angry denial, and the Quickstone shivered upon it in unison. Irissa glanced to Kendric's eyes, remembering then that they had taken root within her own in the quest for the center of a thing that was a peculiarly Torloc trait. She had been wrong to charge Kendric with avarice for anything; it was not his nature. But to see a part of oneself, of a fragmented and bereft self, in the casual possession of another . . .

She reached nearer, feeling an icy heat emanating from her one-time tear. She was appalled by the greed she felt for this thing and by the calculated care with which she would reclaim it, as if expecting it to disown her if it could speak. Her fingertips were almost upon the argent Stone that shone as if all the silver distilled from her magical vision had gathered there. She felt that she dared not breathe, pause, or think. She touched it. Ice ran from her forefinger straight to her heart and through her legs and feet to the ground. She reared away from the Stone as if burned, but yet would have reached for it again. Kendric caught her hand in the iron encompass of his own and held it prisoner but inches away from her desire. His narrowed amber eyes were as adamant as iron. She looked to Chaundre, but knew she would find the same judgment.

She had never seen Chaundre's dark eyes as sober or as sad.

"It is yours, but it is no longer of you," he said. "It has shaped itself to Kendric's particular powers and will tolerate no other owner. I do not know its properties and I doubt that he does. Had you not been separated from your own sorrow, perhaps this one surviving tear would have become a talisman for you. But it is his, because he found it."

"I shed it!"

"It often happens that our own grief takes root and blossoms in another's garden, in ordinary as well as magical matters. Take comfort, Torloc, for your kind has come here before. Some say they came to find wisdom, but it is my observation that the empowered travel so far and so dangerously only to find more power. I think you can yet restore yourself—without tears or stones. I think the path that the seeresses of your kind have taken before can still lead you to a conclusion you can bear better. And I know that I can help you on that quest. And Kendric, if he will."

"I will," Kendric said shortly. "For her charge is true; all that I have, whether I value it or not, was once hers."

Chaundre's face broke into the gentle glow that made him almost handsome. He reached for Amozel's hand and shook it happily. "Then, my friends, you have but to perform one small quest for me, and I can send you on your way to a place that may solve all your problems."

"Quest?" Kendric asked alertly.

"Sit, my friend. And you, seeress. I think you have touched more of yourself than is wise."

Irissa let her shaking knees collapse suddenly until she was seated again on the simple wooden bench where but moments ago she had been diverted by the cavorting of Chaundre's Stone. Now she had seen a Stone of her own making, and it was not for her. Beside her, Kendric allowed his vigilance to fold itself into a seated position. The stool creaked mightily under his weight but held.

"Tell us straight," Kendric instructed, folding his arms on the table as if listening to a slightly larcenous offer being extended across a tavern tabletop.

Chaundre sighed. "Where to begin? Perhaps by telling you, Amozel, that, though I desire another Stone of power, it is not for magical reasons, but to continue . . . extend . . . my exploration of natural wonders."

"I find I do not so loathe magic in the right hands," she answered. "Perhaps even in my own."

"Magic is a dog that will always bite its owner," Irissa

cautioned. "And the loss of it makes one most vulnerable to its blackest aspects. Or to one's own."

Kendric, who had discreetly tucked the controversial Quick-stone back into the sheltering boarhide, shifted on his stool. "It is not so great a flaw to desire that whatever comes easily to others should come as docilely to oneself. I long resented my fellow Wrathmen's easy command of magical talismans while I had none, though I never coveted one; I think I scorn what magic clings to me now because it was another's and came to me not of itself. And that is perhaps overprideful."

No one disagreed, and Kendric squirmed again at such un-challenged acceptance of his confession. "So where do we go? A quest always involves a journey—and that as far and un-pleasant as possible."

"Not too far or unpleasant, I trust. I wish you to obtain the mate—and opposite—of my Drawstone. The Shunstone."

"The Shunstone? That which Fanis Sisterslayer took?" Irissa was indignant.

"And why not? It did not come to him and his heirlings by right, but by wrong. And murderous wrong, at that. But I do not want it for reasons of justice, but for curiosity only, I admit. With the Shunstone and the Drawstone together, I might solve the riddle of the Rynx, prove how the ice-arch holds the Over-stone up, even find a gate—"

"A Torloc gate?"

Chaundre's dark eyes looked directly into Irissa's gray ones. "A Torloc gate," he confirmed. "There must be another; though the seeresses come through the Inlands, they do not return."

"How far is this Fanis' Keep?" Kendric still sounded skep-tical.

Chaundre's long hands spread disarmingly. "Not too far."

"Did not the rim-runners say in the Stonelore that the Draw-stone and the Shunstone kept to opposite ends of the Inlands?" Kendric was frowning now and looming very large over the table. Chaundre cleared his throat, momentarily speechless.

"Chaundre is being optimistic, as is his nature and as I can testify to," Amozel said with a stern smile reminiscent of her Unkept self. "Fanis' Keep stands where you say, Kendric, but you are a man of mighty strength, and Chaundre does not ask more than you can venture."

"Then if it is so far, Irissa can stay here—"

"No. If I am indeed worth so little unmagicked that I would be of no use on such a quest, there is no point in making it. I will seek no gate; and should it spring up before me, I would not take it."

"I meant only to spare you," Kendric began.

"As well consign me to a bevy and be done with it."

"If there is a Torloc gate, it is now mine to take as well as yours. And this time no Eldress shall challenge my right to take it. And if I find it and take it, I shall invite you through, and pity take them who would bar either of us. So, if you insist on making another long march through the cursed Rynth, you are welcome to join me, useful or not. I have grown used to your company."

Chaundre was unwilling to let their discussion take any volatile turns and inserted his demands into it. "You agree, then, the two of you, to seek and bring back the Shunstone? I would seek for it myself, but a Stonekeeper cannot rob another of his Stone. That is the condition of our order and why peace obtains between the Keeps."

"I agree," Kendric said.

"We agree," Irissa said.

Chaundre smiled and reached for Amozel's hand again, which she was most uncharacteristically docile about extending. "Then I think we had better cease our demonstrations and prepare you for your journey—and also ensure that there is some food and libation below." He looked at Amozel. "I think your Unkept women grow hungry."

"And I as well," Kendric noted pointedly. "If I'm going to march the length of the Rynth, it might as well be on a full stomach."

Chapter Twenty-one

◆◆◆

Demimondana and the Unkept accompanied Kendric and Irissa to the edge of the Rynth. If the first leg of their journey—climbing out of the downward spiral that formed Chaundre's Keeplands—was any indication of the remainder, their way would be arduous indeed.

Kendric said as much to Irissa.

She, however, had begun the trek with the nimble gait and lofty spirits of a rock ram, having resolved that if she could offer no talents within the magical realm, she would be of no trouble whatsoever in any aspect of the physical realm.

"We have brought you a gift," Demimondana said at the Unkept's farewell. She took a bulky, wrapped object from one of the women and extended it to Irissa.

Its shape and weight were unmistakable; Irissa pulled away the fabric to unveil a scabbarded sword and leather belt.

"That was offered once from a rim-runner who had raided a Keep. We prefer our bows and daggers in the Rynth," Demimondana explained. "But you are questing to the Keep of the Shunned One himself, the Sisterslayer, and it is well you go equipped to slay in turn."

"Oh, I do not think it will come to that," Irissa demurred even while buckling the sword around her waist.

Kendric's comment was more sound than word, but took issue with her optimism.

"Thank you," Irissa told the women, touched at getting something gratis from those who lived every aspect of their lives in hardheaded trade. She sensed their confusion, their disorientation at Amozel's puzzling about-face, their utter lack of direction. "And you stay here?"

They stirred in concert, their rude clothing chafing against itself like an uneasy whisper. As usual, it was their spokes-woman who answered.

"We stay. Awhile. Amozel, like you, insists she is not kept, though she keeps company with Chaundre." Demimon-dana's light green eyes grew troubled. "It is unsettling, this defection of Amozel. She has become like you, a woman be-tween kinds, who cleaves to one unlike herself. Chaundre is hospitable. But we will not stay long under these circumstances. We wish to be beholden to no one man's hospitality, and there is always the Rynth. Besides, I owe Gryff four more nights for the fowlen hood. Amozel has given it to me."

"As you have given me the sword," Irissa said. "I wish I could offer you something in return."

"Between women, there is no need of trade," Demimondana declared. "Good journey to you and your giant. May the fowlen keep from your footsteps and the meanders always run free of fleshfins to your mouth."

On such formalistic good wishes for protection from dire afflictions, Irissa and Kendric began walking into the Rynth.

"I am not used to a sword at my side," Irissa said after some minutes. "It is more likely to trip me and bruise me than defend me. And my mind-forged short sword in Rule was lighter."

"Bear this one awhile," Kendric suggested, tapping the sling he wore.

"No, I well know how heavy it must weigh." She gave him an amused glance. "You could have conjured it to its shape of old, but lighter, you know. Save you are so literal—"

"Its weight is what makes it the weapon it is and works with me on the downstroke, which is the critical one. I've no wish to wield a five-foot-long needle."

Irissa sighed. "Well, I've a wish. I've been thinking it since we began pulling ourselves out of the funnel that Chaundre calls his Keeplands."

Kendric stopped. "Does your wish wear legs?"

"Many legs," Irissa answered solemnly. "And yet it goes as one."

He gestured to the horizon. "I believe your wish is riddle and it has found you."

The Rynth was gray and flat. On its farthest visible edge, an agitation of black flyspots buzzed toward them. They waited, watching while the apparition slowly swelled into the shape of their expectation.

"The lorryk dislike the Rynth," Irissa objected, with still a hopeful note in her voice. "Demimondana told me once that it was an act against their nature to carry us to the rim-runner camp, that they cross the Rynth at its narrowest points only to emigrate into another sphere."

"They've come through a length of Rynth to reach us here," he pointed out. "Perhaps your wish drew them."

She watched the dark mass separate into dots as it swept on, finally detecting Bounder's bonewood diadem rising above the black wave like a many-pronged lance and seeing the flash of pale, almost silver hooves. The oncoming thunder of those hooves thrummed toward them, until the stones under their boots seemed to throb with it. Irissa felt her heart quickening to the rhythmic beat of the lorryk's advance, as if she were part of the herd, were running with it, her hair whipping behind her, her knees clamped to Lithe's rough, heaving sides, and her fingers clenched in the thick, coarse hair of a lorryk ruff. Kendric felt it, too, beastrider that he was. Irissa glanced up at his impassive face and saw that his jaw had tensed with excitement at the sight, no matter how laconically he hailed it.

Yet he could never feel what she felt toward and with the herd. For a moment, her unfettered magic and their mute, animal oneness had met and blended into an event that astounded belief—had merged into the recalling of the dead stag who even now played crest to the oncoming lorryk tide. She watched Bounder's familiar conformation grow in her sight with emotions impossible to name. She was both chooser and chosen; the beast was her creature and she was its, as it was both herd leader and of the herd. She knew the pride of the maker and the humility of one who remained to be yet fully made.

The gentle Rynthian moon waxed Bounder's diadem opaline as he abruptly slowed to a walk. The herd, like a wide black train, swirled to a stop behind him. His eyes stared with an animal's aloof recognition into Irissa's as his massive hooves minced precisely over the broken shale toward them. He came and stopped before Irissa, waiting. Beside him, a lorryk Irissa somehow knew was Lithe brushed a burnished black side against the unacknowledging stag.

"I take it we have transportation." Kendric's comment did not quite break the spell between Irissa and the lorryk; the thrust of the littlest lorryk's familiarly cold nose into her palm did.

She looked down to find it at her hip again—at her stomach, actually, for it had grown since she saw it last, its forehead blaze turning more silver than plain pewter, its narrow legs straighter and stronger. She patted its neck absently.

"I wonder if they will be willing to carry us as far as the Keep of the Shunstone. From Chaundre's maps, that was the length of the Rynth, even beyond Sofistron's Keep." Her speculation went unanswered, except by the unblinking regard of Bounder and the other lorryk.

"How did they come to us—or you, rather?" Kendric asked. "I still do not believe in wishes, even when I see them walking."

"I think . . ." Irissa patted the little lorryk on the withers and walked over to touch Lithe on the forehead. The doe lowered her head in recognition and nudged Bounder's shoulder with her nose. The stag finally turned his horn-crowned head to favor Kendric with a grudging regard. The lorryk's loyalty, extraordinarily extended, encompassed only one mortal; Kendric shared in it on sufferance.

"I've ridden smoother-gaited mounts," he announced to no one in particular, but simply to make his position clear. He would not refuse the service of four feet in place of his own two, but he was no more eager for this alliance than the untamed lorryk stag. Yet Bounder was the only lorryk large enough to carry him, so they both would have to bear the chafe of union their mutual uncommon size had laid upon them.

Bounder looked back to Irissa, his duty of acknowledging his rider's existence done.

"You still don't explain how they came," Kendric persisted. "They are not creatures of magic, despite your intervention; and besides, you have no magic strong enough to call them."

She sighed. "I think that Bounder brought them."

"Of course he brought them!"

"No. I mean the—original—Bounder, who spoke to us in Sofistron's hall. He said that the residue of what magic I worked there in the meadow took refuge in the head, since a living Bounder, to be true to his kind, could not harbor so much magic. I think the head that hangs in Sofistron's hall hears much of what happens in the Inlands—and knows much of me beyond natural means. I wished for the herd, and the head heard and sent them. But if they've been drawn here by magical means, rest easy that from now on they will serve us quite naturally and quit our services with little real regret."

"Then if we have mounts, we ride," Kendric said trenchantly, moving to give Irissa a leg up on Lithe's narrow-spined back. He looked Bounder in the one glowing eye, then crimped his fingers into the stag's full ruff and pulled himself up behind the beast's withers. "Do they know where we go?"

Irissa smiled as she curled her own fingers into the familiar nap of Lithe's ruff. "I think we shall soon find out."

The lorryk tensed as soon as the two were installed upon their mounts. Bounder wheeled so suddenly that Kendric's long, back-hung blade slapped his rider in the calf; then the stag sprang back across the same Rynth ground he had just traveled. The herd curved itself into a comma as it followed him in a fluid stream of close-packed black bodies and darted for the distance ever opening up before it.

The lorryk took them back the way they had traveled to Chaundre's Keep. At first it was an unremitting landscape of Rynth they transversed, so that the bone-jarring passage seemed endless and featureless to Irissa and Kendric.

But soon the Rynth took one of its abrupt plunges into a totally different sphere as the lorryk pounded over the stones and onto the watery lowlands of Lacustrine.

"Marshes," Kendric shouted disparagingly over the plash of hooves striking water.

"Not so. The ground beneath is rock-firm," Irissa returned. "How deep do you think it gets?"

"Not deep. The lorryk seem to know their way, and thank the Overstone for it, as Ivrium would say, for we have no method of guiding their course. Magic-spawned means seem imprecise by nature—" He stopped shouting as one of Bounder's particularly spirited leaps sent spray crashing over Kendric from forehead to knees.

Around them, water spewed up in dozens of hoof-made

geysers, but still the lorryk did not slow their pace. Lacustrine's distant, magic-made fountains performed their acrobatic leaps skyward without the benefit of the watching wonder of Kendric and Irissa; the riders were the center of a waterworks of their own, and soon the water around them was churned into a head-high, lacy mist that surrounded them as persistently as fog and made it impossible to see even their own mounts' heads, much less each other.

Their passage through the waters seemed endless; although the lorryk never sank deeper than hock-high, the unchanging drone of the herd's lake-muted hooves and the rhythmic pelt of waterdrops on the faces of Kendric and Irissa soon numbed the riders into a weariness they knew they shared without having to see each other.

Then, without a warning change of pace, lorryk hooves were beating on dry land, the Inlands' moon bloomed into view overhead like a sky-hung flower, and gray Rynth unrolled past the lorryk's muscle-roiled shoulders.

Irissa saw Kendric, as grim-faced as the beastrider called Death, his dark hair slick about his ears. Her own had separated into long, water-heavy ropes that bounced about her shoulders, lashing drops of icy water into her eyes and mouth. The lorryk themselves shone like ebony satin, but the hair deep within their ruffs, where Irissa's and Kendric's fingers anchored, was dry.

Soon they were drying all over, the wind of their passage combing their hairs separate again. The lorryk lengthened stride and leaned into their fleet, forward progress. Irissa and Kendric found their teeth chattering, their clothes lying heavy and damp upon them, and their weariness seeping through their bones like rust through unpolished steel. The lorryk pulsed on through the Rynth in a solid wave of flesh, bone, and speed.

They never seemed to touch hooves to Rynthian stone longer than they could help it, though. With another dizzying flash through the invisible limits of yet another Stonekeep, the herd pounded onto the dune-rippled landscape of Ivrium's red desert. Soon their riders were powdered with a fine miasma of sand, and the herd's own coats were dulled with carmine dust.

And so the journey went—longer and at greater speed than Irissa and Kendric had dreamed could be maintained naturally, through every Stonekeep land the length of the Inlands between Chaundre's remote Keep and the equally remote Keep of the holder of the dreaded Shunstone.

"Quest," Kendric shouted once over the drum of lorryk hooves. "A small distance. For a simple Stone. Lucky transportation. Magic!"

Every word was an accusation, but Irissa read good humor in the tone, too, and a warrior's resignation to unexpected hardships. She herself felt as if every bone in her body had been carved into dice and then ungently shaken in the sack of her skin until time itself had grown weary of marking the distinction between now and forever.

When the golden meadows of Sofistron's Keep rose in an amber ripple before her, she didn't even respond to their familiar beauty or to the fact that she had first seen them—and this Inlands world—as a seeress of power. Then they were racing along the great forest's edge and she saw the moon-white promontories of Sofistron's turreted Keep out of her eye's edge—perhaps out of the slender silver rim at her eye's edge—and remembered the icy-walled ring of mirror that had driven her back from her magical self. She shuddered finally at the cold touch of that memory on her mind. Coldstone or commonstone—whatever world one wandered or whatever they called it in that world—it seemed only to do her harm, the chill white stone the earth made in its depths and that she mined deep within the well of her Torloc tears...

She heard a familiar sound then, a lilting, mellow note struck over the meadows, and remembered its source too late. A half-dozen long-armed dark forms were dropping out of the pine branches above them, falling onto lorryk backs and riders indiscriminately. Such a one landed facing Irissa, its taloned, leathery fingers rolling into the fabric of her tunic and its fanged, pink mouth a foul-scented cave of carnivore yearning.

She screamed in disgust, then remembered Demimondana's sword at her side. One hand must cling to the lorryk ruff, no matter what. But the other—she drew the sword and slashed sideways, an awkward thrust in close quarters. The blade took its first blood, and the lemurai grunted in pain as a line of red opened up just beneath the gaily embroidered leather vest it wore about its stringy shoulders. Irissa struck again, with the sword point, not its edge, though it was overlong to use as a dagger. The lemurai screeched rage as her steel pricked. It jumped up and down on Lithe's withers, black-clawed toes digging into the doe's shoulder fat. There was a sudden buck Irissa was unprepared for. The lemurai hung for a moment in only air. With the point of her blade, Irissa pushed into its stomach, hoping to sweep it aside. A dark, hairy hand tipped in bloody claws clenched her sword arm. She felt the sting of its possession burn her skin and heard the fine, worm-woven silk shred hissingly. Her sword drove forward, more push than pierce, but suddenly the lemurai was draped over the length of the blade and sucked behind her. Its hand was the last to vanish, tightening spasmodically on her flesh and raking away in five separate furrows of fire. The pain ran down to her fingertips; she almost lost her grip on the hilt, but the next sensation of pain was sharper, and her hold tightened in mindless response.

Irissa looked around. The lorryk had veered from the treacherous forest edge, but many backs were still burdened with the lightweight but clinging lemurai. Kendric had somehow unfastened his longsword and was using it lancelike to unseat lemurai from neighboring lorryk, knocking them off like a knight in a macabre joust. Once ground-bound, the vicious hounds of Sofistron were game for the unimpeded hooves of the charging lorryk. Kendric's clothes ran red with the parallel tracks of lemurai claws, and Bounder's shoulder was soaked crimson-black. Most of the lemurai had fallen behind, and the lorryk kept up their unshaken pace. Irissa twisted on Lithe's back and sought anxiously among the press of black bodies swaying beside her. There! The little one was still with them, the stretch of its neck and head protruding past a lorryk's chest point. Somehow, she had thought the lemurai might attack the smallest one in force—and with the most success.

The lorryk did not slow, despite the length of the journey, until they were in open Rynth again.

"I never thought I would so welcome the sight of so much nothingness," Kendric said heartily. He finally relaxed his grip on Bounder now that the great beast walked and reinstalled the sword on his back, after carefully wiping the blade across his trousers fabric.

Irissa eyed the addition of a new red trail to his aspect with
distress, even though it was likely lemurai blood. Her own
sword hung uncleaned in the scabbard at her side, but when
they dismounted, she would find some long grasses... In the
barren Rynth? she asked herself dubiously. Kendric the practical had once again taken the most obvious, if distasteful,
course.

Bounder now ambled at the head of the herd as if merely
minded to take a stroll. Yet his coat was sweat-darkened, as
were those of all the lorryk, and Lithe's winded sides heaved
bellowlike between Irissa's knees. The doe managed to quicken
pace enough to join Bounder, as if she somehow sensed it was
necessary for Kendric and Irissa to converse.

He began by frowning at her tattered sleeve. "You tire of
wearing plain gray and must have a gaudier design?"

"Mere scratches," she said, ignoring a burning throb along
her forearm. "Your Rulian blue runs more crimson than my
gray."

"*Lemurai* blood, not mine. Though one dug its evil, thorned
feet into Bounder before I dispatched it." Here, Kendric patted
the massive black shoulder under him, a gesture Bounder endured without change of pace or notice.

"Lithe seems all right. And the little one—I saw it somewhere in the herd."

"You're certain your arm—"

"Nothing," she insisted, waving the arm in question as if
to discount it. "Surely *you* have endured a prick or two in your
adventures; may I not be afforded some scars of my own? It
seems this is all that is left to me," she added a bit bitterly.
"Scars and honorable bleeding."

"There is no honor in bleeding," Kendric said, "except in
legends, and they have the advantage of being long distant and
likely false."

"Yet it is better than weeping."

He shrugged, then winced.

"I thought you said it was all *lemurai* blood." She had
detected the wince.

Kendric grinned. "Hard to tell sometimes, in the heat of
battle. Whosever's crimson we wear, we are fortunate to have
come through Sofistron's Keeplands so unscathed, and I am

pleased to have accounted for the end of a few more of his filthy lemurai."

"The lorryk seemed to relish having them underfoot more than on their backs," Irissa noted. "I must say I don't fancy them as riding companions."

"Well, we're past them, and past most of the Inlands' length, I think. Fanis' Keep must be near. We should have no more trouble until we confront the reasons why he is called the Shunned One. And then the lemurai may look lovable by comparison."

Irissa shuddered, remembering the nightmarish face perched in front of her own only minutes before. "Never," she said.

Kendric started to shrug again, thought better of it, and went so far as to urge Bounder on with his boot heels. The stag appeared not to notice the indignity, but picked up his pace; soon the herd was trotting past the last golden swell of Sofistron's lands, fully absorbed into the Rynth's harsh monotone landscape.

After the brush with the lemurai, the lorryk no longer seemed to spurn this desolation. They walked now, weariness evident only in that their pace was so sedate for a herd not grazing. The littlest one came to Lithe's side, its delicate muzzle lifted to sniff inquiringly at Irissa's boot toe.

"You scent the earth of many spheres," she told it, laughing, "some of which you would not love at all, like Chaundre's sinkhole of a Keep. It is lucky you need not accompany us past the border of Fanis' lands—"

The small lorryk wrinkled its silver-napped muzzle then and sneezed.

"You think they really take us there?" Kendric inquired. "We never told them where we went."

"If they came without calling, they will take us without telling," she answered.

"The magic of the lorryk."

"Not magic, but a knowing deeper than magic . . . Oh, you do not understand."

"No. That is the pity of all of it."

Had they been riding domesticated bearing-beasts, it would have been possible for Kendric to have spurred his mount on at this point, or for Irissa to have pulled back subtly on the reins and let him ride ahead. Instead, they were caught in the uncontrollable pace of the lorryk, Lithe and Bounder walking side by side for now and bringing Kendric and Irissa face to face with what they perhaps would avoid—each other.

"Understand?" Kendric repeated her word. "Do you understand this?" With an adept twist, he unanchored the sword from his back and spun it over his head. He laid it across his thighs as he rode, his hands spread along its naked length, and Lithe swept wide to give it room. "You say I do not understand your magic—and mine. But what do you know of unmagical things? This is my implement, as magic is yours. It is a heavy burden to carry, to wield. It—or its original—was given me, as mine, when I was fourteen and the men of the marshes decided I was as likely to grow tall enough to bear it as any marshland lad. Thus I was sent to the City of Rule to claim my role—and my sword.

"It is easier to understand than magic. Sometimes it seems to weigh like the world. By carrying it, I call no man friend but foe. It delivers death and defense. The rim-runners talk of make- and break-magic. I may have rebuilt it from make-magic, but break-magic was ever its strength. With one blow—when I am properly standing to give full thrust to it—I could sever Bounder's head from his shoulders and undo all your Torloc seerery and sorcery. I know every notch upon the metal, every head accounted to its toll. We have wept and bled together, this sword and I, and yet I would have left it gladly in Rule to rust in Rindell lake. It is visible and looks no more magical than mortal blood and muscle can make metal, and whatever magic it once bore or I put into it by calling it back to my service, it is still at bottom only a sword, only a weapon pure and simple, and that is what makes it most magical of all. Do you understand this?"

"Weapons I understand, and blood and tears. But the romance of the weapon—" Irissa shook her dark head mutely, at a loss even to put into words what eluded her. "That is where we differ. To me, the magic within it makes it more than a sword; to you, it makes it less of a sword, as if its capacity to inflict hurt is diminished by its being other than a simple cutting edge."

Kendric ran his palm along the pitted steel that his memory

and some unwanted wellspring of magic had restored to him. "I like it better without mummery being whispered over it, without powers being ascribed to it, when it stands as what it is."

"You glory in it," Irissa accused. "In the simple brute force of it—"

"Yes! When I raise my hand against another, I know it. This heavy weight of steel tells my every muscle so. Yet you would use a sword and lighten it with your look, as you once did, to wield it as easily as a wand—and there would be nothing to tell you when you wrought power and how well or ill you used it but yourself. You sorcerers risk nothing," he added contemptuously.

Irissa rode in silence. Lithe so perfectly paced Bounder that Irissa and Kendric remained opposite each other, relentlessly yoked by their mounts into a conversation Irissa began to regret.

"I am a seeress," she finally said. "If I do not see true to the nature of a thing before altering it or let another see ill through my eyes, the consequences will turn upon me as sharply as any sword. I lost my vision so once, for a while . . . It is true that when power is internal rather than external, it is more difficult to measure, perhaps even more easy to abuse, but—"

"You do not understand simple brute force," Kendric finished, cheerful once again at having found a way to turn her argument back on herself. "If you did, you would not call it simple. Let us resolve, then, that I will cleave to my brute steel and you will remain master of complex subtleties like magic."

"It is not possible," she objected. "For now, like it or not, you bear the best of both."

"You have a sword." He pointed to Demimondana's gift hanging at her side.

"A mere stinger," she said, dismissing it.

Kendric's dark eyebrows arched. "Ah, not simple and brutish enough for you?"

"Apparently the exercise of magic is too complex for you," she shot back.

He laughed, a laugh so deep and easy that the lorryk picked up their hooves and capered a bit to the ring of it. "And so we go 'round and 'round. Well, I will say this: a journey with a Torloc seeress, powered or unempowered, is never dull."

"And your wit, Sir Wrathman, is as sharp as your blade," she returned demurely under lowered eyelashes.

Kendric's fingers drummed along the naked steel; it had not tasted a whetstone in some time, as Irissa well knew, but it was as effective at crushing as at cutting. "One would think that with all the various and talented Stones in these Inlands, an ordinary whetstone would be easy to acquire," he grumbled aloud.

"Perhaps Fanis' infamous Shunstone will sharpen all our weapons—internal or external."

Kendric hefted the sword back into position on his shoulder, being careful not to prod Bounder with the point. "Fanis is undoubtably some mousy little fellow as eager to see our backs as we would be to see his. These outcasts are always exaggerated into monsters by the public repute, until a flea can cast the shadow of an empress falgon. And even if he is as fearsome as folk would have us think, you and I have faced worse in Rule than anything this puny world can offer. Besides," he finished, grinning and flexing his lemurai-scratched hands, "I could use some more simple, brutish exercise."

Chapter Twenty-two

Night came to the Rynth, as it always did, in the lowering of various shades of violet over the horizon ahead. Soon the Overstone was glimmering softly in a dark heliotrope sky and tinting the lorryk blazes quicksilver-bright.

The herd still walked, or ambled, rather. It was as if the entire party had been wearied into a mood that mimicked content. Irissa and Kendric had not debated the merits of magic versus might for hours; when their glances crossed, they smiled. The small lorryk now stayed close to Lithe's side, its long legs easily keeping up with the strolling herd.

No one, apparently, was in any hurry to get to Fanis' Keep.

"Listen." Kendric held up his hand, whitewashed by the moonlight of all its battle scratches. Even the lorryk pricked their ears at his command.

"What?" Irissa asked. "I hear nothing."

"Nothing?" Kendric's face wore trouble as a floor might wear a wrinkled rug. "I could swear I had heard it again—that soulless distant cry."

"But this is the other end of the Rynth, of the Inlands."

"Perhaps it is in all places equally . . . or perhaps it echoes off the Overstone," he added lightly. "Or perhaps I am hearing things."

"You? Who know what you see so adamantly? Yet Torloc seeresses are reputed to possess sharp ears, from a lifetime of having to look to the edges of things—and I hear nothing." Irissa absently massaged her lemurai-clawed forearm. She could feel the skin drawing taut over the wounds, the first sign of healing, but the area still burned. Kendric would have asked about her arm if he had noticed the gesture, but he was too busy squinting into the hyacinth horizon and listening for the return of the spectral shriek that still rang, dimly, in his ears.

It was while they rode on through the Rynth, lulled and weary, man, woman, and beasts, that the Overstone spawned a sudden clot of white shadow on the gray ground. Like liquid the pale shadow flowed, quick and quiet, and like some milky stream, forked into two branches that curved wide and apart and then swung back to meet each other. They made a circle at last, and in that circle's center walked the lorryk with Kendric and Irissa on their backs.

"You hear nothing yet?" Kendric demanded, even as Irissa's moon-white face frowned.

"No . . . But I *see* something. A flash of white, beyond you."

"No. It is beyond *you*. There!"

The white foamed up like a wave and rushed inward. Harsh screeches ripped the air into tatters around them. The lorryk bolted in one tardy mass, Bounder nearly unseating Kendric. The oncoming white licked the beasts' heels and rose up to their bellies. A new shriek, wild and shrill, echoed in the Rynth. Somehow Irissa knew it for the cry of a mortally wounded lorryk.

The lorryk wheeled with their uncanny speed and darted in another direction, but the white wave was there also; Irissa saw a feathery, snowlike spray at her boot heel and drew the blade she had dismissed a few hours earlier. The metal glittered with her motion, where the dried blood had not dimmed it.

But the attackers were not swayed by the brandishing of swords or the slice of hooves in a mad, many-legged foray. The lorryk twisted and ran, dodged and bucked, nickered and screamed, always in an ever-tighter circle, against an ever-higher-leaping flurry of white.

"Dismount!" Kendric's voice sounded strained but imperative.

Irissa let her uncertain purchase on Lithe's back take its natural course and slid her legs to the ground. Her fingers were still curled in the lorryk's ruff, but in moments Lithe's frantic lurchings broke them loose. The doe was gone, but other lorryk roiled around Irissa, the nick of a flying hoof constant on her legs and feet. Kendric came shoving his way through the panicked animals, the hilt of his sword still riding above his shoulder.

"What is it?" she asked.

"Fowlen," he answered grimly, overseeing the chaos from his great height. "There's a rock face yonder, if we can fight our way to it."

Irissa turned immediately, still facing into milling lorryk, and met dark eyes rolled back to white and saw flared nostrils and heads thrown back contortedly. With the press of Kendric's bulk behind her, there was nothing to do but press forward. The lorryk always gave ahead of her, unaware of who or what she was, but yielding to any force in their frantic attempt at escape.

"Now!" Kendric thrust Irissa hard against the stone, glanced approvingly to her drawn sword, then unleashed his own from his back. He had room to wield it finally, for the lorryk flowed away from such natural obstacles as rock, and there was a clearing before Kendric.

In it, the lorryk wheeled, Bounder's big head lowered and breaking the wave of attacking fowlen into individual members with one mighty toss of his diadem after another. Still the fowlen came on. Irissa saw them clearly now, thickly furred, lean, white bodies surmounted by feather-maned heads that reminded her inescapably of Amozel. They were the size of the littlest lorryk; Irissa could not comprehend their faces. She saw only great, round, staring eyes and the dark below them of a ferocious black maw, like a beak. Those beaks tore lorryk hide, and the half-strangled squeals that came from these normally mute animals in their terror sent Irissa's free hand to her ear. This was one cry of agony she could hear.

Kendric had waded back into the fray, ignoring the danger of kicks from the wild-eyed herd. He grasped his sword two-handed and swung it in a huge circle before him. It sliced into the white wave and the fowlen ebbed. They flowed inward again, but Kendric brought the huge sword curving around from the opposite direction, and they kept themselves ever dancing near the point of it. He moved constantly so no ring could close on him, yet the fowlen encircled him, as if recognizing the sword as a thing to be surmounted before they could claim their true prey.

Irissa was horribly reminded of the struggle she had seen from a distance in Sofistron's meadow, of the dark navel that was Bounder surrounded by the hungry, milling hounds of the Keep. Kendric used his longsword like a club—to drive them off, not to kill them; they were too numerous. He drove them back into a semicircle, herded them, actually, with the ponderous, rhythmic swipe of his blade and his inexorable press forward.

Around the edges of the battle, the lorryk slipped into a single-file stream and leaped away, in moments becoming one with the dark ground of the Rynth.

Irissa clung to the rock face behind her. Her dainty sword was useless against such large creatures as the fowlen, as Kendric would be the first to tell her. To interject herself into the battle would only distract him. And magic—that internal well of wonder that had gone utterly dry on her—was no longer hers with which to help Kendric, who thought that magic rode on mounts as primitive as wishes. If wish alone would make magic mind, she would have commanded a mountain of it at that moment. But she had none, and Kendric was too raw at the use of his own to rely upon it on the spur of this or any other moment.

Yet he was doing well without it, Irissa saw. His sword rose and fell with superhuman regularity. From time to time, a fowlen came flying off the end of it, howling rage, and the pack had backed off enough to let the lorryk escape. Kendric unexpectedly waded deep into their center and sliced around him in a savage circle. Fowlen fur and feathers flew. A lucky blow among the agitated pack brought one fowlen head lifted high above its shoulders; it hung suspended in the air for the veriest moment, it seemed, before falling back to earth, trailing a comet tail of red blood.

The fowlen ebbed abruptly out of sight, leaving one headless carcass crumpled at Kendric's feet.

He finally let the sword find ground, like a needle its magnet, and rested the great weight there a moment. Then he turned and came lumbering back to Irissa, as if each step were hard enough to be his last.

"You drove them off."

"Brute force has its uses," he said, wiping his brow on his sleeve and leaving a red trail across it.

"And you've freed the lorryk."

"Not all of them."

She glanced around and saw that what she had taken to be an island of low gray rock was the prone belly of a doe. A smaller island lay beside it.

"The little one!" She rushed over to kneel by the beast. The piquant head lifted, and a silver muzzle rested on her knee. "It's still alive."

"Not this one." Kendric stood, grim as death, above the doe's motionless body. Not Lithe, Irissa noted with guilty relief.

"But this one is all right. It doesn't seem to bleed. It could rejoin the herd . . ."

"Not with that leg." Kendric pointed wearily with the bloody tip of his sword, and Irissa resentfully followed his gesture with her eyes to see what she didn't want to see—a long, delicate leg, twisted grotesquely.

"It's only broken."

"The lorryk live by their legs."

"But only a broken leg— It's fine otherwise." The head stirred in her lap as if in agreement.

Kendric made a motion then, short, abrupt, and somehow violent. They looked up at him, over the body of the dead doe, the limpid eyes of the lorryk and Irissa's dark-pupiled ones rimmed in silver.

He cleared his throat. "We've got to move on. The fowlen are likely to return; the loss of one, even so spectacularly, is not enough to stop the many. There's enough here to keep them—busy—until we're far enough away to be safe from further attack."

Irissa looked incredulously around the sterile landscape; above her, the Overstone shone undimmed and illuminated her every feature. Kendric winced.

"Leave the lorryk? Alone and alive? For those beaks to come tearing—?"

"Not—alive." The sword, balanced on its point, stirred.

"No! I tire of your 'nots.' 'Not possible, not practical, not—anything.' It is *not* always necessary to kill to solve an impasse. There is the other side of it."

"Other side?" Kendric stiffened. "You mean magic. Nothing else challenges fate."

"You could . . ."

"No! We have no time to risk in saving ourselves. The beast is dazed and broken; it would not even feel the end—"

"But *I* would." Irissa gathered the lorryk's shoulders into her arms, its forebody more fully onto her lap. "I would do it myself, if I could. A broken leg is but a trifle to straighten, no more than a snapped thread in a tapestry."

"A thread has undone a warrior before now, if the right one snaps."

Irissa had never seen Kendric look so forbidding, so implacable. He glared down at her in the uncertain light of the moon, shadows painting his features heavy and unrelenting. She felt she beseeched a statue. Her wounded arm throbbed with the pressure the lorryk put upon it, but she did not slacken her grip on its panting body. She had no power to move Kendric but persuasion, and that was as trifling as a thread, too. She was not used to pleading.

"Kendric. It would not take long."

"For you!"

"I could not rest safe elsewhere, knowing we had not tried."

"But *I* must try. Alone, unguided."

"You are a warrior. You do much alone."

"I do not—meddle—with what-must-be."

"And I would tell you how."

"The fowlen would return for the telling and wolf us both down along with the lorryk."

"I—I will stand guard while you . . . work."

"You!"

"I will hold your sword. It seemed to discourage them."

Kendric laughed, a harsh sound that made the little lorryk shiver in Irissa's arms. "Keeping it slashing through air and hide discouraged them. If you can wield my sword, I would believe that I could mend flesh and bone."

Irissa let the lorryk slide off her lap and stood. "Then give it me."

He held it balanced on its point, the hilt before his chest. He released it suddenly to let it fall, and it fell toward Irissa. Her hands reached out for it and grasped the massive hilt. Already the weight was pulling it past her; only by bracing her body did she halt its heavy progress. She balanced it, too, finding that relieved her of the already obvious burden of it; the hilt reached high enough to brush her cheekbone. But he had not expected her to manage even so much as holding it. He looked down at the fallen lorryk, and his swordless hands made an awkward, half-formed gesture.

"I do not know what to do," he confessed.

"Nor I. We shall simply have to tell each other."

She sounded relieved and enthusiastic; Kendric didn't have the heart to tell her he held out no more hope for them now than he did for the disabled lorryk. A gallant last stand, ending in death and devouring. "Take the sword," he told her, "and stand by yon fowlen body. Then it is only a matter of slicing at every fowlen that ventures near."

"And you must look upon the lorryk leg and see it straight and sound. There is not much to its legs, not much to rejoin . . ."

Kendric's laugh was short and more denial than agreement. He watched to see her take the sword. She slowly backed away from it, letting it tip more horizontal than vertical, until her hands tightened on the leather-bound hilt and she raised it from the ground for perhaps a foot. Her shoulders tautened with the strain, but she backed away from Kendric and turned, almost dragging the sword with her. She took her post above the fowlen carcass that lay dead white on the stones.

Kendric sighed and looked down again to the lorryk at his feet. He squatted beside it and studied the twisted leg. A Torloc seeress might trust to magic in restoring shattered bone, but he preferred a natural edge. His big hands reached out to wrench the fractured leg back into normal position. The creature was too shocked to do more than whimper, and Kendric confronted the leg more hopefully. Cure it. Fix it. Will it well again. Kendric felt foolish, and more than that, in danger of paying dearly for this foolishness.

Irissa had said that he did not understand the ways of magic, and he would be the first to admit so. Nor did he always understand the ways of women, though he knew that Irissa's adamant defense of the lorryk was more than mere feminine sentimentality. She had been linked with the lorryk since her arrival in this world. In some way, her sense of self-worth in survival depended on helping this lorryk now. Kendric could understand standing by a fallen comrade, even when the attempt was doomed, but that was the loyalty between man and man in a common cause, not between man and beast who shared nothing but the same earth and sky and overarching moon . . .

Look it well? He smelled doom in it, knew it was beyond him. He was a render, not a mender; he had spent his life learning to hack things apart with dispatch. How was he of all people to restore?

He glanced up. Irissa stood in the moonlight, her back to him, vigilant at the agreed-upon guard duty, the sword still in her hands but its length resting on the ground before her. Kendric knew the heft of that sword, knew the sound of his bone and muscle cracking as he made a pass with it when he was exhausted beyond the making of all blows. But even then he would strike again. And again. And yet again. Surely a bit of mental stitching of lorryk hide could not be so difficult, he told himself. He was a bad liar, but a good judge of lies.

Irissa for her part faced the limitless gray night. She glanced up at the Overstone. It was an impartial observer, and she guessed it wished as well to fowlen as to lorryk or Torloc. Perhaps Kendric was wrong, and the fowlen would leave them alone now. She stood above the bloody trophy of his prowess, reluctant but knowing it was necessary. And she would show no fear if they came; it was said that wild things scented fear. But likely they would not come, and Kendric would soon have restored the little lorryk and—

"They come," she announced. She had not meant her voice to range into that higher register.

"Then you must hold them off," Kendric said flatly behind her. She dared not turn to measure his progress, for the first white froth of fowlen head had risen over some distant, low stones. Total darkness never reigned in the Rynth, thanks to the Overstone's constant shimmer, but the night was dim enough for the distant eyes to reflect back a gemlike gleam of pure, carnivore red.

The first fowlen slunk over the rock, its lupine body seeming to slither over the rough surface as smoothly as a snake's. Its head was kept level and staring toward Irissa, the huge, round eyes never blinking, the profile of two erect ear tufts making it appear horned, its expression amid the regal ruff of feathers both beautiful and terrible.

Irissa licked her lips, already long since dry, and tightened her grip on the sword hilt. Her palms were wet, and she could scent her sweat mingling with that which already seasoned the leather. She kept her eyes as steadily on the fowlen as it fixed her with its gaze, and she wondered if her eyes gleamed any threatening undercolor, though once their surface silver would have been enough to outlook any alien creature . . .

Without preamble, the fowlen began trotting toward her. Its gait so much resembled that of a large and friendly dog that for a moment she almost felt toward it as to a beloved pet. But the dark claws clicked on the rocks and the feral head remained expressionlessly avid. Irissa elevated the sword a foot or two. The fowlen stopped and watched her gravely. Lifting the sword had been a mistake; her shoulders shook with the effort and she let the point droop back to ground, hoping the motion looked deliberate, like a relaxing of guard since the fowlen had halted. And the creature did not come farther, but sat on its snowy white haunches and cocked the terrible face in its feathered setting.

No fugitive light reflected a nighttime color in the eyes still round and unblinking. She finally perceived them as a bright, burning blue, gemstone-pure, with black, star-shaped pupils. Irissa had never possessed or worn jewels or desired to. The eyes of the fowlen made her aware of the pull of such things. She envisioned a necklace of such glittering, lethal beauty, a ring... She relaxed enough to let her eyes wander from the burning gaze she both feared and coveted in a most uncharacteristic way. Beyond the dead and the living fowlen, two more raised their heads over the rocks, watching. They slowly parted and walked around the low barrier. Onward they came, till they stopped behind the first fowlen and sat, watching with their azure eyes and waiting. Irissa was no tactician, but she saw that the fowlen formed a wedge and that, if she were to strike at the first, she would miss the second and third behind it; if she were to avoid the first and strike the second or third, it would not matter much, once the first beak met her flesh.

The desire to shout over her shoulder to ask Kendric how he fared with the lorryk was so strong her head began turning that way, even though her eyes remained forward and fastened on the trio of fowlen confronting her. She knew that if Kendric were free to talk or take notice of whether fowlen of any feather came or went, he would have done so already. So she held her tongue and cursed her nature and stood still and ready to wield the sword.

Kendric had given up squatting and sat, his legs folded under him like a child. He supposed he looked ridiculous, but for the moment that didn't trouble him. In his hands he held the delicate turn of lorryk leg. It was as gracefully modeled as a weaver's spindle. Kendric's eyes couldn't help but appreciate the dainty strength he held in his hands. Yet he could crush it with one wrenching gesture; he knew that as he knew the exact exertion of his own strength it would take to accomplish that. Now it seemed all that he knew was worthless, and what he did not know—the limits and the use and the ways of the power he had inherited inadvertently from Irissa—was what he must depend upon.

Every time he had exercised his unbidden magic, the results had been flawed. There was no room for flaws in the imperious natural shape of a lorryk leg, no room for weakness. If he would restore it, he must restore it perfectly, as surely, swiftly, and delicately as he would sever a limb from a trunk with his sword. And he must accomplish this as a near-blind man moving foggily through some terrain utterly alien to him.

He almost thought to pause and hail Irissa, to take the sword she so ludicrously clung to and tell her to spend the last silver of her eyes, that tiny rind of power he had once seen within her and that the world could still see surrounding her irises, on the lorryk she would have him save. And he would have his sword back and would slice and hack and slay until the fowlen piled chest-high around him and all would be right with the world—as he saw it.

It was no longer enough to rely upon the powers he knew so well, those of might, main, and mayhem. Like it or not, he knew he bore other powers now, as fragile in their way as a lorryk leg and as strong as anything natural to that which claimed it. He had made the dagger grow a longer fang in the lemurai pit to protect himself. He had made flame leap between his fingers to cook the food the Unkept would have had themselves consume raw. He had made the rain run yellow on their heads to startle them and prove to Irissa that he was not such a fool as she thought. Yet each of these acts welled from an impulse of the unmagicked Kendric. He knew self-protection, he knew an empty belly hungry for edible fare, and he knew the temptation to vain display of old. What it took to heal a mute thing's broken leg he did not know. He did not understand. .

Behind him, there came the grating scrape of steel on rock, and he knew that Irissa brought the heavy blade around to lift it and strike at attacking fowlen. Kendric the Wrathman would have sprung to his feet and reclaimed the sword and slain fowlen by the score and saved the woman from her folly. Kendric who had magic could not afford to worry about that now. Irissa had chosen the sword, and he could not release her from it until he had released the lorryk from the trap of its leg and himself from the silent, deadly struggle he had always waged against the magic within him.

The sword rang on rock, again and again. Kendric the Wrathman would have cringed at the unhoning of good metal that clumsy handling made. Kendric the swordsman would have felt the effort of every raising of the sword, the relief when each fading blow was allowed to fall impotent to the ground.

Kendric who had no imagination would even have speculated at how many fowlen came, and how close, and if the sword sometimes nicked their feathers or fur.

Kendric who had magic had no intentions but doubt, no duty but the mending of the limb in his hands, no fear but that it should remain broken. See it sound, she had said. See it. But to see it, he must wish it, and wish was the most chimerical of things. Or did to see it mean to see the lorryk whole, as a thing that was beyond the shape and surface of it? Kendric looked into the liquid, frozen dark eyes. The lorryk was a gentle, graceful thing, and there had been little in Kendric's life that was that. It was a beast with four legs, and he had ridden such. They had served him well; he had felt a fond regard for some of similar kind, and the sweep of any fleet, four-legged thing had always stirred something deep within him that was not magic, but something like it.

The lorryk lifted its head to look into his eyes and suddenly rested its head on the crook of his arm.

He dared not move. He was close, so close to it—as close as to the final, killing blow in a duel, which one must dance near to for fear it will elude one. The same skills, but opposite, she had said. Kendric heard a nearing birdlike chatter, raucous and threatening, but ignored it, as he ignored the scrape of metal on rock, rhythmically lethargic.

The same strength, the same delicacy, but woven from the will to preserve, not destroy. Kendric looked at the torn lorryk hide and saw the splinter of bone below, the tear of muscle and vein. He saw beyond that to the pain and the fear and the frightful thing it was to be a fleet creature and to have no legs to depend upon. He saw these things part before his eyes, as a series of veils, and beyond each veil was another and another. And his eyes would not stop until they had lightly brushed by all of the veils and until all that they saw was lorryk and life. The veils wafted shut as he withdrew, healed and sealing.

The lorryk raised its head from his arm. Then all of its limbs were flailing. It awkwardly levered its narrow body to its feet, until it looked as if it stood on four splayed stilts. Kendric laughed and caught it around the middle and hoisted it erect. It paused for the moment before flight, and he had time to shout over his shoulder, "Wield your blade hard, Torloc swordswoman, for your lorryk has new wings and would fly!"

It was going already, the white of its upraised tail and fleeing hocks kissing the night a hundred quick farewells. Kendric did not take his eyes off the faint, pale zigzag it made across the Rynth until he could no longer see it. Behind him, the blade scraped madly as if admonishing a whetstone, and the sound finally ran a shudder along his spine. He rose and turned.

Irissa was nearer than she should be, the dead fowlen now ebbed well past its kind. The fowlen regrouped and came on in a blue-fire-eyed pack, their owlish heads lowered so that their shoulders loomed sharp and strong over their stern faces, their beaks working soundlessly except for sharp bursts of screeches. Irissa retreated, though she sensed it not, swinging the sword from side to side like a ground-hugging pendulum, each time letting it rise less high and sink to earth again sooner. It was amazing how much harm a seeress could render to a decent edge in so little time.

Kendric stalked over and wrested it away with one hand, wading into the complacent fowlen and sweeping the sword so high over his head and then down into them that it seemed sometimes to make a circle. Those fowlen that neared him on the upswing he caught in the kick of a sillac-hide boot. They soon dropped the proud pennants of their curled tails between their legs and retreated to the low, distant rocks.

The great sword swung down and touched earth with a final rasp.

"It's gone?" Irissa turned to face the length of Rynth she had kept at her back.

"Gone, perhaps to rejoin the herd, perhaps to slip into a gully and break its silly leg again," he gasped in answer. "I think we had better retreat. I'd feel more secure with a wall of rock at my back."

Their return to the rocks a few feet away was slow. Irissa's boots dragged and scraped ground more monotonously than the sword had when she wielded it. Kendric carried it more laboriously than he was wont, and by the time they reached the rocks, they both put their backs to them and slowly sank against them. Kendric laid the sword askew on the ground beside him.

"I thought we must make a farther retreat than this to avoid the fowlen," Irissa finally managed to say between her labored breaths.

Kendric rested his head against the stone and stared at the impassive moon. "We must. But we can't. Or I can't. I feel more weary than if I had fought a thousand of Ivrium's heirlings. I could not rise again for all the Iridesium in Rule. You could follow the lorryk, and I will stay and show the fowlen the taste of steel down their throats." He brandished the sword, about a foot from the ground.

Irissa sighed wearily. "I could not walk the distance to yonder rocks right now, even if the source of all my powers resided there instead of fowlen. I have never been so deep within the very bones of will and feel as if I have no bones of my own anymore. But I have a sword, however light and short, and can use it on the fowlen." She slowly drew the short sword at her side and held it up in demonstration. Her arms shook so much the blade quivered as if infected by the ague.

"You'll saw them to death," Kendric predicted. "Well," he told the moon as much as her, for they were both too tired so much as to lift their heads off the rock to look at each other, "if death is to be the next we encounter in this strange place, I am glad at least that I became acquainted with the life within myself, even if it is magical."

There was a pause. "I cannot say the same. I met death within me; I never dreamed I could so wish to slay some living thing, but the sword was so burdensome, and the fowlen so greedy—and I was so tired . . . I would have slashed them to crimson ribbons if I could."

"You may yet get your bloodthirsty wish." Kendric jerked his chin to draw her eyes into the distance. A clot of reassembling fowlen, newly bold at their prey's half-prone positions, was advancing.

"Their eyes are so blue," Irissa said dreamily. "Like the skies of Rule that I took for granted until I came to dwell under a lavender one." She sighed. "I do not think I have the strength to stab them. I hope their beaks are efficient and swift."

"It is my nature to defend myself," Kendric said, drawing his sword nearer, "no matter how many lorryk I restore to their feet."

The fowlen came on toward the now strangely immobile pair and the sword that stung and sawed the air and scraped the stone. They were fowlen, they were a pack. They were hungry.

"Hoods for a dozen Amozels," Kendric jested, pulling himself up a bit. Irissa knew the draining he battled, the aftermath of magic, whether working good or ill. She had not known that the weariness of facing one's physical limits would be so like it. She raised her head.

About two dozen fowlen made a frothy white semicircle, penning them to the rocks. The blue eyes were rimmed in skin like black satin, Irissa noticed at this distance, and the dark beaks shone like polished ebony.

Kendric and Irissa wearily rolled their heads toward each other and began to speak farewell at once. A third voice overrode their last words.

"Wait," it commanded. "We do not approve."

Kendric looked up at the moon. It had finally done what he had almost expected, this world's extraordinary orb, and had spoken. It was the thing that had witnessed his awaking in this world and thus it would usher him out of it with a phenomenon worth dying to see.

Irissa looked around sharply, not sure why, but with something small and white and feline in her mind.

Instead, a large furry white something arched over them from the rock lip above to land lightly amid the packed fowlen. It seemed to be merely another fowlen, but it faced the pack commandingly, switching its plumy tail.

"Back to the Cincture," it ordered. "A snow-slug large enough to feed you and all your unborn cubs sleeps near the ice-fountain at Delevant's Maw; you need not range this far for prey."

The fowlen's blue eyes blinked in meek unison; they turned and trotted off into the Rynth without a backward glance at Irissa and Kendric.

The seeming fowlen who spoke turned and confronted the two.

"Are you all right, friends?" it inquired courteously. Its voice was oddly vibrant, almost slurred, and pitched both high and low at the same time, so it sounded as if two spoke in unison. And while it sat quite docilely upon its haunches and cocked its feathered head at them inquisitively, its eyes blinked differing shades of amber and silver and looked slightly askew, as if pulled in two directions. "The fowlen must forage far for food at times," the creature explained, "but do not ordinarily dine on human flesh, save in leanest times. Though you are not quite the Inlands human that we know—"

"We are from . . . afar," Irissa said.

"From the Far Keep," Kendric added, drawing on the formula that had appeared to satisfy the rim-runners.

"The Far Keep . . ." The speaking fowlen assumed an expression very odd and difficult to explain. It appeared to smile. "The Far Keep lies far beyond the ice-arch, friends, farther than I think you hail from. But you are outlanders indeed, and we are pleased to welcome you to the Inlands and the Cincture."

"We?"

The fowlen looked to Kendric. "We," it said, and said no more.

"We seek the Keep of Fanis—" Irissa began.

The fowlen's fur and feathers bristled simultaneously, and it both growled and cawed, the first primitive sounds to issue from that odd-eyed visage. These startled Irissa and Kendric more than the creature's speech had.

"Fanis. May the snow-slugs burrow in his bones. Why seek you him?"

"The Shunstone," Kendric explained promptly. "A—friend desires it."

The fowlen's ruff rose into a glacial sunburst around the fierce avian face. "Strangers though you be to Inlands, Rynth, and Cincture, have you not noticed how appropriately the Stones are named? Beware, friends. We cannot help you there."

"But we have promised—"

The fowlen turned its mismatched eyes on Irissa. "Yes. Promises are fine things, and we would not interfere with yours. Go. Good fortune to you. Fanis' Keep lies in yon direction. May the Overstone light your footsteps. But we cannot do more than wish you well."

"Who are—we? You?"

The thing inclined its regal head. "We are Rynx," it said and stood, to turn and dart off into the semidark like an ordinary fowlen.

Chapter Twenty-three

They walked in the direction the speaking fowlen had indicated for a long time.

They were still fatigued, but with the fowlen pack ordered back into the Cincture and only the Overstone for company, there seemed no need for haste. Kendric's shoulders were not as straight as they were wont to be under the diagonal slant of steel across his back, and Irissa fastened her palm to the pommel of the sword at her hip, so it should not swing so punishingly at her steps.

The night was ebbing into the day's clouded violet glow, now still a deep purple bruise at the horizon. Soon the Overstone would pale into its albino daylight self and the entire sky would lighten to lavender.

"Are you sure that this is the way the Rynx pointed?" Irissa finally asked.

"With so sharp a beak there's little mistaking where it points," Kendric answered. "Besides, all these Keep spheres are round, so it matters not where we touch the border; it is the same distance to the center from any point."

"It matters that we not overshoot the border entirely," she pointed out. "I wish these spheres had not the habit of opening so suddenly before one but were detectable from a distance."

"Perhaps if we saw Fanis' Keep from afar, we should abandon our quest," he speculated. "From what even a four-pawed, odd-eyed enigma has to say of it, nothing sensible would go there if it could help it."

"Then from past performance, I would say we are the ideal envoys to such a realm."

"Aye." Kendric's hearty agreement changed into a resigned grin. "And from what I've seen pass as sense in this or any world, to be unsensible does not strike me as the worst course."

"You seem to have become accustomed to an unstable world."

"Which Rule itself was, after all, though we did not think so, since it was familiar to us. Now that I have seen the strange, I see how much of the strange there was in the familiar, and how much familiar there is to be found in the strange. The Stonekeepers are as jealous of their powers and as eager for more of someone else's as Geronfrey was ever ambitious of yours..."

Irissa's face clouded, like the day. "You still find this a wrong that rides you ill, that I eluded Geronfrey through you—?"

Kendric frowned in thought, his dark brows plunging to the valley formed just as his nose turned aquiline. He looked fowlen-fierce in profile, and Irissa was sorry she had asked the question again, even though she must ask it until she got an answer that she liked.

"Better me than he," Kendric said shortly. His strides lengthened, and Irissa had to hasten to keep pace with his next words. "Besides, it appears your powers have *some* practicality. The healing, for instance. I must admit that there is something exhilarating about seeing what was broken flying away from one, whole and fleet."

Irissa smiled. She, too, had felt that surge of pride at the little lorryk's winged retreat, though she had not had a hand in the healing beyond the urging of it.

Kendric stopped abruptly and turned to her. "I could try your arm," he offered.

Her left hand clasped her forearm almost protectively. She had thought he had forgotten about that, as she was trying to do, although the flesh still ached with a steady, dull tenaciousness.

"It—it is only flesh wound."

"They sting the most."

"And you are weary from healing the lorryk."

"I heal." He sounded amused.

"It is not necessary."

Kendric no longer looked amused. His face grew sober, darkly handsome, and unavoidable. "Do you *fear* my magic— that I will weave your flesh awry?"

"No! No, not that . . ." She would have said more but did not dare. Instead, she thrust her arm at him, drawing back the long sleeve to expose a quintet of ragged red tracks embedded in an angry puff of inflamed skin.

Kendric whistled softly through his teeth. "Sofistron's hounds must wear some irritant poison upon their claws, as the archers of Tolech-Nal would dip their arrowheads in fleshbane for battle. Why did you not tell me of this earlier?"

She shrugged evasively. "We had more important things to deal with. I simply—forgot."

"You would outwarrior a Wrathman, and yet you would risk both our lives for a lorryk. Well, I will fix it."

He held her forearm, his large hands supporting its entire length, and bent his dark head down to study the wounds' crimson stitchery.

Irissa averted her face. It was not his magic's ineffectiveness she feared, nor the sight of her own flesh writhing whole again. She felt mortified and helpless. She had never been the passive object of another's power before, and it was an intimacy that touched her more rawly than the lemurai rakes. She felt the first restoring tingle of her flesh and would have jerked away from Kendric's light grasp, except that she knew he would take it for mistrust, and that would be fatal to his developing confidence in the magic he must learn to use. It was not that she feared his magic would not work, but that it *would*. As they paused there in their trek across the Rynth, Irissa faced the lesson that was the hardest-learned in all her travels, harder even than the loss of magic. She understood that it was a burden to be helped, more than it was to help.

"There." Kendric sounded pleased. Irissa turned hastily back to roll down her sleeve. "Don't you want to see it?"

She didn't. "Of course." She peeked. "Perfect." Enough surprise crept into her tone to satisfy Kendric and to mask the distaste that underlay it. She rolled down her sleeve without looking again at her arm, which was white and smooth, a seamless expanse of restored flesh—a job any Torloc could take pride in. Except her.

"Irissa?" He expected something, some acknowledgment. She looked up at him, into the dark amber eyes that had stared her skin whole again and that had delved deep within her to draw out the essence that was life and self. She knew that only Kendric, who had been the recipient of much of her magic, would understand what she felt now, and she dared not remind him for fear of discouraging the use of that magic in him.

"Perfect," she told him softly, truthfully, concealing her revulsion of perfection borrowed from another. Already she felt the restoring tingle of health journeying up her arm and along the rest of her body, that buoying overflow common to the healed, which had permitted the lorryk to leap longer and faster than usual as it fled. To Irissa, the effect felt like invasion, foreign and out of control.

"You will have no scars," he pointed out.

"No. Nothing to show for it."

"And you should be feeling restored in general." He could not seem to refrain from enumerating the effects of his feat.

"Yes, yes!" She began walking again, so rapidly that even Kendric's long strides had trouble catching up to hers. It was as if she felt an eagerness to leave some passive shadow of herself behind. Poor Kendric! She understood his reluctance to use his inherited magic now, his feeling of being a mere vassal to another's will. And the irony was that the more he came to accept the benefits of his unwanted magic, the more she came to see the price of using all magic.

He was bewildered by her reaction to his boon and panting very slightly as he strode alongside her. Even a man of Wrathman height could not easily keep up with one who was running away from herself, Irissa thought, reining herself back to a more normal pace.

"I do not feel very depleted," he finally huffed, satisfaction tinging his deep voice. She had not bothered to inquire about his after-healing state.

"That is wonderful. And I do—feel—stronger."

"I see that. Slow a bit more; surely we are not in great haste to arrive at the Keep of the Shunned One."

"No. No great haste."

Kendric nodded, apparently convinced that all was well with Irissa. "Well, I for one am eager to see what this Shunstone is and how many nails Chaundre can make dance, once he has both it and his own Drawstone. And then I am eager to learn where we can go to solve the puzzle of where and why the Torloc seeresses go—and go there."

Irissa smiled. "The idea of rushing from one world to another no longer appears to discomfit you. Chaundre would be pleased; you have become a seeker after knowledge instead of mere egress."

"Are not you?"

Irissa slowed and stopped. She shook her head. "I think I crave neither knowledge nor escape now."

"You have no choice. You must at least seek the knowledge of why you and your kind come to the Inlands. And I think, once finding that, you will have no choice but to leave."

"And you?"

His eyes were very steady. "My choices wear their own chains, and I am not certain how long they are. I will make them when the time comes."

It was a disadvantage to be able to look into another's eyes without fear of finding herself reflected there. It was good to have an excuse for the averting of eyes, and she no longer had one. They looked at each other a long time, and Irissa was not sure what Kendric saw, except that it was not magic.

An hour or two later, Kendric stopped marching and wrinkled his aquiline nose, an effect that was half-comical. "Fanis' Keep."

"I don't see anything."

"I smell it," he said sourly.

Irissa sniffed the air delicately, then choked.

"Foul," Kendric said. "Enough to drive a stenchbug back to its rotting nest."

They walked on nevertheless, through an invisible barrier of the most putrid odors, as haphazardly assembled in their way as the patchwork landscape of Chaundre. Decay, stink, and plain noxiousness mingled before them and twined into an unseen heavy curtain that assailed them as much through the pores of their skins as through their nostrils.

"I'm glad we walk now, not ride," Kendric said, able occasionally to find a bright side to the darkest eventuality. "No bearing-beast worth its hooves would tolerate such an odor. Only man."

"And only one man, I fear. The present Fanis."

"A sword is not much proof against sheer stink. Perhaps there's some magic—"

"All your magic could be absorbed into counteracting this stench, and still it would continue. No doubt Fanis keeps intruders off by using their noses against them and has done so for years."

"It's a well-steeped stink, I'll give the fellow credit for that," Kendric conceded. "Then there's nothing to do but prove our noses and our stomachs too stern for it."

The unhealthy atmosphere ended as abruptly as it had begun, and the ingestion of unsullied air into their bodies for an instant made what they had been inhaling hang more odiferous by contrast, so that the fresh air momentarily almost made them retch.

And now they saw the border of Fanis' Keeplands as well as sniffed it. Again, the landscape had changed utterly in an instant. Before them, a thin line of filthy hovels extended as far as the eye could see in either direction, curved into the distance as they diminished.

The roofs were made from sodden thatch that stank of wet putrefaction. Animals of indeterminate breed wallowed in the dung-islanded puddles that gathered outside the slovenly huts. People lounged there as well, or poked dirt-stained faces through tumbledown doors.

"Fanis' folk are as appetizing as his perfumery," Kendric observed, threading an assertive but careful path over the fouled ground. Irissa stepped carefully in the big tracks made by his sillac-hide boots.

The people had gathered to watch them pass and made a squint-eyed, ragged gauntlet for Kendric and Irissa to funnel through. There were both men and women, all equally dirty, many somehow twisted-looking. A too-careful scrutiny would reveal a face missing an eye, nose, or ear, or a handless arm or footless leg. Many faces were caked with disease sores as well as dirt. But Kendric's bulk and the sword hanging diagonally across his back forged through them as a ship's prow might part even the foulest of seas. Though the line of hovels extended far, it was not deep. He and Irissa were soon past the worst of the folk. Only a few snot-faced children bothered to follow and stare at them. These soon gave up, as if loath to leave their untoothsome settlement too far behind.

"In the other Keeps," Irissa said, "we did not see much of the population at large. They were far flung throughout the sphere lands, tending to the Stonekeepers' crops and wants. But they always seemed a wholesome kind."

Kendric nodded grimly. "These cluster here, at the very rim of the Keeplands, as if wishing to press out of them if they could... but if as foul a lot as this disdains the inner Keep, what can await us?"

"Chaundre's 'small' quest."

"And the Shunstone," he returned. "Think what a beauty *that* must be."

Irissa just grimaced.

The lands were deserted now, broken into sulfurous-reeking marshy patches. Luckily, or by design, some higher ground wove its way through the muck. Irissa and Kendric kept to this narrow path, along the sides of which grew stark trees reminiscent of bonewood in shape and size, save that lurid fungi blossomed like fat-petaled flowers along the limbs. One flower fanned its glossy green petals as Irissa passed by and nipped at her sleeve.

"It lives!"

"So does that." Kendric pointed to a wart-ridden toad the size of small cat in the path ahead. It was lolling there unafraid, its segmented, pink tongue extended and as long as a rat's tail, waiting for some airborne insect to land. Kendric's big boot kicked out a crushing blow, but the amphibian catapulted five feet high on muscular back legs just as his boot landed and flew over Irissa's shoulder into the marsh behind her.

She screamed impulsively, then stopped herself by pressing her hands to her mouth. "It is just that everything here is so loathsome," she apologized, nevertheless sweeping her long hair in front of her shoulders and braiding it hastily, lest something slimy leap up and entangle in it.

They saw many more nameless creatures on their passage, some resembling prey-bloated, wise-eyed spiders as huge as

platters. These skittered around the roots of the fungi-
blossomed trees and spun webs between the leprous branches
with filaments as thick as one of Irissa's braids.

There was a constant sound of agitation in the murky water;
odd chirps, hisses, and slithers echoed over the otherwise still
marshscape. The air above them hummed, too, with a rasp
quite unpleasant to hear. Occasionally, some large, swooping
thing would beat down past their faces, but it seemed the flying
things were as eager to avoid ground creatures as Kendric and
Irissa were to remain ignorant of the airborne ones.

Even the sounds of Fanis' Keep appeared calculated for
repulsion—the scrape as of scales, the beat as of glassy insect
wings, and the mud-sucking slither of the dark things that roiled
the murky brown-green waters. Nothing pretty or bright moved
here. The sky seemed dulled, its mantle of pale cloud taking
on a deathly pallor. The Overstone had turned slightly bilious,
like a round of moldy cheese.

Irissa cast a wistful glance over her back and regretted it.
An appalling amount of fetid marshland lay behind them, and
she could see great mists of wide-winged insects buzzing over
the distant marshes. What had looked deserted within the range
of the few feet they had traversed moved everywhere with life
once they had passed, so the whole landscape seemed to quiver.
She shuddered and resolutely turned to face forward to the
stable expanse of Kendric's back with the sword riding across
the fowlen-fur vest that Gryff had presented to him. Irissa would
have given a great deal for the presence of any furred creature
now—even a fowlen.

That back stopped its rhythmic motion abruptly. "Fanis'
sinkhole, I take it."

High ground stood before them, rising like an anthill from
the flat swamp. It looked to be shaped of clay—damp, mottled,
red-gray clay. Some phosphorescent growth riddled the surface, gleaming sickly.

"It looks armored in blood-rusted Iridesium."

"Or some perverse opposite of Iridesium," Irissa speculated.
"Some alien metal that anyone wholesome would shun working."

"More like the genuine thing decayed. All smacks here of
decay, of good turned ill for a long, long time, so that even

what is natural becomes rancid—air, water, earth, and those that crawl and fly upon it."

"We have not been challenged," she noted.

Kendric snorted. "What do you think the hellish stretch of dire marsh we just passed through was, if not a challenge?"

"I meant by force of arms or magic."

"When one's entire Keep is a gauntlet cast at mortal sanity, one does not need swords or spells. No wonder they call him 'Shunned.'"

"He shall not be unchallenged for much longer." Irissa took the lead for the first time, as if welcoming a more concrete adversary than the muck around her and the distaste it spawned within her.

Kendric was content to follow. So far, he had seen nothing that had made his hand itch to reach for the mighty pommel riding over his back. Boots were better defense than steel in this fetid place.

At the oval entrance to Fanis' foothill-high Keep, they met their first barrier—a door. It had no handle or latch, as if never used; though made of wood, it was visibly rotted.

"Why do I feel this will not be as simple to pass as it looks?" Kendric wondered aloud.

"Instinct," Irissa answered promptly. "I think you can open it more easily with your magic than your might."

As was his wont, he ignored her advice. He strode up to the door, examined the slimy surface distastefully, then spread his fingers and pushed hard. They pressed a half inch deep into a substance like greasy yellow tallow, then met utter resistance. He backed off, his hands fanned and held, momentarily disowned, before him. Kendric passed Irissa without comment and went to a small standing pool, where he knelt and gingerly laved his hands in the green-scummed water.

"Beware behind you!"

He turned, still on his heels, to see a band of creatures pouring through a now-open door. Irissa had drawn her sword to engage the one that advanced on her, but most of them were oozing toward Kendric, and his present position made it very difficult for him to draw his sword from its anchorage on his back. He stood, knowing he'd have to back calf-deep into the muddy water. Something curled around his boots, something strong, sleek, and scaled. He ignored it and pulled the great sword off his shoulders in time to sweep it across the bellies of three of the oncoming creatures—he could not call them men, though they walked upright, for their arms ended in un-articulated, fingerlike stumps, their faces were made up of a series of corroded fleshy pits instead of features, and for clothing they wore strips of linen wound around their trunks, heads, and flailing limbs. Kendric's heavy-edged blade cut through their bindings as if through mush; like mush, they collapsed into yellowed lumps on the ground. Yet more came on behind them.

Irissa was not perceived to be the threat that Kendric was, for they streamed past her, and her thrusts of blade into them were as ineffective as sticking pins into pudding. Kendric knew only that under no circumstances would he permit the touch of these beings, that by no means must they reach him. Contamination emanated from them; an instinct either magical or self-preserving told him that one contact would convert him into a taller, broader version of walking rot. Better the swamp-things, he thought, feeling a pulse in one ankle where the underwater leech had wound tight and now squeezed harder still. In minutes his numb foot would give under him and he would be on his knees in the stagnant marsh pool, still beating off waves of attacking mush.

"Magic," he heard Irissa half-call, half-command from behind the putrid fellowship. Before him, at the steady swing of his blade, limbs lopped off, heads rolled away as softly as cabbages, and linen split to ooze a sickly yellow ichor. Yet still more creatures came, ever closer.

"My muscles move faster than my brain," he protested while relentlessly swinging his sword. The bodies obligingly crumbled at its touch, only to serve as a rank carpet for the next line of their fellows. "I've no time to think of magic."

"That's when one needs it most," returned Irissa, who was attacking the mush-men from the rear.

Kendric realized that meant that their number was finite; the thought gave new wings to his heavy blade. Though he backed thigh-high into the rank water and the nearest of the creatures fell with a splash into its murky embrace, the sword made one final sweep. Three figures dissolved into one another as they fell, forming a sodden foothill at the pool's edge. Irissa stood on the water's verge, her own sword still held before her and her makeshift braids half-unraveled by their swing in time to her weapon strokes.

Kendric slogged out of the water, careful to edge around the piled bodies of what he was not sure was living when it had moved. There was no doubt of their state now. As Kendric passed them, the leech loosened on his boot and streaked in their direction. He watched as the whole mass sank as an agitation into the water.

"Were they spelled?" he asked Irissa, but she only shook her disheveled head in uncertainty. "Well, live or dead, spelled or simply hungry, they and that which sucked the color from my boot deserve to dine upon one another." He elevated his foot to show the sturdy sillac-hide bleached white as bone in an ankle-wide ring. "I'm glad I had to retreat no deeper."

Irissa shuddered. "Fanis' Keep is foul to the last drop of water that pools upon it. If the exterior is so noxious, I wonder what waits within?"

They turned to find the decaying door open, unguarded, sagging limply upon its rusted hinges. Beyond was a dark expanse. Across the unmarked line that was a threshold lay a wetly gleaming, mottled serpent, its long lines prey-swelled about the middle. It was shaded all the colors of the rainbow.

Chapter Twenty-four

❖❖❖

The serpent would have been a pretty thing, had all its colors not run together in a muddied, multishaded swirl, giving it a tainted appearance.

Yet it was no longer than Kendric's sword, and looked too belly-bloated to challenge them. They took a step in unison

toward the door—and a similar snake sprang up before their
boot toes.

Kendric and Irissa exchanged warning glances, then moved
to step past it. The serpent's mottled surface stirred. In an
instant, it had swollen to twice its length and more than four
times its circumference. Dark-fanged jaws split open, and the
great head came rising up at Kendric on the expanding ladder
of its rainbow-hued body, so that it looked him eye to eye. He
was so startled that he stared back at the thing's purple iris,
even now shifting through a dozen different shades. He did not
move for a moment, the serpent being too close for a sword
stroke. Magic was a thing he was not used to evoking glibly.

The snake's engorged, soft body began twining Kendric,
seeming to absorb him from without in a pulsating length of
polychromatic coils. It was almost a beautiful sight, the expanding snake with its scaled colors stretching thinner and
brighter along its body as it swelled, and it entranced Irissa
even as she knew that nothing in Fanis' Keep brought anything
but death and decay. With more reflex than hope, she plunged
her sword into the gorgeous dilating body, between a swirl of
red and indigo...

A shrill hiss sliced the newly odor-heavy air and knifed back
and forth like a blade in a duel. The serpent's body swayed
violently from left to right before Kendric, perhaps enchanting
him further. The hiss grew softer as the snake sank lower. It
dwindled to Kendric's boot tops, then shrank with a last rattling
sibilancy into a puckered shred of empty skin at his feet. Kendric shook his head for clarity and kicked the finger-long remnant away.

"You go first," he told Irissa. "Your small sword is a better
weapon against these blow-hards."

She did not object, and in moments the air around them
sang with a hissing chorus as serpent after serpent swelled up
from the ground's soft recesses and Irissa's sword point punctured them in mid-swell. There was nothing gory in their passing, only the small, shriveled, multicolored skins, and Irissa
waded into their midst with a warrior's blitheness, finding a
certain exhilaration in anticipating the spot where the next one
would appear, in allowing them to reach fully expanded proportion and then pricking them into nothingness just as the

shifting green or blood-red or bright yellow eyes focused and a huge-jawed head unhinged to its fullest...

Only the threshold-clinging first serpent remained; Irissa bent down to pierce it before it could swell.

"Nicely done," approved Kendric, who had come behind and kicked the empty skins away for aesthetic reasons, thinking of his and Irissa's return passage from this place. When he was not being a pessimist, he was an unremitting optimist. "I told you this Keep would be mostly bootwork; I've yet to see a foe worthy of the feel of my blade." He glanced at the yellow ichor congealing along the shining steel's length. "A bath of clean red blood would wash it of the stench of this place."

"You may need it yet. Fanis slew his own sister for possession of the Shunstone, remember? I warrant his heirlings will be as jealous of the Stone as their ancestor was."

"Then let's meet this latter-day womanslayer and be done with it." Kendric stepped resolutely over the unguarded threshold into darkness.

By the time Irissa followed him, a warm, golden glow illuminated Fanis' antechamber and the sheepish features of Kendric, who held the selfsame glow upright before his face. It took Irissa a moment to realize that the torch-shaped light caster was the hilt of Kendric's sword, beaming light as it had not done since Rule.

"It shines by itself," he was quick to disclaim. "I did nothing—merely stepped into darkness. It has done nothing but what I expect of a fire-forged sword since I made it. Until now."

"You were not in utter dark until now," Irissa responded. "It answers your needs."

"What if I should be in utter dark and wish it so?"

"It would still shine, for only a fool would prefer dark to light, and magic does not cling long to fools. So if you plan any nocturnal adventures of a private nature, leave your sword behind."

He frowned. "That is another nettle of magic—no privacy."

"Yes," Irissa said, clutching her forearm in a spasm of raw memory. The flesh felt whole, unhurt. It was odd that she did not also feel that way.

"It makes a long-stemmed and heavy torch," he grumbled.

"At least we shall see the nature of this Fanis, which I must admit myself curious of—the kind of man who would surround himself with so much that is repugnant."

Kendric started down the dark hall, if hall it was, holding his sword upright before him. Despite the lambent hilt, nothing could be seen but the rind of darkness surrounding the small pool of light in which they walked. Nothing further challenged them, except the emptiness of the place and its length. It seemed constructed like a sinuous snake, for their path bore left, then right in smooth gradations. And they appeared to go lower. Water dripped morosely in the distance, as if the clay of this construction wept eternally.

"Why build a Keep that towers to the sky, then burrow as deep within it as it rises above?" Kendric's query was more complaint than question, but Irissa answered it anyway.

"Perhaps he fears the sky, the eye of the Overstone, or anything human."

"Perhaps. He does not fear the things that creep and crawl and move in other, less natural ways. Will he fear us, or even a sword that sheds light? And how are we to wrest the Shunstone from him if he will not give it up?"

She had no answer and merely shook her head, a gesture Kendric could not see, since she walked behind him. She had walked behind him through most of this world, she realized, because her powers had paled.

The lower they wended their way, the more damply warm it became, until the air ahead seemed to dance more redly. They came finally to another door, this one carved from lichen-draped stone in the shape of a gaping serpent mouth. The down-shot fangs were as long as Irissa's sword, and some oozing substance dripped like golden honey off their curved tips.

Kendric thrust his sword hilt under the infinitely slow, golden rain. The liquid sizzled on the glowing metal like water on a white-hot forge and vanished in a puff of sulfurous smoke.

"Avoid the ichor. It is some venom and is what fed the veins of the leprous men who attacked us outside."

Irissa was happy to bow to Kendric's advice. Catching her hair close about her shoulders like a cloak, she stooped and stepped through the portcullis of fangs. Kendric had to hand his sword through first, double himself over, and step sideways to avoid the dripping poison. The instant Irissa's hands alone held the sword, the hilt light dampened. She heard the hiss of Kendric's indrawn breath as he passed under the fangs in sudden, utter dark and the relieved, softer hiss of her own when his hands encompassed hers around the hilt and it sprang to light again.

A vast and gloomy earth-hewed chamber surrounded them, but at its center was a huge, dim hearth glow. They walked to it, Kendric changing his grasp upon the sword from beneath to a more aggressive clutch around the hilt. A low, rocky wall met them, the lip of the deep pit it surrounded. Below, a river of liquid rock flickered flamelike against the pit walls. On an island in this fiery channel sat a man.

At least it sat and seemed a man. It wore robes so gray and tattered it appeared more draped within a web than clothed. But an elongated hand clung white-knuckled to a staff as gnarled as the knuckles encircling it. Between the sharp peaks of bony shoulders, a ruin of a face lay sunken on a concave chest.

"Is—is he dead?" Irissa whispered. At the sibilant start of her sentence, the lolling head elevated slightly and a dull glimmer of eyes groped their way.

"Hiss, hiss, my pets. Yes. I hear you. Ears are still sharp, relatively. Guard the threshold, yes. Though no one comes to challenge it. I like to feel my Stone secure."

"*We* come," Kendric challenged. The head jerked a bit higher, though it still sagged lamentably below the shoulders. Eyes dead as a fish belly rolled unfocusedly from right to left.

"We? Someone is here? More than someone. Where?"

"Here."

The head, bobbling on its stringy neck like a puppet's, finally angled itself in their direction. The eyes looked their way, but seemed glazed over. "I see, now. An Inlands lout, a slighter fellow, and one very thin one indeed." Fanis squinted intently toward the sword Kendric held balanced at his side.

"This should be a simple quest, like taking a pacifying stone from the mouth of a Rulian baby," Kendric whispered to Irissa.

"Hiss again. And take? No one takes from Fanis. Where are my pets, my pretty hissers?"

"If you mean the serpents at your door, they have all perished of an inflated opinion of themselves—and a sword point."

"You have passed the bloatsnakes? And my outcast army—all those who were driven from the Keeps for crimes and came to me for a kind of immortality?"

"They feed the things that thrive in your rancid pools."

"Who would bother to slay the defenders of Fanis, when all who dwell in the Inlands would rather die than come nigh?" The voice quavered with age and perhaps with something more surprising—self-pity.

"I, Kendric of the Far Keep, come and I—"

"Far Keep? Far Keep?" The creature shifted on the seat of rocks it seemed carved upon. "No Far Keep in the Inlands, no. You come from afar... a Far Keep." Its laugh at its feeble play on words was high-pitched, more giggle than guffaw. The shrill cacophony died. "That is why you slay my outcasts, my bloatsnakes, why you come across the swamp that no man treads, into my Keep, into my company. You are a stranger."

Kendric didn't answer. Fanis appeared to have forgotten the two other "figures" his feeble vision had discerned. Like those of many aged people, his senses discerned mostly through the predominance of the soundest one left to him—obviously his ears. Kendric studied these organs and noted that Fanis' were elfinly elongated, like his hands, and generously fanned for funneling every sound into them.

"I like company," Fanis announced abruptly. "I have not had company for many, many—years." He chuckled then, a thin, watery chuckle.

"I can see why," Kendric retorted.

"Who requires company?" Fanis said defiantly. "Company comes for only one reason—to steal my Shunstone. Is that your reason, stranger?"

"Steal? No..."

"All of them. Would have naught to do with me or my Keep. Lofty Sofistron, with his pretty, rolling lands. Betokens an empty, rolling mind, methinks. And Ivrium and his eternal quest for new bevywomen. And Lacustrine and his pure, dancing waters. Had no thought for Fanis, no. They all held and wielded their Stones. And Fanis Firstborn was shoved aside for want of finding a plain, round stone. Sheer luck that *she* reached the meander before I had recovered from my evening's revelry, mere luck that *she* went waterward at sunclimb to

pound the clothing on some rock and found instead a stone—
the Stone. And she would not give it up to my right. It changed
her, you see. She took the Stone most seriously. Was forever
experimenting with turning this meander that way and that
meander this way. Wanted to bring the waters rushing strongly
with the fleshfins diverted, so that the village women could do
their wash more speedily! Such a waste of power. *I* would not
have bothered turning the Shunstone to such trifling matters.
I would have used it to turn those proud and mighty upland
Inlanders back on themselves, so that their arrows would turn
and strike right to their haughty, proud hearts.

"But then it was no use, after all," Fanis added with melancholy. "They would direct nothing my way. No arrows, no
enmity. They shunned me. Me! The holder of the Shunstone.
But one cannot turn a thing against itself unless it first makes
a move against one. And they moved to leave me well enough
alone, and with me my lands and my Keep and my—people.
I have not had much company."

Irissa pulled urgently on Kendric's sleeve. She leaned up
on tiptoe to whisper directly against his ear so Fanis should
not overhear. "Ask him if he has a bevy. Ask him!"

"Sometimes I hear the wind whistle, even down here," Fanis
said, stirring. "Even the wind is against me and turns from me
before I feel it, so I have not known wind for a long, long
time. All are against me. All turn from me. All."

"What of your bevy?" Kendric suggested.

Fanis laughed again, harsh and low this time. "Bevy. What
Stonekeeper would send even a daughter to Fanis Sist— But
it doesn't matter. Lies, all lies. They called me names; my ears
were sharp enough to detect that, though I never laid eyes on
an Inlander after—after I assumed my Stone. Do you want my
Stone? You can't have it. I keep it forever. I am Stonekeeper."

The old man—and he must have been older than old—
dropped his sharp chin upon his sunken chest and dozed. A bit
of drool ran down his chin like a tear.

Irissa tugged Kendric away from the pit lip and back into
the dark passageway.

"We will never wrest the Stone away from him unless we
bridge the river of fire. And he will never willingly give up
the Shunstone, for he has had it a long time, a very long time."

"Yet he must be at the very verge of surrendering it to his One Son heirling; even the magic cannot shield him from the decrepitudes of age."

"There *is* no heirling, Kendric," Irissa said, careful not to hiss unduly on the "is" and awaken Fanis. "You heard him yourself. No other Stonekeeper would send him the start of a bevy. He was shunned, utterly shunned, for the murder he had wrought—of a sister, yes, but most importantly of one of the original Stonekeepers. They all held Stones and could tolerate no Stonetaker among them. Hariantha may have been only a female to them, but she found the Stone honestly. If she were vulnerable, so were they all—to Fanis and each other."

"But if he has no bevy, no heirling—"

"He has nothing but himself."

"Then he is the original Fanis, not a successor?"

"Yes, and no power in the Inlands has yet succeeded in wresting his ill-gotten Stone away. Quite honestly, I do not know how we shall do it, though it would be a mercy, for he must have sickened of the Stone many lifetimes ago, though he does not know it. No force in this world can wrest it from him."

Kendric leaned his sword against the wall, as if recognizing a barrier that required neither steel nor brawn. "What of magic out of this world?" he asked.

"You bear that, but you are untried, and Fanis has held and coveted his Stone for an inestimable time. He has managed to prolong his life many times over the other original Stoneholders. Perhaps avarice is the greatest immortality potion of all."

"And what is its antidote?" Kendric demanded, his voice rising triumphantly. Behind them, Fanis coughed. Kendric pulled Irissa close by the sleeves and bent down to whisper conspiratorially. "Its antidote, Torloc. All things have antidotes, even emotions."

"You have thought of something."

"Guilt. I could smell it stronger than the river's sulfur steam. You say he holds on to life only from habit, that he holds the Stone only to keep everyone else in the Inlands or Rynth from possessing it. What if he could surrender it to someone not of the Inlands or Rynth—"

"To us? He would never give it up to strangers."

"Not a stranger. A sister."

She was speechless.

"What's-her-name! The sister whose eyes are the evening and morning stars and whose hair is the clouds above us, as in that unpretty tale that Amozel told at the rim-runners' fire."

"I did not think you listened so closely." Irissa smiled. "Hariantha," she said softly. "I am not likely to forget the name."

"Good. It would not do to visit his long-dead sister upon Fanis and have her call herself by the wrong name."

"But how can we evoke her? Even if we—you—had the kind of power to summon her here, to reassemble her in the very place the Shunstone that banished her is held, it would be impossible—"

"No. I would not attempt such foolishness. Besides, I do not believe the tale. Oh, Fanis murdered her for the Stone, all right, and likely with an arrow driven daggerlike into her back. That sounds true enough and, from what I've seen of the creature, most like him. But scattering her bones to the bonetrees and her eyes and hair to the sky—mere embellishment. Hariantha's bones no doubt lie beneath our feet, and she has dwindled to dust motes ages ago."

"Then how—?"

"It is not necessary to produce Hariantha, only her likeness. And I've been thinking. Fanis has not noticed you beyond a vague personage accompanying me. I believe, if I concentrate properly, that I can...cloud your shape with the likeness of Hariantha."

"But you have never seen her, and Fanis is her brother."

"Her nearly blind brother, who has outlived his span more times than even magicians should attempt. No, his greed and guilt keep him alive, and perhaps the Stone. If we would have it, extraordinary measures are required. And I have no qualms about relieving a murderer of his gain."

"And how shall I be made to resemble Hariantha?"

"If you will trust to—my—magic, I have been thinking that I could call down the clouds for your hair, the stars for your eyes. The use of this imagery must mean that the real Hariantha was light-eyed and light-haired, and if I evoked the illusion of these legendary traits over your natural visage, it should provoke quite a start, even in a hardened old magician like Fanis."

Irissa sighed. "It is your idea, and you seem confident in it, which is the beginning of potent magic. Very well, do what you think."

"Remember, you must persuade him to *give* you the Shunstone. I fear that more thievery can only increase the shunning effect that surrounds us."

Irissa nodded resignedly and watched as Kendric stepped back from her so her entire form was visible to him. He licked his lips, glanced once to the glowing hilt that illuminated his task, then stared at her. His eyes, such a warm amber-brown by nature, burned almost black. They drilled into her from head to foot, and soon Irissa felt swathed in some numbing fog. Something very light and invisible wafted over her, a sort of gauzy skin, and she felt obliged to move measuredly so as not to dislodge it.

"Has it worked?" The apparition spoke in Irissa's voice, further disorienting him. But Fanis was old beyond imagining and had not heard his sister's voice since her final, death-denying scream.

"Unless I spell my own eyes."

"I do feel some light web veiling me." Irissa spun in demonstration and felt something flutter around her.

Kendric's hand went to shield his eyes. "Move slowly! I cannot keep you draped in my illusion unless you remain within it. If your likeness to Hariantha should drop in Fanis' presence, who knows how punishingly he could wield his Shunstone?"

"Or how he might wield it at the very sight of Hariantha?"

"That's true." Kendric looked crestfallen. "We must forget this masquerade. It is too dangerous—"

"Nonsense! Crossing the swamp that no man treads was dangerous. At least here is something I can do." Irissa turned and floated gracefully in her gauzy illusion back into the cavern where Fanis dozed and dreamed.

Kendric lingered at the passage entrance, his eyes ever on Irissa's back and the long, light hair that covered it. As long as she seemed other than herself to his eyes, he could hope that his magic held.

"Fanis. Fanissss!" Irissa's voice came silken and sibilant

from the darkness. It called softly out over the red-churning river, snaked down to the lonely island, wove in and around Fanis' shrunken cheekbones, and whispered in one ear and out the other. "Fannnn-isss!"

"Sleeping," he told no one. "Did I hear a hisser, pretty bloatsnake? No. Dreamed. Dreamed strangers came and killed my guardians. Dream too much."

"Fanis!"

The feeble head finally rolled back enough to look up to the pit lip and the pale, glittering figure poised there. Fanis' milky eyes were caught like cabochon opals in the bezel of his lids, frozen, nearly sightless but disbelieving. Something light and wispy stood there, trailing strands of hair and gown and clouds. Something with piercing bright eyes like twin, shiny arrowheads, unused and aching for the kill. Something—familiar.

"Fanis. Brother!"

He jerked upon his uncushioned seat, a puppet whose single string was his lifeline, and that was rudely twitched at the moment. "Who calls?"

"I. Hariantha. Your sister."

His gnarled hand dropped the staff with a start. It clutched on air, then sought some deep inner pocket in his tattered robe and sheltered there. "She—she is—gone."

"Dead, Fanis. They say I am dead. But I am not. How can I be, for I see, and see farther than I even did when I walked upon the Rynth. I see all the Inlands over, even to the Cincture, and I see all that is done upon it by morning and by evening. When was it that you came to me by the meander's edge and—?"

"Morning! It was morning!"

"You see. I see by both morning and night, and nothing is forgotten to me. And I hear, I hear a great deal. The birds come and brush my face and whisper to me with their wings. I hear the wind rushing past me, sweeping my long, pale hair from one side of the Rynth to the other. Sometimes it sweeps my hair so wildly that I cannot see for a time. But my vision always returns. And now I can see in all directions—west, east, north to Chaundre's Keep, south to yours. I see ahead of me, behind me . . . They say you can feel no wind, that even the air shuns you now."

"Yes! Yes!"

"They say you are a lonely man and less than a man. They say you are an old man beyond the farthest shores of age. They say you have no bevy, no heirling, no kin, no parent, no sister—"

"Who is this *they*?"

"The birds, the lorryk, the people of the Inlands and Rynth. All things speak to me now, Fanis, all things but my Stone. They say you hoard it still, and take no comfort in it."

He stood, the old creature, stage by stage, one aching, unbending joint by another. He did not look like one of magical life span, but like a victim of cruel, extended mortality. His hand came out of his robe, clenched and palsied. He extended it slowly, the fist white-knuckled as if holding the haft of a dirk.

"I have it here. My Stone. It has been with me always."

"Not always," she intoned calmly.

His hand trembled so violently he extended his other to steady it. Kendric watched cautiously from near the passage mouth. The aura he had cast around Irissa grew steadily more dazzling. Her hair seemed to be growing and flowing around her in a windswept cloud. She had found precisely the proper words to unravel the avaricious old magician and spoke with a remote majesty that even had Kendric a bit ashiver in what seemed the presence of something beyond life—and beyond death. He kept all of his attention focused on the surface he had created for Irissa, knowing that if he faltered, she might bear the brunt of Fanis' rage, which history had long ago proved fatal to another woman.

"My Stone," came the querulous voice from the pit. "Mine alone. Me alone. Always. A long time."

The light-mantled hair that was Irissa's nodded graciously. "A long time. Almost as long as the winds have blown the clouds and the stars have shone."

"I could—I could—" The old man tottered to the molten river's edge, his figure reflecting a hellish heat he seemed unable to feel. "I could . . ." The sentence did not seem to have an end, and he fell into senile vacancy, staring with his clouded eyes into the wavering lava, his fingers working against something clasped within his palm.

"There is only one thing you can yet do, Fanis Sisterslayer," came the voice from above, stern as the sky and as distant.

"I could—give it back!" He looked up then, head cocked defensively into one humped shoulder.

Hariantha's head nodded solemnly, sending her flowing locks into vaporous tresses that foamed around her face. A pale hand reached out, from a long distance away, it seemed, and Fanis' hand reached forward in response, as if drawn by an invisible line.

His fist clenched and he beat his hollow breast with it once. "No. You must come down to take it from me."

Alarm made Kendric's concentration waver, and for a moment he glimpsed Irissa's dark hair lying its normal length along her back. Then he must have found some steady interior strand of magic, for the clouded image asserted itself more impressively than ever. Kendric saw Irissa step to the low, rocky wall, saw it melt before her. She moved down into the pit, slowly, as if suspended.

He started forward, unable to allow Irissa out of his sight, trying to beat back the idea that she had somehow plummeted over the pit edge into the fiery river. Had Fanis claimed his victim a second time, in another guise?

Kendric found he could approach the pit edge without attracting the old magician's attention. For Fanis could watch only the vision of Hariantha that walked toward him, and when Kendric saw it, too, he was as riveted. She trod the air between Kendric and Fanis as if descending an invisible stair, the hem of her pale robes falling to outline each invisible riser's shape for a moment before she moved on and lower, toward Fanis. She crossed the flaming river, and not a glimmer of it reflected on her snowy robes or in her lucent eyes. She touched the rude earth of Fanis' island and held out one hand.

With aching slowness, Fanis unbent his arm from his breast and tremblingly extended his hand. His tattered gray robe looked tawdrier than ever near the icy, pristine glow of Hariantha. Behind her, the raging river dulled and gradually cooled to a gray like Fanis' clothing. Fanis' fingers still clung to the Stone. Even though his hand was extended above Hariantha's outstretched palm, his fingers would not seem to relinquish the Stone, but dug clawlike into his very hand, until the blood ran like red flame down his wrist.

"Take it!" he begged suddenly, one watery eye sending something like a tear streaking across a seamed and filthy cheek.

"You must give it," she said, waiting.

One by one, his fingers unfurled. A small, dull Stone fell into the white palm extended. Her white fingers closed upon it. Hariantha turned without pause and began walking up an airy staircase again, above the river that had hardened into a choked gray mass of frozen rock.

Kendric waited at the pit edge, no longer fearing detection. He had seen Fanis' fragile body crumple at the surrender of the Stone and the turning of Hariantha's back upon him. Kendric's eyes were only on Irissa, and he wondered that she should have so successfully drawn upon his flawed magic as to turn the air into a ladder for her will. He made himself maintain the Hariantha likeness, fearing that, should Irissa return to her own unamplified form while still suspended over the pit, she would fall, like a sleepwaker awakened too rudely. So Hariantha as he had envisioned her walked toward him—measuredly, calmly, unacknowledgingly. Kendric admired the icy fire of her eyes, the streaming abundance of her hair, her regal poise, and her sweeping robes. For one new to magic, he had evoked a legend well. And Irissa—Irissa had had the exquisite wit to say just the proper thing to wrest the Stone from its Keeper. In a moment she would touch solid ground. Kendric extended a hand to her. She slowly swept her arm up and placed her closed fist in his open palm. He clasped both hand and Shunstone and drew her toward him by them.

They stood together on the pit edge, Irissa still wearing the likeness of Hariantha. A sound below, something of a croak, made them turn. Fanis lay prone, his limbs askew, his clouded eyes turned up at the dark cave roof. And then those limbs, so narrow and twisted, began to swell and straighten. The feathery wisps of white hair on his age-freckled pate fluffed in an unseen wind and whipped long and thick about his shoulders. Those shoulders had swollen, too, to a young man's dimensions. Before their eyes, Fanis grew younger and stronger as he lay dead. And the sightless eyes that stared up lost their opacity and shone bright, youthful blue. It was a handsome youth who lay there, empty-handed, and the face that was turned to the dark earth above smiled.

Kendric looked uncomfortably at Irissa. She still wore Hariantha's likeness, as if it were a cloak she had forgotten to toss off. But it was not her magic that wrapped her in another's shape; it was *his*. And he was not thinking magic now.

His hand tightened on Irissa's and the Shunstone within it. He sought some way to call her back to herself, but could feel himself stumbling in the labyrinth of his unexplored magic. A cold thought took root, that perhaps he could not call back Irissa, perhaps he had doomed her . . .

He looked for her eyes beneath the bright, starry gaze he had called down for his mock Hariantha. He saw nothing but a remote arctic twinkle. As he strove to penetrate it, the cloud dissipated in flying strands that whirled tighter and tighter around the form at its center, then flew off into the corners of the cave. With rising confidence, Kendric glimpsed pieces of Irissa behind the unwinding strands and saw her gray eyes and dark hair.

The last of the mist swirled away from her and rose up to the cave roof, where it swelled into an ocean of cloud and swept down upon them all again. Icy air wed to a shrill wind surged through the cavern, whipping Irissa's dark hair into spiky strands and driving Kendric's eyes momentarily shut.

The wind was gone, and with it the cloud. So was the mortal flesh of Fanis, young or old.

Irissa looked down at the pit. "Kendric, did you—?"

"No. And you—?"

She shook her head, thankfully its full dark self again. "It was as if I saw it all from some place very high and chill and remote. After I stood at the pit lip, it's all . . . hazy. But we have the Shunstone."

"And Fanis has his freedom, whether he knew it or not—"

"And I think," Irissa finished, "I think Hariantha has justice."

They looked down on the residue of Fanis Sisterslayer, who

had held a Stone that was not his, and who had lived the longest of all the long-lived Stonekeepers. All that lingered of that blood-bought longevity was a pale geography of bone and some lengths of light hair as ethereal as a cloud.

Chapter Twenty-five

Something of the brightness of Hariantha's eyes lingered in Irissa's, cruelly mimicking the lost silver of her powers. Kendric did not tell her that, for he was her only mirror now and would rather dull his own perceptions than reflect back too sharp a truth.

They rushed back up the coiled passage in single file, Irissa ahead with the Shunstone still clenched in her fingers. The light from the sword's hilt rode above Kendric's shoulder, gilding her dark hair here and there. She had not spoken since their discussion over the remains of Fanis. He feared that, like most raw magic wielders, he had drawn on a magic beyond his own to turn the trick.

Yet she paused artfully at the fanged archway to slide sideways through the venom-glazed fangs and waited for him to make his slower, more dangerous way through. Then she turned and sped forward, as if demon-pursued.

In the daylight, they stood blinking. The ichorous residue of the guardians had dried into an antihill of yellow powder, and all the water-soaked, oozing lands around them were desiccating so quickly that a sulfurous steam sizzled up from the swamps.

Irissa held her Stone-bearing arm stiff before her, apparently needing to thrust it as far from herself as possible.

"It—it is ..." Her fingers uncurled, one by one, forcibly.

A dun-colored stone fell to the ground. "I cannot hold it any longer."

Kendric crouched to regard the object of their quest. Egg-shaped, bland-colored, it was the mate of Chaundre's Draw-stone for plainness. A pincer of his thumb and forefinger hovered, curved and ready to close over the simple surface. The cords of his hands sharpened and his forearm muscles swelled with equal effort.

Kendric sat back on his haunches with a grunt and shook his head. "You cannot continue to hold it, and I cannot begin to. With all the force I command, I cannot close my fingers on it."

"Chaundre didn't bother to tell us how we should carry back to him a thing which forces all things from it." Irissa had crouched beside him, her elbows braced on her knees and her dark hair brushing the ground. Her eyes were only silver-rimmed now and she was completely herself—as much so as could be in these days when the core of that self was held hostage somewhere with her lost powers.

"A typical quest," Kendric said glumly. "One rushes off to where one doesn't know one is going, to acquire something that is good for Overstone-knows-what, with no inkling of how to deal with it. Leave it to what's left of Fanis."

"We promised Chaundre. Besides, I think we were meant to have it for the nonce. I could not have carried it from the cavern, had not some lingering spirit of Hariantha made it possible for me to hold it even that long."

"Hariantha should have lingered a little longer. Well, I will try to pick it up again."

Irissa's long white fingers plucked cautiously at his tunic sleeve. "Magic, I think, will master it. Perhaps you could cloud me as Hariantha again, and I could bear it in that guise back to Chaundre."

"And perhaps Hariantha is hoping I do just that, being eager to live the Inlands existence denied her by Fanis' arrow. She would have her Stone back, a fresh new body to dwell in, and only an untried magic wielder to drive her out again, if he could. No, I think not. I have had enough of clouds of glowing, gilded hair and star-sharp eyes."

Irissa's dark glance slid his way under veiling lashes. "If

you had a taste for such Mauvedona-ish coloring, perhaps you would not be so reluctant."

"I like things the way they are," he growled back to her teasing. "I want to know that what I see is what I see."

"What you see now is one small stone that can defeat you until you magic your way around it."

Kendric frowned. "Well, what would contain a Shunstone? Water?"

"It flows away from it. Remember, Hariantha originally used the Stone to turn meanders *away* from her people to their advantage."

"So one must think of what one wishes to accomplish, then do the opposite. A contrary thing, like most talismans—perhaps if I wished it as far from me as possible . . ."

"It has no will to defy you, nor feet to come dogging your footsteps unwanted."

"Then what shall I do with it, other than abandon it?"

Irissa sighed. "I have no solution either, except—it is a Stone, and Chaundre had hopes of using it in tandem with his Drawstone. Perhaps another Stone's power will tame it."

"Then Chaundre can leave his cursed, crazy-pattern Stonekeep and bring his own Stone here!" Kendric exploded. "We have no Stone, a long journey ahead of us to fetch one, and trouble enough with the first, if you ask me."

Irissa's glance was again oblique, again significant beyond Kendric's understanding. "*We* have no Stone. But you do."

He remembered; remembering, he flushed. "That. It is nothing I claim, merely a trinket—"

"Souvenir, I think you told Chaundre before."

"It is—of another's manufacture. I do not need to use it to establish Keeps I do not want in lands I do not like or to carry Stones I do not covet!"

"Consider it on loan," Irissa urged softly. "And use it."

Kendric wrenched his purse strings open unhappily and sent a forefinger searching within until it touched a cold, smooth spot. He brought what Chaundre had named the Quickstone from the dark. It sparkled between his fingerpads, tiny in comparison to any of the Inlands Stones, because it was an outlands stone and once had been only a tear.

With a dubious look to Irissa, he brought the Quickstone

nearer to the dormant but oddly defiant Shunstone. The Quick-stone's surface shifted, and Kendric felt the droplet between his fingers quiver. His hand hovered over the Shunstone again, as close as it could come. His fingertips tightened on the elusive Quickstone, pinching so tight he felt his flesh rub flesh. The Quickstone had narrowed to an eel of silver liquid. It slithered from his fingers, a serpentine length that elongated like spit until it touched the Shunstone.

The Shunstone ran silver and swelled a bit; like a snake, the Quickstone had a maw more formidable than its size.

"It—it ate it!" Kendric complained.

"Quenched it, rather, with its own properties. I think you can safely carry the Shunstone now, and no one will know, for not a scintilla of its powers will leak past the Quickstone surface. You appear to have acquired a Stone of wit and imagination."

"Mere Torloc embellishment," he retorted. "And it is only an insentient Stone, as you pointed out. I shall look for imagination elsewhere."

"At least you have the wit to do so," she answered, finally rising.

They surveyed the steaming marshland side by side.

"A long walk," Kendric said, fastening the boarskin purse, now heavily weighted by the double Stones, onto his belt. "And a hungry one."

"And longer and hungrier once we emerge into the Rynth again," Irissa added. "I will not wish for lorryk and draw the herd into the fowlen beaks again."

"Then we must begin." Kendric started across the reeking marshes, finding better foot purchase on the even-now-extending high ground, but also discovering that the vaporizing swamp water made a noxious barrier to breathing.

By the time they reached the fringe village, both were bent double from coughing. This time no villagers stood out to watch them pass. Perhaps the wretched huts were some protection against the rising stench.

Once across the invisible threshold between Stonekeep lands and Rynth, the air cleared. Kendric and Irissa inhaled in relieved unison.

"Does the Shunstone weigh heavily?" she asked.

"No more than an ordinary stone of its size." He turned back to study the Keeplands still visible behind them. "What will happen to Fanis' forlorn people now?"

"I think they will become less forlorn and perhaps even find they do not need a Stonekeeper, but can keep themselves very well. Look, the cloud rises."

It was true; a heavy yellow-gray mass hovered above the newly dry ground, moving ponderously upward.

"Good riddance," Kendric bade it farewell, "Yet I hate to see it rise to pollute the skies of this place. Perhaps the Overstone will swallow it."

"You are beginning to believe in the Overstone, like a rim-runner."

"I am one," Kendric answered jovially, "who may yet come to make my home in the Rynth, if we find no Torloc gate. And you can rejoin the Unkept—"

"I never joined them," she objected. "And if we stay, I would advise you to consider the benefits of erecting a Stone-keep on my stolen tear."

"How stolen? You shed it for me."

"Not for you. For—leaving Rule. And you."

"Is there any difference?"

"No, save that I was young and foolish then—"

"And would not weep now?" He had stopped walking to confront her evasive eyes.

"And *cannot* weep now," she reminded him.

"Perhaps that is why I had the foresight to take a souvenir. A man cannot love a woman who cannot weep."

"Who spoke of love?" Irissa demanded, her face frozen in distress, wild and dry-eyed.

Kendric shrugged. "We spoke of tears; it is the same."

"No! Until you have lost the magic you hold so tightly, you will know nothing of love or tears. Or Torlocs."

She spun as if eluding an unwelcome grasp, when all he did was look at her, and ran directionless into the yawning Rynth that obliged her need for flight by stretching in all directions equally.

Kendric watched her go, sorry he had turned their guarded, uneasy intimacy into a challenge. Everything he knew of women, tears, and Torlocs told him she wept. Everything he knew of magic told him she could not. Finally, he followed.

They walked the Rynth for a day and into a night, coming near no Stonekeep and beginning to appreciate the lorryk's fleet progress. They did not speak of anything other than the distance before them or share information beyond that one felt the need of a rest, the other a sudden stab of hunger. Such mutual silence would seem to indicate deep thought, but only the Overstone was there to commune with either of them, and it kept its own counsel, as they each kept theirs.

"If we do not touch upon a Stonekeep soon, we shall be in danger of walking ourselves to death in the Rynth." Kendric had finally come alongside Irissa again after allowing her to set the relentless, driven pace she seemed to require. He had no difficulty keeping up with her; it was more difficult to ebb behind, discreetly out of sight and out of her troubled mind.

"There must be one near," she noted dully. "And then it is only a matter of walking to the center of it, as someone once told me."

As if to oblige them, the Rynth took a dazzling change of nature before their eyes not many steps farther on. A range of broken, jet-black mountains towered sky-high, glittering deep obsidian in the Overstone's icy, nighttime sheen.

"What Keep is this?" Kendric wondered. "I sift my brains for the Stonelore tale about it, but remember no black peaks and no black stone."

"It is the oddest land that we have seen yet in a place usually so flat," Irissa agreed, wonder rinsing her voice of the strangled note that had webbed it of late. "But can anyone live here?"

It was a good question. The land was upthrust, sharp, and crystallized, brittle and shiny as a beetle's back. Walking upon it would be arduous and living off it impossible. It was all glassy, jagged rock, thrust into fenestrated towers so high it seemed their peaks would rake the ice-arch—if they could. There was something sentient about the dead landscape, the glimmer of it as cunning as the glint of a cutpurse's eye when it spied an unguarded treasure and waited to pounce upon it.

"We cannot live long untended in the Rynth," Kendric finally decreed. "I say we explore it, at least."

Irissa nodded and set first foot upon the shards of shiny

black rock before her. Instantly she was climbing, though the ground had not appeared to rise so steeply, and in minutes their progress was made with all four limbs as they half-clawed, half-crawled their way up a deceptive rock face so dark and steep that going up became the only option. Each look down revealed a dizzying plunge into a darkness that glittered like a star-lined abyss.

They said nothing—Kendric because the sword's free-swinging weight across his back acted as an anchor that could pull him into the dangerous darkness below. His mind had to provide the counterweight for every motion. Irissa, he thought, did not speak because she was afraid and afraid of saying so. He himself felt that fear rode on his back and goaded him with unseen spurs to make the ill-thought move that should turn his own bulk into a weight to drown him in the ragged dark below. This was not terrain that lorryk could spring over, bearing-beast could clamber, or even humankind could hope to live upon and cultivate for anything but adversity. A need for rest and restoring food had brought them to a place that allowed no pause and fed nothing but the dead.

"Kendric! Above us, did you see it?"

He shifted his hands on the slick yet sharp surface he clung to and dared leaning his head back enough to look up. Only the darkest, sheerest face of the mountain loomed over him. High to the right, he could see the Overstone's round, non-committal countenance reflected dimly in it.

"The moon?"

"No. The falgon.. The dwarf falgon. It flew from the rocks just above me."

Even as he watched, flinching, his mouth half open to shout caution, Irissa's slight figure angled more sharply upward. What she had seen—or thought she had seen—gave her heart. He could see the sharp, gray points of her elbows and knees working as she clawed across sheer rock, and he saw when one elbow hooked itself over a piece of the dark cliff and remained there.

"A ledge," she announced. "And one large enough—" There was no further sound but her hard-working gasps. And then the mountain swallowed her, gulping the gray in one instant. Kendric looked up again at the Overstone's reflection, to make certain that only Irissa had vanished, and not all things bright. The moon shone on, blandly unsurprised.

Then the moon had a twin, a smaller, pale ovoid that popped into view just above Kendric.

"It's a ledge, a low cavern, and big enough for even a Wrathman of Rule, if you can climb up it."

He did not think he could. Yet he shifted farther to the right, seeking handholds. There were those and fissures in the rocks to hold a bit of boot, save that his were so large and clumsy. Sheer strength and size were no advantage when one wrestled adamantine rock; it took a certain agile lightness of spirit to better a rock face. Lightness was not one of Kendric's attributes, and his every muscle told him so.

"Make a mind-rope," Irissa said from above, her face hanging deceptively near.

His mind was empty of all but the press of knife-sharp rock into his palms and knees and of his right foot slipping inexorably off the tiny ridge it clung to. He was too distracted to mind-make anything; yet Irissa had found a goad to drive her up to safety—an illusion in feathers, or perhaps not an illusion.

"Kendric! If you do not come quickly, I shall . . . I shall weep!"

It was half threat, half jest, and wholly a lie. Yet he heard the desperation in it and risked a clamber up to another set of fragile holds and yet another. If she could survive by pursuing dwarf falgons from an old world, he could try to survive by pursuing Torloc tears in a new one. Both were, he feared, merely the stuff of legendry now, as surely he would be if he fell—the Rynthian outlander giant who could not climb rocks, solemnly pointed out by rim-runner and Unkept alike whenever they passed this spot on their wanderings . . .

He saw the white flutter of wings above him—no, only Irissa's hands swooping down as far as they could. No falgons, only her.

"Quickly," she was urging. "There's only a bit more to go. Take my hands."

Dangle all his recalcitrant weight as well as that of his sword upon the slim white hands of an unmagicked Torloc seeress? He was so appalled he made one last scramble up the cliff and found, as he had suspected, no handholds at all. Her arms stretched before him like pale braids.

"Trust me," she insisted, though he knew it was himself he likely could not trust to keep her from entangling in his downward plunge.

His boot toes scrubbed rock, sounding like flint striking steel. He prepared for the sudden fall away he would feel first in his stomach, then in each of his limbs. But his grasp on her hands held. He was not too surprised to pull harder with one hand and stretch upward with the free hand for any purchase. His elbow banged rock ledge and swung over it. His hand found a small, unmoving hummock of rock and clung. His knee scrabbled up over the edge with the rest of him, even the sword, and his hand slid sweatily down the length of Irissa's, feeling every articulation of bone and joint within it. He hoisted himself the last distance until solid ledge made a bed for his effort-pounding body.

Irissa was there; she had hooked her body around a large hummock of rock. Now she was unwinding her legs, sitting up, raising a pale palm she had scraped along the rock ledge, and saying matter-of-factly, "You see. Dwarf falcon." Something white glistened against her skin, almost pearlescent. "I think they roost here."

Kendric rolled himself over on his back and laughed until the black rock above laughed with him.

Chapter Twenty-six

◆◆◆

"Some native variety of bird, that's all. Amozel would tell you which."

"Falgon," Irissa said.

It was a moot point. They were following a dark tunnel in the mountain ever downward, though no steps were carved into the passage. Kendric's sword hilt obligingly had illuminated itself when their path had plunged into total darkness.

Kendric was weary and bruised beyond all counting, and Irissa limped a little, but was far too forbidding to allow him to call attention to it. Doubtless she had injured her foot when she had made herself into a human anchor for him. Now they were expending what little strength they had left on a course through a dark-hearted mountain to whatever untenanted pit awaited them at the end of it. But they were human—or predominantly human—and they would try.

A sound shattered their mutual silence and echoed itself out of existence. They stopped—and stopped breathing at the same time. It came again—a distant, rhythmic click that reminded Kendric of the chip of flint on steel. Or of steel on flint . . .

He turned to Irissa. In the hilt light, his teeth shone white in a grin. "Perhaps we shall have food. And rest and refuge. If what I think awaits us around that turn—"

She followed him without comment, though his pace quickened. But Kendric was drawn by his own lure—not some remnant of another world, but a thing common to many worlds, a sound that explained why this Keep had such an uninhabitable exterior, why such a tunnel delved deep within the forbidding mountains, why . . .

He turned the indicated corner, then lunged back to catch Irissa before she overshot the turn. One large hand muffled her mouth from any speech; the other held her still against his side.

"Tell me, Torloc, what had your people done near Rindell in Rule?" he whispered.

Her eyes were widened circles of mystification. "Lived. We lived near Rindell."

"On what? On what trade?"

"On—on the coldstones found deep in the rins . . ."

"Found?"

"Mined. Oh!"

Kendric swung her around then so she could see beyond the corner. A vista of carved-out rock lighted by lurid, flickering torches opened to them. The torchlight reflected on the silver rails running arrow-straight through the tunnel mouths honeycombing the dark ahead. Empty carts stood in line like docile bearing-beasts at the top of a steep incline. In the distance, they could see the figures of men hammering at the midnight rock, making a sound like flint on steel.

"Oh, I am so hungry..." was Irissa's only remark at this sign of human habitation and industry.

They moved into the wide tunnels, stepping over the humming silver rails upon which the carts apparently moved. The humming explained itself when a cart came crashing out of the dark above to hurtle by, its whirlwind passage stirring their garments.

"But what do they mine?" Irissa asked.

Kendric bent to press his fingers against a cart bottom. They came up glitter-dusted. "I think the same thing that you mined in Rindell. Coldstones."

"But coldstones are commonstones in this world and riddle the Rynth. Why bother mining them?"

Kendric frowned and thought. "If water runs from anywhere in this world, it is from these dark peaks. The meanders must pass from above us, washing commonstones with them. Or perhaps the stones have always been here, hidden away, and this Stonekeeper is an eccentric like Chaundre. Perhaps he likes their glitter. I imagine he would be a magpie sort, to dwell in such gloomy surroundings. Be glad you can no longer weep, Torloc, or you would be in the hands of another Stonekeeper who would be loath to let you go—this time for tears."

"Just hope he does not discover what you bear in the boarskin at your side," Irissa responded, refusing to rise to any further mention of her tears or lack of them.

The atmosphere hung heavy with torch smoke and the uncirculated inner air of the mountain. They moved slowly deeper into the mine, nearer the dark figures that grew no lighter as they approached. It was clear that, while all the common folk of the Keeps worked at the will of their Stonekeeper, some had a softer lot than others. These black-garbed men and women—and children and beasts—as Irissa pointed out, delved listlessly in the deepest dark, the only sounds among them the scrape of their picks and the whine of the rails.

Irissa and Kendric approached the miners cautiously, knowing the need to contact humankind, but knowing also the leeriness of most people against strangers. Their focus was only ahead. Irissa trailed a guiding hand along the rock wall beside her, taking some comfort in its rough certainty. That certainty changed surfaces so quickly that only her hand perceived it.

"Oh!"

Kendric spun to face the wall, ready to engage man, beast, or anything in between. Instead of the dark tunnel mouth he expected with an attacker springing from it, he saw a wide, glittering vein of crystal ore, the opposite of the midnight rock that formed the mountain. Distant torchlight played strongly on the fractured surface, as if having leaked so far only to create this spectacular effect. From the quartzite surface, the light rebounded in sharp flashes of crimson, indigo, and deep, bright Borgia green. Kendric shaded his eyes and studied Irissa. "All well?"

"I nearly cut my palm on this rock; it is as sharp as a snow-season ice-dagger and as cold to the touch." She sucked fretfully on her abraded flesh, annoyed by this littlest of discomforts as she had not been by the greatest.

Kendric folded his arms across the fowlen-fur vest. "No wonder it cuts, chills, and blinds. It is pure, uncut coldstone, and a Wrathman-wide vein large enough to purchase a better part of the City of Rule, were we in Rule now and were the City of Rule spared the fire and flood of the last days."

"Coldstone!" Irissa dropped her injured hand reverentially to the sharp, solid curtain of crystal. "I have never seen it raw, only sliced into stones suitable for trading. And only in my few, small tears . . . I had no idea it was so cold, so impervious, so cutting."

"It is dangerous," Kendric conceded. "In any form."

"You can cut yourself another Quickstone," she suggested, her voice momentarily as brittle as the crystal around them.

"The Quickstone is a hybrid born of your tear, my possession of it, and this land we find ourselves in that stores its magic in stones. I do not think its like will come again, and I am not sorry for it."

"But—" Irissa's brow knitted under the Iridesium circlet and made Kendric wonder about the properties of the magical metal she still wore. "But there are no coldstones as we knew them in Rule here, only the commonstones found in the meanders, and they are different—smooth but not sharp, clear but not brilliant."

"They are water-washed coldstones, as your tears are woe-rinsed, and thus the cutting edge is taken off the crystal. And, of course, they are valueless here, for their truest, most valuable properties have been muted."

Irissa let her hand stroke the coldstone wall consideringly, as she would the flank of a favorite bearing-beast. "Then I wonder, Kendric, since the Inlands Stonekeepers trade among themselves, with whom does this particular Stonekeeper trade—in a world where what he mines is unesteemed?"

"A question worthy of Sofistron's admiration," Kendric agreed. "I think we should take care not to fall into this one's hands until we know his nature."

They skirted the party of miners, despite the tightening of their stomachs at the idea of food. Yet it seemed likely that these dull-moving delvers had little enough of their own to eat in this unfertile mountain. Always the paths lay downward along the tunnels dug for the passing of the coldstone-laden carts. Many times Irissa and Kendric had to flatten themselves to the dark walls behind them when an oncoming clatter announced another cart. Kendric even had to hold his breath in the narrow passage; often a cart brushed his clothing on its breakneck way down the mountain's gullet. Coldstones piled to overflowing flashed by with brief, dazzling rainbow clarity as they caught the sword hilt's gentle glow. Then the darkness that sat upon Kendric and Irissa returned, as heavy as a cloak, and they moved on again, aware of it dragging behind them in great, weighted folds.

The deeper they went, the grimmer weighed the darkness, until it seemed to have palpable texture, hanging so leaden that the air lay still and warm around them, as if curtained in.

"Oh!" Irissa, with her fondness for trailing her hands along the wall, had met another surprising change in surface.

"Cut again?" Kendric asked, reaching for her hand in the dimness.

She pulled away impatiently from his solicitousness. "Quite the contrary. Feel it, feel the wall." Kendric moved so cautiously to do so that she caught his hand in both of hers and pushed it into the deepest blackness they knew as wall. It sank inward as if swallowed.

"Not—wall," he said, amazed.

"Not wall, not rock." Irissa was moving along it, almost out of the pale circle cast by the hilt light, her hands swimming into the wall as if into water. "It is fabric, as black and soft as a Clymerindian night, as—"

The blackness had swallowed her whole. It took Kendric only an instant to hurl his warrior's bulk at the last place he had seen her, leading with the full brunt of his shoulder, willing to crash through rock if need be; such will was a formidable kind of magic in a man of his size.

The blackness gave as if bowing courteously away before him, instantly receptive. Its folds momentarily smothered his senses—eyes, ears, mouth, skin—and his impetus tripped him on the ridge of some impeding softness, so he went stuttering over an unseen threshold and came rolling awkwardly into the well-lighted chamber before him.

That chamber was furnished, lighted—and occupied.

"*Another* visitor! This is an occasion of note in a Stone-keeper's generation. Welcome. I would ask you to sit, but suggest that you stand first," a voice commented, sounding amused.

Kendric lumbered to his feet in no good mood. His agile, defensive roll had pressed the blunt length of the sword upon his back into the tenderer parts of his body, and he felt a fool. Irissa already sat, calm, in some ceiling-hung sling of black velvet, and watched him with a most irritatingly startled expression.

The chamber was black also and lighted by lamps suspended from chains of beaten gold that glinted as high into the darkness as Kendric's eyes could see and still showed no anchor. It was a chamber only in the sense that Ivrium's silk-hung cubicles were chambers. Yet it seemed infinitely more solid, for the walls draped gracefully down from the limitless darkness above, shaped like the hollow inside a mountain and made entirely of seamless lengths of midnight-black velvet that shimmered softly at the folds.

The floor was carpeted in some black-dyed hide so plush and thick that Kendric could not see his boot toes. Even the tables were swathed in black carpeting, and the brass serving pieces that stood upon them tilted precariously. Serving pieces? Kendric suddenly remembered how hungry and tired he was and considered hurling himself, sword and all, into the chain-hung sling opposite Irissa's. Being by nature a warrior, he instead surveyed the premises fiercely, folded his arms adamantly on his chest, and stared at the man who commanded this Keep.

"I am Reygand," the Stonekeeper said cordially, "and while travelers seldom stumble across my stoop, I am pleased to make you welcome. Please sit, Sir—"

"Wrathman," Kendric answered, glowering and reluctant to reveal his name to an unaligned magician. But he threw his great length into the indicated sling, first pushing the sword askew so it should not tangle with him further. He regretted even this the instant he realized how hard it would be to extricate himself from such soft surroundings. The sling swung rhythmically, and Kendric felt as helpless as a baby in a cradle.

The Stonekeeper, he noticed, did not allow himself to be wafted by his seating arrangement, but sat unmoving on a black, velvet-draped seat of some kind with a towering back. Against this background, Reygand blended with what bore him. He, too, was draped in black folds that coiled around his head and curtained his face, then hung loosely from the rest of his frame. It was possible to tell only that he was a man and seemed granted the usual number of limbs and features customary to humankind. His face was a bland, pale-skinned oval, neither puckered with age nor marked by any outstanding feature. He reminded Kendric of a lean-legged black spider at the center of its web, one whose reach was as long as the tendrils from which it constructed its trap.

"Your Keep is most—unusual," Kendric said proddingly.

Reygand's cloth-swathed face tautened in amusement. "Yes. I am, you see, the possessor of the Nightstone—"

"Of course!" Irissa interrupted, turning eagerly to Kendric. "The rim-runners mentioned something of it during their Stone-lore."

"I thought you were of the Rynth," Reygand said. "But it is most inconvenient for us Stonekeepers—I refer to my forebears and the Founding Father of my kind—for the Nightstone is efficacious only under the condition its name implies, and there is no true night in the Inlands, thanks to the Overstone's ever-open eye. Though some say once there was night and no Overstone."

"That is why your Keep is mountain-deep," Irissa said, "and why you drape yourself in darkness."

"Of course. And why I welcome visitors, no matter how haphazard, for no one seeks eternal night but the dead."

"We are living." Kendric made a point of this. "And we did not seek you but—"

"Stumbled upon me. I know." Reygand lifted one hand deprecatingly. It was black as well, gloved to the elbow in a gauntlet embroidered with patterns of tiny black beads. "But you will not live long without sustenance. I will call my bevy." The gauntleted hand rose higher to wrench a lampless brass chain hanging nearby. No sound came then, nor moments later when a black-draped procession of women appeared, bearing fresh dishes to lay upon the rug-hung tabletop.

"Oh, I am hungry . . ." Irissa struggled in the soft sling to twist her feet onto the floor.

"Peace, woman of the Rynth. You can have what the man leaves. It is custom here."

Irissa flashed Kendric a look of pure poison, but he shrugged, setting his infernal sling in motion. It was best that he extricate himself from the contraption first, anyway, for it took more strength to do it than one might think, and on his feet he could defend them both against this dark-garbed magician. The motions it took to release him from the velvet's insistent grasp were not dignified; but once his boots were on the dark carpets, the string of bevywomen bowed away from him. Their sheer black veils fluttered above their pale lips, and their pale hands gestured to the table. He complied, being hungry and uncertain what else to do. Besides, Irissa had been a bit cavalier of late, and a short fast upon his bounty might do her good.

The food was laid on dull black platters with braided brass rims and seemed toothsome in every respect but its presentation. When a bevywoman poured a deep garnet stream from an ebony ewer, Kendric was not slow to take the equally black cup she offered. If a Stonekeeper wished to surround himself with night, it was not more unusual than one who surrounded himself with water, like Lacustrine, or madness, like Chaundre.

"You may wish to lay your weapon upon the table while

you eat, swordsman," Reygand suggested. "You look sore used, and there is a bench at your back."

Kendric turned. He had not seen it, black against the black, but a small, x-framed bench stood empty behind him, its seat a drum-tight length of black fabric. Kendric unfastened the sword and set it softly on the rumpled velvet at his right hand. He sat and began to reconsider eating the food. Irissa, after all, had complained of hunger several times, and her only way to it was through him . . .

Reygand rose. Kendric noted that the man's height was unremarkable and let his body sink deeper on the bench. The Stonekeeper walked into the space between Kendric and Irissa, his gauntleted fingers reaching for something in his robes.

"I thought you would care to see my Stone. There is not its like in the Inlands, and few have seen it." He flourished a shiny black rock, spherical yet large enough to stretch his thumb and forefinger wide. He came to show it first to Kendric, which was only proper to Inlands etiquette.

Kendric pursed his lips. He still had not made up his mind to eat, but had resolved not to do so unless Irissa could join him. It was time to teach these Stonekeepers a few civilities . . . Reygand thrust the Stone under Kendric's nose.

Kendric saw black—encompassing, solid, shiny black. It was black that should not be, being both utterly reflective and utterly absorptive. He saw himself, as if in a dark mirror, and this was no distress, for even with secondhand Torloc powers he was not image-forbidden.

He looked up and saw himself faint yet life-sized, sitting beside himself, eating from the dark dishes and drinking ruby-black wine from the inky cup. He opened his mouth to speak and could not talk, made gesture to move, and could not. He could only see himself, doing what he had thought to do in very few moments, and beyond this—willful reflection—of himself, the tiny, pale visage of Reygand and the lighter, charcoal-gray figure of Irissa. And he saw his sword, lying just beyond the right hand of the mock Kendric that was his dining partner. The hilt was shining a beacon-bright warning.

Irissa turned her dimly seen face to him. Kendric could not read much well beyond the Nightstone wall that webbed him, but he could read the displeasure upon her features perfectly.

* * *

Irissa frowned. Kendric, she saw, had tackled Reygand's offering with his usual culinary gusto. A Wrathman could eat heartily in any circumstance, including inequity, apparently. Her glance rested on the sword that lay docile beside him. With a sword and a square meal, Kendric would be content till doomsday. She was mad to rely upon such a one for anything but the most predictable of services, a strong arm and a weak head for magic.

"You must be hungry after your travail," Reygand said sympathetically. "At least let me show you my Keep; by then, yon giant will have had his supper and you can dine."

Irissa lifted her chin. She was sure that Kendric would break even custom if she asked to share his meal, but she would not ask. And Reygand had promised to show her the Nightstone, yet had stopped at showing it to Kendric. No doubt she didn't merit more than a courteous tour of the premises. She nodded assent. He gestured to the chamber's draped corner.

"You will have to hold on to the ropes," Reygand told her. "Our way is up."

There was no stair, only a suspended black velvet bridge leading upward. Brass-ringed ropes as thick as her wrist stretched at hand height on either side of the passage. She caught hold of their soft lengths and began walking upward on the cloth that sagged with her every step.

In a way, it was a journey as draining as the climb up the rock face, walking on that which was half-solid. But Reygand toiled up behind her, a part of the dark in his night-shaded robes, and there was nothing better to do but continue. Each glimpse over her shoulder showed her Kendric absorbed in his solitary dinner, his dark brown hair swallowed by the blackness, so she saw only his pale profile, his hands, and the white blur of his fowlen-fur vest. She could not say how devastating was the indifference implied by his simple, cheerful, animal self-absorption, but she suddenly felt that she came as close to shedding a true coldstone or at the very least some stinging salt as she had ever come in the Inlands.

And so she climbed on, mindless and desolate, regretting the distance between herself and Kendric and embracing it with a cold, stony-hearted pride, feeling an ordinary hunger that gnawed relentlessly at her body and surfeit with emotions that overflowed her mind.

"We are arrived." Reygand's gauntlet plucked Irissa's sleeve. A corporeal touch from him amazed her; she had thought him utterly part of the disembodied night they walked through. It began to occur to her that all might not be what it seemed—that nothing might be.

"Raventop," he announced. "The heart of my Keep."

Irissa looked around. They were in an ordinary tower, its walls formed of blocks of stone, save that this stone was the same shiny substance that made the outer mountain. It appeared to be the magician's bedchamber-cum-lookout, for a velvet-draped bed hugged the inner, windowless wall and a semicircle of windows occupied the outer curve. At least the apertures wore the shape of windows; Irissa could see nothing but blackness out of them, though they ringed her almost as thoroughly as Sofistron's coldstone chamber had. And there was—it was as tall as a window, as narrow and vertical, yet it was not a window, but a mirror. She had not seen a mirror since Rule. It was odd to confront such a thing, knowing she need no longer fear it, and regretting her safety.

"I am not an original Stonekeeper, you know," Reygand was telling her softly. "There are many gates to every world, and I was ever wont to find gates first, Torloc."

She stared at him.

"Even when Finorian was young, I had slipped from time to time from Rule and found my other mountain fasthold here."

Finorian? Rule? Torloc? Irissa stared into the pale face that it seemed she had overlooked in all the ebony of this place. He wore pleasant features, this Reygand, and his eyes were blue. She thought of the Rynx then, though she knew that was the wrong memory, from the wrong world. He spoke of another world, a former world.

"I have not yet shown you my Stone, as promised." He sighed, heavily, and began working the fingers of his gauntlets off his hands, inch by tight-gloved inch, as if the process were painful. The flesh revealed was bone-sharp and shriveled, that of hands exposed to the full mortality of an inordinately long life.

Irissa stared at them and saw them reaching for her, through stone, through time, through a magic wall that should never have been breached. "Geronfrey!" she said and looked to the blue eyes.

They were mild, resigned. "Yes. Geronfrey. But I have been Reygand here for almost as long as I was Geronfrey in Rule. There is some Inlands superstition that only a descendant can claim and carry a Stonekeeper's Stone. It is not true. Reygand the Sixth had few and feeble heirlings; it was not hard to supplant them. And I had time and Rule to hie to for a change of scene. The Stonekeepers keep to themselves, so I kept to my Keep and my—"

"Coldstones! You mine the coldstone here, where it is worthless, and carry it to worlds where it—"

"Can buy me what my magic cannot master. You were the one thing impervious to my powers, Irissa. You carried your own wealth in your tears and magic in your eyes."

"And do so no longer," she admitted. "So perhaps you can at last forgive that I was not as malleable as you thought me."

"No longer coldstones, no longer magic." He cocked his head as inquiringly as a mimicking bird at her.

Irissa felt no need to pretend to powers she no longer had or to deny Geronfrey his savoring that. After all, it was her power he had craved, not her person, though the means to her powers were as personal as anything that passed between man and woman, whether magicked or not. And it was an old, long-dead betrayal. He had courted her when Kendric and she had come to stay in his under-mountain hold in Falgontooth. He had courted her for her silver eyes and the powers that seeped through them, which were transferable only once and to only one man—the first. And she, knowing only that power was not the price she put on her heart, had fled Geronfrey, seeking one untainted by any but the most ordinary, the most human, of powers. And so she had found Kendric in the dark of night and given to him who would not take what Geronfrey would have given much to take.

She had merely deceived Geronfrey as to her willingness to consider his courtship, and who could blame her, trapped as she had been by her own nature and his insight into it? Yet Geronfrey had blamed her, and she and Kendric had escaped him only by the finest of hairs. Now he had them both within his grasp again. She looked at his aged hands; they were another sin to her account, for had he not tried to reach his revenge through sheer matter, this, too, would not have been his loss.

Irissa swept her own hands wide, helplessly. "You have us. For what it is worth. An unempowered Torloc seeress, a homeless Wrathman of Rule."

"Yes. I have you. And you are right. It is worth nothing to me. A magician of my subtlety is too proud to waste time revenging myself upon some brute of flesh and bone who but acts as he is led; and I find that wreaking my power upon the unempowered for the sake of it is an empty exercise. I learned that long ago. So. We are well met, then. Old friends. Old adversaries. Old emigrants from Rule." Geronfrey let his blue eyes study the tops of his aged hands. "Old merely, at least in my case."

"I was not aware that you were unempowered," he continued.

Irissa nodded dolefully, hoping that he was also unaware that Kendric had eventually inherited the powers that Geronfrey had so coveted.

"You can do nothing?"

She nodded her head. Admitting so to a sorcerer like Geronfrey was a painful confrontation with a loss she was virtually inarticulate to explain to Kendric. Whether he went by the name of Geronfrey or Reygand, he was a wielder of magic and he knew what the loss of it meant more intimately than any in this world or another. He had won over her after all, Irissa thought, and raised bitter gray eyes to his.

Geronfrey's bony fingers brushed her dark hair back, as if the man were eager to read her loss in all its details. "Yes. All gray but for the narrowest rim." His sharp fingers tightened on her chin, so that she could not look down, but only into his so-young blue eyes. "I could . . . I could help you, I think. If I cared to."

He pushed her face away and turned to pace along his vistaless windows. Irissa felt numb. She should have recognized the tower, so like in some respects to Geronfrey's tower in Rule. She should have remained below with Kendric, waiting for—what? For Geronfrey to reveal himself to them both and perhaps wreak his vengeance on both? She should not have come docilely here with an alien sorcerer. Alone. Especially now that he had proved himself to be less alien than she had thought.

"Help?" The word was hollow, empty on her lips.

Geronfrey nodded solemnly, the black drapings around his face shifting like curtains around a stage. There was something poised and vacant about Geronfrey's face, too. Perhaps he felt all this was as empty as she did.

Geronfrey tented his fingers before his face, so that they made a bony steeple upon which his blandly youthful features balanced like a ball. His head nodded again, and his eyes narrowed speculatively until she could no longer discern their color.

"I—retain—a portion of you. I would assume that I retain a portion of your powers also—useless to me."

"You have had nothing of me but the sight of my back as I fled," Irissa said fiercely. It was enough that she had lost her powers; she should not lose her pride.

"I demur, Torloc. I offered you a unique vision of yourself, remember? Your first glimpse of your outer self in my dark mirror. That night in my stronghold was one of many firsts for you," he added dryly. "But long before you lost yourself in a Wrathman's embrace, you found yourself in my mirror. I suppose I should take some comfort in that, now that I am resigned to your rejection. One does not live as long as I without taking resignation for a bedfellow. I have that mirror still. Behold it."

His dark robes swirled around the white flourish of one skeletal hand. Irissa's glance followed his gesture before she could stop herself. She was facing the one dark window that she knew was a mirror.

It was as empty as an ebony pool. Now that she dared face her own reflection without fear of lessening her powers, it appeared that she cast none. The faultlessly sleek, dark surface remained unrippled, impervious to motion within the chamber.

Irissa snapped an accusing look at Geronfrey, feeling both defrauded and relieved.

"I believe I like you better when you can look direct, Torloc. I would not have misread you in Rule, had you spoken so eloquently with your eyes then. No, I am not tricking you, promising you hope for the pleasure of taking it away. I am holding what I possess of you. I believe it retains your powers, and that by . . . joining . . . with this lost slice of yourself, you might empower your true self again. But there is no guarantee, and I am an honest seducer, as you admitted once. You must decide whether you wish to see that long-lost, mere surface of yourself again."

Her lips parted, ready to refuse. She paused. Below her, Kendric ate and drank in the dark, as content with his physical lot as her magical one discontented her. She risked confronting a disruption of the physical, her own image in another's hands, to chase the chimera of magic. But what had been done once . . .

"Yes," she told Geronfrey, and it was there before she had articulated the word's final, sibilant consonant—herself. The image was faint in the dark mirror, the muted paleness of face, throat, and hands floating almost disembodied. The Iridesium circlet cast so dense a reflection that it sliced off a white triangle of forehead from the rest of her features. Her eyes were dark holes in the mirror, though the very edges of the irises seeped a sickly phosphorescent glow . . .

Irissa turned her real face away. "It is a travesty of image. Release it."

"Wait! You have seen only a meld of your current reflection and that which has lain long uncalled. It asserts itself now."

She looked back, loathing her weakness. The silver rims were swelling inward, drowning black pupil to a mere pinprick. Irissa stepped toward the mirror, seeing then that the image wore not only the Torloc seeress' unabated silver eyes but also the heavy robe of sable velvet she had worn on that occasion so long before, when she had eluded Geronfrey but not herself or Kendric . . .

"Yes. Step close. Nothing prevents you now, Torloc. You have no powers to shield, nothing to lose but your loss. If you wish to draw from this sliver of yourself, you must step nearer, you must draw it to you."

Irissa's fingers, fanned and cautious, reached out. Her image raised a similar starfish of hand so slowly through the dark, reflective waters that it did not precisely mirror the position of Irissa's fingers. The image's fingertips trembled and then matched Irissa's. Only the slightest distance separated them.

Irissa felt that the mirror surface was not solid, but liquid, that this vision of herself was like a wailwraith called up from the bottom of her shadowed pool to mock reflection with a vain mortal woman caught leaning too near the water. Yet . . . The silver eyes met her own, burning through her deadened gaze with a hot, magic, white light. She was near enough to see the great golden brooch holding the gown together between the image's breasts, dimmed by the dark mirror to an Overstone-bland sheen.

Before, Geronfrey had warned her against touching her own image, against breaching this distance. She heard no warnings now; she heard nothing. It was as if Geronfrey had ceased to breathe, as she had—as if he, too, hung upon her gradual, soft sinking into her own image. Fingertips touched. Irissa felt a brush of cold, then nothing. She felt her foot lift to the mirror frame and use it as a step. For an instant she felt plunged in icy winter water to the ankle. Then her entire body made that chilling, drowning contact, and she was embracing a seamless surround of cold and dark that adhered to and swallowed her. Silver eyes burned into hers with such unswerving intensity that she felt them eat to the back of her skull and drive screaming out into the gulf behind her hair. It was emptiness beyond imagining that she was sealed into, that she faced on all sides. Against such limitless, unforgiving, terrifying nothingness, even regret was a redundancy.

Irissa was walking slowly in the heavy, train-trailing black robe, down a hall in Geronfrey's under-mountain tower. Her hair, as dark as damp black velvet, hung to either side of her face, fell cloaklike over her shoulders and back, and lay upon her like a conscience. Yet she walked, dragging the dark of herself and her garb behind her. The stones around were gray and echoed not even her footfalls, but that was because her feet were bare and silent. They felt chilled.

She walked down the hall with great purpose and great fear in her heart. She was not sure what or whom she feared, for she had come lately from only a warm bath and the leisure of combing her damp hair smooth with an ivory comb and primping of a sort alien to one whose vanity was centered in her mind, not in any outer aspect.

Still she moved, purposefully, heart pounding, until she came to a wide wooden door that she had and had not seen before. She felt she had done this endlessly, seen and not seen herself in these precise circumstances. She felt she lived memory and relived what had never been. Her fingers stretched and brushed the heavy door. It swung away before her as lightly as a cobweb. She was in a chamber with an ember-warmed fireplace yawning luridly against the farther wall and a huge, tester-hung bed on the other.

She walked toward the bed, clenched her fingers in the fabric—heavy, unyielding brocade—and swept it back. Something stirred in the smothered dark, something large and unknown. An arm reached out to hold back the curtain; she recognized the blue of a certain tunic. A tousled, dark brown head thrust through the rent in the fabric. Irissa felt the first emotion she had experienced in this empty, selfless state—relief. It was only Kendric, and she was, as usual, disturbing his simple comfort with her complicated presence. Why? She herself could not answer, could not remember. And then he was reaching for her, drawing her into the dark; she could feel the bed curtains hushing shut upon her, behind her, and she was dragged down into the deepest dark depths of memory and that-which-was-not-quite-memory. The dark closed upon her again, this time soft and comforting, warm and as privately enveloping as night.

This was memory, not reality, she told herself, but she had forgotten the sweet security that she had sought and found in Kendric, comfort enough to keep her warm even within the icy confines of a night-blasted mirror. She remembered, too, her lost powers, which the Irissa whose motions she relived had possessed then. But it was more than the memory of then-powers that warmed Irissa now, and it was good to have delved into this shadow of herself to remember that. It was odd, though, that in all this so-familiar reenactment of a choice made long before in another place, she had not noticed the sword. It was always by Kendric, and on this occasion had announced itself with a particularly persistent glow. Yet all here was dark. The arms tightened around her, and Irissa of the Mirror gave herself up to them.

* * *

Irissa was walking slowly in the heavy, train-trailing black robe, down a hall in Geronfrey's under-mountain tower. Her hair, as dark as ebony velvet, hung to either side of her face, fell cloaklike over her shoulders and back, and lay upon her like a conscience. Yet she walked, dragging the dark of herself and her garb behind her. The stones around were gray and echoed not even her footfalls, but that was because her feet were bare and silent. They felt chilled.

She was walking away from some place, someone, with great purpose, but also with a deadness of emotion. She recalled other emotions, warm and sustaining, but they came from a great distance, of time as well as of place. She herself felt garbed in ice. It seemed to thicken upon her, to swell upon the black velvet train dragging like a tail behind her. Her hands hung at her sides, too heavy to lift. She could feel the ice forming over her face, hanging in shiny jet ice-daggers from the strands of her hair. Her temples throbbed where the Iridesium circlet melted the forming crystals until they ran like water past her eyes and down her cheeks, until they ran like icy tears. Then even they froze and glazed her features motionless.

Her bare feet still shuffled forward beneath the robe whose folds had grown hard and cold and immobile as iron. They grew chiller and she paused. She could not move now, could do nothing but stand frozen in the dark heart of something utterly alien. She contemplated the icy, empty darkness, stretching around her to all limits of whatever there was, and was glad so little of her remained alive and remembering to know this place, this state, for what it was.

Chapter Twenty-seven

———◆◆◆———

Kendric's stomach growled. He was distressed that such a mundane matter should assert itself at such a moment, but then this Reygand *would* afflict him with the sight of an unreachable dinner while trapping him within some black, glassy emanation of the Nightstone.

The image of himself was still consuming happily. Kendric was not sure how much time had elapsed since Reygand had bowed Irissa into the dark, curtained corner of the fabric-hung hall, but it was certainly more than he wished. He himself felt no real sense of time or motion, for he was as oddly leaden as before, as if he had been draped with an invisible cloth of great weight—not wholly invisible, Kendric reminded himself, studying the brittle gossamer webbing him.

How did one undo the effects of a Nightstone? As one undid night with light? It might not even have to be magical light, for Reygand's devotion to underground living and the funereal black with which he fashioned his walls both bespoke a need for utter, smothering dark. The sword hilt might suffice to rend the dark, but it lay far from Kendric and the substance that trapped him, still glowing fitfully. If he could move enough to extract the flint and steel from his purse, he might produce an even more spectacular effect.

Kendric had never tried to use his strength against the physical power of a magical spell. But magic often drew on the natural, and whatever hung around him had a natural trait or two, such as reflection. He guessed that Reygand's false Kendric could not move and eat so convincingly, had it not had a natural Kendric near to give shape to the illusion.

He flexed his arm muscles and felt a reassuring tautening. As he guessed, that which was deepest within himself would

285

be most resistant to the spell. That which was most upon the surface was most bespelled, since the purpose of the thing was deceptive appearance. Kendric didn't stop to think of why. He was occupied, as Irissa when she had been imprisoned, with how.

Luckily, his arm had been bent, elbow flexed, and his hand resting near the needed boarskin at the moment of enchantment. If he could only drive his stiff fingers through the purse's drawstring throat and wrest the tiny bits of stone and metal from its gullet... If only! He roamed the land of wish-for-it again. He would have shrugged at his folly, but he could not. Instead, his first two fingers curled by a concentration of his will—he could feel inner muscles shaking with effort up his arm and deep into his back. Then it was merely a matter of driving the entire arm forward so he could reach into the purse... The trembling spread to his other arm and down to his hips. He had never exerted so much effort into so little movement, and it seemed for a moment that his whole body might shudder apart. Then his fingertips closed on what he needed, both pieces, and he slowly withdrew them, holding them pinched above the cup of his palm.

False Kendric beside him drove a knife lustily into a slab of meat, seemingly capable not only of undisturbed eating but of ceaseless eating.

Kendric's other hand was frozen curled at his waist. He shifted his struggle to the other arm and slowly forced that hand to meet the first. It pleased him to discover that mere force could dislodge magic, however slightly, and he did not mind the sweat that rolled stinging into his eyes.

With both hands together, it was merely a matter of striking flint and steel... Telling himself that this was a "mere" matter made it appear more possible. Besides, it was here he planned to supplement his strategy.

His palsied hands made one opposing pass against each other, flint and steel clenched separately. They kissed with a faint, metallic rasp, too weak to produce a spark. Kendric produced it, from his mind, as he had so often aided recalcitrant flint and steel at the Unkept women's campfire. A searing red comet leaped off the dull-colored metal and sizzled upward.

Kendric impelled its progress with his eyes and watched it erupt on the polished translucent dome arching over him.

Now came sound—hiss and crackle and snap. The Nightstone's web rent into tatters of falling flame, and false Kendric disappeared in a ruddy instant that made his original shudder a bit. Ashes fell across the orange of his sillac-hide boots and dusted Kendric's knees and hair. They seasoned the full platters of food lying cold and congealed before him.

He rose, seized his sword, and bolted for the corner where the veiled images of Reygand and Irissa had gone. There was nothing there but heavy, ocean-swelled folds of black velvet, towering high above him like the sleek prow of some colossal dark ship. He beat his way against the cloth, and rippled length after length of it curled back against him, as muscular and seductive in texture as a moonweasel. He caught it in one fist and shook it, as if to pull a curtain down by its rings. Whatever rod supported these gigantic draperies was driven firm high above in the mountain's peak.

Then he noticed a furtive golden gleam. His hand closed around a ring big enough to fill his palm, one that in turn clasped a snake of stuffed velvet. Kendric fastened his sword across his back and began drawing himself up a ladder of velvet, the fabric beneath his boots sagging heavily with every step upward. It was like swimming in full Iridesium mail through a dark, curdled-cream sea; but having once found a path, whatever its nature, Kendric resolved to take it until he saw Irissa again.

The chamber at the top of the shifting staircase was reassuringly solid. Kendric stood studying it suspiciously, dubious even of its apparent emptiness. He unfastened his sword and thrust fitfully into the ground-sweeping folds of midnight velvet testering a princely bed along one curtained wall. He walked to each of the blank, black windows and stared out them. He walked back to the chamber's center, to turn slowly and methodically in its middle. It was an odd environment, yet of a piece with the rest of Reygand's Keep, with windows overlooking the mountain's obsidian heart—an odd fancy and one that was not entirely new to him. Aside from the luxuriant bed and a small chest at its foot, there was no other furniture but the mirror on the wall—

Kendric could see only a slender dark slice of mirror, narrow as a bloatsnake before it swelled. In two thundering steps he had put himself face to face with it. Finally, he saw Irissa.

She stood, life-sized, at the very front of the mirror, slightly elevated by the frame so that they were eye to eye. But she was not looking at him; her eyes roamed searchingly past him, as if he were the unreal image, not she. And then he saw that she wore the robe of Rule, the handsome, trailing gown Geronfrey had thought to tempt her vanity with, and he saw the long stone hall of Geronfrey's tower in Rule arrowing into the distance behind her. She could have been standing in the same place she had stood but months ago, wearing what she had worn then, save that her eyes shifted color as he watched, from dark gray to silver.

His hand fisted upon the sword just below the hilt, and he raised it to shatter the dark glass. No. She might shatter behind it. His thoughts collided madly, veering between two worlds, two halls, two magicians, two Irissas...

Kendric turned his back upon the mirror, strode over to the bed, and sat at its foot to contemplate her, his hands folded over his sword hilt, his chin propped upon his hands, and the weapon's great length angling away between his splayed legs. It pained him to watch this mirror-trapped Irissa, her changeable eyes always reflecting the panic of the trapped. They reminded him of the eyes of the littlest lorryk as he had held it and first tried to heal it. It was horrible to face such mute despair; seeing it in well-known eyes was more terrible still. He must think, then act and act rightly, or they would both forever face the consequences. He must use magic, no fooling himself about that, no tricks with flint and steel. And proper magic, to free her without destroying her. For she was not here, as near as the image he could touch if he dared. She was somewhere very far away, and he must bring her back.

Kendric sighed, stood, and went over to study the mirror again. He laid the sword carefully against the wall, so gingerly it seemed he wondered if he would ever pick it up again. And then he reached into the handy boarskin and brought out the Shunstone-hearted Quickstone, his Stone of power in a land that was not his. He doubted it, and thus doubted himself, yet could no longer afford that luxury. It was dark, this mirror, but every reflective surface must wear light somewhere. He held the swollen Quickstone in his fist. It was smooth and cool to his skin, aloof. Why did he think it would bend any part of itself to his needs? He held it and thought the mirror melting, softening into molten silver, like rain.

The transitory silver of Irissa's eyes arrested, then expanded until her whole figure was bathed in an argent glow. It swelled outward to the mirror frame, the whole surface shining bright and obscuring Irissa, hall, and all. Kendric held to the Quickstone, which now had warmed to his flesh until it seemed likely to seep between his knuckles. The mirror vibrated before him and swelled into three dimensions. Something was stepping through, something that wore the worm-woven silver-gray silks of Rule. Irissa was stepping through, her gray boot poised on the frame bottom, her face surfacing through a wavering sheet of sheer silver as a wailwraith was said to rise to a pond's top; now her dark hair was visible, roped with weeds of quicksilver.

With his other hand he grasped hers and pulled her through. He had not thought he pulled so hard, but she catapulted into his body, and he had to use his free arm to steady her. His other hand felt frozen to the elbow, and he slowly dropped the Quickstone back into the purse at his belt.

Irissa had hidden her head in his shoulder, as if she never wanted to see more than the dark of his body again. He disappointed her long enough to pull her head back roughly by the hair. Her eyes were unshifting gray again, narrowly rimmed with silver. He sighed and began awkwardly brushing snaky strands of quicksilver from her hair. Irissa burrowed her face into his fowlen-fur vest again and moved to the light strokes of his hand like a cat to a caress.

"Kendric! How did you free me? It was horrible, that void where I was held, neither here nor there, neither past nor future, and not even present. I was like some spider's prey, silk-tethered and hung spinning over eternity." She shuddered and stopped talking.

He did not know this Irissa—not that he doubted he had freed the real Irissa, only that she was not the same. Now she was clinging to him and murmuring his name over and over, as if it held a special magical virtue. Kendric tightened his arms around her. Irissa pressed herself more warmly against him. He was not minded to object, but she had misinterpreted his gesture.

Behind her, the shimmering mirror had gradually resolved itself into a dark, reflective surface. As it had returned to its own consistency, so, too, had the long expanse of Geronfrey's hall reappeared. And in the foreground was a figure. This was another Irissa, gowned in trailing black, wearing her silver eyes. Those eyes no longer darted about in a mad attempt at escape from what they saw. They looked clear, steady, and unafraid into Kendric's, at the same level as Kendric's, for the figure was life-sized and elevated by the mirror hanging upon the wall. There was something dreamlike and dazed to the figure, something insubstantial about it, though every detail was as real as those that made up the Irissa he held in his arms and even now held tighter, as if to impress her realness into his flesh.

She smiled at him vacantly, the mirrored lady with the silver eyes, as if she had known him once but no longer remembered where or when. Far behind her, in the hall's deepest shadows, another figure stepped forward. And the mirrored woman majestically turned, swinging her dark train into a tail, and began walking down the hall until her gown and hair vied with the shadows for blackness. Kendric reached for the sword he had leaned against the wall and plunged the hilt through the mirror until it rebounded on stone.

Irissa started against him as shimmering black cracked away in a thousand ragged pieces. Only the wall remained, with an empty frame and a jet glimmer at his feet.

"You broke it." Irissa's voice sounded thick, velvet-smothered, but he was glad she was ready to confront what lay behind her.

"Yes." He laid the sword against the wall again so he could enfold her with both arms.

"How did you release me?"

"I'll tell you some other time."

She finally looked up at him, and he saw why her voice had sounded so sodden. Her cheeks were shiny with the passage of tears.

He brought his hand to her face; his fingertips came away wet. He put his question into his eyes.

"I have not got my magic back," she said, her ordinary gray eyes brimming extraordinarily full of salt water, "but I think I have recovered my share of mortal tears."

"You weep—" He was still awed by it, having learned to expect anything from her but the obvious.

"For joy. I am so glad to be able to *see* you again, Kendric." She weighted the word "see" with more than ordinary meaning. "I have been far into my past and future. I have remembered things only a stubborn Torloc would forget. I have been—"

He pressed his fingertips to her mouth and watched the tear tracks dry on her face. "It was Geronfrey? Reygand, that is?"

She nodded and would have spoken, but his fingers remained in place. "Some other time," he said and backed into the soft black velvet he knew was waiting behind them, drawing her with him. There was one element of Reygand's hospitality that he had no fear of using. A Wrathman liked his comforts, as Irissa would be the first to point out.

Chapter Twenty-eight

———◆◆———

"Marvelous, marvelous!"

The Quickstone slid serpent-supple from the Shunstone and pooled into its original shape in Kendric's palm. He tucked it away unobtrusively, for everyone's attention was focused on the ordinary-appearing Stone left as a dun-colored island on the broad surface of Chaundre's tower's tabletop.

Chaundre was clucking and peering at the Stone, his commonstone appliance perched upon his long nose and threatening to slip off as he leaned nearer. Amozel sat by him, her firm chin supported by her dainty but strong hands, an expression of uncommitted curiosity warming her brown eyes.

Kendric and Irissa stood side by side, in a stance reflecting a certain impatience to be off and a definite disinterest in the Stone they had brought.

"Was it a difficult journey?" Chaundre asked with that absent tone that indicated courtesy rather than true interest. His eyes remained fastened on the Shunstone.

"Yes and no," Kendric said.

"Most . . . instructive," Irissa answered.

Chaundre nodded without looking up. "And how shall we use it, eh? In conjunction with the other, or first by itself, or—"

"You promised us guidance on Irissa's quest to find where her fellow Torlocs go," Kendric interrupted.

Chaundre glanced up from under woolly eyebrows. "Sister Torlocs, technically. Only the females journey here. Interesting, eh?" He smiled mysteriously. "But I promised you help and, truth to tell, the sooner you are on your way, the sooner we can begin our experiments on the Shunstone."

Kendric and Irissa exchanged a tolerant glance. Amozel and Chaundre's alliance seemed but more cemented than ever, and, in the mutual glow of their own reunion, this seemed a happy thing.

"I'll get you the maps," Chaundre promised, still lingering over the Stone, his trailing sleeves carefully rolled back so they would not inadvertently sweep its surface.

Kendric cast his eyes to the tower's unroofed ceiling and exchanged a kindred look with the Overstone, which had doubtless spent more time than he watching Chaundre's attention wander.

"The maps. Yes." Chaundre whirled away with the sudden, uncoiling burst of energy characteristic of him, then returned from a nearby chest with more of his foolscap scrolls. He unrolled several before spying the right one. This he laid carefully on the table's very end, so it should not disturb the Shunstone, which at the moment looked so utterly rockish it seemed incapable of being disturbed by doomsday.

"We are here." Chaundre's long finger pinioned a point near the map's top. "And you must go to the Cincture, which is only a half-day's journey." Chaundre unbent and beamed happily at them.

"You mean . . ." Here Kendric's blunt finger speared a point at the map's bottom. "You mean we traveled all the way to the other end of the Inlands to fetch your silly Stone when we only needed to walk a few miles north to be about our own business?"

Chaundre shrugged ingratiatingly. "But I needed the Stone, and an Inlands-born cannot take another's Stone, ever since Fanis . . . Be glad your journey is short now, for that is all that is optimistic about it."

"He means that the Cincture is shunned by all Inlands folk and beasts," Amozel said seriously. "And that only the fowlen roam it. It is sure death."

"Yet the Torloc seeresses have gone there—" Irissa began.

"And have never returned," Chaundre warned, his eyes sharp over the top of his commonstone appliance. He smiled. "But I think that is because they know where they are going. And so do I, in a sense. They go here—" Chaundre walked his fingers spider-fashion to a blank part of the map. "The Cincture, though uncharted, surrounds all the Inlands, like a ring. Yet I have calculated that the meanders spring from the Cincture and—according to their courses—must merge somewhere here! And that is where I infer the Torlocs go, for they all must pass by me, and I have watched their routes."

"And what is there?" Irissa asked, indicating the place with her own long, pale finger.

Chaundre's eyes widened. "I don't know."

Kendric exchanged another look with the Overstone. "Well, if you will be so kind as to equip us, we will be on our way to find out."

"You will find death and fowlen in the Cincture and the bones of your Torloc seeresses," Amozel predicted.

"Fowlen are not so bad," Kendric said cavalierly. "The Rynx seems to have them well controlled."

"Aha! The Rynx has shown itself?" Chaundre's attention was finally fully distracted from the Stone. "You saw it?"

"Spoke with it." Kendric sounded casually boastful. After all, he who had spoken with a cat in Rule would not be non-plussed by speaking with a bird-headed wolf in the Inlands.

One of Chaundre's unruly eyebrows rose. "Spoke with it. Hmmmm. The Rynx never appears unless some disturbance affects both Inlands and Cincture, and I have concluded that coincides with the passage of a Torloc seeress. But usually

such a presence causes endless upset among the Stonekeeps—
the swelling of meanders, the drying up of marshes and lakes,
the death of cattle and birds, and the souring of wine and other
such things."

"Thank you," Irissa said demurely.

"You have not caused such disruptions, perhaps because
your powers ebbed in Sofistron's chamber, before they had an
opportunity to set the Inlands spinning. But if the Rynx appears,
it is apparent that the Cincture is not exempt from feeling your
presence."

"Or possibly his."

They all turned to stare at Amozel, who was looking speculatively at Kendric. She smiled. "You forget, he bears magic,
more than she, and although I have shunned its use, I have
seen enough of it to know it works in unanticipated ways."

"Whether it is me or not," Kendric burst out, "we shall
know nothing more until Irissa and I get on the road to Rynx
or ruin or whatever awaits us in the Cincture."

Chaundre smiled benignly, as at an impatient child. "And
so you shall go and, we hope, know more and return. We are
planning on your attendance at our wedding five days hence.
Among Inlands Stonekeepers, it has been thought that only
common folk wed, but Amozel and I wish to dispute that."
Their hands joined across the table, over the Shunstone.

"It is hard to believe, Chaundre and Amozel to wed." Irissa
shook her head bewilderedly.

She and Kendric were trudging into the Rynthian distance,
Chaundre's patchwork Keep already vanished behind them and
nothing ahead of them to indicate that an utterly blank space
on Chaundre's map labeled the Cincture even existed.

They walked on in companionable silence, used to being
alone in the Rynth now, used even to the Rynth. After a bit,
Kendric spoke.

"Do Torlocs wed?"

Irissa stopped and kicked her boot toe consideringly at a
few loose stones. "I was pledged to Thrangar, the Torloc
Wrathman, had he not disappeared, remember? It was
Finorian's plan, anyway, though as usual she told no one

of it. But that was a formal alliance, and nothing might have come of it."

"These things are never simple," Kendric reminded her gently.

She dropped her head and nodded.

They had not discussed the events in Reygand's Keep, beyond admitting that the sorcerer was Geronfrey of Rule as well, and that they had somehow escaped him again, thanks to Kendric's application of magic.

Irissa had resolved never to confess to Kendric that Geronfrey had tempted her into the mirror with a false promise of restoring her powers. It was a weakness she was truly ashamed of, and she feared that Kendric would not understand until he, too, lost magic and mourned it. Whatever ill for her and good for him Geronfrey had intended by tricking Irissa into reliving her first rejection of him, the result had been to rekindle the warmth between herself and Kendric. That she could never regret.

And Kendric bore the burden of his vision of a shadow Irissa still moving in the mirror like an invisible sword upon his back. To tell one who had lost so much of herself that yet another piece of self lived in another place, in another person's hands, would be cruel. Besides, he hoped his crashing hilt had ended shadows. He knew enough of magic to doubt it, but he hoped.

So they walked together, toward what they hoped was the Cincture, the most forbidding edge of the Inlands. They went, feeling strong and serene in themselves, in each other, to where the Torloc seeresses always went when they passed through the Inlands. They went, they hoped, to find Irissa's knowledge and Kendric's egress.

Just when Chaundre's half-day's journey began to seem like a day's and when the Rynth unrolled before them in endless, Rynthian similarity, they crossed into the Cincture.

Inlanders called it the Cincture, as if it had a finite, almost corporeal presence. Irissa and Kendric found it the most overwhelming place on the Inlands—one great unbordered landscape of ice and snow, still as death. The ice-arch and Overstone above reflected this arctic pallor, and no birds swept wings across the quiet, clouded sky. Snow curdled in blue-white dunes to the farthest horizon, unyellowed and unmarked by the passing of common creatures. Ice had clashed in some immemorial past, pushing itself into frozen white hillocks that disrupted the eternal snow dunes as a wound might flesh. Now all was immobile as the Overstone and somehow as expectant, as watchful.

A nearby meander flowed silently under a thin, clear icy shell that, but a few steps farther on, hardened to a milky slab under which no water ran. The air was cold but crystalline, and details in the distance seemed as sharply edged as the ice-cast shadow at their feet. It was a land that would appear to have an echo, and only echo, for a voice.

Irissa shivered. Kendric put his arm over her shoulders, but she shook her head. "Not cold. Only—"

"I know." Kendric stared into the albino emptiness. The air was chill enough to turn breath into threads of fog, to keep ice and snow unmelted, but not truly freezing. A person could walk long in this white waste without losing fingers or toes, and that was the pity of it. It was relentless, the Cincture. There was not even the excuse of disintegration to keep one from facing this land, pacing out its limitless distances, and still losing to it.

"I should hate to come here alone," Irissa said. "Yet my kind did."

"Well, you are not alone, for your good or my ill," Kendric said, grinning. "I suggest we begin our trek across this death's-head of a land and find the place where the meanders merge, as Chaundre said." His hand, curled around her shoulder, tightened encouragingly.

"I do not think even the fowlen would care to dwell here," she noted. "Amozel was overoptimistic."

They walked on, cheered when another meander track—a level curving road of ice across the uneven land—was visible in the distance. If Chaundre was right, and the meanders, frozen or not, converged, then there very well might be something at the center of that conjoining . . .

"Perhaps we'll find even a Torloc gate," Kendric jested.

"I thought you had lost your taste for things Torloc."

"I vacillate."

Night came subtly to the Cincture, like a gray curtain rung

down so softly its coming was hardly visible. The white seemed to intensify with the deepening of blue shadows across it. Overstone shine polished the snow into cut-stone fragments of dazzling sparkle. And, above them, the ice-arch shimmered with a faint rainbow of constantly changing color.

"How do we know in which direction we go?" Irissa asked. "This land is a ring, and we could tread it endlessly from north to west to south to east, over and over, and not even know it."

"Follow the meanders." Kendric pointed to the three slashes of smooth ice now snaking through the dunes. "They seem to be drawing into one body."

"And what if we find only a place where all meanders meet, a great frozen lake that is gate merely to its own stillness?"

"Then we will be the only exiles of the Rynth to have set boot on the Cincture and will have a tale worth telling to our grandchildren around a rim-runner campfire."

Irissa stopped and fixed Kendric with her charcoal-gray eyes, a challenging glint lightening them almost to their old silver. "You take too much for granted, Wrathman."

He looked alarmed. "The grandchildren?"

"The Rynth. *I* do not choose to dwell in a wilderness when one I know has a Quickstone and an entire Keep to erect upon it. It would be amusing to consider what kind of Keep a Quickstone would build—perhaps ever-changing, with walls of running water-ice . . ."

A sound came then, both thankfully distant and distressingly near, the oddly pitched howl that had shrieked even into the Rynth. Now it sounded unbearably lonely, insufferably shrill. Irissa clapped both hands to her ears, her face drawn into a mask of pain.

"Oh, it is dire, dire loss. A mourning as high as the Overstone, as deep as the ice that penetrates to the very heart of this land. I cannot bear it."

"Hush, it is over."

"I hear it still—"

"Echo only, and that dying. But it is a fell sort of keening, part human, part bestial, part more than either. It is a nearer version of what we heard in the Rynth, and then, as now, I feel a fearful kinship with it."

Irissa looked in wonder at Kendric, who seemed placid despite the shriek.

"You had your eyes cast down during the worst of it," he explained. "I didn't. I saw the ice-arch colors deepen to the tone of it, until it seemed a rainbow entire danced there, holding up the Overstone on misty bands."

"A rainbow?"

He nodded solemnly. "Not really. But rainbow-shaded, like a certain arching gate in Rule. I think we take the right path."

They turned again to follow the meanders' frozen course ever northward and walked until the waves of crust-crested snow appeared to move toward them with an oceanic rhythm, until the squeak of packed ice beneath their feet became so commonplace they could no longer hear it, and until the air-rending wail was only a memory.

Another low dune of snow gathered to rush toward them, or they toward it, casting cobalt shadows on the ground, breaking into a diadem of fanciful shapes upon its crest, like a wave.

It was not snow but fowlen, an entire pack strung out singly and rushing toward Kendric and Irissa on lean white legs, their feathered faces intent amid sprays of ruff.

Irissa and Kendric reached for their swords in unison, then heard the unrestrained howl of the wretched thing they could not name reverberate again over the snow, the sky, and their own skins. It echoed into the ends of the Cincture and seemed to urge the fowlen on.

Chapter Twenty-nine

———◆◆◆———

The fowlen circled them, the pack large enough to form a roomy noose around them. Irissa had not felt so captive since Sofistron's coldstone-walled chamber, though the fowlen made a living wall and threatened her life, not her powers.

Behind her, Kendric had flexed his knees to a warrior's crouch and held the great sword cocked over one shoulder, ready to slice into a swatch of fowlen fur and feather. The pack crowded in, rubbing feathered ruff against ruff and white, muscle-rippled shoulder against shoulder. Unlike the ordinary wolves their bodies resembled, they did not drop nose to the snow to scent their victims; beaks made poor organs of smell. Instead, they kept their fierce, dazzlingly blue eyes fast on Kendric and Irissa and pressed inward.

Irissa felt, rather than saw, every muscle in Kendric's body coil tighter. She whirled in his direction, despite leaving an unguarded rear, in time to see a pale shadow bound over the ring of fowlen and land lightly within the circle.

It was the creature who had called itself—itselves—the Rynx, and it sat immediately on its powerful haunches, as if demonstrating peaceful intentions. Kendric let the long blade rest on snow in turn. Around them, the fowlen also sat, one by one, and tilted inquisitive, impassive faces.

The Rynx lifted one white paw. Kendric and Irissa took it for a signal, since the fowlen raised first one front foot, then another, as they sat—not as signal, but as mere animal nature relieving at least one extremity from the continuous icy press of the cold beneath their toes.

Kendric's and Irissa's mutual sighs of relief momentarily painted the air before them white. If the fowlen felt the cold, it meant that the creatures were merely beasts—alien, oddly composed beasts, but beasts. About the Rynx they were not so sure. Seeing it here, in repose, against others of its appearance, they were struck again by its size—twice that of the fowlen—and by the unblinking oddity of its one silver and one amber eye.

Its pupils were catlike pointed ovals, dark as woodland pools.

"Welcome to the Cincture," it said, switching its weight consideringly to the opposite foot. "In other times, our duty would have been to impede you, seeress, as we did the others."

"And now?" Irissa demanded. Unlike Kendric, she had not lowered her upraised sword, though it was but a stickpin to a creature of the Rynx's size.

"Now is another season, the penultimate season. Now I guide you to Delevant's Maw itself. Your predecessors won their medals vying with me for the privilege. For you and your companion, I have conjured a sled to speed your journey. I fear we do not have much time. It stirs, and my duties have come full circle on themselves. I bring Torlocs of power to the heart of the Cincture."

The ring of fowlen split behind the Rynx. A low-slung sleigh of crystal-clear ice stood there on gleaming runners.

"The fowlen will pull you," the Rynx said; at the words, the pack trotted two by two into a long line before the sleigh.

"With what?" Kendric asked skeptically. "And more to the point—where?"

"To Delevant's Maw," the creature repeated, a slight, impatient note in its voice—or rather its voices, for the tones still vibrated between high and low simultaneously. "And fear not, my elongated friend. I took your length into account when shaping the sleigh and I will even now summon some warmer, softer seating than ice."

A mist formed over the sleigh's interior, mounded like a cloud. Irissa was tempted to near the sledge and plunge her ungloved hand into it. "There is no feel but softness and no cold within it," she said.

Kendric fastened the sword upon his back again, but pointedly folded challenging arms over the fowlen-fur vest on his chest. "And I suppose your white wolves here will push us?"

The Rynx looked as self-satisfied as a creature with virtually no means to change its expression could. Wreaths of pale mist appeared and draped themselves over the waiting fowlen chests and shoulders.

Kendric frowned and unfolded his arms slowly. "It looks like—"

"I, too, have found 'Hariantha hair' a useful thing to draw upon, sorcerer. Nothing lends itself so neatly to magic as a legend. Yet it is not my purpose to dazzle you, but to bring you to where your own purpose awaits you, for the good or ill of all of us and this world. Will you ride?" the Rynx demanded in its disconcerting double voice.

Kendric would have exchanged a consulting look with Irissa, but she had settled the matter by sinking down upon the cloudy stuff.

"Oh, I am so *weary* of walking in this world!" Irissa smiled at him from the froth, looking no worse for wear and much more comfortable. Kendric folded himself into the sleigh's contours after making sure there was room for the sword alongside him.

At a sharp caw from the Rynx, the fowlen bounded forward, white paws flashing and ruffs ruffled by the wind. Kendric and Irissa half-reclined, like jewels in a richly padded box, and hurtled forward with no sensation of it but the wind in their faces.

The Rynx ran lazily alongside them, its massive head on the same level as theirs, its feet making no noise in the soft snow that blanketed the underlying ice.

"Has the Cincture always been like this?" Irissa asked.

The Rynx blinked consideringly and answered in its two-toned voice. "The Cincture never changes. It grows neither warmer nor colder—"

"But snow must fall here from the sky, else how did it come to be?" Kendric's question was more a statement.

The Rynx answered promptly. "Snow and ice have always been the Cincture's carpet. Fowlen have always ranged the snow and ice. Nothing falls from the sky—except a bit of Hariantha hair when I call it. We have always ruled the Cincture and humankind has always kept out of it—except for those who must come to take their birthright."

Irissa turned to Kendric. "Their birthright. Of course. The

Cincture is the place of Far Focus, where a Torloc seeress must go to make the rite of passage to greater power. I—we—are not here because of a mistake, but because it was necessary."

"Why here? Why the most desolate limits of another world?"

"I do not know," Irissa admitted.

"Because *he* is here," the Rynx interrupted.

"He?"

"It, then," the Rynx conceded. "The onetime Torloc wizard."

"Torloc wizard? But only Torloc women have powers." Irissa spoke on, as much to Kendric as to the Rynx. "It is true Thrangar had some slight magical skills through his sword, and that you have—contracted—some powers through me, but it was always the Torloc women who held the reins of power—"

"Not always," the Rynx said shortly. It increased its lope to a full run and vanished into the distance ahead.

"Well." Irissa stared into the whiteness that masked the Rynx and seemed to hide even their white-shrouded coursers beyond the first few. She settled back less easily than before into the cushioning white softness. "It behaves as if it knows a great deal—"

"And tells us nothing. Always the way with the magicked, even the four-footed ones," Kendric grumbled. "I am not sure we should have tumbled so unwary into this creature's downy conveyance . . ."

"*We* did not. I did."

Kendric shrugged. "At least you are able to make a distinction between we and thee, something yon chitchatting bird head seems incapable of."

"But if it takes us to the place of Far Focus, where all Torloc seeresses must journey to receive full use of their powers—?"

"It was set here as an obstacle to such missions; it admits as much itself. Why should it now glide us so politely on our way? And what will happen to me if I come unwelcome to such a place of power for your kind? And to you if you do not recover at least what powers you have lost? I see the hope of that in your eyes."

"Had I my powers, you would not dare to read my eyes," she challenged.

Kendric's warm amber gaze remained as steady as a fowlen's. "Do not be so sure of that."

Irissa blinked and looked away, though only the same, unending white landscape sped by them. "And you should not be so certain that you will be unwelcome in a Torloc place of power now. We drink from different sides of the same well."

"Then I am in equal danger. Good." Kendric folded his arms. "If we choose to rush headlong into uncertainty, at least we share the risks."

"And the benefits." Irissa elevated one bare hand from the fog misting her lap and rested her long, unringed fingers lightly on Kendric's arm. "If my powers can be restored here, perhaps yours can be refined, amplified . . . You do not object?"

"Just worry about your own powers; I am content to remain as I am—a maker of fires and rains and other small, practical things."

"All somewhat impractically made," she reminded him. "And none of us can remain as we are, no matter how it contents us."

"We shall see," he responded mysteriously.

"Now you sound like the Rynx."

"A noble creature," he declared.

Whether the Rynx sensed it figured in their discussion or not, it spent the rest of the journey at the head of the fowlen, perhaps urging them on to greater speed. The whitewashed landscape flashed by with dreary regularity. It was odd how such paleness could weigh heavy on the brain after a while. Irissa laid her dark head on Kendric's shoulder and did not move after that. He peered down to see if she slept, his eyes watering once he lowered them from looking directly into the wind, as if the wind itself held its own effects at bay. Her dark hair whipped constantly at the white of his fowlen-fur vest, and her hand still lay lightly along his arm. Her eyes were closed, her face bleached white except for her dark eyelashes and the slash of Iridesium circlet across her forehead. The variescent metal was drained of color now, with so little sunlight to send it dancing. It merely looked blue-black. The sky was uttery opaque, though the Overstone still showed, a dull white jewel caught in a rainbowed ring. Waves of violet and crimson and saffron and green rippled along the arches' icy length, a fugitive dazzle that ebbed and flowed within them, like multicolored water seen through a thick layer of ice.

Kendric was reminded of power caught and held away from the surface, from its true element. Something shifted within the ice-arch. The Rynx had warned that it stirred. He remembered that Irissa had been quenched in some similar cold, steely way by Sofistron's chamber and he thought what it would mean if she never raised more than an ember of her previous powers again. Could he mimic them through her, as he had used flint and steel for Amozel's benefit to mask the fact that he started a fire by magic? Perhaps, whatever happened, wherever the Rynx led them, Kendric could use his own borrowed powers to restore a semblance of power to Irissa. But that would be a lie, and magic did not work well around lies. As she herself had warned him, it was dangerous to continue thinking of his own powers as a mere loan. No, one could not fight another's battles for him—or her. That he had long ago learned as a Wrathman of Rule. As a rudimentary Torloc, he had much more to learn.

The whirlwind of movement stopped. Irissa stirred, sat up, and rubbed her silver-rimmed eyes. "Mountains?"

"Foothills, certainly," Kendric agreed, tracing with his forefinger the low ridges of ice extending forward on either side of them, at perhaps a distance of two miles from one another.

The Rynx returned and sat, pausing to preen its windblown ruff a bit officiously. "We have arrived at Ringlost, where all meanders join."

"Chaundre was right!"

The Rynx wagged its black beak and turned to Irissa. "We have heard of this Chaundre. We think he takes an interest in our comings and goings."

"He is interested in the comings and goings of all things," Kendric pointed out, "which is why he is called mad."

The Rynx nodded solemnly. "If you care to walk again, I will show you a ring."

"All this way to gawk at a ring," Kendric mumbled, thrusting himself stiffly out of the sleigh. "More work for madmen."

They followed the Rynx across the uneven ground; the creature was as large as a middle-size cow from the rear and carried its feather-barbed tail over its back in a prideful curl.

Soon their boots were slipping on the smooth sheet ice of a frozen meander. The Rynx's massive claws clicked calmly over the treacherous surface; it finally stopped at the point where an upjut of crusted snow, the very beginning of the foothills, rose from the level ice.

"Below," the Rynx portentously said, its voice sounding both high and sweet, low and harsh, half trill, half growl.

They looked below, directly at the ice, frozen with thousands of tiny bubbles suspended like stars massing in a night sky, but otherwise clear.

Something round and gold lay embedded there, a perfect winking circle, precious as sunlight and perhaps as huge in circumference as the ring of fowlen that had originally surrounded them.

"Ring?" Kendric scoffed. "It is a ring large enough to encircle the fingers of the mountains."

"From this ring and the empty bezel in it—which is that swelling you can half-see a Wrathman's length away from us—came Sofistron's Lunestone," the Rynx said.

"I have seen Sofistron's Lunestone," Irissa challenged. "I could hold it in my palm, thus." She shook her cupped, long-fingered hand demonstratively under the Rynx's very beak. "The stone that sat the bezel of the ring below us would have been huge, as huge as—"

"Even the Overstone, or as the Overstone is to the eye from here below," the Rynx agreed. "The Lunestone was washed through long time and much distance in the waters of the meander. By the time it had been carried into mid-Rynth, it was diminished."

"You expect us to believe that one small stone came from as mighty a ring as this?" Kendric was indignant.

"This is Ringlost," the Rynx repeated, and, despite the way it served as its own echo, Kendric had grown accustomed enough to its tones to read a tinge of melancholy into its words. "We stand, as you said, at the fingers of the mountains, between the first and the next finger of the left hand, to be precise. At each fingertip a meander ends—or begins, depending on whether your reference point is Rynth or Cincture. And at each place sits a similiar ring, plain and worked of gold, with an empty bezel. All the Stones of the Rynth sprang from these rings; all washed themselves away in the meanders, save for some slight remnants. All were claimed by the Rynthians who found them and erected Keeps upon what powers still accrued to them. There are ten, as there are ten fingers to the hands of a wizard."

Irissa shuddered so violently that Kendric took it for an alerting to danger. But there were only the three of them standing carefully still on ice, with two staring down as if through a window at a great gold ring far below. Irissa was staring up, along the ice ridge growing in the distance to greater heights.

"I was remembering Geronfrey's hands," she said dreamily, "as they had been stripped of their flesh for the folly of thrusting them through a stone pillar in Rule. White, they were, ridged to little more than bone. Very old, as old as the inner man and then older even than that somehow. If what the Rynx says is true, we stand, we stand—"

"Picture this pooling ice as the fingernail," the Rynx encouraged, and there was something sinister about its genial specificity. "The ridge is the first joint, with another behind it and another. Then comes the flat and fairly gentle glacial slope of the wrists and arms, and the more difficult passage of the snow-mantled shoulders, though Delevant's Maw has sunk somewhat below the shoulders, and we shall not have to travel that high."

"The mountain is a *man*?" Kendric bawled.

"The man is a mountain, or a chain of such," the Rynx replied. "Surely you of all people are used to outsized things."

"The wizard Delevant?" Irissa inquired sharply.

"The Torloc wizard Delevant," the Rynx affirmed in its trilling growl. "Or what remains of him."

"Do you know what a contradiction to all things Torloc that is? A Torloc wizard. Only the seeresses have held the powers for unremembered generations. Why would they journey here to a man-made mountain to enhance their magic?"

"Things change," the Rynx remarked.

Kendric shrugged his shoulders at the overcast sky. "I hope you have the honor of meeting Chaundre. I think you two would deal well together."

The Rynx ignored the implication or was simply ignorant of Chaundre's reputation as mad. From a seating position, it slid gracefully down on its belly, long front legs extended.

"Mount us," it ordered. "It is a long, rough way to Dele-vant's Maw, and will be faster on four feet than on two."

Kendric shrugged and straddled the broad back, his feet easily dragging on the ice. Irissa clambered on in front of him, just behind the sharp shoulder bones. But the Rynx was both well muscled and well furred and offered a far softer seat than the lorryk. It rose, seemingly unimpeded by its burden, and began trotting past the ends of three more parallel ridges. Kendric and Irissa peered hard at the clear ice they crossed. At the bottom of each meander root, they sighted a glint of gold. When four ridges had been passed, the Rynx veered true north and broke into a rolling lope.

Irissa curled her hands into the slack neck skin just below the feather ruff; behind her, Kendric braced his hands on his thighs after checking the secure lashing of his sword to his back. The Rynx's gait was more fluid than that of a bearing-beast, and its speed, as promised, was businesslike.

It obviously knew its way across this landscape, blandly white as it was. On either side of them, the ridges gradually sloped into low mountains. Ahead loomed the highest mountain of all, a strange, dome-topped mound of untracked snow. The nearer they got, the larger loomed the summit, and they could see yawning cavities that blackened and grew bigger with the Rynx's every forward bound.

Two caves sat socketlike halfway up the mount. The third was the largest, and appeared at ground level. The Rynx bolted straight for this darkness, then paused on the brink of it.

It was a great, grinning slash in the glacier, and some sun must have shone on it, for melting ice-daggers large enough to mast a warship dripped icily down from above, looking like monstrous fangs. Kendric and Irissa sat and stared at it word-lessly.

"Enough," the Rynx said. "We are not a rocking beast nor invincible. You may dismount." It sat abruptly, so that they almost slid off backward; Kendric quickly got his long legs to the ground and pulled Irissa off with him.

"Delevant's Maw," the Rynx iterated.

"So we gather." Kendric began to readjust his sword with little good grace.

"Draw your blades," the Rynx said. "You do not go to meet a lorryk."

Kendric pointed out sourly that his blade was unlashed, not strictly drawn, but the Rynx seemed uninterested in fine points.

"Must we?" Irissa was contemplating the drooling dark with little liking.

Kendric shrugged.

The Rynx stood and trotted into the cavern.

They followed.

Chapter Thirty

Chill and dark assailed them with a nearly tangible presence. From ahead came the measured click of the Rynx's sharp nails. The sound stopped, and nothing interrupted the dark. Kendric and Irissa could feel a shield of icy bright light from the cavern mouth behind them. But their bodies blocked it, though it lay on their backs as hotly as sunlight would in a warmer world.

Ahead was the dark. Delevant's Maw. They knew they stood in the delicate arching interior of a frost-formed skull. They could feel almost sentient space vaulting around them, interrogating them silently.

"Now that I need it, where is my hilt light?" Kendric whispered in deference to the dark, but the sound fractured into brittle bits of echo, as if even syllables would shatter in the motionless cold that filled this empty place.

A faint luminescence, almost liquid, leaked from between his interlaced fingers. But the light was cold and feeble here and fell only far enough to draw a steely white line along the beveled edge of his blade, so it seemed only another oversized ice-dagger, somehow crystalline.

"Follow our footfalls," the Rynx suggested, moving forward again to the beat of its staccato self-percussion.

So they followed sound into a blackness deeper than Reygand's eternal night, blackness that had no warmth and smothering softness, but only icy distance in its touch. The Rynx's claws tapped the floors with the stuttering chatter of a blind beggar's cane along an often-traversed alleyway, but they saw no glimpse of it; not even its feather sheen reflected the hilt's dampened light.

The way went up, and soon they were stumbling against rudely carved ice risers. Deep beneath their boots, frozen into the limpid ice, lay the carapace of some huge, coiling creature. Each giant step seemed to be erected upon a segment of its articulated body. They finally came to a broad landing of ice so clear not even bubbles hung suspended in it, and here the hilt light shone down at full brilliance. Below them lay the creature's terrifying featureless face—merely a coronet of smooth white feelers radiating from a gaping maw.

"Delevant?" Kendric asked, experimentally tapping his sword point on the ice to ensure that its pellucid depths were no illusion. The party seemed suspended above the Maw, mere instants from dropping down into it.

"You have no high opinion of Torloc wizards if you think that," Irissa whispered back. "I think a snow-slug, long dead. It is what the fowlen eat in the Cincture."

"Better them it than it them," Kendric answered, ever practical. "This giant worm seems to have insinuated itself into the very curves of this skull-place. Perhaps there was something to devour here once, and then nothing, so it starved."

Irissa shuddered. "A dire end to a mighty wizard. But I cannot believe this landscape *is* Delevant. It may be a metaphor *of* Delevant, some symbolic formation . . . ."

"Who formed it?"

"Perhaps he had servants once, who later died."

"Hmmm. Anyone who would serve anything in the Cincture would be madder than Chaundre—or than us for confronting this strangeness. Do you hear the Rynx any longer?"

Irissa lifted her head into the darkness, as if smelling it. "I hear nothing now."

"Perhaps we've lost the creature, and I'm not certain that isn't to the good. But I see a faint thread of blue light ahead;

let's make for it. At the least, it may be a chimney out of the mountain."

The icy cobalt dawn on the darkness' horizon broadened like a sun-cast light, eventually suffusing upward against the smooth, white, concave cavern dome. It seemed as if a sky of Rule stretched above them, unwrinkled and serene.

"Better," Kendric commented.

"The Rynx," Irissa returned, pointing out the silhouette of a seated creature against the vibrant blue where it burned most brightly.

They joined their guide and saw why it had stopped. It sat on the very brink of a sheer waterfall of ice—two waterfalls, facing each other, with only the deepest darkness between them and that illuminated by a blaze of blue light, which turned the frozen, unfurling pillars into ribbons of reflected cerulean and silver. Even the Rynx glowed faintly blue, and its one silver eye shone azure as it turned its feathered head to them.

"The Chasm of Blue Fire," it announced, the timbre of its two-tongued voice more husky than lilting, which gave it a morose quality.

"You've been here before," Irissa said.

"Many times," the Rynx answered in melancholy agreement. "Each time to face a revenant of Delevant across this chasm. It will come again soon, for it is as drawn to the presence of a Torloc seeress as one is drawn to it."

"I am unempowered," Irissa pointed out in deadly, even tones.

"So much the worse for you. But perhaps this time we will triumph—look, it stirs, it stirs."

Kendric came to stand beside them, struck by the unlikely steps of descending size they made: one tall man with a long-sword; one less-tall woman with silver-ringed eyes and a short sword; and one odd-eyed lupine mongrel with no sword that came only to Irissa's shoulder as it sat.

They faced a plain of ice that lay sinisterly still under the unstarred blue sky above them. The light lapped against the pale cavern dome, giving it a watery appearance. And now the ice across the chasm buckled, snapped, and thrust a finger of itself upward. The ice pillar grew as if being expelled by intense pressure from below, until it stood man-high, bathed in a gentle blue glow. It split, with the sound of bone splintering between grinding teeth.

A figure stood birthed in the shattering ice around it—or the impression of a figure. Its face, its long, flowing hair, and its garments were frosted and translucent by turn. Its aspect revolved between male and female, between youth and age. For one instant it looked the twin of the cloud-haired Hariantha whom Kendric had draped over Irissa in Fanis' Keep; in another, it was a wild-bearded and dull-eyed old man, stringy of limb and sharp of bone. In yet another, it was the image of the Torloc Eldress, Finorian, with her high-cheekboned closeness of face and her hair tossing around her in ice-dagger-sharp strands. Then the face was young, milky smooth as the Overstone, and Irissa thought she saw herself in it, or a dozen selves, had she been bleached to this utter whiteness.

She almost stepped toward this pale reflection of herself; she even reached out a hand. The visage shifted and stayed young, but grew more chiseled of feature, haughty, and certain. A young man stood there, in great arrogance and beauty, and Irissa was ashamed that she had made a move of kinship toward a creature so capable of taking such gestures for tribute.

"Delevant," the Rynx said when this last likeness had appeared.

The young man's face grew icier and haughtier. "Watchcur! Have you come again to test yourself for naught?"

"It is not for naught that you remain here, icebound both within and without."

"But my pilgrims have come and have come again, bringing me tribute."

"We are not pilgrims," Kendric interrupted indignantly, grinding his sword point into the ice for emphasis.

A quick blue flick from icy eyes danced his way. They rested instead on Irissa. "She of power has come, she of my kind has come. Has come again as she always comes, seeking something and bringing something in return."

"This time you will not find your exchange so even," the Rynx warned. "This one is flawed." Irissa flinched.

Delevant was silent, but his face grew cunning, as if he were so certain of himself he need not veil his intentions. "So was I once, I am told, and see what has become of me," he mocked. The arms swung innocently, openly wide on frosted wings of sleeve. He looked like a heroic statue in a plaza, glowing with pride and perfection through a stony medium. And then the aspect shifted, and the startling round of visages careened through its changes until it revolved into young Delevant again, and the arms slowly enfolded themselves.

The Rynx stood, braced its four feet, and began speaking. "You had the ten rings of potency that you had gathered from the worlds within and without, one for every finger. You had outdone every wizard of your kind, until they ceased competing with you and all the Torlocs were reduced to your dependents. None could contest your powers; and finding none against, you turned against all. Your will became the Torlocs' sun and moon; you drove them hither and yon across the gates to many worlds, refugees at your command, sent at your whim to return with magical trinkets to your vanity. The living mind of a Rengarthian crystal-caster, the soul of a death-delver from the Dark Sun, even something as trivial as the wind-compass of a Clymerindian master steersman. Then you overreached yourself. Swollen with the pride of your easy ascendancy, you magically expanded your very body to reach through the Uncommon Gate and take the Overstone itself from Those Without."

"And did it!" Delevant's voice rang powerfully from the ice all around, clear and precise, not double-edged and muddy, as was that of the Rynx. "All you have done is lisp a history lesson; doubtless that is all a featherhead like you can contain."

"We were given your history with our charge; and we have contained you sufficiently for many unfolding lengths of the tapestry humankind calls time." Now the Rynx sounded slightly smug. "And though you brought the Overstone to the orifice of this world, you never succeeded in drawing it fully through. So it remains fixed where you brought it, as cold, white, and dead as yourself. And that is why Those Without in justice hurled your giant body back to the Inlands earth as a broken mountain range, icebound and empty."

"Empty? You call me empty? I contain all that I was and more—a piece of all who came to take from me an intensification of their own powers." The figure began its whirling progress of likenesses again, its voice changing with each word it uttered to reflect the quality it boasted. "I am male, female, young, old—more than ever I was before I reached for the Overstone. Through me, the Torloc seeresses have gone back to their trivial worlds with powers enough to see their kind through whatever petty challenges remain for them. And I have taken a bit of fresh, unfettered power from each. How long do you think you can contain me, watchcur? Have you grown enough with the years, as I have, to leap the Chasm of Blue Fire and grapple with me eye to eye? You stand between me and my supplicants. Advance or retreat."

And Delevant moved, placing one foot before the other to stride from the ice shards encasing his body to the knees. The Rynx drew in a hiss of breath, then spat it out as mist. Its haunches tensed, the ruff expanding into a fierce bristle of feathers. It turned its eyes, all pupil now with a dim rim of silver and gold around each, to Kendric and Irissa. "You see. It stirs. Immobile as the Overstone it has long been, since we were first a featherling pup and set guard upon it. There is no hope for it but—"

The Rynx sprang, fur rippling like shifting snow on its muscular flanks. The great bird head lanced the air over the chasm. For a breathless moment Kendric and Irissa leaned forward with it, certain somehow that it could fly, that the chasm's wide, yawning mouth—many times the length of its body—was a distance its will could span. Almost it made the leap, tremendous as it was. Almost. The front claws dug deep in the ice lip opposite, and the hind claws alighted an instant after, peddling at the sheer ice wall, chipping ice away into a coldstone-bright spray. Delevant strode over to the edge and folded his arms to watch. The head strained forward at an impossible angle and the great black beak buried itself in ice like a pick. But air had done with supporting the dangling rear legs; the Rynx and a great chunk of ice broke away from the frozen falls simultaneously, plunging deep into the blue light flaming far below.

Delevant extended a foot as white as his garb and nudged a loose slab of ice below also. It flashed vivid blue as it fell. One white feather drifted with a pendulum's lazy swing from side to side. It seemed unnaturally suspended in the air, as the Rynx had been for a few desperate moments, but it slowly and surely spiraled into the flickering blue depths.

Delevant, or the semblance he had become of that entity, wore the likeness of the young, prideful wizard. Yet he strode around the opposite chasm shore as if stiff with age or cold and unused to his new freedom. He ignored Irissa and Kendric.

"Perhaps," Kendric quietly suggested, "we should leave."

"It is the place of Far Focus," she answered calmly. "And I have come far to see just this thing. He—it said it gave powers to seeresses who came..."

"And *took* powers from them. You have none to give. He's welcome to mine, but I doubt they're developed enough to give the fellow anything on the scale he's used to, unless he craves a fire on his icy island and doesn't mind scorched fingertips."

"Kendric. Don't be irreverent. This—man—is the highest of my kind."

"No recommendation to me, from what I've seen of Finorian, unless high-handedness is a virtue. Look, the fellow pays us no mind, as if we were vermin. Were we on the same side of the chasm, I'd venture he'd pay attention to the flat of my blade."

"And brute force will carry no weight here."

"I'll keep my sword handy nevertheless; even the Rynx suggested we go armed, and it struck me as a wise old bird, so to speak."

Irissa sighed. "The poor Rynx. It seemed doomed to an endless strife with the spirit of this wizard. And now it seems that spirit is made man again. Or woman again. Whatever its constitution, I must try to make my peace with it."

She stepped near the chasm edge, so near that Kendric swung his blade as a bar in front of her. She smiled and pushed it away with her bare hand. "Delevant."

The figure turned. "None but the two-voiced Rynx has spoken my name in more time than even I can remember. This is pleasant. Say it again."

"Delevant. I am Irissa, a seeress of your kind. I come seeking—"

"I know. I know." He came and stood opposite her, each on a separate edge.

Kendric, chafing again in the role of observer, couldn't help observing a similarity of feature between Irissa and the handsome youth on the opposite shore, save that Delevant still wore the absolute, even pallor of the dead, so that he seemed hewn from animated white marble. It was Kendric's turn to shudder, but no one noticed.

"Can you give me what I seek?" Irissa asked.

"Of course. The question is, what can you give me?"

"You are a powerful wizard—"

"Yes."

"You do not need anything that I can give."

Delevant laughed, and it was a lonely sound. "Do not attempt to flatter me, Irissa. It is true that I have dwelled apart for a great time, but I am my own best flatterer. Do not try to convince me that I want nothing from you simply because you have nothing to give."

"My powers were considered the most promising of my kind—"

"A debased kind. Can you not see from me what Torlocs were, what *I* was—and am again?" he added hastily.

Kendric, watching, thought that haste was not a trait necessary to the omnipotent wizard Delevant represented himself to be.

Irissa was silent, then fanned her ring-naked hands and began again. "Delevant. You know what it is to be stripped of your powers. Can you not at least, now that you are released, pause to share a bit of yours? I ask only restoration; you need not amplify—"

Delevant laughed again. It sounded like something that would come from the throat of the lonely, distant thing that howled, but in another, more dangerous mood. Kendric rested his sword blade lightly on the ice and observed that a pale reflection of it drove deep into the frosted surface.

"Surely you have a softness for your kind?" Irissa pressed.

"I am all kinds now and none," Delevant said. His white eyes glittered with the chasm's cobalt light, and Irissa was momentarily reminded of Geronfrey. He came to the very verge of the drop. "You have only the slightest scum of power upon your eyes, but it is sufficient." A long, icy-white finger pointed to the chasm at his feet. "Make me a bridge; you have power enough to do it if you have will enough."

"I cannot! And if I could—it would surely draw the last of my powers from me."

"Make me a bridge, Torloc, and I will cross it and give you back powers you have never dreamed of."

"No," Kendric said. Delevant didn't even glance at him.

Irissa looked at Kendric for the first time, her eyes beseechingly dark. "I must try. Any means—"

Kendric closed his eyes wearily for a moment, but said no more.

Irissa looked down. There below, what was left of the Rynx likely burned on a fiery blue spit. There the azure waves came crashing up on cold, blue silence. A bridge. Made by her who had always come to bridges as they were breaking and gates as they were closing. If a wizard as powerful as Delevant said she could do it while she still had a veneer of silver on her eyes to spend on magic, she could try. She had not built with her eyes since raising the lorryk, though she had prattled much advice at Kendric about doing it. See true, she had said, see with all of your memory and will down to the bottom of both and then deeper. Her own advice sounded meager. She looked to her feet and saw the ice melting and flowing, shaping into strands, spun like glass on the air, interlacing into a web and stretching, thinning, yearning out to the other side. It was no bridge, but rather a lace of ice, an airy, delicate construct that pulled itself finer and finer until at last it touched the opposite ice and held there, trembling along every strand, as she trembled along every limb.

It was a thing of firm and fragile beauty. Kendric stared at it open-mouthed, and Irissa stared at it empty-eyed, for it was the last of her magic, but Delevant set one cold foot after another upon it and crossed.

The bridge turned brittle and broke as his foot spurned it on the last step. It splintered into a thousand bright fragments and fell like glittering, sharp snowflakes, knifing through the blue light.

Irissa clasped her arms to her stomach and made a sound as if she had been stabbed.

Delevant stepped nearer her, his face shining like the Overstone's. "Mourn not, seeress, for now you are free to contain a thousand kinds of magic. Now I, whose body has become ice and rock, can live and walk again—"

Kendric stepped in front of him and barred his way. "You are not Delevant," he challenged.

"I am the sorrow of Delevant. I am Delevant's spirit. And I am every Torloc seeress who ever crossed the threshold of Delevant's Maw. I am waiting. I am patience. I am power. I am chained. I need only a living vessel to contain me, and she has no magic now and will welcome me."

"No!" Kendric said, but he glanced over his shoulder to Irissa. He had never seen her eyes so remorselessly dark, her face so set. She shook her head slowly from side to side; beneath the bitterness of her eyes at her loss and Delevant's deception, there was a will of such adamant human dimensions that it shook even Kendric.

"Never," Irissa said, her voice as hoarse as that of the Rynx.

Kendric turned back to Delevant, feeling oddly pleased for a man as worried as he now was.

The creature was spinning likenesses again, all of them frozen into masks of disbelieving fury. The image of Irissa spun by and then that of Finorian, both turning angry silver-struck eyes directly and dangerously upon Kendric. He backed away instinctively, to give himself sword-wielding room. The entities laughed in sequence, now changing character so rapidly that soprano mixed with baritone in a grating cacophony that made the Rynx's double voice seem mellifluous by comparision

Kendric heard hysteria in the laughter and some of the same mad, lonely notes that had so riveted him in the Rynth. Irissa was backing up behind him, not so much in deference to his defense, but because the sound was driving her back. Her palms were pressed over her ears, her white fingers fanned over her dark hair, and her body bent at the waist.

"The wailraith," she shouted in warning, more loudly than necessary, for she could not hear her own words. "It is the wailraith, the water spirit in every world that would drown our souls if it could catch them. They are all a piece of Delevant, and Delevant of them. They are his voice."

Kendric nodded, not really listening. He did not even pay heed to the maniacal, tormented laughter. He had been standing by, merely watching—and thinking. If it had taken him a little while, well, he had at least arrived at a conclusion. He thought he knew what magical trick would take the whey-faced projections of Delevant apart limb from icy limb. He tightened his palms on the hilt until the light was quenched, but he felt the hilt's warmth nevertheless and drew it into him as an ally.

Delevant ceased presenting his many faces and settled on the likeness of Finorian. "Fool!" it thundered.

"I cannot quarrel with you there," Kendric said amiably, backing warily away as the figure advanced a step.

"A sword cannot stop me."

"It bears some magic."

"Some magic cannot stop the bearer of all magic." The Finorian semblance advanced yet nearer.

Kendric dug in his boot heels and raised the blade. "*I* bear some magic."

"You? You are nothing." Finorian had looked awesome enough in the flesh; now, her very robes salted with hoary age, she was overwhelming.

Kendric let the magic he had summoned and husbanded shoot free down the length of his blade. The dull silver metal turned into a long red tongue of flame; he swung it in a mighty blow, and the flickering length of it sliced Finorian's head from her shoulders at the juncture of her scrawny neck. Finorian's face splintered into shards at Kendric's feet as the head hit the ground. The ice body wept water and stopped moving, freezing into the likeness of a headless statue. Where the head had been was a spinning cloud of mist. A new head formed over the motionless body, that of the young Delevant. By now Kendric's blade had cooled to lead-color and felt as heavy. He was no longer sure that he could command it to run molten again, and wondered if he could even lift it. Delevant came upon him wordlessly, naked hands outstretched. Kendric summoned all his strength, inner and outer, and saw the blade flare into flame again as he swept it as high as he could lift it toward Delevant. Fire seared ice, and the fiery blade cut Delevant in twain at the waist. The upper trunk rolled to the ground, its severed edge already smoothed by melting water.

Behind the unmoving lower trunk, a mist swirled and became another familiar, icy form, another facet of Delevant. "Once more at the knees," Kendric threatened it grimly before it had fully formed, "and let us see you rise from that blow, sorcerer." He watched the mist assemble into a face and let the heavy sword point sag. The visage was Irissa's.

Kendric was as momentarily confused as he had been when facing the dark mirror image of Irissa in Geronfrey's mirror. No one had ever told him what ownership a likeness had in an original, or if a blow to the one was a blow to the other, either corporeal or figurative. And he had no time to think now. The likeness advanced on him and he bowed away from it, stunned.

It veered immediately for the true Irissa, its eyes gleaming softly silver. But she was backing away, shaking her head in mute revulsion, beyond the tempting of even seeing her own empowered eyes before her. The figure closed with her bodily, and they were struggling there, the ice Irissa in flowing white garments, the living Irissa in good gray garb.

She had the thing by the arms, and it was like her in every respect, including height and weight; they seemed hardly to move as they contended, so matched were they. And Kendric was constrained from lifting his sword against them, for fear of striking awry—or striking aright and regretting it.

It was a fierce, silent struggle. Delevant's Irissa strained her choke-poised hands toward her double's throat. It was life she wanted and, to get it for herself, she had to take it from another. But the real Irissa was fighting only for the humanness in her now, and survival was the largest part of that. She held the icy image of herself off at a distance too great for it to do any physical harm. Then the ice Irissa's fingers grew gnarled and elongated, until they stretched to living flesh and seemed ready to sink themselves into Irissa's neck. Desperate, Irissa lowered her head like a rock ram and butted it into the ice-hewn figure before her with all the physical force at her command. There was an unexpected metallic ring, and shards of the ice-wrought Irissa scattered before the flesh-made Irissa into a thousand dancing pieces.

Kendric stared. All the colors of the rainbow were circling madly over the dark surface of Irissa's Iridesium circlet. Even now she was putting her shaking hands to it and saying breathlessly, "It hurt. I haven't had such a headache since Sofistron's . . ."

Kendric came over and put his hands on her shoulders and laughed, pulling her to him and kissing her resoundingly on the forehead, or rather on the metal that circled her forehead. "One last, feeble remnant of Rulian magic—and it worked against the mightiest Torloc of all, were Delevant male, female, old, young, wailwraith, or only the imitation of one. Look, he runs, like so many meanders, into a simple sheet of water."

It was true. The blocks of inanimate ice around them, the pieces left of Delevant's many manifestations, were dwindling to water-smoothed lumps in standing pools, until they were commonstone-small, no more than opaque white pebbles.

The chasm's blue light danced higher and higher; tatters of it licked the air like cold flame, and Kendric rushed over to pull his abandoned sword well away from it. From a distance came a sound of cataclysmic cracking, like a great backbone snapping into many pieces.

A wind came keening through the cavern, tearing Irissa's hair into shreds that obscured the Iridesium circlet, pushing even Kendric's warrior-short locks into his eyes. They stood blinded by the wind, their garments whipping around them, feeling the cool, silken touch of the azure light on their bodies.

Irissa put a hand to her forehead and tossed back her flailing hair so she could see. Beneath her palm, the Iridesium tingled in a shifting pattern. She could feel its colors etched on her flesh and could discern from the intensity of tingle whether crimson or cobalt or green vibrated beneath her skin.

"Kendric. Something is happening, something comes to me—" She stretched out her right hand, fingers splayed, until the cords of her hands stood like ridges across them. *Snap!* A gold band appeared on her small finger and clamped shut. *Snap!* Other Circles ringed her third finger, her second, and her first; then the large joint of her thumb was surrounded by a crown of gold. Each plain gold band wore a bezel, and each bezel held a small stone of a different color.

Irissa stared at her hand as if it were not her hand. Kendric's left hand hovered over hers, hesitant to touch it. The keening wind accelerated and drove Irissa's hair back into her eyes. But she heard another irrefutable series of metallic snaps; when she had swept her face free again, she saw Kendric holding his left hand by the wrist as if disowning it, or wrestling with himself, and five gold rings glinting on his broad, hair-sprinkled knuckles from small finger to thumb. Kendric tried to wring

his fingers free of the perfectly fitting rings with a desperate
pull from his unringed right hand.

This time Irissa laughed. "It is an inheritance, Kendric. Do
not be so ungracious. I think Ringlost is no longer Ringlost.
Delevant came by these stones honestly at least, if not the
Overstone, and we are the logical bearers of them now."

"If we were logical, we would not be here," Kendric growled,
flexing his newly metal-bound fingers. "At least whatever force
shackles us was good enough to stay away from my best sword
hand."

"Shackles? No, freedom. Don't you feel it? The wind is
warm and all that has been held captive is released, even Delevant, I think, in its way. And I think . . ."

Irissa's head was down amid the dark windstorm of her hair,
and Kendric was still staring at his beringed fingers. Something
clicked to the ice at their feet; Kendric bent automatically to
retrieve it, as he would a lost button.

"I am very free with talismans for Wrathmen of Rule. Do
not feel obliged to keep it." Irissa's voice carried a note of
apology and something very different.

Kendric looked at the thing in his hand, a common-looking
stone really, a clear cabochon of no great size. A mere teardrop.
He looked up, into eyes of sheer silver, and saw both salt water
and coldstones catching on her smile.

Chapter Thirty-one

———◆◆◆———

"It is a pity about the Rynx." Chaundre leaned his morose
face on his hand. "I had always wanted to commune with one,
and now it will be hundreds of years before one appears again.
Or perhaps never." Chaundre straightened. "Besides, my friends,
you must have had a terrible journey back, with the Cincture

itself cracking, and ice melting, and the meanders rising at your very feet."

Irissa and Kendric exchanged a knowing glance. "The fowlen remained our docile sled dogs," Kendric reassured him. "After all, they were in as much haste as we to attain the safety of the Rynth; it must be their home now that the Cincture has dissolved."

Chaundre waggled a disagreeing hand. "Not dissolved—gone liquid. We are surrounded by a circle of freshwater sea now, from what my devices discern, and a good thing, too, else the meanders would swell to the very base of the Stone-keeps and drown us all."

"The poor rim-runners," Irissa noted half-humorously. "Are they to become fishermen?"

"No, farmers." Chaundre looked amused. "Now the only fertile land of the Inlands is no longer magically spawned. The Rynth shows signs of flowering into quite ordinary fields. Besides, the fleshfins have been swept into the Cincture Sea."

Irissa cradled a serious face on her hand in turn. "Was the Rynx really plural?" she asked Chaundre. "I grew rather fond of them, or it."

"You have a weakness for four-footed things." Chaundre smiled. "I know you fret for the lorryk gathered around my Keep."

"The fowlen haunt the Rynth now and must eat. That has always been the law of ordinary things," she answered.

Chaundre's eyes twinkled over the arched bridge of his nose as he looked down at Irissa. "Then you will be pleased to know that, while Sofistron has not bestirred himself to come to this, er, celebration, he has sent the head of the lorryk stag I've installed over yon door, along with a promise never to hunt the lorryk again on his Stonekeep lands. It is a present to his daughter Amozel on the occasion of her, er, investiture."

"You mean marriage," Kendric interrupted. "Why can't you magicians call a sword a sword?"

Chaundre shrugged happily and glanced up at the unroofed top of his great hall, where the pale ice-arch seemed to form a spine to support the light lavender veiling of the sky itself. "Overstone only knows," he answered and looked back at his seated guests. "But I am glad you are here to witness a day,

whatever we call it, of great satisfaction to myself and Amozel—
and of great import to the Inlands' future affairs. Look at old
Ivrium there, litter-borne across the Rynth on the shoulders of
his overeager and contending heirlings. I fear even the best-
scented fruits of my orangery will not content the old glutton.
And there, that tall stripling who has forsaken magicianly robes
for the rude-style trousers of a rim-runner—Lacustrine is ailing,
but has sent his One Son, Fennloch, as emissary. Only Reygand
has not responded in some way to my invitation . . ."

Chaundre frowned and examined the crowded great hall in
momentary discontent while Kendric's and Irissa's glances met,
shifted away from each other, and met again. "But Reygand
always was something of a recluse, of his own nature, unlike
Fanis, who was driven to exile," Chaundre continued. "I was
glad to hear of the method of Fanis' passing and of his return
to the youth his greed dishonored. Let us hope there will be
less contention in the Inlands now that we meet each other face
to face. For now, indulge yourselves, friends. I swear no lorryk
decks my platters, Irissa. And, Kendric, my orangery leaves
are as good for a warrior as any roasted flesh."

With that, Chaundre bowed away to mingle with his other
guests, leaving Irissa and Kendric to overlook a chamber full
of strangers interspersed with a few familiar faces that were
already beginning to look strange again.

"Demimondana is a commanding figure in the fowlen-fur
hood." Irissa nodded toward the statuesque woman standing
near them, the lick of flame-red hair flashing out from beneath
the ceremonial white ruff.

"Not as inspiring as Amozel, though," Kendric returned,
"or a certain silver-eyed seeress."

Irissa dropped her eyes to the leafy heaping on her platter.
She had regained her magic with her silver eyes, but found
both awkward to use now. Since she had been to the Torloc
place of Far Focus, Delevant's Maw, she could look at things
directly without fear of losing her powers to her own reflection.
Now she must be wary that she not stare overlong at a tardy
servingman, lest he melt into the slow-running syrup Irissa's
momentary impatience imagined him to be; and she had once
been tempted to stare Ivrium's high-heaped servings into stone,

so he should know what it was like to be present at a feast and forbidden to eat.

One of the Unkept women came by with a knowing, conspiratorial look and offered Irissa a serving of the barrenberry wine she wore slung in a skin over her shoulder. As Amozel before her, Irissa shook her head and fanned her fingers over the empty circle of her goblet. The rings clinked on the white stone surface. Irissa glanced at them. She had tried using her magic to melt them off, but they would not be gone. Kendric, trusting to the natural, had braved the heat of Chaundre's forge to unbind his unbidden rings and had nothing to show for it but singed hair upon his hands.

Kendric! Irissa smiled. There was one thing she could look at without worrying about underlying magical intention. She glanced back at him.

His eyes gleamed more gold than amber since Delevant's Maw; she suspected his own share of Torloc powers had multiplied after they had wrested Delevant free of himself, but he showed no sign of it. He was looking at her now with ordinary seriousness.

"You never finished telling me if Torlocs wed," he noted.

Irissa toyed with the handle of her eating dagger, realizing then that it was made from lorryk horn. Her fingers retracted as if scorched.

"We call it bed-bond," she answered, her eyes shy despite their directness, "and I suppose it can be honored with a ceremonial of sorts. But I think the fact is more important than the formality."

"I also," Kendric agreed heartily, "prefer facts to formalities. It is a fact, then, you and I." He grinned and slapped the timbered table with his palms, wincing irritably when the customary gesture crushed the unaccustomed hardness of the rings into his flesh. "Curse these uncanny rings; they seem to wear me, rather than I them."

Irissa fanned her right hand next to his on the table. "Chaundre says each stone is an authentic fragment of a Stonekeeper's talisman. I have not yet studied their allotment. You have copper, silver, green, plain, and black." Irissa paused. "I am glad you bear the black. I should always fear seeing myself in its dark surface."

Kendric said nothing, but rubbed his right forefinger contemplatively over the obsidian cabochon.

"And have you mastered your Stonelore, Wrathman? Can you tell me what stones you wear?" Irissa asked playfully.

Kendric frowned. "The rim-runners' fire and the night we sat around it with the Unkept seem years ago. But copper—copper is easy. I remember yon mountainous man across from us hoisting a copper stone from the depths of his greasy robes. Copper is Sandstone. And since I bore the Shunstone back from Fanis' Keep, I warrant I carry it still, so that accounts for the plain one. See, you wear its like on your small finger—that must be the Drawstone."

"We are telling off the Stones on *your* hand," she reminded him sternly.

"The silver is the Lunestone, of course. And the green . . . green must be the Gladestone. Lambard's, wasn't it? And black, of course . . ."

Kendric seemed inclined to say no more, and Irissa was not inclined to encourage him. They remained silent, staring at the alien Stones upon their hands. "And yours?" Kendric asked finally.

"Drawstone—I think you are right. The red is the Bloodstone, the gold the Shinestone of Jacine. Blue must be Skystone, and the clear one, almost like one of my human tears, must be Floodstone."

"Yes, you are prone to rain heavily when you precipitate," he admitted wryly. "Well, they are not so bulky, these rings, and perhaps will prove more useful than their inconvenience suggests."

They paused to look around the hall. Every long table was burdened with the best of Chaundre's magical or ordinary agricultural labors. Every bench along each table side was crowded with an assortment of Ivrium's heirlings, rim-runners, and Unkept women, though this last party kept aloof not far down the board from where Irissa and Kendric sat in the festive new clothes Chaundre had provided for them.

"I understand their withdrawal," Irissa whispered to Kendric. "I, too, feel no part of this."

He fixed her with a stern, disconcertingly golden eye. "You

shall have to. Is this the Torloc who bade me erect a Stonekeep on a tear?"

"I know we must make our way in this world we have come to as best we can—and we have many friends. And yet, none else of our kind..."

"It is the way of any world," Kendric said. "We are fortunate that, like the Rynx, we can say 'we.'"

"Poor Rynx." Irissa shook her head sadly, but leaned nearer to eavesdrop on the approach of Lacustrine's One Son, Fennloch, to Demimondana. When one felt an outsider at a festivity, one acted as audience to a play.

The young man bowed his blond head, his bronzed features politely noncommittal. "You lead the Unkept now, Ivrium's daughter."

Demimondana nodded, looking puzzled.

"It is a great conundrum," the young man burst out, "how one so, so...lumpish as Ivrium could generate one as... supple...as yourself."

"My mother was Elodien's fairest daughter, though none but the bevy knew it. She died young. Sometimes I think the bevy shivan-cloth smothered her...but you are Fennloch. I heard of your elevation to One Son. No doubt you will be establishing your own bevy soon," she added with polite but barely concealed distaste.

Fennloch rubbed a square copper hand over his shaven chin and glanced to the high table, where Chaundre had joined Amozel. The pair looked distantly serene, yet their joy seemed to halo them as a ring sometimes might circle the sun. Fennloch shifted his stance consideringly and did not look back at Demimondana, though he ostensibly talked to her.

"I see no need for haste to establish either a bevy or a brood of heirlings to contest with one another for precedence. I won Lacustrine's favor finally, but the effort was expensive to all; in fact, I think that is why he declines so rapidly. I do not wish his death, despite my assuming his Stone on it. What mad Chaundre has dared to do shows us all that there are ways other than those we cast in Stonelore. If there must be One Son—" He glanced back at Demimondana, to find her eyes raptly watching his. "—why not...One Daughter? Or both? Or many?"

"It has never been done!"

Fennloch shrugged. "I am young, as you are. We do what has never been done. No daughter of Ivrium had walked unshod into the Rynth until you—he was too jealous of his bevy-right to let any escape. Were you not intended to my father Lacustrine's bevy?" he asked abruptly. "There was great sorrow when you went into the Rynth," he continued without waiting for her answer. "We had all heard of your beauty." Demimondana was speechless, and Fennloch smiled. "But had you not gone, we never would have known of your bravery."

"It is not a trait valued in a female," she said stiffly.

"Perhaps that will change in the next generation of Stonekeepers." Fennloch was watching her warmly, but with great care.

Demimondana took a deep breath. "Your father, Lacustrine . . . I understand his Keep is very fair, all fountains and water-borne pavilions."

"Very fair," Fennloch answered significantly.

Irissa found herself simultaneously holding her breath and clutching Kendric's arm, as she had done once before in Chaundre's Keep.

Demimondana nodded slowly and came around the table to Fennloch's side. "Since my . . . father has been carried so far, I think I will greet him." She began walking regally across the stone floor to where Ivrium reclined on an avalanche of pillows. Fennloch turned and watched her admiringly.

Two hammy hands descended confidentially on the shoulders of Irissa and Kendric. A low, rough voice spoke in their ears. "There go my promised four nights for the fowlen fur to that stripling of a One Son," Gryff growled.

But the three remained silent as Demimondana came to the very carpet edge of Ivrium's installation and paused. Ivrium himself was occupied in tearing meat from bone and looked up only a moment later. He chewed on mechanically as his eyes took in the tall, upright figure that was his daughter. His jowl-draped jaws finally paused.

"You can advance into my presence booted," he conceded, "but don't expect a morsel till I'm done." Demimondana's boot hesitated over the lavish fringe as if it were a barrier, then she crossed the carpeting to her father. Fennloch followed her.

"That Chaundre is an evil influence," Gryff complained,

his hands squeezing their shoulders for emphasis. He sat down between them, forcing them to make room, his back to the table and his elbows resting upon it.

"There are other Unkept women," Kendric consoled.

"Perhaps," Irissa suggested, with a wicked glance at Kendric, "now that bevywomen are not in such demand among the younger Stonekeepers, you can persuade a Stonekeeper to give a rim-runner one. Or two."

"One woman is enough," Gryff said. "And I will find my own, as I would have earned my right to a Stone. In the meantime, the Rynth waxes green, and it appears that we exiles have inherited a lusher land than the mincing heirlings who remained behind are ever likely to come by."

Gryff rose and gave them a final, rude blow on their backs. "Well, farewell. If you need anything in the Rynth, seek me out."

"Poor Gryff," Irissa said.

"I thought it was the Rynx you mourned."

"I did. I do. But the Rynx is merely dead; and final as that is, it is not as dire as what Gryff and the others here face—change."

"We, too." Kendric was sober. "We remain marooned here, with new powers, true, but still an old problem." He sighed and cast his gaze across the chamber. "I see faces I know and like here, but I do not know this land. It does not feel like—home."

"I sought my true home, and look where it has led me—and us. To a place neither of us feels at home in. That is why I could not bear the cry of Delevant's wraith when I heard it. It was the moan of the lost, a loss beyond magic—a loss of connection with one's kind."

"You at least have a kind with which to reunite," Kendric said, quaffing from the goblet that a servingman had filled with a purple stream of wine. "There is no longer a place for me in Rule, especially now that I bear magic and Rule has lost its last particle of magic—" He shook off his melancholy with a burst of rough appreciation. "This wine is excellent, alien but hearty. Try some."

Irissa, troubled by Kendric's introspection, nodded to the servingman and watched her white goblet foam full with a

purple pool. In mid-pour the stream flowed startlingly green—
bright, poisonous Borgia green, like the wine of Rule that was
lethal when ill-vinted.

Irissa stood and stared down at the still surface of her cup.
Beside her, Kendric quenched his longing for home in several
swallows of a wine that kept its purple color. Behind her, the
servingman brushed by on his way to another cup, another
quaffer. Before her, in the goblet's liquid green surface, a face
formed—pale, almost icy. It was a face familiar to her from
not many days past and from an almost unreachable time before
in the snapping-shut hinges of a rainbowed gate.

"Finorian!" she whispered.

"At last." The voice was faint, remote; it barely wafted to
Irissa's ears over the banquet din. "Irissa, I have been trying
to slip through a rung into this world to seek you. But I found
only darkness until now. We are in great peril, we Torlocs.
Our paradise has turned crucible and our magic burns against
us. If you have power enough to hear me, come through, come
to us, come to the gate—"

A shadow fell over the face in the cup, clouding the bright
green liquid to dark emerald. Kendric had stood to peer into
what had transfixed Irissa and now leaned inquiringly over the
cup.

"You!" Finorian's voice reached his ears, too; he reared
back in surprise for a moment.

"Well met, hag," he rejoined, his voice soft yet undercut
with iron. "I have a bone to pick with you. Why did you not
let me pass the gate with Irissa when I had powers within me
that permitted it?"

"They were not apparent then," Finorian began, her icy eyes
darting from side to side and seeming to make the Borgia bestir
itself.

"But it is apparent now?" Kendric's question was not a
question.

"Yes." Finorian spoke so softly both Irissa and Kendric
leaned nearer to hear her. "I need Irissa," she began again.

"*Now* she needs us," Kendric noted in a sour aside to Irissa.

"Not both—"

"Both or none," he answered.

Finorian paused so long they thought her image frozen into Borgia-green ice. "Both," she finally conceded in a dead tone.

"How?" Irissa demanded.

"A gate." The old seeress sighed.

"It refused us."

"There is another."

"How do we find it?"

"You have found it—once. Look beyond Far Focus." Finorian's visage dissolved into a few bright reflections in the Borgia.

Irissa sat numbly. "A gate. We do not have to remain here."

Kendric sat also, sniffed the Borgia, tasted it gingerly, and took a deep swallow. "Excellent vintage. Credit Finorian with knowing her Borgia, at least."

He passed the goblet to Irissa and she took a small, unsavoring sip, then made an approving moue. "Not bad." She took a deeper, more leisurely draught. "What could be the danger?"

"Rather, where could be the gate?"

"Somewhere we have already been."

"If we can trust Finorian," Kendric interjected. "I grow weary of such cosseting," he said consideringly. "Borgia, banquets...I feel the need of another journey, Torloc—more hardship, danger, uncertainty..."

Irissa's right hand, white although no longer unringed, rested cobweb-light on his forearm. "Do you truly wish to leave?"

He regarded her solemnly. "It is not a place I feel I can call mine."

She sighed relief. "Nor I. But perhaps we will never find such a place."

"At least we will look. That is more than most do."

"That sounds like a Torloc trait, Wrathman, to quest for home, with no guarantee it is any better than where one is. It may even be worse."

He nodded, rose, and fastened on the sword that lay beside him on the bench.

Something in their faces spelled farewell; as they paused before Amozel and Chaundre, the banqueting board din suddenly hushed.

"My friends," Amozel said, not noticing Kendric's raised

eyebrows at his inclusion in the plural address, "you have wearied of our feast?"

"Not wearied, but become restless to create our own cause for celebration—to find the place that was denied us," Irissa answered.

"A pity." Chaundre halted his coldstone appliance in its habitual slide down his nose. "There is much of interest I could show you with the combined powers of the Shunstone and the Drawstone, if you would linger."

"I'm sure," Kendric answered quickly. "But we have our own riddles to solve, ones that began in Rule and must end somewhere else. We fear the Inlands are only a pleasant pause upon our journey."

Amozel laughed. "Pleasant! Stay much longer and we will make a diplomat of you, Kendric. No, pray be gone, both of you, and keep your natures undiluted. But I think the Inlands will be a far pleasanter place in future. You and Irissa will always find fair welcome here."

They chorused their thanks and withdrew, pausing at the threshold to survey Chaundre's roofless great hall one last time. Already the faces were growing unfamiliar, like dream aspects fading in daylight.

"There are those I shall miss," Irissa admitted.

"Then we stay," Kendric asserted, "and I will erect a Keep upon my Quickstone."

"Or perhaps I could erect a Keep upon my Fivestones," Irissa returned, waggling the fingers of her hand as a reminder. "And you could come to visit. I may wish to start a bevy of my own—with certain innovations . . . After all, Hariantha never had a proper chance at erecting her Stonekeep—"

"And a good thing, too, if she was as embellishment-prone as a certain Torloc seeress . . ."

"Great silly children, you quarrel again," came a voice from above, a voice they had not heard since lost in the dark byways of another Stonekeeper's Keep.

"Not quarrel—discuss," Irissa told the majestic head of Bounder looming over them. "As you do not command, but merely direct."

"There will be little to command or direct now," the head said with melancholy. "None will consult me, since my voice stems from a magic alien to the Inlands. Only you can hear me."

"That is a pity," Kendric said, not sounding sincere. "But at least you can see all that transpires in this place where so much has shifted. You should have an interesting time of it."

"Yes. It should divert me for a few centuries or so."

"Perhaps we shall return," Irissa consoled, "and you can tell us what has come of all this."

"Not likely," Bounder said solemnly. "A world worth leaving is seldom worth returning to."

They bade the beast farewell and crossed under it to begin their descent through Chaundre's jumbled Keep. Kendric leaned down to whisper a confession in Irissa's ear.

"I know you are fond of the lorryk and that they have served us well in this world, but I cannot say I am sorry that yon speaking head is tacked to the wall and thus barred from accompanying us."

"No," Irissa agreed. Then she laughed at their harmony. It could not last in little things, though the greater seemed sealed.

They went out onto Chaundre's patchwork grounds, which even now grew more chaotic as the influences of the Shunstone and the Drawstone warred with one another. The lorryk were grazing on the proudest efforts of Chaundre's gardening; Kendric shook his head as Irissa called them away from gnawed orangery trees.

The littlest one, no longer so little, loped over on strong, straight legs and ritually greeted Irissa by butting her chest.

"Ouch!" She rubbed a palm across the silver-blazed forehead and brought it away, amazed. "Horns," she said, pointing to a pair of velvety swells above the eyes. "Someday he'll be challenging Bounder. Perhaps we were wrong—*I* was wrong . . ."

The touch of Kendric's hand on her shoulder stopped her. "Using magic has its price, and even nature exacts its toll, as Chaundre would be the first—"

"And last—"

"—and last to tell you. Now, how do we go about finding what lies beyond Far Focus, Torloc? I'm a novice at this."

They stood among the grazing lorryk and stared up at the cataract-clouded moon. It stared back.

"Overstone only knows," Irissa conceded. "Where did my predecessors go?"

"Straight into the teeth of Delevant's Maw," Kendric answered promptly. "Torlocs have a great taste for disaster."

"But we have been there—"

"As Finorian said—"

"And it exists no more. If the gate was indeed there, it is destroyed. Perhaps Finorian did not realize . . ." Irissa mulled.

"There's not much that one misses, including a few things you and I have not thought of. Perhaps we were overhasty in returning here; perhaps the gate was just beyond the chasm. Delevant, after all, was gatekeeper."

"Back again?" Irissa sounded dismayed. "It seems this world has done naught but pull us from one pole to another for no avail."

"So does any world," Kendric muttered philosophically. "Including, no doubt, your Torloc haven, Evendaunt."

"Edanvant," she corrected automatically.

"Do you even know what awaits you there, or why the Torlocs have yearned toward it through many worlds and for many centuries?"

"No . . ." They were walking as they talked, wending their crooked way out of Chaundre's Keeplands. Irissa paused to look back down on the lorryk, already ranged around the orangery again. They had left Chaundre's Keep without even being aware of it. She looked to the unbespelled land ahead.

It was wet from the swollen meanders' overflow, from the icy sheets of tears shed by the dissolving Cincture. Kendric fisted his hands on hips and sighed as he surveyed it.

"Marshes again. Shall I never be rid of damp boot leather?"

"In Edanvant," Irissa said by saucy rote, "it never rains—"

"It never rains here, but that did not prevent you from turning its outer limits into one huge floodplain. Overstone only knows what you will do to Edanvant."

"Or you will," she retorted, glancing sideways with silver eyes that never needed to fear mirroring again.

He narrowed his own at her, nevertheless feeling a savored satisfaction that he finally would meet the formidable Finorian face to face—not as a vanishing mist or a shivering image in a goblet. Kendric flexed his beringed hand as if preparing to wrap it around a dagger pommel.

"Let us march, then," he suggested, "since that is all the imperative the Inlands ever gave us."

They set out with long, loose strides over the last of Chaundre's jumbled land and onto the flat, open plain that led only to the Cincture that once was.

The wet earth sucked in its breath in juicy gulps at their every step; soon the gray and orange leathers of Rule were soaked black around their boot soles.

Above, the Overstone turned the same bland face upon them that it always did, and the land showed the identical featureless surface, endless and flat, colorless and odorless, save for a waterlogged scent. No birds fanned across the ice-arch; no creatures stirred on the soggy landscape. Fowlen feet would disdain the brackish land until time had dried it firm again.

The place had a new, untried look to it, unshaped by the hand of man, track of animal, or passage of magic. There was no meander flow to follow, as they had done before, for it was all shallow meander. Nothing green grew beneath their feet, for the earth had been icebound until recently.

Irissa had the oddest feeling she trod on some giant, empty map, but that was doubtless a Torlockian fancy and not worth reporting.

They walked the rest of the day, setting a steady pace, and on through the Overstone-lighted night. There was little point in pausing, for there was no place to seek shelter and no dry spot to sit or sleep upon.

Their feet became chilled and then their knees. The land's very emptiness seemed to suck the warmth and confidence from them; although they knew it was unmagicked land with no Stonekeep within miles to affect it, it exerted its own, unspelled power. It was the power of vastness and emptiness, of raw newness, of sheer freedom from magic. It had become a place not where magic was simply absent, but where the temptation to use magic might rebound upon itself.

Even Kendric's sword-long stride slowed finally under the endless, draining pull of it, and Irissa no longer maintained the pretense of keeping up with him.

"How do we find what no longer is?" she asked, standing still in the unrippled terrain. Kendric looked back and saw her mirrored in a compass' worth of directions by the dark water surrounding them.

"There was earth and rock below the ice, the skeleton of that once-mighty worm we climbed." He turned ahead. "We should see such soon."

"Should? That is a traitor word, Kendric."

He shrugged and adjusted the drag of longsword in the sling across his back. "May, then. Or might."

"Perhaps magic . . ."

"No!" Kendric's voice softened as he explained. "This is new-rinsed land. It had overmuch of magic. If we burden it now, perhaps it will close to us utterly."

"And this is not closed to us?" The wide sweep of Irissa's hands created comets of ring-reflection that echoed in the water-bound land beneath her.

Kendric looked down to his mired feet and saw the reflected ice-arch grinning over his shoulders and the Overstone riding half-hidden behind his head.

"We will find some landmark soon," he promised doggedly.

She did not argue, mindful perhaps of Bounder's parting words, but slogged ahead to join him on the march ever forward into nowhere.

The second day dawned as featureless, and their trackless journey continued as disconcertingly pointless. By now their legs had stiffened into icy pillars that strutted forward more out of habit than volition, and Kendric was minded more than once to sling off his sword and use it as staff, despite the ruin that water would work upon the blade.

Irissa gasped and went stumbling past him, hair and heels flying. He snagged one arm to keep her from plunging face-first into the marsh.

"What is it, some swamp-eel?" he demanded, slinging his great sword around and squinting into the placid water.

"No, something hard," Irissa complained, balancing herself by one hand on his shoulder and lifting a foot that ached despite the boot protecting it. "I stubbed my toe on something."

They peered into the water as into a window, but it was

like a great, frosted looking glass reflecting the clouded sky; nothing below seemed visible.

Kendric raked his sword tip through the water, expecting to dredge up some weedy ribbon of slime. Instead, metal rang on metal. He handed Irissa the sword without a word, though she staggered under its stewardship, and squatted in the shallow water, feeling with his hands.

"What has no end, is cold and gold, and wears the girth of a moonweasel?" he asked at last.

"A golden moonweasel consuming its own tail," she snapped. "I don't know. What?"

For answer, Kendric's arms spread wide, hands hidden by water and his shoulder muscles tautened. With a tremendous heave, he pulled a huge, curved bar of gold momentarily free of the water.

"One of the Ringlost we saw through the ice." Irissa answered his riddle in awed tones.

"And lost again!" As Kendric released the metal, it splashed back into invisibility. "That thing's size is a most effective deterrent to greed. Cursed will be he who ever tries to haul those things free of their watery graves."

"But it means we are near Delevant's Maw, whatever is left of it. And if the rings remain, why not the gate?"

"Ask Finorian," Kendric suggested, wiping his sword blade on his tunic hem, though even that was soaked from the ring's backsplash.

"That means we must only go forward—"

"Or backward. I know not which is which anymore," Kendric complained.

They studied the scene again, flat, mirroring water stretching in all directions and thus nullifying any direction.

"Oh, for a compass," said Kendric the man of Rule.

"Oh, for Chaundre's Drawstone," sighed Irissa the would-be seeress of Edanvant.

"We wear a miniature of many Stones on our fingers," Kendric reminded her.

Irissa shook her head. "For once I agree with you. I would not care to be the first to unleash magic into this new-made land. And besides, neither of us knows the ways of our rings.

No, it's walk we must, knowing we are nearer. It's only that I get so weary of not sitting..."

"Well, there's a small hummock there. It may be just a mound of mud, but then again, it may be rock. If you can walk there, you may be able to sit."

Irissa turned eagerly to look where he pointed. There was indeed a virtually minuscule hump of something protruding above the limitless, level expanse. Her smile of relief soon drooped.

"Kendric, I do not think that I shall have to walk to it— it appears to be moving toward us."

"I knew this unrippled land concealed something fell." Kendric sounded almost pleased as he wrapped both hands around the sword haft and braced his feet in the ankle-deep water.

The hummock came on, appearing to float until it was much closer, and then seeming to take step by muck-sucking step. It was almost the color of the landscape—pale, muddied white—and whatever head it had hung low between its sharp shoulders. The nearer it came the larger it loomed, until it could have stood wither to wither with a lorryk.

It paused a few yards from them, remained very still, then suddenly shivered violently from fore to aft.

"Ahhh!" Irissa and Kendric retreated as one under a rainfall of muddy drops, their eyes squeezed shut while loop after loop of moisture hurled their way, binding them to temporary inaction.

"What kind of beast attacks by shaking itself?" Kendric muttered, forcing his eyes open and shaking his own wet hair.

Irissa pulled several sopped strands back from her face to regard their challenger. It no longer stood bedraggled and sinisterly shapeless. The body was white and well furred, though still damp. Its four feet were hidden by water, but its head was no longer concealed. That rose impassively from a wolf-muscled neck, aureoled by a fanned ruff of glossy white feathers.

The Rynx, somewhat larger than before and apparently twice as self-satisfied, if that were possible, cocked its snowy head and regarded them with unblinking eyes—one silver, one gold.

"We journey to the gate," it announced.

"*We* do," Irissa answered.

"We as well," the Rynx replied in its two-level voice. "It is a long walk for two legs." The eyes blinked pointedly at their muddy trousers stuffed into water-soaked boots.

"You're . . . alive," Kendric ventured.

"So our sorry condition tells us," the Rynx affirmed. "Alive. Wet. Muddied. Yet no worse off than you." The Rynx paused while it appeared to be considering something very seriously. It sighed, if anything as sibilant as a sigh could be said to whisper through that huge, hard maw of a beak.

The Rynx sank abruptly to its snow-white belly in the mud. "Mount," it ordered.

Irissa did not hesitate; she had little fear of the four-footed, save for the terrifying empress falgon she and Kendric had ridden once in desperation in Rule.

Kendric hesitated. It seemed half his life had been a hesitation, but then, he was still here to live it, and many who had not hesitated were not. He was suspicious of this Rynx that grew larger at each reappearance and had survived apparent death. Where would it convey them—and why?

"Mount," the Rynx instructed wearily. "You are a lengthy creature, but I can bear longer. Hasten. My undercoat grows damp."

Kendric reluctantly straddled the beast behind Irissa. It rose, bearing him far enough off the ground so that his boots hung above the waterline. They rolled their fingers into the thick pelt folds at the Rynx's shoulders as the creature trotted off at a canine pace.

"How did you survive the Chasm of Blue Fire?" Irissa asked.

"We did not. We never do. Yet we return. Each time we contended with Delevant, we held it at the cost of our selves. Yet the struggle gave us strength and the fire forged new selves, and we returned stronger than before. Now you have banished Delevant utterly, as we were unable to do, and we are returned for no purpose to a place washed clean of all scent of itself. Only the gate remains. We will carry you to it, if you will take us through to your world beyond."

"You could not even carry *me* through a Torloc gate," Kendric whispered into Irissa's ear. "How are we to navigate this one through?"

She considered. "It has some native magic; I am fully restored; you have powers of your own—" He snorted. "—and we owe it our aid, as it aided us."

The Rynx trotted on, unworried by how its fate weighed in their mutual balance. In time, some gray hummocks arched out of the surrounding waters. Unlike the Rynx, these neither advanced nor shook themselves dry. Yet they grew in size—naturally—as the party neared them, the hard rocks curving toward them like embracing, bony arms. In their midst, a tumbled basalt pyramid gnashed boulder against boulder.

"It's all so changed, so diminished." Irissa's fingers tightened on the Rynx pelt, and it stopped as if by command.

"Delevant's bones, I warrant," Kendric said grimly. He dismounted, his boots touching dry rock. The ice structure that had mocked the skull of a man was gone, melted away with the ancient Torloc wizard's power. There was only the deserted, drenched landscape and this barren island of rock rising from it like something rejected.

Kendric took a thoughtful tour of the lowest rocks, looking for some familiar formation, some pathway to any place that might be termed a gate.

"We end where we begin, on rock," he told Irissa. "There's even a rainbowed arch above us, albeit a bit remote." He jerked his dark head at the now familiar ice-arch that had canopied all their Inlands days and nights.

A constant, delicate play of shades danced across it, a phenomenon they had noticed before in this northern extremity of the Inlands. The place was still and quiet, except for the shifting colors above them. In that stillness, Irissa, then Kendric, heard a faint, rhythmic susurration.

Irissa sprang to the pinnacle of the rocks, leaping with the agility of a rock ram among them. At the top she stood transfixed, her beringed hand pointing to some horizon only she saw.

Kendric followed her up more cautiously, but paused, as

amazed as she. Ahead lay the milky crescent of a softly heaving sea, water churning itself foamy as it licked endlessly at the raw rim of what remained of the Cincture.

"Chaundre was right," Irissa said. "The Cincture has become an ocean, a rope of water ringing all the Inlands, and soon this land we stand upon will be only a rocky coast."

"A marshy, rocky coast," Kendric corrected.

"And there, Kendric, what is that, that last upthrust of ice standing alone?" Her forefinger pointed imperiously, the blue Skystone upon it seeming almost to quiver in the diffused daylight.

He reluctantly turned his attention upon a pillar standing solitary and somehow purposeful on the rocky, level plain that stretched from the back of Delevant's skull to the new-melted sea. It stood, as commanding a presence as if it lived, and it reminded Kendric all too accurately of the ice-born images Delevant had hurled at them not many days past.

"Some remnant," he guessed. "We should avoid it."

The Rynx settled silently on its huge haunches beside them. "I say it is a hinge, swordsman, that turns the mechanism of your gate, if you have but the heart to take it."

There was no mistaking the intent that shaped the ice-carved plinth. It was a reassembling of the many visages consumed by Delevant in his endless years, a haphazard stacking of odd and alien faces looking to all directions and to none with their pupilless, icy eyes.

Irissa had started down the rocks toward it, so Kendric bounded down to join her, the Rynx overtaking him with a graceful plunge.

When they were on level ground, it was obvious the column towered over them all and that it was some final remnant of Delevant's ancient and empty realm.

The image of a great bird head was carved at the foot of the column, holding in its beak an egg, a huge egg like a jewel—or perhaps it was a jewel shaped like an egg—in which veins of color pulsated as if alive under the marble-white surface. Every shade of the rainbow shifted there—bright, Borgia green, almost phosphorescent violet, crimson, and gold.

Irissa reached for it.

"Don't touch it," Kendric warned, his old dislike of magic rising to his throat.

"Why not? It must be the latch to our gate." She plucked the thing from the icy carven beak, and the beak snapped shut on where her fingers had been.

Kendric caught her arm and hauled her back rudely, his eyes ever on the column. Above them, the sculpted faces began collapsing, feature into feature, blending bizarrely as they fell, ice smashing to stone below and smashing further.

It was like a second slaying of Delevant, like drawing the key stick out of a tower constructed of toothpicks. A grinding sound louder than the shattering of the pillar before them drew their glances up.

The Overstone groaned and slowly rotated, as if wrenching itself from a vise. Its supporting arches ran riot with color, oddly becoming more insubstantial the more violently shaded. Their taken-for-granted solidity shifted; the color bars floated like clouds, like veils on the sky, and then began slowly settling to earth.

Irissa pointed at the phenomenon, clutching the egg-shaped-stone against her stomach and sensing the same colors stirring within it.

"Kendric! You aren't conjuring Hariantha hair—?"

"And my coloration ran amok? I think not. I think we stand as before, on rock amid water with a rainbow curving above us . . . as we meant to leave Rule. And did. As we will now leave the Inlands for whatever paradise awaits Torlocs and their fellow travelers."

It was inescapable now. The moon was loosed to follow some leisurely, foreordained path through the sky. It was no longer the Overstone, and Irissa wondered if the throbbing stone in her palm was. The ice-arch had melted into rainbow, and those brilliant strands were shrinking and drifting slowly down to Inlands earth, down to Irissa and Kendric—and the Rynx— standing calm and waiting below.

Above the sinking rainbow, the sky grew gray and misty. Irissa felt a soft, chill sensation, as if being rubbed against by a great, cold, invisible cat.

She glanced to Kendric and found his features dewed with tiny drops, coldstone-clear.

He grimaced. "Your parting gesture to the Inlands, Torloc," he announced, sounding oddly choked. "Rain. I trust it is not yellow and that it doesn't fall to land as commonstones, but as simply plain, pure water."

Irissa clapped her free hand over her mouth. "Chaundre and Amozel's banquet! Chaundre's roofless great hall . . . !"

"It will not remain roofless long, I warrant. The Inlanders will have to learn to live with rain like the rest of humankind. And we, I fear, will have to face another of these treacherous, color-shifting gates—It had better open onto the right world, or Finorian will face more than she bargained for."

The Rynx moved silently to Irissa's other side, as if expecting mere propinquity to propel it through whatever aperture opened. Irissa felt the colors in the stone tingle against her palm, felt a tightening around her forehead. Kendric leaned close, his lips against her ear.

"Your Iridesium circlet runs multicolored again."

She nodded wildly. She felt it all, the pulsing, descending rainbow, the almost palpable presence of a gate—unseen, inescapable now. She reached out a hand for Kendric and met his mirroring gesture. Their rings chimed together, the sound alien, but the warmth of their tightening grips familiar. The colors settled over them in misty, elusive rings. Somewhere there was a sound, a sea-sent roar foaming at their senses.

"A gate is only a gate," Irissa warned Kendric, into the chaos already seizing them, into the noise rising to swallow them. "It can lead to good or ill or much in between. I cannot promise—"

"I can." Kendric was again the felt presence, the thread that bound. His voice came from the colors and melded with them, weaving in and out of the self Irissa perceived. "I can promise that anyone or anything that attempts to sever us again in midgate shall regret it."

She felt determination quiver along the thin thread of connection and sensed the throb of magic in that message.

"At least we go," he said, "wherever we thought we wanted to go, where we will find—"

"The rest of the Torlocs," she interrupted joyfully, feeling the imminent completion of a quest so long denied.

"That. And Finorian," he added less happily.

"And the future," Irissa said, laughing until the tears came and they could both hear them shattering on the unseen rocks at their feet.

Kendric cupped a hand under her chin and felt a palmful of salt-damp coldstones plummet there. One sweep of his arm cast them away, into the rainbow. They arched outward in a dazzling scythe of gemstones. For an instant, they took gaudy shape and shade. A flock of birds, each in bright contrast to the others, winged away into the Inlands mist for Inlanders to marvel at.

Irissa challenged the rainbow. "Did you do that?"

"You haven't begun to see what I can do," Kendric promised, laughing. "Do you object?"

"No," she answered. "But Torlocs were ever prone to embellishment."

"You call that mere embellishment?"

"I fear so, Wrathman."

"No," he said firmly. "I know what I see. It is magic."

The gate swirled around them and took them and the Rynx as well. There was confusion and color and always the terrible, strong pull of the gate.

There was no up, no down, no forward, no back. Finorian had been wrong. There had never been any going back. There was only the gate, with them in it, and the certain grip of their hands, which no gate could break.

Where they had stood, a bright dervish of rainbow whirled, dissipating slowly into the drizzle that rained from a sky gone charcoal. In the distance, winging unerringly for the Inlands, a flock of bright birds grew small against the horizon.

ABOUT THE AUTHOR

Born the daughter of a Pacific Northwest salmon fisherman, Carole Nelson Douglas grew up in landlocked Minnesota with an affinity for water, cats, and writing, not necessarily in that order.

Her majors at The College of St. Catherine, St. Paul, were theater and English. A finalist in the *Vogue* magazine Prix de Paris writing competition, she gravitated into journalism upon graduation in 1966, was an award-winning feature writer for the *St. Paul Pioneer Press and Dispatch,* and later became copy and makeup editor for the newspaper's opinion pages.

She treasures an extensive collection of vintage clothing and jewelry almost as much as her Arkham House editions and hard-cover Lord Peter Wimsey set. She and her husband, an artist and furniture designer, make their home on sufferance with a trio of white cats, one of whom made a guest appearance in *Six of Swords,* the predecessor to this book.

Douglas has written all her remembered life, but began writing novels in 1976. She is the author of three historical novels and writes contemporary women's fiction as well as fantasy.